THE UNTOUCHABLE

GERALD SEYMOUR
theUntouchable

BANTAM PRESS

LONDON · NEW YORK · TORONTO · SYDNEY · AUCKLAND

TRANSWORLD PUBLISHERS
61–63 Uxbridge Road, London W5 5SA
a division of The Random House Group Ltd

RANDOM HOUSE AUSTRALIA (PTY) LTD
20 Alfred Street, Milsons Point, Sydney,
New South Wales 2061, Australia

RANDOM HOUSE NEW ZEALAND LTD
18 Poland Road, Glenfield, Auckland 10, New Zealand

RANDOM HOUSE SOUTH AFRICA (PTY) LTD
Endulini, 5a Jubilee Road, Parktown 2193, South Africa

Published 2001 by Bantam Press
a division of Transworld Publishers

A catalogue record for this book is available
from the British Library
ISBN (cased) 0593 046501
(tpb) 0593 046528

Typeset in 10½/13pt Palatino by Falcon Oast Graphic Art Ltd

Printed in Great Britain
by Mackays of Chatham plc, Chatham, Kent

1 3 5 7 9 10 8 6 4 2

For Georgia

Prologue

'I think I can live with that – yes . . .'

It was, Henry Arbuthnot thought, a moment of almost classical symbolism – not that Dubbs would have noticed, and certainly not Albert William Packer. The words marked the transfer of power.

'. . . Yes – I don't have a difficulty with what you're suggesting. You'll not find a problem with me.'

The man sidled out of the room. They heard his footsteps scramble down the steep staircase. The door on to the street slammed shut and there was the noise of a powerful car accelerating away, then the quiet that was broken only by the rumble of the machines spinning in the launderette below. It was a fine afternoon in early winter and the windows of the first-floor room were open. The launderette was always busy on a Friday and the motion of the machines shook the room above, making the dust from the files and the leatherbound books dance in the light. The room was seldom cleaned. Arbuthnot rarely used a vacuum cleaner, and he would never have allowed casual staff into his office.

Three men had come that day to visit the premises rented by Henry Arbuthnot, Solicitor at Law. He had expected a fourth visitor until he had noticed the cuffs of Albert William Packer's shirt where they peeped out from under his jacket sleeves. There was blood on them, still rich red, not yet darkened with age. It was fresh, and the fourth visitor was conspicuous by his absence.

Three men had come, and had pledged that their commercial activities would in no way impinge on the business dealings of his employer. The transference of such power – the granting by rivals of control of the capital city – should have been celebrated with a good bottle of Veuve Clicquot, but that would have offended his employer. Dubbs swung his shoes off the table and grinned then slapped the employer's back. Arbuthnot offered a pudgy hand that was held, squeezed, and dropped. There was no triumphalism. Flanked by his accountant and his solicitor, Packer had listened as three men, shuffling and mumbling, had acknowledged his superiority.

'Good as gold, weren't they?' Dubbs's little voice trilled in the shadowed office. 'Well, that's it, isn't it? We run London. We got there – we got to the top of the tree . . . I do the money, he does the law and keeps us clean, and you do what you do best – keep the business flowing . . . A day to remember.'

And that was it. That was the end of the moment of victory.

A short, heavily built, florid-faced balding man, Arbuthnot – three days short of his forty-first birthday – took the opportunity to reflect that he was now the legal representative of a man who exercised supreme power with chilling ruthlessness. Not that day, but in a week or a fortnight, he would find the opportunity to raise the question of increased remuneration with his employer. He thought he was now worth a minimum of a fifty per cent hike. Cheap at the price. His job for nearly twenty years had been to keep that employer's liberty intact, and he had no doubt that he had the skills to accomplish the same role in the future, but then the stakes would be higher. He rubbed his hands together and smiled wanly. He knew what he should say, but it would be a cold douse for the others, and he hesitated.

He looked at Dubbs. Couldn't stand the little bastard. His mind raced. He thought Dubbs a chimpanzee with a fresh banana. Dubbs's grin split his narrow lips. But just as an employer of status needed a legal adviser, so he needed a totally trustworthy man to mind his assets, and they were considerable. Dubbs was short, slight, sallow and neat, and his hair, probably dyed, fell lank on his forehead. He smelt of a pungent body lotion. He wouldn't have invited Dubbs, common little creature, across the threshold of his home, however acute the need. But as he was brilliant in his understanding of the law, so Dubbs was expert in his manipulation of money.

They were both, the solicitor and the accountant, of equal importance to their employer, and though their dislike of each other was mutual, it was hidden, suppressed.

His glance roved on until it rested on the face of his employer. Albert William Packer's appearance was ordinary. His was of medium height and medium build, his hair was carefully cut, his hands were neither heavy nor lightweight, his clothes were . . . Arbuthnot looked away. His employer did not like to be stared at, and always focused his eyes on the target who watched him. A cobra's eyes, Arbuthnot thought. If he had ever been asked, and he sincerely hoped he never would be, to help in the creation of a photo-fit image of Packer, he would have concentrated on the eyes as the only distinguishing feature of the man. The brutality that had taken his employer to the top of the heap was in those eyes. They never ceased to frighten him.

'What I'd like to say, before you both leave, Crime Squad and the Church, they'll hear soon enough about the new order of things. I would urge a period of consolidation, nothing flash too soon. Build on what we have, then expand. Sort of one step at a time. Great caution should be exercised . . .' Arbuthnot looked at the mouth, not the eyes '. . . because, from today, they will chuck at you every resource they can muster. You are, now, their Target One.'

Dubbs giggled, but Packer was silent, merely gave a wintry little smile.

The meeting was concluded.

Arbuthnot escorted them to the street, watched as they checked for tails, went through the basic but thorough counter-surveillance drills, and they were gone, Dubbs turning right on the pavement, Packer going left. Slowly, because they were steep and the carpet was threadbare and loose, Arbuthnot mounted the stairs. He was trembling and his knees were weak. It took him an age to get back to his office. His client was now the king of the capital's criminal world. And he felt its implications keenly. He had made a pact with the Devil: he was Faust.

When would the Devil come for him?

He had sold his soul for wealth. Back in his office, he used a grubby handkerchief to wipe off the table the smears from the heels of Dubbs's shoes, and then he moved back the chair that Packer had used, lifted it from behind the desk to its usual place against a bank of shelves that bent under the weight of legal texts. There was a knock at the door and his clerk brought in a tray to clear away the coffee cups and the water jug, left him the evening newspaper, and backed out respectfully. He had attached himself, voluntarily, to serious money. He picked up the newspaper . . . Margaret Thatcher had left Downing Street that day . . . The Iron Lady was gone with a tear in her eye, usurped in a palace coup . . . Vicious, but bloodless? He turned the pages. That transference of power was of secondary importance to the one that had been played out in his small office. He found the news item.

A man from south-east London had been discovered in the early hours of the morning in Epping Forest. His legs had been severed by what police believed to have been a chain-saw. Death was due to shock and blood loss, a Scotland Yard spokesman had said, and added that the murder was assumed to have been a further atrocity in the capital's current gangland turf war.

He put the newspaper in his brimming wastepaper bin.

In his mind, he recited,

> The stars move still, time runs, the clock will strike,
> The Devil will come, and Faustus must be damned.

Not today – not tomorrow, old cocker – not ever. He was entwined with Albert William Packer. Packer was a clever bastard, the top man. Packer would look after him. Of course he would . . . The light was slipping. The room seemed darker.

Chapter One

When dawn came, the body was snagged in the branches of a tree. Not that it was easily recognizable as a corpse.

In spite of the foreigners' alternate pleading, threatening, and throwing money at the city's municipal authorities, refuse collection had again broken down. In many of the streets back from the river rubbish was piled high outside business premises and at the doors of the old apartment blocks. The residents of the blocks facing the river, not believing that the dispute between the foreigners who nominally ran the city's affairs and local officials was about to be settled, had taken to heaving their plastic bags into the water. The body was wedged between two plastic bags, and was disguised.

The tree, holding it fast, was marooned on a spit of gravel half-way between two of the bridges straddling the river. One bridge was overlooked by the scaffolded and screened building where the National Library of historic documents without price had been housed before being hit by incendiary shells, and the second bridge marked the position taken by Gavrilo Princep eighty-seven years earlier in the moments before he had raised a handgun and fired the bullets that killed an archduke and an archduchess, and condemned Europe to a conflagration of a scale unknown before.

The roads running either side of the Miljacka river – the Obala Kulina bana on the north side, and the Obala isa-bega Isakovica on the south side – were already jammed with cars, vans, lorries and the foreigners' military jeeps and trucks. No driver had time to waste peering down into the river to notice the tree. Pedestrians crowded the bridges, smoking and hurrying, gossiping and continuing last night's arguments, and none of them, young or elderly, paused to stop and stand against the rush of movement to look down at the mud-brown water, the spit of gravel and the tree beached on it. As they had in the recent siege of the city, people hurried to complete their journey. To linger and look around them had been to court death; for four years the city had been called the most dangerous place on earth and habits of survival died hard, but now the tide of inhumanity washed on other more distant shores: Dili in East Timor, and Grozny, and Mitrovica in Kosovo.

There had been five successive bright spring days over the city. The piled snow banks on the pavements beside the river, compacted by bulldozers in the winter months, were finally dribbling away. High above the city, dominating it, where the siege guns had been sited with a clear view of the river, the bridges and the streets, the ski slopes were melting. Mountain streams seeking escape into the Miljacka cascaded down steep escarpments, and the river running through the heart of the city swelled and rose. Its force grew. As the early rush of foot-sloggers and vehicles thinned, the strength of the water's flow lifted the body sufficiently for it to break free of the tree's branches.

There was nothing romantic or noble about the Miljacka. It was not a Thames or a Seine, a Tiber or a Danube; perhaps that was why none had bothered to stop and gaze down at its movement. Flanked with concrete and stone bank walls, fifty paces wide, if measured by a man who had a good stride and had not lost a leg in the shelling, broken up by weirs, it was more of a dirty drain than a majestic waterway. As it continued its journey down-river, the body was sometimes submerged, caught in powerful deep currents, sometimes swirled to the surface before it was again dragged down and sometimes just the buttocks of the dark grey trousers protruded above the water.

There was no dignity for the body as it was taken through the unseeing city.

Behind him, he heard the scrape of the spy hatch being opened, then the clatter as it was dropped on its hinge against the outside of the door. He didn't look up.

'Coffee, *Mister* Packer. Cappuccino. Two measures of sugar, granulated and brown.'

He pushed himself off the floor, wiped the dust from the knees of his trousers and went to the cell door. He reached out and took the polystyrene beaker from the hand stretched through the hatch. He didn't thank the prison officer for bringing him the coffee, with two measures of sugar, but then he hadn't asked for it to be brought him, not that day or on any of the days that he had been in the Central Criminal Court. He smiled briefly, as if that were sufficient indication of his gratitude. He could see the prison officer's face through the hatch, the blinking eyes and the flash of teeth, and he knew that his smile had been sufficient to lighten the stupid bastard's day. He understood why he was brought coffee, why this and others of the stupid bastards apologized to him for the dirt in the cell and the state of the toilet, and why they always grimaced when they put the handcuffs on him before leading him back to the wagon for the evening journey to HMP Brixton. They were all, every last one of them, frightened of him. They feared that he would remember rudeness, sarcasm, a sneer, and they thought he would have a good memory. They also knew that he could find out where they lived, what car they drove, where their women worked, at the snap of a finger. His reputation went before him. More importantly, he was going to walk, as certain as night follows day, and they all knew it. He was always brought coffee with sugar from their canteen when he was first put in the holding cell before being escorted up to Number 7 Court, and at the lunch recess, and in the evening after the court had risen and before he was loaded into the wagon.

'I'll let you know as soon as there's signs of movement, Mr Packer.'

His back was to the hatch. He took the top off the coffee, poured it down the toilet, and went back to his work on the floor. Laid across the concrete were sheets of a tabloid newspaper and on the sheets were the clothes and possessions he had used in the last eight months on remand since his arrest. His suit jacket was hitched on the back of the cell's single wooden chair. On the newspaper were his second suit, conservative and grey with a light stripe, three button-down shirts, two ties, his three spare sets of underwear, five pairs of socks, and an extra pair of plain black shoes. They were all laundered, pressed or polished, because when he walked he didn't want to bring back soiled or creased clothes to the Princess. Neither of his suits was particularly expensive, not hand-made, off the peg. His shirts were decent, not monogrammed, his ties were sober, his shoes ordinary. Nothing about his clothes or his appearance was flamboyant. His confidence that he would walk had caused him to send home his trainers, T-shirts and the tracksuit he had worn during the long months on remand in Brixton's maximum-security wing before the start of the trial. There were no books, no magazines, no photographs in frames, only a plain washbag and a small clock radio. Early that morning the prison staff had been surprised when he had cleared his cell, loaded everything that was his into a plastic bin liner and carried it to the wagon that was escorted to and from the court by policemen armed with Heckler & Koch machine pistols. The trial was half-way through, the prosecution case was concluded, and the previous afternoon his brief had made the proposition to the judge that the client had no case to answer.

At the time of his arrest, the newspapers had written that he was worth in excess of a hundred million pounds, that he had headed the capital's top crime family for a decade, that he was targeted by the National Criminal Intelligence Service, the National Crime Squad, Customs & Excise's National Investigation Service, GCHQ, the Security Service and the Secret Intelligence Service. But, he was going to walk. He was an Untouchable. He knew he was going to walk because the Eagle had told him he would.

He sat on the chair and faced the door, glancing over the graffiti on the walls written by Provos and Yardies, murderers and rapists. A brief involuntary action, but he touched in turn each of the pockets of his jacket hitched on the chair. They were all empty. There were no cigarettes because he did not smoke, no keys because he did not need them, no wallet with cash because tough men in Brixton queued to give him anything he wanted, no credit cards or cheque book because no card company or bank had accounts in the name of Albert William Packer.

'Just been told, Mr Packer, judge'll be back in five minutes.' The face was again at the open hatch.

He nodded, then sucked a long gulp of air into his lungs. On life's ladder, Mister, as he insisted on being called by those who worked for him and those who spoke to him on his constantly changing mobile phones, had learned to trust few. Among the few was the Eagle, his lawyer on a heavy retainer, his 'legal eagle'. The Eagle had promised him he was going to walk and he trusted that prediction. It hadn't crossed his mind until that moment that such trust might be misplaced. It would go bad for the Eagle if it were. He breathed out steadily, then stood and took his suit jacket from the chair back and slipped his arms into the sleeves. He walked towards the cell door, then straightened his tie.

Through the hatch the voice said, 'Right, Mr Packer, if you're ready I'll take you up – oh, don't worry about your bag, I'll see it's minded.'

He smoothed his hair against his scalp as the key was turned in the door's lock, and put the dirt and squalor of the past eight months behind him.

In the themed Irish pub, across the street from the Old Bailey, the Eagle lingered over his lunch of steak and Guinness pie, with a side salad. A hack called over to him, with the familiarity of his trade, 'Henry, the judge is coming back in, going to rule on it.'

The Eagle merely nodded. Other than to deny his client's guilt, and then only cursorily, he never spoke to court journalists and crime reporters. He regarded them as parasitical scum, and it irked him that his given name should be used by a complete stranger. There had been others, at the top of the tree before his client, Mister Packer, had climbed into the upper branches, who enjoyed the company of hacks and liked to read their names in the newspapers. A long, long time back, he had advised his client that newspapers and their writers should be avoided. In the Eagle's opinion, newspapers were symptomatic of vanity, and vanity was dangerous. He carried on pecking at his pie.

His clerk, close to him, mobile phone at the ear, murmured, 'Three or four minutes, Mr Arbuthnot, and the judge'll be back in.'

'No panic, Josh,' the Eagle said quietly. 'I'll follow you over.'

His clerk, Josh, ran for the pub door. The Eagle laid down his knife and fork on the small round bar table at which he was perched, then changed his mind and hooked up a final piece of lettuce leaf. He was an ample man and his backside splayed over the rim of his stool. He wore an old suit that carried the stains of other meals, his shirt was far from new and the collar was slightly frayed; the tie had the crumple creases of frequent use. With what the Eagle earned from his solicitor's practice, and the retainer paid him by Mister, he could have worn as good a suit and shirt as might be found in Jermyn Street. Tucked under his knees on the stool's foot bar were his scarred tan suede shoes. When he left his home in the country to come up to London on a Monday morning he wore gentlemen's clothes, and his first act on reaching his office over a launderette in Clerkenwell was to strip off those clothes with their fancy labels, consign them to a hanger in the cupboard, and change into the tired suit, shirts and ties of better days, and ease on the suedes; his last act on a Friday afternoon was to reverse the process. It was as if he switched identities before taking the train to Guildford. His London suit, shirts, ties and shoes were an essential part of what he preached to Mister: nothing should be flamboyant, nothing should draw attention to wealth that could not be easily explained.

Henry Arbuthnot had only been twenty-two when he had first met the man who now paid him that healthy retainer, introduced to him by his black sheep brother, David, who had done twenty-seven months, fraud, in Pentonville prison and met Packer there – twenty-four months, aggravated robbery. In the twenty-eight years since then his client had never been convicted. He finished his glass of Pepsi and lemonade, wiped his mouth with the paper napkin, and eased himself heavily off the high stool. As a twenty-two-year-old, fresh from college and his degree, learning criminal-case law, he had been a fierce drinker; not any more. He had been 'dry' since he had met Mister. He was on call twenty-four hours, day and night. For his retainer, which ratcheted up each year, it was demanded of him that he be constantly available. Mister was his meal ticket, and abstinence from alcohol was the price to be paid.

He left the pub and sheltered for a moment in the doorway to gauge the strength of the rain.

Opposite was the main entrance to the Old Bailey, the Central Criminal Court. Word travelled fast. Photographers were gathering at the principal security entrance. Two police cars were parked at the kerb in front of the entrance, and the armed men were already loading their machine pistols into the secure compartments behind the front seats, their job over. There had been armed police on the corners of the building since the trial had started. He shuffled across the street. Because of his heavy gut he walked badly.

He went inside and flashed his card. The Eagle knew the way it would end, had known for days.

The prosecution case had originally involved the identification by Customs & Excise – the Eagle called it the Church – of his client in a car, his client's fingerprints in the car, and the evidence of an informer also in the car. While Mister had been on remand, the Eagle had systematically demolished the case with the help of the big man's enforcers. The Protected Witness Unit was supposedly secure and secret. Money had bought the location of the gaol where the PWU was housed, and the number given inside the unit to the informer. Big money had bought the prison officer who had contaminated the man's food. A stomach pump had saved his life, but not his resolve. 'If they can get me here,' he had whined, 'they can get me anywhere.' He had withdrawn his evidence, refused to testify.

Mister was standing at the far end of the corridor, wreathed in dull light. The cell door beside his client was the only one in the block that was open. At his shoulder were the clerk, Josh, and a prison officer who clutched the bin bag, as if he were a hotel porter.

The Home Office Forensic Laboratory was at Chepstow, across the Welsh border. The fingerprint evidence had been there. A technician with a predilection for gambling at the roulette tables of a Newport casino had been offered a choice: for co-operation his debt of nine thousand pounds would be paid off, for obstruction his mother's legs would be broken with such baseball-bat severity that she would not walk again. The fingerprint evidence had gone missing.

'All right, then – shall we go?' There was a watery smile at the Eagle's mouth.

The Church's identification of his client by their surveillance team had been a greater challenge. He couldn't buy the Church and couldn't threaten it, so the Eagle had had to burn late-night oil to work meticulously through the surveillance logs for the fissure in that part of the case. Having found the point of weakness, he had then diverted the attention of the enforcers, the Cards – Mister's hard men – to the leafy suburban detached home of the Crown

Prosecution Service lawyer on the special-case desk . . . It was all worked out, it was the power of his client.

Mister never looked round. The prison officer passed the bag to the clerk. The Eagle led them back up the steps. At the first landing, instead of turning left and waiting at a barred grille gate for it to be unlocked and taking the route up to Number 7 Court, he turned right. At that gate, he showed his pass, as did his clerk, and the youngster pushed the discharge document under the face of the security man with the keys to Mister's freedom, a big, bluff, red-faced ex-Guardsman who wouldn't have brought coffee to a prisoner or carried his bag for him. The Eagle sensed that the security man wanted to sneer, spit, but didn't.

They emerged into the great lobby area of the building.

'Did you get the taxi, Josh?'

'Yes, Mr Arbuthnot – side door, like you said.'

No way that the Eagle would have Albert William Packer photographed close-up by a scrum of snappers, then have the pictures used every time a low-life hack wrote an organized-crime story on the capital. Anonymity was what the Eagle sought, for his client and for himself.

Two groups of men and women were watching them. They'd have to pass them on their way to the side exit.

'Just walk past, Mister, no eye-contact.'

The first group were the detectives from the National Crime Squad. As the Eagle knew, they'd have had a watching brief because the targeting of his client had been taken away from them and given to the Church. Only fools played games when they walked past the detectives after a prosecution had failed. He recognized most of them, but behind him Mister, who had the keenest memory the Eagle had ever come across, would know their names, their ages, their addresses, their children's names . . . and there was one, who looked away, that Mister owned. The Eagle waddled past the detectives and towards the second group, rolling on his feet, and panting a little from the climb up the steps.

'You know what the Church say, Mister?' The Eagle spoke out of the side of his mouth. ' "Of course there are professional jealousies between them and us, Church and Crime Squad. We're professionals and they're jealous." That's what the Church says.'

There might have been a death in the family. The Church people stood hangdog, close to the side exit. There was a senior investigation officer and what the Eagle reckoned were all of the higher executive officers and executive officers who made up the Sierra Quebec Golf team, and they looked like they were too shattered to throw up. Sierra Quebec Golf had been assigned exclusively to his client for three years prior to Mister's arrest. It was all budget sheets, these days. The Eagle could snap the figures through his head. He estimated that the Church had committed a minimum of five million pounds to the investigation, then all the extras of Crown Prosecution Service and an Old Bailey trial. The men and women of Sierra Quebec Golf had good reason to think the ground had opened under their feet. He couldn't help but look at them as he went to the side exit. Set in the frustration of their faces, men and women, was deep, sincere hatred. They weren't like policemen. The Eagle had walked his client many times out of police stations, no charges offered, and had witnessed close up the resigned shrugs of men going through the form and 'doing something'. This was different, personal. He had to look down at his feet as he went past them because the loathing bled from their eyes. He went through the door, stampeded down a narrow set of steps, and behind him was Mister's measured tread. Mister wouldn't have been intimidated by the Church men and women.

The taxi was idling at the side door. He dived for the security of the back seat. He saw the way the driver looked nervously at the client following him, then away. All the cabbies in London would know that the quietly dressed man with an unremarkable face, his client, was Albert William Packer. He gave the destination to the cabbie. The Eagle realized then that Mister had not yet thanked him, had not squeezed his arm in gratitude, nor muttered a kind word to him.

As the taxi pulled out from the shadowy passage behind the Central Criminal Court, Mister asked softly, 'Where's Cruncher?'

The first time the Sarajevo firemen had managed to get the grab hook on to the body and pull it out of the Miljacka's central flow and into slower side waters, they had ripped off a sleeve of its jacket. Their rope went slack, and they hauled it in to find the length of cloth.

The chief fireman steadied himself, checked the coiled rope at his feet then swung the grab hook in faster circles above his helmet. The trees restricted the length of rope he could swing to gain the necessary momentum. There was a crowd behind them, and another on the far side of the river. Frank Williams, wearing the light blue uniform of the International Police Task Force, was enough of a student of the recent war to understand why there were trees on this section of the bank. This point in the river had been the front line. The burned-out apartments over the water had been the home of the sniper nests, crouched with their telescopic sights and looking down at a perfect view of the trees. All over the city, even in the worst of the shelling, men had gone out with axes and saws to fell trees for basic warmth, and take a chance with death. Here the trees had survived because death would not have been a lottery, but certain. He went to night classes to learn the language of Serbo-Croat-Bosnian; he was not especially bright, not formally intelligent, and the learning was difficult to him, but his slight knowledge of their language was always appreciated by the local men he worked with. It made an impossible bloody job marginally less difficult.

Painstakingly, but fervently, in Welsh-accented *patois* he urged them: 'Come on, guys, let's get this shit business over with.'

The chief fireman launched the grab hook. It was a good throw. He had made a clever calculation of the speed with which the river carried the body. It was now on its back, arms out as if floating at leisure in a swimming-pool. The hook splashed into the water downriver of the body's legs and caught the trousers. He took the strain. There was a ripple of applause on the far side of the river and a cheer from behind them.

Frank Williams winced. When a body came out of the Taff or the Ebbw, the Usk or the Tawe, it would at least be accorded a degree of respect, compassion. Here, it was a diversion, a brief show. The body made a bow wave as it was dragged against the current.

He lapsed, as he always did when stressed, into English: 'For Christ's sake, do it with a bit of bloody care.'

Three of the firemen scrambled down the stones of the river's wall, gaining purchase on the footholds where shells had splintered the masonry, or the weight of machine-gun fire had chipped the stones. They caught the rope and hauled the body over the slimy stones at the river's edge. Frank leaned over the wall and peered down at the white face, the big eyes and gaping mouth. He had been thirteen years in the South Wales Constabulary and a week short of seven months on secondment to the United Nations mission to Bosnia-Herzegovina, and he had not yet learned to be caustically removed from emotion at the sight of a stranger's corpse. The body was lifted up, heaved on to the wall, then lowered casually to the pavement, where the river water subsided from it. An ambulance pulled up behind them. The crowd pressed forward to get a better view.

As he wound up the rope, the fire chief said dismissively, 'It is a foreigner . . .'

'How can you tell?'

Frank had been driving by twenty-seven minutes earlier when he had seen a bunch of street kids pelting something in the water. He had stopped, reflex action, as he would have stopped in Cardiff, expecting to find the kids' target was a wing-damaged swan, a duck or a drowning dog. He had been on his way back to his base at Kula, beside the end of the airport runway, from an early-morning shopping raid at a coppersmith in the old quarter, where he had bought a bracelet for his mother's birthday. He was already late. If the corpse was that of a Muslim, dead in the Muslim sector of Sarajevo, then it was of no concern to the IPTF. If a Serb died in the Muslim sector, there was IPTF involvement. If the body was that of a foreigner, the involvement was heavy.

'Look at the watch on his wrist – it is gold. He is either a politician or a criminal, if there is a difference, or he is a foreigner.'

'So, where's Cruncher?' he asked again and saw the Eagle's eyes flick once in surprise. But his solicitor was never going to be superior with him, would never make a fast jibe. He knew the Eagle was terrified of him, and the combination of terror and greed kept the man in place. Mister's life was about power and control, whether at home, whether free, whether in a cell. He formed few attachments but he was fond of the Cruncher. He had grown up with the Cruncher, him in Cripps House and the Cruncher in Attlee House on the local-authority estate between the Albion and Stoke Newington roads. He had been to school with the Cruncher, lost sight of him, then met him again in Pentonville. He'd once heard the Eagle call the Cruncher, wasn't supposed to hear it, a 'bloody little barrow-boy'.

The cab turned off the North Circular and drifted into tree-lined streets where the first spring blossom was showing. He'd been in maximum security since the last day of the previous July when the trees had been heavy in leaf; he had missed the autumn gold and the Christmas stripped bareness. Now the daffodils were out in full glory under the blossom trees, but the crocuses were waning. It was a time of year the Princess liked . . . They were at the top of his own road. The houses were wide, detached buildings, brick, stucco or mock-Tudor, and there were Neighbourhood Watch stickers on many of the ground-floor front windows. Bumps in the road prevented illegal speeding by cut-through drivers. It was a quiet, respectable road, one of hundreds in the capital, just as his own house was like one of thousands of similar properties. Only fools drew attention to themselves: most of those who did were in Long Lartin or Whitemoor, or down on the island at Albany gaol. Other than twice to ask the question about the Cruncher, who should have been there, Mister had not spoken during the journey; he had listened to what had happened in his absence – details of property purchases and sales, and profits too sensitive for the prison-visit booths – and taken a careful mental note of it.

The Eagle tapped the screen behind the driver and pointed up the road to Mister's house, then said, 'He should have been back last night. The Cards were down at the airport to meet him. He wasn't on the flight, didn't come through. The Cards called me. I rang his hotel. They said he hadn't checked out, but his bed hadn't been slept in the last night. I called again this morning, he still hadn't been back in his room. Sorry, Mister, that's as much as I know.'

It should have been a perfect day. He wasn't looking at twenty, twenty-five years, but at coming home to his Princess . . . but Cruncher hadn't been there.

There was a bleat in the Eagle's voice. 'You know what I worry about. I mean it, lose sleep about? One day you overreach – know what I mean – take a step too far. I worry . . . It was close run this time.'

He hit the Eagle with a closed fist, where it hurt, just below the heart. It was a short jabbed punch, and his solicitor let out a little stifled gasp. Mister owned a detective inspector at the heart of organized-crime investigations, a prison officer, telephone engineers in the sections where taps were monitored, had a man in place wherever he was needed; he could strike terror into rivals, turncoats and lawyers. He employed the best of solicitors on retainer, and the best of accounting number crunchers ... so where the hell was Cruncher?

The taxi pulled up. Mister slipped out of the cab with his bin bag, didn't offer an invitation to the Eagle to come in with him. He hadn't thanked the Eagle, the work was well paid for. He would never be in debt – money or for services rendered – to any man, never under obligation.

'Hello, Mr Packer, nice to see you back.'

He smiled at the young woman pushing the buggy with the sleeping baby along the pavement. She was from four doors down and her husband imported Italian fashionwear. 'Good to be back, Rosie.'

A woman was clipping the early spring growth on her hedge two doors up. Her husband owned a garden centre in Edmonton, and her garden was always a picture. They supplied the labour that kept the Princess's lawns and herbaceous borders neat.

'Afternoon, Mr Packer, welcome home.'

'Thanks, Carol, thanks very much.'

Rosie and Carol, and all the rest of the road, would have remembered clearly that morning, the last day of last July, when the road had swarmed with armed police and white-overalled forensics people, as he had been led away in handcuffs by the Church. Every upstairs curtain would have twitched; they'd all have been in their nightdresses and pyjamas, peering down at him as he was escorted to the car and pushed inside. He knew from the Princess that Rosie had been by that morning, when the police and the forensics team had gone, with a cake, and that Carol had brought flowers. They were ordinary neighbours in an ordinary road, and they knew fuck-all about anything.

He heard the taxi pull away behind him, and rang the doorbell. The climbing roses over the porch were in leaf but not yet in bud. The lawn had had its first cut. The door opened.

She had been Primrose Hinds. Their marriage had lasted eighteen years in which time he had never touched another woman. She was the daughter of Charlie 'The Slash' Hinds who had emphysema, a hot temper, and a regular address in the Scrubs, and who was flash. From his father-in-law he had learned all that was wrong about a lifestyle. Primrose was his Princess. She knew everything about him, she was as discreet as her father was not, she was the only person he fully trusted. He could have bought his Princess a castle, covered her with jewellery and lived the celebrity existence, as others did. She had never worked since their marriage, at which no photographs were taken by guests and no official snapper was employed. A year after the wedding, a doctor had told her that she was unable to have children.

'Good to see you, Mister, good to have you home . . .'

He kissed her, on the cheek. It was not a kiss of devotion but of true friendship. Later she would give him the numbers of the new mobile phones that the Cards had dropped off, and when the house was last scanned for bugs, and where the vans were in the road for the cameras. She was a pretty woman, an inch or so taller than him, and had a good throat and good ankles. He had insisted that she never visited him in Brixton, never came to the gallery for the magistrate's committal hearing or travelled down to the Old Bailey. He protected his Princess from prying, peering, stripping eyes.

'. . . I expect you'd like a bath, and how about a nice lasagne then? God, it's good to have you back.'

She closed the door behind him.

As if it were his sole priority, Mister said, 'We don't know where Cruncher is. He wasn't on the plane last night. His hotel don't know where he is . . . It's ridiculous . . . Cruncher's never gone missing.'

The judge paused in the process of his laborious handwriting, shrugged, smiled helplessly and said that his daughter normally did the typing for him, but sadly she was not available. Frank Williams had just looked down at his watch.

'It's not a problem, sir,' Frank said. 'You have my name, number and workplace, yes? My involvement is purely coincidental. I happened to be passing the river and saw the body. It might be that of a foreigner, which would make the death IPTF business. The routine, sir, is that we should have a post-mortem, and that I'll set in motion an investigation to find out the identity of the deceased. It's all pretty straightforward, I don't expect too many earthquakes . . .'

Again there was a self-deprecating gesture with the hands. 'It is because it is routine that you have been sent to me. If earthquakes were anticipated you would have been channelled to someone more appropriate, to someone more worthy.'

'I just need a signature, sir, for the hospital and the pathologist.'

Taking an age, the judge filled out the form. Back at home the work would have been done by a brisk, competent official in a quarter of the time. He wondered where they had dug this old fool out from, which stone they had lifted.

There had been no identification on the body, and no hotel security card. His starting point would be the better hotels in the city. The clothes carried designer labels: an Italian suit, a French shirt, an Italian tie, German shoes, and brief tight underpants of silk with a London label . . . *silk*.

Autumn 1991

He was watched. He had been watched all through the day from the early morning. It was late afternoon now, the sun was low over the golden outlines of the trees on the hills to the west of the valley, and he turned his slight body on the tractor seat to stare back hard at the big man who sat on a wooden chair by the door to the house. The tractor's wheels caught a rut in the field and jolted him, shook his spine through the thinning foam cushion on the iron seat. He lost sight of the hard eyes gazing at him from past the grazing fields, the big mulberry tree and the fencing close to the house that he had put up the previous spring. They were two old, obstinate and opinionated men, and each in a moment of privacy would have called the other a valued friend, grudgingly, but times were difficult and changing for the worse, and on that day neither had called out a greeting or waved. They lived on opposite sides of the valley, separated by the Bunica river, and the events of the summer, now slipping away to autumn, had seemed to widen the differences of politics and culture; no wave and no greeting cry. Each would have thought it the role of the other to make the first gesture.

Above the noise of the engine he whistled to his dog. Years before he could have rounded up the cattle in the morning and the sheep in the afternoon on foot, but age had taken a toll of his knees and hips and he relied now on the tractor and the dog's skill. When the dog looked back to him for instructions he pointed towards the ford. In the morning, with his dog, he had brought the cattle back from the grazing fields, crossed the river with them, and driven them back to the fenced corrals by his barns; now he brought back the sheep. The grass was exhausted, the weather was closing for the winter. His dog harried the flanks of the column of sheep and stampeded them towards and into the river at a place where his father and grand-father, and his grandfather's father and grandfather, had dumped cartloads of stones to create the ford. Husein and the man who watched him had only been away from their own villages, in a whole lifespan, for the two years of conscripted military training, and that was more than forty years ago.

He looked back at the valley floor across the riverbank. He saw the good grazing fields and the arable fields where the summer's maize crop had been harvested, the vegetables grown in strips had been lifted and the stark lines of posts linked with wire above the cut-down vines. He looked beyond the yellowed grazing fields, the ploughed arable land and the weeded corridors between the vines, past the mulberry tree from which the leaves were flaking, and the house with the shallow porch from which Dragan watched him, and up the hill track, by the well, towards the other village where smoke bent from chimneys, and over the ochre of the trees that caught the last of the sun's strength. His hearing was no longer keen, but he thought he had heard strident voices coming from north and south, warring in the few seconds that his tractor had stalled. But with the engine now straining to carry him up the far bank such sounds were blotted out. As the wheels spewed water and slithered on the mud-bank, he saw the pool upstream and the fine trace of the wormed long line he had left out for trout.

It was the fault of the radios. The radios that played in his own village, Vraca, spat out poison, as did the radios in the other village, Ljut. Against the tractor's engine, they were dead. He braked. He allowed the dog to take the sheep ahead. He stood up, to his full short, wiry height. He lifted his frayed cap from his sparse hair. His mouth, filled with ragged teeth, was set in a weathered walnut face below a greyed, drooping moustache. It was, Husein thought, ridiculous to the point of evil, that the radios' poison and hatred should destroy an old grumbled friendship. He waved his cap and shouted, 'Dragan Kovac, can you hear me? Heh, I will be back in two days, if the river has not risen, to plant the apple trees. Heh, can we take coffee? Maybe we take brandy. Heh, I will see you, in two days, if it does not rain.'

He waited to see if his friend would wave back and strained for a far-away call in response, but he saw no movement, heard no answering shout.

For two centuries the ancestors of Husein Bekir had bought land from the ancestors of Dragan Kovac, paid over the odds and bought every scrap, every parcel, every pocket handkerchief. Christian land was now Muslim owned. To Husein it was incredible, as it had been to his grandfather and his grandfather's grandfather, that the Serb village was prepared to sell precious land to a Muslim village for short-term gain. He understood that the Serb people prized a uniform more highly than hectares of grazing and arable ground, orchards and vineyards. The Serbs were bus drivers, hospital porters, clerks in the Revenue, soldiers, Customs men and policemen. Dragan Kovac had been a sergeant in the police before his retirement. They sought the status of the uniform and the security of the pension, not the scarred hands and the arthritis that came from working the land. Husein himself had bought the pocket of land right under the home of Dragan that included the mulberry tree and the field where he hoped next week to plant the apple trees. There was no more land left to buy, and the radio from Belgrade, listened to in Ljut, said each morning, afternoon and evening that Muslims had stolen Serb fields. The radio from Sarajevo, heard on the transistors in Vraca, said every day that Serb tanks, artillery, and atrocities in distant Croatia would not intimidate the Muslim leaders from the prize of Bosnian independence. They killed old friendships.

His wife of thirty-nine years, Lila, chided him for not wearing a thicker coat as protection against the evening chill and his grandchildren, wild little mites, charged excitedly to fence in the sheep. There was a rumble of thunder as grey dark clouds chased the sunset.

The first splatter of rain fell on Husein Bekir's face.

He climbed down stiffly from the tractor.

The sun still shone on the far side of the valley, on the land he owned that stretched from the riverbank to the scrub-covered slopes that rose to the tree-line and the other village. He was a simple man: his formal education had finished on his fourteenth birthday and he could read and write only with difficulty. He claimed that political argument was beyond his comprehension and he followed the simpler instructions of the mullah in the mosque. He knew how to train a dog. He knew also how to work land, and get the heaviest possible weight of crops from the arable fields and grapes from the vineyard. He knew how to catch a trout that would feed five people. He knew how to stalk a bear and shoot it for its skin, how to track a deer and kill it for its meat. The valley was his place. He loved it. He could not have articulated that love, but it burned in him. Because of what the radios said, from Belgrade and Sarajevo, he did not know what was its future.

He thought that Dragan, the retired police sergeant and a monument of a man, separated from him by politics and religion, shared the same love. He walked awkwardly up the hill towards his home. At the door he paused. The sun dipped. The rain came on harder. The beauty of the valley was lost as the squall crossed it. The russet and ochre colours were gone. Husein shivered, then coughed deep in his lungs and spat out the phlegm. He kicked the door shut behind him so that he would no longer see his valley.

The sign on the desk, printed off a PC and stuck to a cardboard strip, said, 'CANN *do* – WILL *do*'.

Sitting at the desk, stamping two-fingered instructions on to his console then staring at his screen, the young man pointedly ignored the chaos around him. It was as if the work he did divorced him from the atmosphere of morose and sour heartache. He was the only member of Sierra Quebec Golf who had not been in court. As SQG12, the dogsbody of the team, he had been left behind to mind the shop when the rest of them had trooped up to the Old Bailey. As he hit the keys and scribbled longhand notes on a pad, he seemed to refuse to accept what all the others knew. The team was finished. Some were packing papers into cardboard boxes, others were going round the walls and stripping down charts and photographs viciously enough for the paint to come away with the Sellotape, downloading computers and stacking disks, collecting the personal radios from the lockers around the room, checking the surveillance cameras' serial numbers against the docket sheets, and those on the telephoto lenses, then putting them roughly into the silver metal protected cases. The senior investigation officer chain-smoked under the no-smoking sign. It was over. The inquest would start in the morning, and it would not be pretty. The SIO would need to watch his back, and the higher executive officers would be making damn sure they didn't have to field the blame. When the inquest started, all of them but the SIO would either be taking the leave they'd postponed till after the trial or beginning life in a new team.

'Don't touch that . . .'

He must have looked up at the moment that the final picture on the wall was about to be ripped down. It was a half life-size picture, full length, of a man in T-shirt and trainers, handcuffed, being escorted down a garden path. At the foot of the picture one word 'Mister' was written in marker pen. It was the venom in the voice that made the man hesitate.

'Leave the damn thing there.'

The room had been ritually cleansed, the boxes and cases filled, all the computers switched off but one. It had taken them long enough for the pubs in the City to be emptying of commuters.

They filed out. Joey could hear their fraudulent laughter in the corridor. The team had been together for three years, for nothing. It was the senior investigation officer's idea of leadership: they were going to the pub to get so drunk they couldn't stand, then they'd fall into rip-off mini-cabs and get home, and in the morning they'd all have mind-bending hangovers, they'd have solved nothing and not eased the hurt.

He was twenty-seven years old. He was the junior. Sierra Quebec Golf, formed to target Albert William Packer, no other purpose for its existence, was the only team Joey Cann had worked for. For those three years he had lived, slept, walked, crapped with Albert William Packer. He had never seen Mister face to face, only looked at photographs and watched video. He had never heard the man's voice clean, only listened to it on tape from the telephone intercepts and directional microphones. Yet he would have said that he knew him. For three years, in the room at the Custom House by the Thames, he had been buried in tapes, surveillance logs, photos, reports, forensic findings, buried so deep he had sometimes needed to gasp for air. It had come without warning. If the SIO had known that the case was about to fold, or the HEOs, or any of the older EOs, then none of them had thought to tell him. Just a call on a mobile phone to say that it was over.

He picked up a phone, dialled. 'Hi, Jen, it's me . . . I'm going to be working late.'

'Tell me something new.'

'Did you hear?'

'About what?'

'About the case, dammit, the case – Packer.'

'Has it finished? It wasn't supposed to finish before—'

'It went down, Jen.'

'Sorry, am I being stupid? Has he gone down? What did he get?'

'Jen, the case went down. He walked.'

'You had it sewn up. From what you told me, it doesn't make sense . . . Look, it's aerobics night, do you want me to skip it?'

'I'm working late.'

'Don't you want to talk?'

'No.'

He rang off. Speaking to Jen had put clutter in his mind. The chaff was cleared when he cut the call. Doggedly, carefully, he began a long night of travelling again through the case work. In the pub they would have thought what he did was futile. Each time the tiredness tugged at his eyelids he blinked it away from behind his big, pebble-lensed spectacles, and looked up at the picture of Mister in its lonely honoured place on the wall. That alone was enough to shift the exhaustion and drive him back to the screen.

Chapter Two

Past nine in the morning and the fingers still beat rhythms on the console's keyboard. Two hours before he had waved away the cleaners. The room was a tomb of stacked boxes around the cleared desks and the locker doors hung open crazily. When he had been fiercely tired, his head sagging, the sight of the photograph on the wall had stiffened him. Joey Cann was near the end.

The computer hummed with the latest instruction, then the format of cross-examination flickered on to the screen and locked. He read.

> *Question:* And you were alone in the surveillance vehicle?
> *Answer:* I was.
> *Question:* It was after eleven o'clock that night?
> *Answer:* It was.
> *Question:* Up to that time, eleven o'clock that evening, how many hours had you worked?
> *Answer:* Seventeen.
> *Question:* How many hours had you worked that week?
> *Answer:* Ninety-four.
> *Question:* You were tired? You were desperately tired?
> *Answer:* I was doing my job.

Question: How many hours' sleep had you had that week – an estimate?

Answer: Thirty-five or forty – I don't know.

Question: What was the weather that night?

Answer: I can't recall, nothing exceptional.

Question: According to the Meteorological Office, there was low cloud and intermittent drizzle – but you don't recall?

Answer: I don't remember.

Question: Had you eaten in that seventeen-hour shift?

Answer: We usually try and get a burger – but I don't remember what I eat.

Question: I'm getting a picture of a tired man, and a hungry man – you are aware that hunger increases tiredness?

Answer: I suppose so.

Question: The distance between yourself and the vehicle in which you 'identified' Mr Packer was seventy-seven metres. Is that correct?

Answer: I believe so.

Question: You were tired, you were hungry, the visibility was poor, you were the length of three cricket pitches from the target of your surveillance, but you maintain that you are certain that you could identify Mr Packer?

Answer: I do, and I am.

Question: Had you, yourself, cleaned the windscreen of your vehicle?

Answer: No.

Question: When was the windscreen last cleaned?

Answer: I don't know.

Question: Don't you have the records that will tell you, records from the vehicle pool?

Answer: I don't have them.

Question: Was there a street-light close to the vehicle in which you allege Mr Packer was sitting?

Answer: There was enough light for me to make an identification . . .

Question: I asked whether there was a street-light close to that vehicle – was there?

Answer: I don't recall.

Question: On the map plan you have provided us with there is a street-light almost directly above the car you had under surveillance. Did you know that?

Answer: The light was satisfactory for an identification.

Question: According to the records of Haringey Council Roads Department, that light had been reported out of action eighteen days before and had not been repaired by the relevant date – does that surprise you?

Answer: I identified Mr Packer.

Question: Did you take photographs that night?

Answer: Yes.

Question: Where are those photographs?

Answer: They didn't come out.

Question: Didn't come out?

Answer: Correct.

Question: I see you wear spectacles – are they for general use?

Answer: Yes.

Question: How long have you been wearing spectacles?

Answer: Since I was a child.

It was a public demolition. The man in the witness box was as good as any of the Sierra Quebec Golf team at surveillance and had been made to appear an unreliable amateur in court. The cool reasonable politeness of Mister's QC dripped off the transcript . . . Joey heard the door open but did not look up.

He scribbled his notes. An informant had retracted, fingerprints had gone missing, the star witness had fallen on his face. It had been the systematic and clinical destruction of three years' work.

There was a spluttered hacking cough behind him.

'Putting the world to rights?'

He recognized the hoarse, guttural voice of the senior investigation officer. Joey closed down the computer, took his time, then swivelled in his chair. 'I was looking for what we did wrong . . .'

'Bollocks . . . I tell you what you are, Cann, you're an arrogant little prick.'

'Am I?'

'An arrogant shite with an attitude problem.'

'Is that right?'

Joey stared at him, his gaze unwavering. He saw the blotched face and the puffy bags under the man's eyes. He saw yesterday's shoes, scuffed and scraped, and a pair of suit trousers that had been thrown on the floor. The man's eyes blazed at him.

'We went to the pub last night – I don't know how many pubs we went to. Some of us threw up, some of us fell over – two pubs put us out. We had a kitty and a banker, fifty quid each, and we packed it in when the banker said he was skint. We stayed together till all the mini-cabs were lined up and ready to go. No one was left behind. We got home. We were a team, the whole of SQG, except you. You were too fucking superior to be a part of the team. "I was looking for what we did wrong." You think you're the only one who cared. You think you're the only one with the intelligence to know what went "wrong". This is a team game, Cann, and until you realize it you're going to stay an arrogant little shite without a friend in the world. We don't have heroes here, we don't bloody want crusaders. Some of the best investigators in the business were in this team, but they're not good enough for you, and you piss on them. I doubt you'll ever learn . . . Stupid bugger, we all care, we all gave three years of our lives to put Packer away. Go home, go and dig your bloody garden.'

'I don't have a garden.'

'Your bloody window-box, then.'

'I don't have a window-box.'

'Then why don't you just fuck right off out of here?'

He knew that the SIO had eight months until retirement. The man would have retired well if he had been able to boast gently that he had prosecuted and put away Albert William Packer, the Untouchable. Little doors would have opened on to the well-paid circuit of security consultancy. The SIO had had the big one within his grasp and he had let it go down the drain. Joey stood, stretched, then went to the wall and carefully took down the photograph of Mister's arrest, prising it slowly away from the paintwork so that the corners weren't torn, then he rolled it up and put it into his bag.

The SIO lurched towards him and the fat finger, bright with last night's mahogany nicotine stains, stabbed at Joey's chest.

'You know why we hate heroes and crusaders, Cann? Why we root them out? Why? They put the safety of the team at risk. They miss the point of what we're trying to do. They're selfish and superior to colleagues. Any creep with a mission is not a team player. Fuck off, and when you've had some sleep, maybe you should reflect on what to do about being too high, too mighty, to get pissed with the rest of us. You've no future here.'

Joey walked out of the room and away down the corridor, his bag banging against his leg. He swiped his card at the door, stepped out on to the pavement, avoided the regular little clutch having their first cigarette of the day, and headed for the Underground station.

From Bank he could have taken a direct Northern line train south to Tooting Bec and his bed-sit, and he could have slept. Instead, he bought a ticket to go north on the Northern line to King's Cross, then to change for the Piccadilly line trains heading out into the suburbs.

Taking advice, good or bad, had never been an especial talent of Joey Cann.

He'd often had coffee in the wide, plant-strewn atrium, but it was the first time that Frank Williams had been into a room at the Holiday Inn. He'd brought two local policemen with him, reckoned it would be a good education for them to watch him at work, would give them a chance to learn basic policing exercises.

The bed was still made. The desk top was empty, except for the hotel's stationery pouch. He found two suits in the wardrobe where two more Italian shirts were hanging, with a pair of soft leather shoes underneath them. Beside the telephone there was a pad for note-taking, and he routinely tore off the top two pages and slipped them into a plastic sachet. He was looking for a passport, a briefcase, anything to put flesh on the occupier of the room, a family photograph; but he found nothing. Sunlight streamed into the room. If he had not been a policeman he would have felt that he intruded on privacy. He had already tried the Saraj, the Grand and the Motel Belveder, but none had a missing foreigner. It was the sort of basic police work that Frank Williams was good at. He was slow and thorough, and he made the local men wear the gloves with which he had provided them. Because they were young they were probably still honest, but they'd soon catch on. Another six months and they wouldn't have been down on the carpet, looking under the bed, or climbing on a chair to peer above the wardrobe, they'd have been out at a road-block, fining motorists, cash only and no receipts, for speeding or having defective lights. No passport, no briefcase, no wallet, no personal organizer, no cheque book or credit cards, no work papers, no mobile telephone, no tourist guides, but the room was held in the name of Duncan Dubbs, of 48 River Mansions, Narrow Street, London E14. The description of the room's occupier was a probable match to the battered face of the man from the river, and the certainty came quickly.

What sort of man, with what sort of business, left a hotel room sterilized of his work, background and personality? He was thinking about it . . . He saw the flash from the sheen of the material and heard the raucous laugh from the younger of the local men – he had the bottom drawer of the chest open and was holding up a pair of underpants to be examined by the older one. Frank Williams reached out and snatched the underpants, checked the label and made the match. They were silk . . . Shitty enough to die far from home, he thought, but worse when your secrets became a joke for strangers.

Mister was back.

For two men, at the top of his priority list, the news of the trial's collapse came too late for them to take flight. Neither had had time to board a plane to Miami, the Algarve, Spain or anywhere. One, during the eight months of Mister's imprisonment on remand, had defaulted on a payment in excess of three-quarters of a million pounds. The other, in Mister's absence, had muscled into the dealer network and imported his own Afghan-produced and Turkish-refined heroin.

To Mister, it was necessary to show that he was back.

The defaulter had been taken from his apartment, with his suitcase only half filled in a scramble of packing, too quickly for him to get to the Uzi submachine-gun kept for emergencies under a floorboard. That morning, he was in the intensive care unit of Charing Cross Hospital where a medical team struggled to keep him alive . . . The muscler lay on a bed in a similar unit at University College Hospital, festooned with monitoring wires and drip tubes. When the Cards had come for him, in the small hours, at the drinking and snooker club he owned in Hackney, he had not known that his minders had flaked away from the front and rear doors.

Liberties had been taken while Mister was away. It had not been expected that he would regain his freedom without warning. It was not possible for Mister to retain his authority, his power, after eight months away, unless his strength was demonstrated. He had sent a message that night, twice.

A detective sergeant, at Charing Cross Hospital, asked a consultant to speculate how the right leg of the victim had been taken off at the knee. Ashen-faced, the consultant suggested the detective should go and look for a heavy-duty industrial strimmer, the sort used by workmen employed by Parks and Gardens to clear light undergrowth and scrub. 'How long would that have taken?'

'To sever it completely? Not less than a minute, maybe a bit more.'

Another detective sat in an alcove close to the cubicle at University College Hospital, alongside the useless presence of an armed police protection team, and had been told the victim had suffered huge abdominal damage from the discharge of a short-barrel shotgun. A doctor had asked him, 'Who does that sort of thing?'

'We call it "bad on bad". For them it's normal business procedure. You and I would fire off a lawyer's letter, they do it with a twelve-bore, sawn-off.'

The body, stitched up, was trolleyed back to the cold store.

The pathologist stripped off his messy gloves and his assistant untied the long apron's back cords and he shrugged out of it.

'Death by drowning,' the pathologist drawled, English language and American accent. 'Considerable alcohol in the stomach, and a meal – I really don't have time to tell you what he ate. There is no indication of criminality. The injuries, abrasions, are consistent with what would happen to a cadaver after thirty hours in the river. There is no reason why the cadaver should not be shipped home to the family for burial.' He paused to look up at Frank Williams. 'Now, please excuse me.'

Frank thought the pathologist would be earning, maximum, five hundred German marks a month. That would equate to around forty pounds sterling a week, before tax. The man was trained, a professional, had probably learned how to cut up bodies at an American university. While he was attached to the IPTF in Bosnia, Frank made six hundred pounds sterling a week, after tax, and had no college education. He believed nothing he was told by a government employee in Sarajevo; it could be that there were no criminal injuries, it could be that there were criminal injuries unnoticed by the pathologist, or perhaps criminal injuries that the pathologist had been paid not to identify. They were in a basement area of the Kosevo Hospital, and he could imagine what it would have been like here, in the candlelight during the siege, like a slaughterhouse, a carnage hell. A young diplomat from the embassy was beside him.

'That's that, is it?' Hearn, the diplomat, asked. He grimaced. 'First time I've been at one, glad I missed lunch.'

Frank said, and overstated the irony, 'Well, isn't that convenient? You're staying in a hotel on business. Problem: none of your business papers are in your room. So, incredibly, you are one of Sarajevo's five tourists a year. Problem: none of your guidebooks or local maps are in your room. All right, you're drunk and incapable. Problem: how do you climb over the railings on the bridges, or the walls on the river's edge, when you're fifty-something, and chuck yourself in after you've lost your wallet and every other piece of identification?'

'So . . . ?'

'Well, it's not good enough.'

'I've marked it, thank you. Leave it with me, and let's see where it runs.'

The SIO stood. The chief investigation officer sat at his desk.

'There's no way round it, Brian.'

'I think I know that.' The SIO sweated.

'Sierra Quebec Golf, in its present form, is dismantled, and you – if you'll forgive my bluntness – are supernumerary.'

'It's been more than thirty years of my life.' He shouldn't have said that, didn't want to sound self-pitying. He'd known he'd be called in, but had hoped it would be later and that the drink would have been further through his system.

'That's a shame, and you have to believe it's sincerely meant . . . But facts have to be faced.'

'I'm familiar with the facts. We were unlucky, that's all.' He heard his own voice and thought it petulant. He'd never been easy with the new man, the outsider, the blow-in from the intelligence community. Never been able to talk to him the way he had with his bosses when they were promoted from inside, closed shop.

'For heaven's sake, Brian, be adult. It's not a time for sulking. Millions of pounds have been spent. We were laughed out of court . . . Packer is the nearest thing we have in this country to a superleague organized-crime player. You had every resource you wanted, everything you asked for.'

'A witch hunt, is that what this is, and I'm the bloody broomstick?' He hadn't combed what hair he had. His head was throbbing, along with his anger. The new man wore a perfect suit, a perfect shirt and a perfect tie with some bloody image on it that the SIO couldn't quite focus on, something from the spook days he supposed. And the CIO was Cambridge and connected, and had the ear of the élite.

'You can either be transferred to VAT investigations for the last few months or, if you think it more appropriate, take early retirement. Pension won't be affected, goes without saying.'

'That's remarkably generous of you.' Sarcasm never came naturally to him. His wife, who'd been with him as long as he'd been in the Church, said that when he tried sarcasm he demeaned himself. It was ignored.

'Looking at you, Brian – I don't get any pleasure from saying this – gives me the impression you slept in a hedgerow last night. Senior men getting drunk with juniors is seldom wise.'

'I took the team out. Bloody hell, don't you understand? It's what we always do when a case goes down. These men, these women, they'd put their lives into this, everything else secondary, and me. We went for a drink or three, so what?'

'Not a habit I sympathize with. I would have thought an assessment of the disaster, and it *was* a disaster, would have been better prepared while minds were clear, not through a hangover . . .'

The SIO laughed, a hoarse snigger.

Glacial eyes gleamed at him. 'Why is that so funny? Enlighten me, please.'

'Cann did that. Cann stayed behind. He was at the computer all night. Why? "To see what we did wrong." We didn't do anything wrong. It was the system, the process . . .'

The CIO had the palms of his hands together, fingers outstretched, a bishop in prayer. 'Always somebody else's fault. I hear you, Brian. Keep saying it often enough and you might gain some comfort from it. Anyway, I'm afraid that's the end of the line. Sorry, there cannot be sentiment, not when a man as prominent as Packer walks free. So, what's it to be?'

There wasn't going to be a party. There might be a carriage clock sent on in the post, and there might be a seedy secretive gathering in a pub and the handing over of a sherry decanter bought with a whip-round. He said quietly, 'I'd like the rest of the day to clear my things up, and say a few goodbyes.'

'Sensible choice. The pension people will be in touch.'

He flared. He was on his way out, headed for the rubbish heap. 'God, look, I wanted to put him down, I wanted it as much as anyone.'

'But you didn't, did you, put him down? That's the difficulty, Brian. Good luck.' The CIO smiled.

'Goodbye. Let's hope others manage where I failed.'

'Yes, with the right people I'm sure we will.'

The SIO was on his way to the door.

The voice behind him was sham matter-of-fact. 'Oh, the one in the team who resisted your leadership demand to get drunk, give me his name again.'

'You don't want to worry about him – he's not a team player, but then he was only the collator, did the archive, kept the paper in order. He's a nobody.'

'What's "nobody's" name?'

'SQG12. Joey Cann.'

Joey turned into the road. He had never been there before. He had filed perhaps two hundred photographs of it; he knew its every detail – when the trees were in blossom, in leaf, or bare, and the gardens when they were stripped down or coming into flower. It was as if he had lived in that road through the lenses of cameras secreted in canvas BT shelters, parked vans and abandoned cars. The road was usually in monochrome but it made little difference to his ability to recognize it.

He was a driven creature. In the world of legal process, a defence brief could have ripped to small pieces the slight-built young man, pale-faced, hair dark and tangled, with the large spectacles and the crumpled jeans who had turned into the southern junction of the road and who now sauntered along it towards the playing-fields at the top end. He had no authorization to be there, no permission for intrusive surveillance. Merely being in the road broke Church practice and bordered on the edge of legality. He could not have stayed away.

'Excuse me,' a voice shrilled behind him.

He drifted to the side of the pavement and a woman pushed a baby buggy past him. She turned and gave him a withering, suspicious glance. He knew her, from photographs, as Rosie Carthew. He understood that he would have looked an out-of-place cuckoo, and she might have smelt his body. Her husband brought into the country Italian top-of-the-range ladies' dresses, skirts, blouses and handbags. He also knew that, eighteen months before, Rosie Carthew had twice phoned the local police to complain about suspicious vehicles in the road, and twice surveillance operations had been killed off.

A woman was sweeping the pavement of hedge clippings. From the pictures he recognized her as Carol Penberthy. Three months before Mister's arrest, at dead of night, the Security Service A Branch 'watchers' had buried a fish-eye camera in the brick gatepost on the drive of the house opposite his. Nothing to do with Neighbourhood Watch but she must have been restless and up at her bedroom window as they worked. The next morning Carol Penberthy had been filmed by the fish-eye trooping out of her own doorway, down the pavement and up to the Packer doorway for a fast, whispered conversation with Mister in his dressing-gown and slippers. That night a ramshackle van had come down the road and the fish-eye's last image had been of its front fender before it had crashed into the brick column and destroyed the camera.

He doubted that either woman was in conspiracy with Packer – just inquisitive, and nosy, with flapping tongues.

Joey was outside the house. He had seen it through all the hours of the clock, days of the week, weeks of the month, months and seasons of the year. He knew the setting and size of the bricks of the walls, the number of glass panes in the front bay windows on either side of the porch, and the positioning of the spyhole in the door, the chimes in the hall from the bell – a year before the arrest a microphone had been set into the bark of the blossom tree by the front gate; it had lasted a week before being prised out; they'd muttered then that either Mister had got lucky, or that the information tap had leaked once again – and the patterns on the curtains, and the mesh on the net. Behind the door and the curtains he knew the layout of the rooms. The house had been 'burgled' by the A Branch watchers, the first time they had been involved. They were the clever cats introduced to go where plodding policemen and mediocre Church men couldn't reach: they'd put a bug behind the cover where the TV aerial came into the living-room wall and a pinhead probe inside the ventilation grille in the bedroom, which had lasted four days. Both had gone out when the rubbish was put in the bin on the pavement. He knew the rubbish went on a Monday morning. The A Branch intruders had been in the house for seven minutes and had had time to photograph every room. He knew everything about the pictures on the walls, fine landscapes in watercolour but not mega-money, and the wallpaper, the pills in the bathroom cupboard and the food in the fridge. It was as if he had been a house guest.

'Can I help you?'

A woman was getting out of her car in the driveway opposite and two doors down. Leonora Govan. Separated, going on divorced, two children. Surveillance said she was more often inside Mister's home for coffee with the Princess than any other woman in the road.

'No,' Joey said.

'May I ask what you think you're doing?' There was an accusing whip in her voice.

'You can ask, it's a free country.' Joey was smiling. It was the first time he had smiled since he had taken the call on the mobile the afternoon before. But he walked on.

Well, it was a good question, which taxed him. What did he think he was doing? He turned once and looked back. In the corner of his vision field was the woman, Leonora Govan, standing in the middle of her unloaded shopping-bags still staring at him. He glanced a last time at the house. He had brought it alive from the photographs simply by walking past it. Joey Cann was not a romantic; those who didn't like him said he was humourless and without feeling, those who cared for him would say he was dedicated and focused. Flights of fantasy did not fill his mind. What did he think he was doing in a north London suburban road looking at a house where the only sign of life was a single upper window an inch open?

He stood stock still on the pavement. Ahead of him, on the playing-fields, was a class of boys learning football and beyond them a class of girls messing at hockey. At the end of the school day they'd be charging for the school gate, smelling of sweat and with dirty knees, and on the street outside the school would be the pushers, who bought and cut from the dealers. The dealers bought and cut from the importers. The importers made available the heroin, crack, cocaine, Ecstasy, LSD and amphetamines produced in the far corners of the world, and sold on for profit to the dealers and pushers. A romantic would have said the importer, an ordinary man from an ordinary house, was *evil*. Not the word Joey Cann would have used. The 'ordinary man', living in an 'ordinary house', was nothing more and nothing less than a *target*, the bloody biggest target the Church had: Target One. He wondered if the bastard, Packer, had laughed as he came out of court, released. He had heard Mister's laugh on the tapes, seen it on the photographs.

What was he doing? By walking past the house he was putting life on to the photographs and tapes. He was making the man real. He rocked with tiredness and leaned against the fence. The man – Mister, Packer – would have thought himself an Untouchable. He turned round. There was no movement in the road.

He whispered, 'What you should know, Mister, wherever you go, I'm with you, I'm following you. Look over your shoulder, and I'm there.'

Joey giggled out loud.

On the Balkans Desk at the Foreign and Commonwealth Office, they read the signal sent by Hearn from Sarajevo.

'Oh, Christ . . .' a woman said. 'Another body, that's all we damn well need. Lead-lined coffins, paperwork like a phone directory. It's like Interflora, isn't it? People shift bodies, undertakers, like florists shift flowers, don't they? It'll take a whole morning and half an afternoon to sort it. Families always say yes, then balk at the cost, right? I suppose Zagreb would be the nearest for an international undertaker, don't you think?'

The man beside her nodded. He was reading the signal for the third time. He said quietly, 'It doesn't seem that Hearn's too happy about this. I'll push it at the men in raincoats across the river. Give them something to do.'

*

It worked away at him, like an itch needed scratching. Where was the Cruncher?

That morning he went to see his father. Other men suffered bad claustrophobia in gaol or deteriorated physically and mentally, became weighed down by the burden of institutionalism, but not Mister. He had survived imprisonment and now he believed his reputation was gold-plated. He had beaten them. He drove the Princess's 5-series BMW, three years old, and had the front windows down so that the street air blew on to his face. Several times on the drive down Green Lanes from the North Circular, his territory, before he had turned off for Cripps House, he had felt that peculiar buzz of excitement, the product of power, but each time as it peaked there had been the itch – Cruncher's absence.

There were eight floors to Cripps House. The estate had been built in 1949 and was ageing, decaying, but the housing authority always found resources to daub new paint on the doors and windows. The lift was regularly maintained. There were no muggings or thievings in that block, no drugs sold and no syringes left on the landings. On the eighth floor, at the end of the open walkway, perched like a sentry tower with a view to the main road and the parking areas, was the home of Herbie Packer, retired bus driver, widower, never in trouble with the police. Elizabeth Packer, who, when she had worked, had cleaned rooms at the Waldorf Hotel, had been dead now for four years. By the time Albert, not yet Mister, had been twelve years old the regular visitors to the top-floor flat had been teachers and social workers. When he was fourteen they'd been replaced by uniformed and plainclothed police. The refrain from Herbie and Elizabeth Packer to them all had been: 'He's a good boy, really, heart of gold, trouble is he's just got caught up with the wrong crowd.' There was no shifting them on that, even when the police came and arrested him and he went down, aged fifteen, for a year in the youth detention centre at Feltham – and at nineteen, when the door was broken open at dawn and he had been taken away to do two years in Pentonville. And still, as he proudly told it, they refused to blame him. He took the lift up. In any of the other blocks on the estate, all named after cabinet ministers of the day, he would have seen graffiti on the lift walls, and the contact numbers of tarts and pushers. There would have been the screwed-up paper balls on the floor that held

44

heroin wraps, and even in daytime there would have been a mugging risk in the airless shadowed hall beside the lift shaft. But his father lived in Cripps House and the use of a pickaxe handle and electric terminals had secured the safety of the older residents, and small sums of money in plain brown envelopes judiciously placed in the right hands ensured that the building stayed clean and painted and that the lift worked.

Out of the lift, he paused on the walkway and looked across Albion Road to the more distant Highbury Grove. His sight line travelled past the Holloway Road and locked on to the central tower of HMP Pentonville. By screwing up his eyes, straining, he could make out the regimented lines of cell windows on the back of D Wing. During his two years there, he had made the critical contacts of his adult life. As a result of time in Pentonville he had met the men who armed him, distributed for him, dealt for him, and the Eagle, and there his ties to the Cruncher had been strengthened. He swore softly . . . His eyes raked back over the dull skyline of towers, church spires and chimneys. Over the wall of the walkway were Dalton House and Morrison House, then the largest of the estate's blocks, Attlee House. Attlee House had been the Cruncher's home.

He could put his life into boxes. To each he allocated a varied amount of time and commitment. One held the matter of the priority of discipline and respect, and had been dealt with. Another box was his father. He rang the doorbell and set the smile on his face.

The matter of the missing Cruncher was isolated in its own box.

He held his father in his arms and felt the thin bones of the old man's shoulders. Years ago he could have bought a bungalow for his parents down on the coast but his mother had always refused to leave Cripps House. Now, in his seventy-fourth year, his father was the same, wouldn't move closer to Vicky, Alex, May and Julie, his daughters. He stayed put: it was his home. They went in through the door and Mister kept his arm round his father's shoulders. The living room was dominated by the outsize widescreen TV and a soap was playing with the sound turned high because the old man's hearing was going.

'You're looking well, son.'

'Not too bad, Dad, considering.'

'I'm not too bad myself.'

'Is there anything you want, Dad?'

'No, nothing, I want for nothing.'

'You just have to shout. You know that.'

'Nothing, you're a good lad . . . I'm pleased to see you back. Hasn't been right without you being around.'

'Just a bit of a mistake, Dad. They was putting two and two together, making five. Nothing for you to worry about.'

It was as close as they ever came to talking about his life. He sat on the settee that had been pulled apart, half a dozen times a year, in the old days by the CID from Caledonian Road, his heels resting on the same carpet that had been lifted by the police so many times. Beside the television was the shelf and cupboard unit that had never fitted together properly since the detectives had dismantled it for the first time thirty-two years before. Whatever the teachers and social workers had said of him, that he was a hooligan and a thug, his father had never criticized him, never raised a hand or a voice in anger to him. All he had been allowed to provide for the flat was a new cooker and fridge for the kitchen, the fancy electric fire with lit artificial coal, and the widescreen television. In turn, he hadn't allowed his father to visit him on remand, for the same reason that the Princess had not been permitted to come to Brixton, or to sit in the public gallery at the trial. They talked about the programmes on the TV, and the new striker from the Cameroons just signed by Arsenal up the road in Highbury, and the weather, and the girls' babies; mostly he listened and his father talked.

When it was time for him to be moving, he said, 'I thought I might call in at St Matthew's, Dad – thought I might do that.'

They were on the walkway. Over his father's shoulder was the looming mass of Attlee House and he could see the boarded-up window where the Cruncher had been a kid. He kissed his father and hurried away.

The diplomat's signal moved electronically to the Secret Intelligence Service building on the south bank of the Thames river. The name, Duncan Dubbs, and the address, 48 River Mansions, Narrow Street, London E14, were fed into their computers. They failed to register a trace. The Sarajevo signal was recopied and passed back over the river to Thames House, home of the Security Service.

He asked for Matron.

'What name is it, please?' the receptionist asked curtly.

'Packer, Albert Packer.'

The receptionist was new. He hadn't seen her before and his name meant nothing to her. 'Do you have an appointment?'

'I just called by.'

'I know she's rather busy this afternoon.'

'Just tell her that Albert Packer's here. Thank you.'

From the outside it was a depressing Victorian building with a high façade of grimed brick. Inside there was all the light and warmth that fresh-cut flowers could muster. With his eldest sister and his father, he had brought his mother here four years ago. The tumour in her stomach had been inoperable. The receptionist spoke on the phone and he saw the surprise she registered. She told him that he should go up, the implication being that Matron would clear her desk for him, and he said he knew the way. His mother had lingered for a week in St Matthew's Hospice before ending her life in peace. He loved the quiet of the building, and the smell of its cleanness, the light in the corridors and on the stairs, the scent of the flowers. It no longer held terrors for him.

Matron met him outside her office, wearing a prim blue uniform always decorated with her medal ribbons from the British army's nursing corps, and from her chest hung an old gold watch. She was a tall, gaunt-faced woman from the west of Ireland. She was formidable until she spoke, severe until a stranger saw the sparkle of wit in her eyes. On a cold February afternoon, four years ago, when he had brought in his mother, and he'd been refusing to accept the doctors' diagnosis, and he'd seen Matron for the first time, he'd asked defiantly, 'Is it ever possible, does it ever happen, that a patient walks out of here?' Looking him straight in the eye, she'd replied, 'No, it never happens, it isn't ever possible and it would not be helpful to think it.' Few people told Mister the truth, unvarnished, with no adornments. In the next bed to his mother had been an artist who had exhibited with the best, and on the other side of her had been a retired colonel from the Brigade of Guards. His mother, the hotel cleaner, had been between talent and status, given equal care, equal love, equal amounts of pain-killing drugs.

'Good to see you back, Mr Packer. I was wondering...' She chuckled.

'Were you now? What, hoping the bad penny wouldn't turn up?'

She held his hand. They were both laughing. With his other hand he reached into his hip pocket, took out a small, thickly filled envelope, and passed it to her. There was never less than two and a half thousand in fifties and twenties in the envelopes he gave her, and seldom more than five thousand. With sleight of hand she slipped it down the V of her uniform under her throat, then winked. She never mentioned his life, or what she read in newspapers. The first time he had gone back to see her, a month after his mother's funeral, he'd asked her what she needed. She'd said that she'd a list as long as her arm, but a cheque would do. He didn't do cheques, but he did cash, as long as there weren't questions. 'How do I put cash through the books if I don't have a donor's name? Do I tell the financial controller that Christmas came early?' she'd asked. He'd grinned. 'You don't tell anybody anything. You do a bit of creative accounting. You buy what you want to have, you don't have to wait on a committee's delay for authorization. It's yours to spend when and how you want to. I'll send along a man. His speciality's creative accounting.' Cruncher was the money man. The cash in the little envelopes bought tilting beds, painted the wards, provided new TVs, paid half the annual salary of a Macmillan nurse, put in the computer that tracked the daycare patients, helped towards decent funerals for the dead without funds, the bus for outings, the comedians for parties, and holidays for carers. No other person knew of his financial contributions to the hospice and Matron never inquired into the source of the money she gratefully spent. He stayed away from public fund-raising occasions. His photograph had never been taken at the hospice. She'd told him once that what he did was 'raw, no frills charity', and told him another time that when, alone, late at night, she struggled with income and expenditure she didn't know what she'd do without his generosity. He'd blushed then, and she'd never said anything like that again.

'What can I do?'

'I don't really like to ask you...'

'Try me.'

She rolled her eyes. 'There's a Mr Thompson who's just joined us.

He might be with us for a couple of weeks, not much more. He's brought in a box of cowboy books, and his eyes aren't up to reading to himself, and he says women can't read cowboy stories aloud . . . I don't like to ask.'

'No problem.'

Half an hour later, Mister closed *Sunset Pass* having read two chapters of Zane Grey's story to a former water-board engineer suffering from terminal lung cancer.

'Well, that's interesting, very interesting.'

At Thames House, the computer registered a trace when fed the name of Duncan Dubbs. They were hard times at the Security Service. The end of the Cold War internal-espionage threat and the reduction in Irish mainland bombings had set in place a furious campaign to find work to justify the ever-climbing budget. A right-wing politician had described the Service as one of 'sound mediocrity'; on the other side of the House a left-winger had called it 'the worst and most ridiculed in the western alliance'. They were 'grey-shoed plodders' suffering 'institutional inertia'. They were 'boringly parochial' and unable to bring 'intellectual debate' to their future role. As an apology of employment, organized crime had now been dumped on their desks. The computer clattered out the secrets of a man hauled from the Miljacka river in Sarajevo. Success bloomed, a reason for existence.

The line manager pored over the printout. 'Fascinating stuff. What will Mister say? Dear me. Poor old Cruncher. Best bit of news I've heard all day, all week – Cruncher gone to his Maker . . . but in Sarajevo. What the hell was he doing in Sarajevo? I tell you what – "what" is going to cast a certain pall over Mister's face, going to wipe all that joy at walking out of the Old Bailey.' He turned to the young woman who had brought him the printout. 'Cruncher was at Mister's right hand – number cruncher, got it, Irene? – his accountant. That's quite a victory, for us, him losing Cruncher. Can't figure it, what he would have thought he was doing in Sarajevo. I do hope the word spreads that Mister's right-hand scumbag wore silk knickers. Wish it was me who was going to pass on the good news.'

It was twenty-five minutes to midnight when the 5-series BMW turned into the drive. The SIO sat in the passenger seat beside Freddie, the most loyal of his HEOs. Slowly, after Packer and the Princess had gone into the house, he counted to fifty. Then he eased himself up and pushed open the car door. He stood up, coughed, and checked that his ID, in a slightly worn leather case, was in his breast pocket; the card had twenty-four minutes validity left. In the windows the lights blazed. He made his way across the road. He walked up the drive and rang the bell, heard the chimes as footsteps approached the door. He stood flush in front of the spyhole, opened the leather case and displayed the card.

'Brian Finch, senior investigation officer, Customs and Excise. Sorry to disturb you, sir, or ma'am, but I'm afraid it's important. It's about a death. Could you let me in, please?'

The door opened to the extent of the chain and again he displayed the card. The chain was released. He assumed a CCTV camera was on him.

'Good evening, Mrs Packer. It's your husband I've come to see.'

Mister was standing in a doorway off the hall. He'd loosened his tie and discarded his jacket. He seemed taller than he had in the dock at the Old Bailey. There seemed to be a cast in his right eye for the lid was lower than the left, and a finger went to the scar as if that were a nervous tic. Not particularly big, or particularly powerful. No display of threatening muscles in his arms or shoulders, no show of strength in his stature. Rather ordinary, and pale-skinned from the months locked up. And this was a man who, as Brian Finch well knew, created terror.

'What do you want?'

'Came to share a spot of bad news with you, Mr Packer.'

'You got a warrant?'

'I doubt I need a warrant for what I've got to say, Mr Packer.'

'It's intrusion and harassment. I'll call my solicitor.'

'Almost a family bereavement, Mr Packer, I'm afraid. They've fished a body out of the river in Sarajevo, wearing silk underpants – takes all sorts in this life. We think it's the body of your very good friend, Mr Duncan Dubbs. Drowned, probably pissed, no suggestion of foul play. We need a bit of help, Mr Packer, next of kin, that sort of thing . . .'.

Later, the SIO would count this as one of the more extraordinary moments of his professional life. He was telling a major figure in organized crime that his principal lieutenant, his financial guru, his genius at hiding the laundered money, was dead. His eyes never left the face in front of him. There was no reaction. He'd tried, with his words, to belt the man in the most vulnerable place, as if he kicked the softness of the stomach. No gasp, no flicker, no foot shift, no tongue on the lips, no looking away.

'And also, Mr Packer, we can't figure out what Cruncher – sorry, Mr Dubbs – was doing there, a dangerous place like that. Why would he have been in Bosnia?'

The door was closed in his face.

Early summer 1992
'Who is he?'

'It is Husein Bekir.'

'What does he think he's doing?'

'I think he's bringing apple trees. He tried to bring them last autumn, but the water rose too quickly and defeated him. It is the first time the water has been down.'

'Tell him to go back.'

The regular army unit had moved into Ljut the previous afternoon, and in the early evening the captain, Vokic, had used the time to reconnoitre the land leading down from the village to the natural barrier of the river. His orders stated that he should prepare the village as a defensive position, and deny the enemy the chance to take it and so dominate the road behind. In the late evening a woman had come down the hill to Dragan Kovac's house and cooked a meal for him and the retired policeman. Then the two men had sat on the porch, waved away the flies, and drunk brandy.

Captain Vokic was a professional soldier of the Yugoslav National Army; looking on to the valley in the falling light he had been struck both by its beauty and by the simplicity of its defence. At first light, while Dragan Kovac still snored on a cot bed in the living room, the captain had risen from his host's bed, offered to him with enthusiasm, washed, shaved and eaten a plate of bread, cheese and an apple. He had gone up to the village and found his senior NCO and a detail of troops, commandeered two wheelbarrows, and supervised the unloading of the mines from the lorries into the wheelbarrows.

An old tractor, pulling a rattling trailer, was coming down the road beyond the river heading for the ford, where the river flow boiled and charged over the shallow stones. It came towards the fields in front of where the retired policeman now stood beside the captain. In the sunshine the fields glistened with dew and the light caught the brightness of the wild flowers.

'He has bought the fields. They belong to him. He bought them, and his grandfather, and his grandfather's grandfather.'

'He does not come across the river – tell him.'

Dragan Kovac did as he was ordered by the captain. He cupped his hands around his mouth and bellowed into the early-morning air. His friend, Husein Bekir, was not permitted to cross the ford, and should go back. But the tractor kept coming. The instruction was ignored. The captain peered through his binoculars into the early-morning light. He saw a short, thin little man hunched over the tractor wheel. The exhaust fumes hung in a trail behind the tractor's slow advance. It kept on coming towards the Bunica river.

'I think he is deaf. I think he cannot hear me over the noise of the tractor.'

The captain turned, pointed to the rifle slung on a soldier's shoulder, then reached out his hand for it. He took it, armed it, heard the bullet engage in the breech, depressed the safety, and aimed.

The retired policeman protested: 'He is a friend, he is deaf, he owns the fields.'

Dragan Kovac was not to know that the aim taken by the captain was into mud and grass on the track in front of the tractor. The captain squinted over the open sights, then fired a single shot. His shoulder rocked on the recoil. There was a momentary disturbance in the track, five or six paces in front of the tractor, but the high velocity bullet did not bury itself, a spent force, in mud. It hit a smoothed stone and ricocheted upwards into the tractor's radiator. The tractor jerked to a halt. The bullet's discharge echoed through the valley, and then silence. The bullet had killed the engine. Silence hung over them, and over the dark ploughed fields, the lush green meadows, the vineyard that needed weeding and where posts and wires needed maintenance, over the water in the river, and over the villages of Ljut and Vraca.

The war had now been alive in Sarajevo for a month.

On that day in Sarajevo eight civilians would be killed and forty-nine injured by shells fired from tanks and artillery; the airport was closed; the maternity hospital lost power until barrels with a precious two hundred litres of kerosene were fed into an emergency generator; residential areas came under sustained attack. Tickets were issued, that day, for the rationing of basic foods . . . but it had been the first shot fired over the valley.

A few metres short of the ford, the old man sat starkly upright on his motionless tractor.

'You think he can hear you now?'

'I don't know,' the retired policeman said sourly.

'Try. Tell him he should go back. Tell him that if he approaches the river again he will be shot. Tell him this side of the river is now a prohibited area, under the control of the military.'

Dragan Kovac shouted into the silence. He had no heart in what he was ordered to do, yet he was not a sensitive enough man to feel that the one shot had destroyed, perhaps fatally, the innocence of the valley in which he had spent his life and which was home to Husein Bekir. His friend across the river heard him out, then stood on the tractor's footplates and shook his fist at them, before trying to start the tractor again. There was neither a cough from the tractor's engine nor a turn-over whine. He watched the farmer step down clumsily, then turn away and start to trudge back towards his home and his village.

'I don't think you need me,' Dragan Kovac said grimly.

'Correct, I don't. But there is something you should not forget. We are here for your protection. If we are not here they will come across in the night and slit your throats as you sleep, and if they let you live you will be the servants of their religion. You will be dominated by fundamentalists.'

'I suppose so . . .' What the officer said was only what they were forever repeating on TV and the radio. He saw the diminishing back of Husein Bekir, and the tractor marooned near the river, then went back to his home.

The captain supervised the laying of the mines. The previous evening he had drawn a close-detail map of the village, the track down to the river, the fields, the mulberry tree and the riverbank. The two wheelbarrows carried forty-seven mines, and when each one was buried he drew a circle to identify its resting place on the map that filled the greater part of the printed page, marked Zapisnik Minskoeksplozivne Prepreke (MEP). Thirty-one of the mines were designated as PMA2, the remaining sixteen were classified as PMR3. They were anti-personnel mines. First the PMA2s were buried. They were circular, painted brown-green, and ten centimetres in diameter. They went into shallow pits, scooped out by trowels so that only the three-centimetre-wide six-pointed crown protruded. They would take a five-kilo pressure to detonate ninety grams of Hexogen/TNT. At a metre, on exploding, they were reckoned fatal; at five metres they would maim and mutilate, at twenty-five metres they were in-effective. The captain had six locations for them. They were settled in the ground, position noted, then armed. No mine markers or fences needed to be placed around them: the soldiers who would guard the village knew where they were.

The PMR3s required more care to site. They stood thirty centi-metres off the ground and were fastened to a wooden holding stake. From each the soldiers played out twenty-five metres of fine wire, tightened it, then staked the end. The trip-wire, taut, was six inches above the ground. Inside the ribbed metal container, which would fragment into shrapnel, was a core of TNT. They could kill anyone within a twenty-five metre radius of the detonated charge. The positioning of each was marked on the captain's map, and the location of two PROMs and their trip-wires.

As the war stretched out its greedy arms to them, the villages and the valley were now contaminated.

Chapter Three

'What are you going to do? Go on, or step back?'

'I'm thinking.'

At a few minutes short of five o'clock in the morning, the sparrows, tits and chaffinches were starting to sing and, with the smear of grey softening the city's lights, Mister paced in the back garden. The Princess was now beside him. She had been to bed, had woken, found he wasn't beside her – panicked before clarity took over from the weariness – thrown on her dressing-gown, and come to find him. He did most of his thinking in the back garden, and made all of his calls on the mobile phones from behind the screen of conifers that would block out their cameras.

'Can you do it without Cruncher?' she murmured.

He was two years younger than Cruncher. At school he had made the money and Cruncher had been his banker; he had put the frighteners on the kids and they'd taken money from home, and Cruncher had minded it for him and told him where to put it; good old conservative Cruncher, then aged fifteen, had put his first hundred and his first thousand into Channel Island-based bonds, a numbered anonymous account. He'd lost touch with Cruncher when he'd gone to the young-offenders prison, and Cruncher had moved out of Attlee House. If Cruncher had been physically strong, and a hard man, he would eventually have taken over his parents' fruit and vegetable stall in Dalston market. If he'd had money, real money, he would have gone off to accountancy school. He hadn't been strong, hadn't had the resources, so he'd taken a flat south of the river and a clerk's job in the City. The way Cruncher told it, the supervising clerk was embezzling, and doing it cleverly because when the books bounced the blame seemed to fall at Cruncher's feet. A fraud conviction had put Cruncher into Pentonville, and an old friendship had been resumed. Mister, and he'd always acknowledged it, was fascinated – in Pentonville and afterwards – by Cruncher's encyclopedic knowledge of the routes for moving covert money. The day after he'd been released, two weeks before Cruncher came out, he'd gone down to a suburban Blackheath road, kicked in the supervising clerk's door, beaten the man half to death, good enough for him never to work again, and Cruncher had become his man.

'I never backed off.'

'Is it that important, to you?'

'Seems to be.'

'But you've never done anything big – and this is the biggest – without Cruncher.'

Cruncher organized the network of bankers and dealers who would ignore the Disclosure regulations and flush the money into the legal financial system. Cruncher liked to say that the size of the globe had been reduced to that of a computer screen. Accounts were held in the Caymans, Cyprus, Panama, Mexico, Nigeria, Venezuela and Canada, and still there was the old Jersey nest-egg. Cruncher talked a language, foreign enough to Mister, of cost flow, franchising, front companies and offshore. Half the year Cruncher was in the air or swanning in the best hotels on Mister's business, moving money and identifying the property investments that the Eagle made legitimate. If there had been records available to public scrutiny, and there were not, Mister would have figured on any list of Great Britain's top twenty for wealth. It had been Cruncher's idea that he should move on, soar upwards, do his biggest deal. The thought of the deal, in the eight months in Brixton, had sustained Mister.

'Have to learn then, won't I?'

'Like the start again of the good days : . . ?'

'The best days.'

The good days, the best days, the days he loved, were the early ones when he had made his turf sacred and cut down the legs of rivals. The days of security vans and factory payrolls, monitoring the competitors to rip off their trade, enforcing respect with the sawn-off shotguns and Magnum pistols, buying the first drinking clubs, the first bars and the first property in the marinas down on the south coast. He'd made the money, Cruncher had rinsed it, and the Eagle had kept him out of the courts. The best days, when he was on the rise to the top and rivals capitulated, were heady and exhilarating . . . Then the plateau.

More than three years back he had realized he was going nowhere. No more raids and rip-offs because from the middle eighties, when Mister was in his early thirties, the trade had turned to importation, distribution and dealing. Heroin had made the serious money that Cruncher had laundered. Heroin from Afghanistan, imported into the country by the Turks from Green Lanes down the road from the North Circular, had brought in the big money, and the plateau had been reached when the competition had been wiped out. Mister ran the capital's supply, some that went to Birmingham, a bit of what went to Liverpool and Manchester, and most of what went to Newcastle. The only time since he had been on the plateau that he had been hands-on, in a car and taking a sack of stuff to a warehouse, he had been identified and lifted. He hadn't needed to be hands-on, but it was *boredom* that had put him in the car. In the best days he had been in sole control and Cruncher and the Eagle had fed off him; on the plateau there had been little for him to do but read the balance sheets that Cruncher presented to him, and authorize the contracts the Eagle prepared – he couldn't even spend the money because both chorused that yachts, villas, private jets and stakes in football clubs led to investigation and downfall. The week before his arrest, Cruncher had come to him with the plan for the deal, and the boredom had been stifled, killed, scraped out of his system.

The mobile in his pocket warbled quietly. He snapped it on. He listened, then he said, 'I'm sorry, but I don't know what you're talking about. You must have a wrong number.' He switched it off and pocketed it. It was what the Eagle told him he should always say when the Crime Squad man called him.

There was a thin smile on his face. 'The guy who came tonight, he's been fired. He's finished. His time ran out at midnight. I'm still Target One, but his team's wound up.'

Her fingers touched his face. 'You're the top man, you're untouchable. You're walking rings round them.'

'Target One,' he mused, rolled it round his tongue. 'And the Church team's finished . . . Can't do anything about it, not right now, but Cruncher's pad has to be clean.'

Mister knew everything of Cruncher's life. He knew of Cruncher's three loves: rent-boys, luxury, and the handling of money. He tolerated the homosexuality, allowed the luxury and marvelled at the expertise in handling money. The police would be crawling through the terraced Docklands house. He had to hope that the records had been stored safely in the safety-deposit boxes of the small private banks, to which only he and Cruncher had the passwords and entry-code numbers. He didn't think that Cruncher, before he went away, would have left behind evidence that would incriminate him or – worse – lead to the sequestration of his assets.

'So . . . ?'

'I'm going to go with it,' Mister said. 'It's what I want.'

'I'll make a coffee.'

'Don't think I'm not sorry about Cruncher, but I feel good.'

On the first train of the day that clattered down the tracks south from Glasgow a tall, elderly man with a stooping walk came back to his seat from the buffet car.

His seat was in standard class. His rank in Customs & Excise entitled him to pullman or first-class travel, a full English breakfast in the restaurant, and complimentary newspapers. But it was his style that he claimed the minimum of available expenses. The habit was unsettling to his juniors and frowned on by his more senior colleagues. He revelled in the discomfort he caused. He would not have admitted it to anyone he worked with, but he rather prized the ability to create discomfort. No one in the National Investigation Service, whether drunk or hallucinating, would ever suggest there was a possibility that this senior investigation officer had his price. In work practice, he was regarded as a dinosaur from before the Stone

Age, but his incorruptibility was guaranteed. He had demanded, and reluctantly been given, a receipt for the single beaker of coffee. He settled into his seat. A young mother was breastfeeding beside him. A businessman opposite shouted into his mobile. He shared foot-space with a student who'd spread textbooks across the common table. He travelled light. In the rack above him were a small tartan sports bag and a waxed green coat. A thin briefcase lay on the table, close to his hand, as if it were the only thing of importance he had brought with him. He wore highly bossed but worn brown brogues, a heavy check shirt, a quiet braid tie, and a three-piece suit of grey tweed with green flecks. An antique gold watch-chain hung across his upper abdomen. The mother, the businessman and the student would have been hard put to place him in society. From an inside pocket he took a slim, ancient flask and poured a dash of malt into the railway coffee, sipped it, growled in quiet satisfaction, then clamped an unlit pipe in his mouth.

He unzipped his briefcase and took out a single sheet of paper, faxed to him the previous evening after he had been called to London. It was the preliminary report on a drowning in the river running through Sarajevo.

Late summer 1992
When dawn came, the soldiers were nervous and tired after a night of standing-to. An explosion had initiated the alert.

Dragan Kovac found Captain Vokic by the well. He saw the bags under his bleary eyes. The retired policeman no longer lived in his own home: he had been told it was too dangerous for him to stay there now that paramilitary bandits had moved into the village across the river, and he lodged with his nephew, his nephew's wife and their children, an awkward arrangement. The captain now slept in one of the two stone and heavy-timber bunkers, had made a command post in the dank interior of the other. Kovac had come to resent the presence of Captain Vokic in the community because he, the leader, was relegated in importance: all decisions affecting the village and its life were taken by the captain. Not that there was great life in the village. The younger men had all been taken into the Serb army and were scattered through Bosnia, and many of the younger women had left for the heartland of their own people, far distant from the uncertainties of the war's front line.

Dragan Kovac asked for, and was grudgingly given, the captain's binoculars. He stared out into a blur before the captain irritably showed him the focus ring. Clarity came. He was looking at the home of his former friend, Husein Bekir. When he talked with the old men and women who were left in Ljut, or his nephew, or the young soldiers, it was always of the enemy across the valley, and the atrocities that they would commit if they were ever able to come in strength over the Bunica river. There had been no contact with the men and women of Vraca since the soldiers had come to Ljut. He could see the smoke rising from the chimneys, children playing, and men with rifles sitting idly on stones, smoking or reading. He did not see Husein Bekir, though he searched for him among the cattle and the sheep that scavenged the poor ground on that side of the river for fodder. If he had not had the binoculars he would not have seen Lila, Husein's wife, and then he would not have thought of the man whose home faced his. He handed them back to the captain.

'What happened in the night?'

'A mine exploded.'

'Did they try to come through, Captain?'

'I don't know. Perhaps.'

'The soldiers are scared, like women,' Dragan Kovac said dismissively.

'Of course they are frightened . . . They are not like the regulars who first came here, they are not even conscripts. They are village boys. All they have of the army is the uniform. Always I am asked to send more men away for transfer to a more important front line. I don't think that we could resist an attack pressed with determination.'

'How do you give them courage?'

'I put out more mines. The more mines they have in front of them, the braver they are.'

Later in the morning the soldiers carried forward two sacks of PROM mines. The captain fretted around them in the long grass of the grazing fields, in the weeds that had grown up in the ploughed fields, and in the overgrown vineyards. The PROMs were bigger, more lethal. A few were buried in holes hacked out of the grass and weeds so that only four stubby prongs were visible before the plants were worked back over them, and they were hidden; they would be activated by nine kilos of pressure. More were attached to short stakes and had a trip-wire leading from the antenna to a second stake; they also would be hidden when the grass and weeds grew, and were activated by a three-kilo vigorous tug on the wire. Among the military men on both sides of the war, the PROM was the most feared. On firing, a first charge threw the explosive capsule nearly a metre into the air, then came the main detonation. The shrapnel would fly out at a level to hit the genitals or soft lower belly of the victim. It was deadly. If he had not had the detail of his map, the captain would not have been able to take his soldiers down into the fields where the fallen grass and yellowing, seeding weeds covered that earlier sowing. Fourteen new mines were planted, to stiffen the morale of the young soldiers, and the location of each was added to the captain's map.

The pollution of the valley had spread, and other than the map there was no evidence of it.

'We found where the mine exploded, but there was no blood there, no pieces,' the captain later told Dragan Kovic. 'I think it was an animal, probably moving too low, on its stomach, for the shrapnel . . . You should go, you know, you should leave. It is not safe here.'

'It's my home,' the retired policeman said.

'I have heard on the radio – I am transferring in the morning to Sarajevo.' The captain stood outside his bunker. 'You will not have a professional to protect you, only an idiot from Foca, some untrained kids, and a minefield.'

On arrival at Heathrow airport, the body was hijacked.

The slip of paper that authorized its removal was illegibly signed, but that was good enough for the London firm of undertakers. The hearse drove away empty from Cargo, and a closed van took the lined casket to the pathology wing of the West Middlesex Hospital. The man requested by the Home Office to carry out the post-mortem was an expert in the study of corpses retrieved from the water. It was said of him that if there were a chance of the cause of death being learned – suicide, accident or murder – he would find it. On a quiet Saturday morning, the professor of pathology waited for the trolley to be wheeled into his workplace, and for the casket to be unscrewed.

That weekend . . .

. . . Randomly chosen pubs, and the back rooms of the *spieler* Turkish-owned cafés in Green Lanes, were used by Mister for meetings. He set his business operations back on course. On the doors and in the alleyways at the rear and side of these buildings were his Cards. Shipments' movements were authorized, and tables were piled with envelopes of banknotes as debts and obligations were called in. Summoned by staccato calls on mobile phones, men came to pay court to Mister and wished him well. He spoke little, but that was his way. There were three patients now in the capital city's intensive-care beds – sufficient to emphasize his aura of power.

. . . For fourteen hours on the Saturday, and a further thirteen hours the following day, a man in a flecked tweed suit sat undisturbed and unseen in the small backroom annexe behind the chief investigation officer's suite and pored over the papers, profiles and tape transcripts concerning the life and times of Albert William Packer.

. . . Through Saturday, day and night, and Sunday, Joey Cann sat listlessly in the bed-sit that was his south London home, or slept fitfully. The telephone, in the ground-floor hall two floors below, never rang for him: neither did his mobile. On the Saturday afternoon, he should have been on the touchline watching Jen play hockey, but he'd not gone, and without explanation he'd cut the clubhouse disco in the evening. On Sunday, he should have been in Somerset for his mother's birthday lunch, but he'd rung to say he had a cold and didn't want to pass it on. The photograph of the arrest was now Sellotaped to the wall at the foot of his bed.

. . . There was a crowded schedule for Henry Arbuthnot in the Surrey countryside, where nobody had heard of the Eagle. Pigeon shooting on Saturday morning, vulgar but useful for keeping the eye in practice for the serious matter of the pheasant season, a moment of respite before spending the next day with Maureen and the girls at the Chiddingfold Hunters' gymkhana, where his eldest banked on a rosette, and then a couple of solitary hours in his study to prepare for Monday's early journey to London.

. . . A charity's lorry was loaded at the back of a village's church hall in the East Midlands with boxes of woollens and cast-off clothes for adults and outgrown toys for children. An answer to a begging advertisement, placed in a local newspaper, for a haulage transporter to offer the charity a lorry had been answered by a Mr Duncan Dubbs, two months before. Not only would a lorry be provided, at no expense, to help those needy and unhappy people in the heart of Europe, but a driver too, and Mr Dubbs had told the organizing committee that he hoped to be able to add to their generosity with clothes and toys his own community had gathered together.

. . . A sudden squalling blizzard hit Sarajevo. The mountains were masked by grey-black cloud. The streets were icy and treacherous. In premature darkness, gloom and danger fell across the city, and the river running through it rose to a spiteful torrent.

Crossing the main road cautiously into the city, Frank Williams had reached the offices of the judge. He'd skipped indoor football over the weekend, and instead had finalized the pouch of reports relating to the retrieval of a body from the Miljacka river. One more signature and the matter was closed. The judge's chambers were a chaotic mass of paper, and the man was distracted. He needed one more signature, received it, and then there was a final tying up of loose ends. Frank was given three eye-witness statements, the testimonies of three citizens of the city who had told local police that they had actually seen a man staggering from a night-club restaurant beside the river, then leaning alone over the rail of the bridge, and the last witness had heard a dull splash. Well done, the local boys, he thought. Good initiative, good enterprise – a welcome change. In return he gave the judge a telephone number that had been retrieved from a notepad found beside the bed in the hotel room; a Finn he worked with had known the technique of covering paper with the finest grains of black powder to identify the indentation of writing on the lower sheets of a pad after the upper sheets had been used and destroyed. They shook hands.

She found Joey in the unlit room, lying on his bed and staring at the ceiling. She would not have seen him but for the street-lights that beamed through the window.

The bed had not been made and it was now middle evening. The room was usually a temple to orderliness. Her eyes roved over the dirty coffee mugs, tinfoil containers from a takeaway curry, empty beer bottles, and typed papers scattered on the carpet. She had her own keys to the front door of the house and to the room on the second floor. They all said, the girls in her team, that she was lunatic to keep the relationship going. They were right, and she didn't listen . . . She saw the picture on the wall. It was new, hadn't been there last week. He shouldn't have stuck the photograph to the wall. It wasn't fair on Violet, who'd put up good expensive wallpaper for her tenant. Normally she would have said it was a damn fine room, airy and light in the daytime, and even felt something like home when the curtains were drawn. But, this evening, in the shadows cast by the orange street-lighting it seemed to her to hold a threat. She looked back at the picture, as if it were the source, not the mess on the floor and Joey prone on his unmade bed. The room conspired to frighten her.

'How long have you been here?'

He did not answer. His eyes held a point on the ceiling.

'I'm speaking to you, Joey. How long have you been like this?'

The silence beat back at her.

'Joey, I'm not asking much. Aren't I entitled to expect an answer to a civil question – entitled or not?'

She thought she saw a brutishness in his face, and something cruel at his mouth.

'Joey, don't mind me, you're being pathetic. You don't want me here? Right, I'm going.'

Not that she did. The other girls said she was attractive and could have done better. It wasn't love, between them, not the sort of love she'd read of in the magazines from her teenage days, it was just something bloody comfortable, and she'd learned to exist alongside the variations of rudeness or indifference. They'd met when he'd been sent to the school to liaise with the headteacher about setting up a remote surveillance camera in the roof space above the science block that would monitor a house across the road from the school's front gate. She'd had a free period and been deputed to show him the attic trap door. She'd liked him immediately, and liked more the boyish shyness with which he'd asked to see her again. God, the ground didn't move under them, but they slept together, went to the cinema together and watched TV together. The last two years, before and after the arrest of the man Sellotaped to the wallpaper, she'd come to the empty – more often than not – room, cleaned and cooked and sometimes taken his washing to the launderette. All the other girls said she was an idiot.

She knew the answer, but asked: 'Haven't you been to work today?'

'Not wanted. Told to go home. Put my feet up, they said. Relax, enjoy myself, think about something else. So, here I am.'

She was always, couldn't help herself, most an idiot when he seemed so vulnerable. She doubted anyone else in the world saw the fractured, weak aspect of him. For two years he had been unable to think, to her knowledge, of anything else. When they were together, she'd shared him with Sierra Quebec Golf – what a stupid name. No hobbies, no interests. Some of the men she worked with were into sport, or photography, hill rambling, boozing, or skirt-chasing. He only had his team and his target. She didn't count against his team, or the man whose photograph was on the wall. She sat on the bed beside him.

'What's special about him?' She took his hand. 'Why does he matter so much?' With her thumb and forefinger she kneaded the rough skin on the back of his hand. 'Isn't it just another job, another day?'

While she held his hand she turned away from his face, and the pain she saw there, and looked up at the photograph. 'Is it because of corruption?'

She'd hit the cord. His fingers jerked tightly around her hand and his nails gouged her. His mouth slackened then tightened in a spasm.

'Did he buy his way out? That's the worst, isn't it? Corruption hurts most, yes?'

He loosened her hand.

'Corruption's the worst, right? You're all looking at each other, all tainted by suspicion. I suppose men come in and search the files, go through all your assessments, get the computers to hack into your bank accounts, and look at what car you're driving, what your mortgage or your rent is, pry into your lives. There's no answer to it, is there? Can't get rid of the smell. Trust's gone . . . I'm sorry, Joey, believe me. I don't know what else I can say . . .'

She knew the way, from what he'd told her – no confidences but the basics – that the investigation had involved the National Crime Squad, the National Criminal Intelligence Service and, of course, the Crown Prosecution Service, and, the National Investigation Service.

Ferocity in her voice. 'Don't let anyone ever say it was you . . . Don't let anyone ever say the bastard bought you, or frightened you.'

She pushed herself up from the bed, stamped to the door, switched on the light, then went back across the room to the window where she ripped the curtains shut. She seemed to smack her hands together as if it were time to start afresh. She had her back to him as she crouched on the carpet and started to pull together the scattered papers and pack them away, haphazardly, any old order, into the file boxes, then dropped the lot of them beside the door. He didn't protest, had turned to face the wall. She went to the cupboard under the sink, retrieved a bin bag and stuffed the takeaway tinfoil boxes into it. She swept up the bottles and dumped them, too, into the bag. The mugs went into the sink. The clothes from the floor, and the shoes, she threw headlong into the back of the wardrobe. She rinsed the mugs and his knife and fork, then banged them down on the draining-board. She took the vacuum cleaner out of the cupboard beside the shelf on which his crockery was stacked, and ran it over the carpet, searching for rice grains, dust, purging the room. She went to the bed, caught at his T-shirt and spilled him off it, on to the floor. She made the bed, smacked the creases out of the blankets, sheets and pillows, then turned to face the picture on the wall. She reached up to it and carefully, so that Violet's wallpaper would not be damaged, freed it from the floral pattern. She held it in her hands and her fingers quivered.

'That bastard doesn't own you, Joey,' she hissed. 'You leave him there and the bastard dominates you, watches over you. Don't let him, Joey, or he'll destroy you. He may think, the fucking bastard, that he can buy anybody, frighten anybody – but not you, Joey. He's a piece of shit.'

She was crying as she tore the picture into pieces and flung them into the rubbish bag.

'How is it that people like that can have such power?'

The tears streamed down her face. She shrugged into her coat. The telephone was ringing in the hall downstairs. She closed the door after her and stumbled down the stairs with the rubbish bag.

Joey's landlady, Violet, was speaking into the phone. 'His work-place, you say .. Right, I'll go and get him. It's two flights of stairs, so it'll be a moment.'

She should have done it herself, should have gone back up the stairs and saved the elderly lady the trudge, but she could not face the doom atmosphere of his room again. She went out into the street and dropped the bin bag into the dustbin. But she knew that the man's power remained in the room with Joey.

He sauntered a pace behind Atkins, his armourer. For a man hard to surprise it was an eye-opening experience. Mister had never before been to anything like the Defence Systems and Equipment International Exhibition. Outside, the spring morning tipped with rain. Atkins had picked him up at a service station on the north side of the motorway ringing London and brought him down in the four-wheel drive. They'd been clogged in traffic as they'd approached the site and had crawled past demonstrators at the gate, hemmed in by a police cordon, as they held up placards denouncing the 'Death Supermarket'. That he was there, that the arrangements had been put in place, was a reflection of his confidence in the Eagle's assurance that he would walk from the Old Bailey. He seldom spoke, but he listened. His armourer knew enough to initiate conversations that he thought Mister would be interested to hear, but not to involve or introduce him.

They went down the aisles between stands that displayed the pride of military hardware. Everything was on show from tanks and armoured cars to titanium-plated aircraft cockpits, rotating heli-copter mounts for rapid-firing triple-barrel machine-guns, protective clothing for troops in a chemical-warfare environment, land-, air- and sea-launched missiles.

At the main door, as their entry passes were processed, Atkins had asked, 'What in particular, Mister?'

'Just what I'm getting,' had been the laconic reply.

'In how long?'

'No hurry.'

In the past he had taken the Princess to the Ideal Home Exhibition, and the Motor Show. Not a lot of difference. From behind the stands, salesmen, who hooked on to any interest, darted out and tried to pressure drinks into hands. But they stayed dry: Atkins knew enough of Mister to know that alcohol was frowned on. Mister had made a major financial commitment to what he was getting, but he regarded it as necessary if the deal were to go through – the deal had been Cruncher's concept.

It was all about 'peace', Mister noted. Peace-keeping, peace enforcement, peace maintenance were the slogans of the day. He didn't hear the word *kill*, or read it. He hung back when Atkins met a general he'd served under, and who knew his father.

'Hello, hello, how are things going, now that you're out?'

'Struggling along, sir, but not too bad, sir, can't complain – it's an eye-opener, sir, but I haven't seen a bayonet.'

'It's all so damned sophisticated. Easy to forget that fighting is done by men. The better the equipment you give your men, the bigger the chance that it'll crash. If it crashes he's lost. In real combat it's man against man – but all the foreign people want is the best, so they can drool over it and hope to God they never have to use it. Must be getting along. Jolly good to see you . . .'

They came to a mock-up of a 'frontier post' where the British army were 'fighting for peace'. He looked over the Land-Rover with the machine-gun mounted, a sniper in a gillie suit, and a mortar team. In front of him were a cluster of tiny Asians, Chinese and Thais, and towering over them were their escort officers. They were looking down. Mister's eyes ducked, and Atkins eased the small-built men a little to the side, did it with care so that no offence was given. Prone on the ground in front of the 'frontier post' were two camouflaged soldiers who made a tableau with a squat, thuggish piece of gear mounted on a shallow tripod. The dull light reflected from the launcher's lens. A sergeant was telling the Asians the qualities of the anti-tank weapon system: '. . . destroys tanks, helicopters and bunkers. Can fire up to three per minute. Aim point is hit point, and it's effective up to 2,500 yards. You can change target during the missile's flight, and because of its low-launch velocity the chance of detection and counter-measures is minimal. It has a double-charge warhead for penetration, packs a hell of a punch . . .'

Mister's question was whispered: 'Is that what I'm getting?'

'The medium-range Trigat – MR Trigat – that's what you're

getting. Sorry, that's what you've got. It's an excellent weapon, Mister, the best of its kind.'

He had absorbed everything he had heard. *En route* to Bosnia was a weapon that could not be afforded locally, that was sophisticated and would be a prized symbol of superiority. On one of his rare visits to Brixton, Cruncher had told him that he should take with him gear that would turn heads. The gear was an offering, a gift – so Cruncher had explained it – to convince doubters that Mister was top league. When Mister came, bearing gifts, he would be listened to. He was going to ride on the back of the MR Trigat. It was heavy stuff, new to anything he had had before. Atkins, the armourer, had provided him in the past with Uzis and Glocks, Skorpions, Hecklers and a Kalashnikov, and with two-ounce measures of Semtex explosive to blow a reinforced warehouse door for a *protégé*. He liked Atkins, nine years in the Royal Green Jackets with a final rank of captain; the man's leaving his regiment in the wake of a scandal – impregnating a brigadier's daughter and running from the consequences – then setting up as a freelance military consultant had slotted in well with Mister's plans. Atkins had a mannered drawl, offhand, but he took no liberties, and he delivered. Atkins had also done time in Bosnia. Mister had no complaints. Atkins had suggested the way to acquire four MR Trigat launchers, and twenty missiles, as well as seven handsets and the control unit for an ITT-built Advanced Tactical Communications System, combining data and voice-network capability, and security. When Mister travelled, he would be well laden with gifts. He did not understand how the anti-tank weapon or the communications system worked, but that didn't leave him with any feeling of inferiority. The gifts guaranteed that he would win a hearing and respect . . . Cruncher had been laying the ground.

'What about lunch, Mister? You've seen about everything other than the open-air displays, but there's no call for you to get soaked. I expect it'll be a salmon steak in the VIP restaurant.'

'Why not?'

He could beat the legal system, and he could buy into supplies of the latest, most restricted military equipment, and they could not touch him.

'Tell me, all this stuff here, who are the customers?'

'Other than you, Mister, they're governments. That's the level this place is at.'

The pathologist had few illusions as to the technical knowledge of those who would read his reports, so he doubled up: one report for men and women with a medical and forensic background, and a second for policemen, Security Service officers, civil servants from the Home Office and Customs & Excise. The second report, for laypersons, explained the finding of a narrow bruised contusion at an upper position at the back of the cadaver's – Dubbs's – neck. The blow causing the contusion would have been sufficient, in the pathologist's opinion, to cause death or, at least, total disablement. It followed that the cadaver could not, in the pathologist's opinion, have then mounted a railing or a wall and pitched himself into the river. An intervening paragraph stated that the injury had not been sustained during the cadaver's journey down the river. The half-page report concluded: 'The blow was probably effected with the heel of a hand by a man of considerable strength and with a knowledge of where to strike. Assume he is trained or has familiarized himself with the techniques of unarmed combat, as taught to Special Forces. Conclusion: Murder.'

After anxiously telephoning the chief investigation officer, a civil servant agreed to follow the unusual and possibly illegal road of withholding the post-mortem's findings *sine die*. Rank was pulled. The civil servant was left in no doubt as to the importance of the connections of the CIO, and his Whitehall influence, and took a sensible course. The pathologist's conclusion would not enter the public domain. Hardly a month went by without the CIO telling colleagues: 'There's no point having authority if you're not prepared to exercise it.' The final twisting of the civil servant's arm, close to verbal breaking-point, was the CIO's clear message that the findings represented a matter of national security.

Both reports, technical and layperson's, were locked away.

'You come with a backpack of recommendations.'

'I didn't put them there.'

The chief investigation officer, Dennis Cork, poured tea from a silver pot into a bone-china cup. He held up the milk jug, an invitation, but across the desk there was a shake of the head. He pointed to the lemon slices, but there was a hand-gestured refusal. He passed the black tea to his guest. It was passed back.

'I'll take three sugars, please.'

Three sugar cubes went into the cup. It was returned, then stirred vigorously. 'Thank you – it's the way my father always took it.'

'The recommendations wrap round, and protect, a considerable reputation.'

'That's for others to say . . . and I don't believe compliments, sincere or otherwise, ever contributed much.'

The CIO liked him. His office was temperature-controlled: a new system he'd had put in when the suite was refurbished – at expense – enabled him to be shirt-sleeved and comfortable. He thought it displayed eccentricity and character that the guest still wore the heavy tweed jacket and the buttoned waistcoat with its watch-chain. They were bright eyes facing him, a little rheumy with age, but they were hard, and when they were fastened on him he found them difficult to meet.

'You've read yourself in?'

'I've read as much as I can in two and a half days of a three-year investigation.'

'It's wounded us.'

'When a man like that walks it's always hurtful, particularly if you have to account for the expenditure.'

If the CIO had been looking to be rewarded with sympathy he would have been disappointed. He doubted this man was big on commiseration. It was hardness he wanted, and chilling coldness – and leadership. He pressed on. 'You are fifty-nine years old, facing retirement. You have done us the kindness of travelling south at short notice, personal inconvenience, and now I am asking you – it is a request – to spend a few weeks, maybe a month, of your last year with us, to squat down here. A last tilt at Packer while the iron's still moderately warm, if you know what I mean. If it all goes cold then it might be years before I can justify the same level of resources to target him – a final throw. Will you?'

It was a plea for help. He was offering the best and most responsible job in the Service, and the most difficult. Short of getting down on bended bloody knee he could hardly have gilded that particular lily further. The guest pondered, took his time. It seemed an age. The CIO drummed carelessly at his desk top with a pencil. A frown had cut the man's forehead; his fingers were locked together and creaked as he opened and closed the palms of his hands. Then he sipped the tea, and made up his mind.

'My way, without let or hindrance.'

'Any way you want, within the law. I don't know how often you'll get back-up there . . .'

'They'll still be there when I've finished.'

The CIO imagined mountains and sea cliffs that were as remote and inhospitable as the eyes that were again locked on him. The file told him this dour man spent his weekends away on a peninsula up the north-west coast from Glasgow. He supposed, a flight of fancy, that the terrain and the seascape, harsh and without charity, had moulded the character of the man. The response was a challenge.

'It'll be a new team.'

'Agreed.'

'Chosen by me, from outside London, from outside the Custom House.'

'Agreed.' He started to beam his charm. 'But with one exception.'

'I'm not hearing you.'

He hadn't wanted to recruit an easy man to take over Sierra Quebec Golf. He wanted a man who was contrary, awkward and dogmatic, a man who bullied.

'A new team from outside London, chosen by you, is what you'll get – with one exception.'

'I'm not a negotiator.' The response, rasped back, was immediate.

'The record says, which is why you're here, that you don't compromise. The one exception – I think you should consider it – was described to me as "an arrogant shite". At least meet him.'

Joey Cann sat alone in the room, with the empty lockers, clean walls and blank computer screens, and waited. He did not know what to expect.

Chapter Four

His head rested on his hands in front of the screen. He heard the door open and the beat of heavy shoes on the floor. He felt the presence of the man behind him.

'Are you Joey Cann?'

'That's right.'

'The name's Douglas Gough – Dougie to friends, but slow to make them.'

He had used a cold, pebble-rattling voice. It took Joey a few sharp seconds to realize why there was no warmth. They were not friends, pals, chums, mates. He had been told during the phone call bringing him in, from the CIO's personal assistant, that a new team would reactivate Sierra Quebec Golf, and that he was to meet, and brief, the team-leader replacing Finch. He thought that the banter, wit and crack of the old team was dead. He turned to face Gough and saw no welcome offered him.

'I'm lumbered with you.'

'Don't expect me to apologize.'

'I was told I needed you because you're the archivist.'

'I know more about it than anyone else.'

'And that you're an arrogant shite.'

'I do my job as best I can.'

'The "best" is only adequate. Go short of the best and you're out on your neck.'

'Thank you.' He meant it. Joey felt a surge of gratitude and relief. In his room, over the weekend, he had lain on his bed, toyed with a takeaway, sipped and not enjoyed his beers, and imagined a life divorced from Albert William Packer. Anything, he'd thought, other than the work around Packer would be second-rate. He noticed the scrubbed clean, babylike, out-of-doors complexion of Gough; the skin on his cheeks, veined, was the same as his father's down on the estate in Somerset. The shoes, polished and cracked, were the same as his father wore, and the suit when his father went up to the house to meet with the owners. There was the scrape of a match then the face was diffused behind pipesmoke.

A gravelled question. 'How did you come in, Joey?'

'I walked to the Underground, took a tube from Tooting Bec to Bank, then walked.'

'Did you see any soldiers?'

'No.'

'Did you see any police with guns?'

'No.'

'Did you go through any road-blocks, were you body-searched, did you have to produce ID?'

'I didn't.'

'This is just so that we understand each other, so you get to appreciate where I'm coming from, and where I'm going to. If the threat were terrorism, a similar threat, a threat on the scale we face now and today, then there would have been troops on the streets, guns, blocks and identity checks. Headlines in papers, worried faces on TV, pundits chattering – but it's not terrorism. It's crime . . . At the height of a terrorist campaign, assassinations and bombs in railway stations, how many people get hurt, get killed – ten a year, maximum ten? What I'm saying, Joey, terrorism is pine marten's piss compared with the threat of crime. Where I come from, where I was reared, we have a small church, a free church, that makes a deal of laughter from people who don't know us. Our church believes in the power of evil. We don't make excuses for evil, we believe it should be cut out, root and branch, then burned. Crime is narcotics, narcotics are evil. They kill and they destroy. They threaten our values. There are no "sunlit uplands" in crime fighting, no bayonet charges, heroic it is not . . . Do you get where I'm coming from, and where I'm going?'

'I think so.'

'Do you think I'm a mad, daft beggar?'

'I think I'd feel privileged to work on your team.'

'You can walk now.'

'I'd like to stay.'

'Why did the case go down?'

'All the usual suspects: incompetence, intimidation and corruption.'

'Listen hard to me, young man. We are losing the war against the importation of class A drugs. With our seizures we are not even touching the customer's supplies. We are incapable of creating shortages on the street. We are hemmed in by the restrictions of legal process, by the decisions of the European Court of Human Rights, and we can shrug and walk away, and say tomorrow'll be better. It won't, it'll be worse. I don't accept that. I have to win, Joey, and I will walk over people in my way to do it. I'll walk over you, if I have to, and not break stride. What's going on now, the volume of narcotics importation, shames us. It'll destroy us, it's a cancer in us. I'll tell you what I like – when a judge says, "Fifteen years. Take him down." What I like better is when the guy then turns and shouts, "I'll fucking kill you, see if I won't." If you go after them hard you break the power. Without the power they're rubbish. You bin rubbish. When the pressure is exerted on an evil man he makes mistakes. When he makes mistakes you have to be there . . . You may be arrogant – you may have an attitude problem – but it means nothing to me, as long as you're going to be there and ready when the mistake's made.'

Joey said, 'I want to be part of that being there.'

'Do me a cartwheel.'

Joey switched on the computer. A cartwheel was a diagram to show the organization of a criminal enterprise. He drew a box in the centre of the screen. He typed the two names in the centre of the box: Mister and the Princess.

'He's always called Mister. It's the code on the phones and how he expects to be addressed – we think it started off as respect. He wanted to be *Mister* Packer. She's Primrose, her code and what he calls her is the *Princess*. She's a part of his firm, talked to and trusted. He doesn't play about, he's totally loyal to her.'

Joey drew a circle around the box, and then the spokes from the box to the circle. He typed at the end of a spoke the *Cruncher*. 'All the prime associates are coded names. The number cruncher, the accountant, Duncan Dubbs. He does the finance on every significant deal – wasn't at the Old Bailey.'

He was passed a sheet of paper by Gough.

His brow furrowed as he read the pathologist's report, the layperson's version. 'I don't understand what was for them in Sarajevo.'

'It'll keep. Go on.'

He typed another name. 'Henry Arbuthnot is the *Eagle*, that's legal eagle. He's the solicitor on retainer, and he does all the contracts.'

More names and more spokes, and the cartwheel formed. Joey said that *Atkins*, the soldier Tommy Atkins, was Bruce James, ex-Royal Green Jackets, the armourer who produced the weapons used by the *Cards*, the Cardmen/Hardmen, who were the enforcers, and he named the three principals. Then there was the *Mixer*, Mixer/Fixer, who acted as the firm's general manager and made the routine arrangements.

He drew the last spoke line, and he wrote in the *Eels*. 'Eels is wheels – that's Billy Smith and Jason Tyrie. They drive for him. They're both from the block he grew up in, and both from Pentonville days. That's the inner team. Oh, and there's a name I don't have, and a code. It's the information spoke – might be us or the Crime Squad – and it's important. It's on the inside.'

Gough gazed down at the cartwheel.

The drawing represented the fruits of Joey's life over the last weeks, months, years. The cartwheel was the obsession that held him. The hook had caught him from the first day he had been given the archivist job in Sierra Quebec Golf. All the photographs and all the tape transcripts were on the computer, but they needn't have been. They were lodged in Joey Cann's mind. Locked in that room, with the screen for company, he had learned more about Mister than any of the men and women who had tracked the cars, watched the house, tried to follow the money, and who could go out at the end and drink until they couldn't stand. He had overheard it said, but never to his face, that it was obsession, and sad.

Joey thought he had been thrown a lifeline.

'What's the weakest link?'

'There may be one, but we never found it. What I think . . .'

'What do you think, Joey?'

'He reckons he's beaten us, and he'll be running now to catch up on his life – I think the weakest link is *Mister*.'

It was off his tongue, and he wished he hadn't said it. He looked at the cartwheel he'd made laughing at him prettily from the computer screen, and wondered whether Gough thought him foolish.

He looked round to see if his opinion was sneered at but saw only Gough's back, going out.

'I'm taking you with me,' Mister said.

The Eagle's voice fluttered. 'Are you sure? – Is that really necessary?'

'Yes, that's why I'm taking you.'

'Don't you think I'd be more use here?'

'No, or I wouldn't be taking you.'

There were two locations where Mister had always felt talk was safe: one was the Clerkenwell office of Henry Arbuthnot, Solicitor at Law, above the launderette. Under the terms of the published *Intrusive Surveillance – Code of Practice*, authorization for bugs and taps in premises where client met legal adviser could not be given by a policeman or a Customs officer. Section 2 paragraph 7 demanded that authorization came from a commissioner. Section 1 paragraph 8 stated a commissioner was a 'person who holds or has held high judicial office and has been appointed by the Prime Minister for a term of 3 years to undertake functions specified in Part III of the Act (Police Act 1997)'. Serving and retired judges were likely – the Eagle swore to it – most times out of ten to throw back the request. The office was safe territory. Josh, the clerk, was making coffee, and never came in before he'd knocked and been told to enter.

'We go on Thursday. Mixer's doing the tickets.'

'I'm not sure that I've the background or, indeed, the expertise required.'

'Are you turning me down?'

The Eagle never disagreed with Mister. Privately, personally, buried from sight, he had been against the venture from the day the

Cruncher – the barrow-boy – had raised it. With mounting dismay he had noted Mister's ever-growing enthusiasm for the branch-out into new territory. He knew how far to go: there was a line over which he would not step. When he was maudlin – worst when he took the Monday-morning train from Guildford to London and left behind the comfort of his family, his land and his home – he thought of himself as a victim. He could do his own deal, of course, and go Queen's Evidence, but he had no doubt that he would never live to enjoy the parts of his life that mattered to him – the family, the land, the home. He would be killed ruthlessly, and painfully. He knew what the Cards did, and he knew that Mister was more vicious than the men he employed. The Eagle took the money, and did what he was told to do.

'How'd you get that idea? You want me to go with you, I go. It's as simple as that.'

'Just for a moment I thought the old Eagle was giving me the shoulder.'

'Never, Mister, never in a million. It'll be a good trip.'

He was a cautious man and saw the journey as danger. There was the quiet cry of a mobile phone in the dull room, coming back off the booklined walls and off the floor where the files were stacked, the territory of grime and spiders. He liked to work on his own ground, where he had confidence. He needed to be alongside a legal system that he could waltz around, where rules were laid down that could be bent with ease and broken – but he would not have dared to stand up in open opposition. Mister dragged the mobile out of his pocket, listened expressionlessly, then snapped it off.

'Got to be going, something to be dealt with . . . Atkins'll be with us. We'll talk.'

'Yes, Mister. I'll be here and waiting. Just let me know where you want me.'

The Eagle understood but had little sympathy for the new restless drive he saw in Mister. Himself, he was tired, looking for an easier road. He shuddered at the thought of Sarajevo. He remembered the TV images of bodies and wreckage, drunk teenagers with guns.

Autumn 1992
It was first light when the troops began to come back over the river.

He had not seen the fighting but he had heard it. Husein Bekir had let his wife go to their room and had refused her entreaties to follow her. He had switched off the lights in the house, wrapped himself in a thick coat and gone to sit on a fallen log that was half-way between his home and the well that served the village. It was a bright night: there was a star canopy and a wide moon. It was a night when he would have backed his chances, when he was younger, of succeeding in hunting deer.

The troops came out from the trees behind Vraca, went through the village and down the track towards the ford. Earlier in the evening, before the attack was launched, an officer had come to him and expected him, the patriarch authority of the village, to tell where the mines were laid in defence of Ljut. That had been difficult for Husein because there were friends from his whole life across the valley, and he had pleaded that he was old and could not remember where he had seen them sown.

He had thought it the worst problem he had ever confronted, telling where the mines were or not, when he had heard from the darkness the crumpling, echoing crack of the detonations, ear-splitting noise that blasted between the valley's walls, and among the small-arms fire and the shouting, and the officer's whistle had been the awful humbling screaming, as when the dogs caught a fox and could not kill it quickly.

No flares were used in the battle, as he and his friend Dragan Kovac had been taught to use them when they had gone away for conscription training. He had relied on his deteriorating hearing to follow the course of the fighting. Four men had been carried back from the far side of the river: one had lost half a foot; one the whole of a leg below the shred of his uniform trousers at the knee; another, as they had carried him, held his hands across his stomach to keep in his intestines; one had had the side of his face taken away. All of them had screamed, except the one with the stomach wound who called softly for his mother, and the men who brought them back had cursed the mines.

From his place on the log, he had known from the firing that the Muslim troops had reached the village, and then there had been a strange, frightening quiet. He had thought he heard, but could not be certain, shouts and cries from far away. He had pulled the coat tighter around him, and cupped a match in his hand to light a cigarette: he had been careful not to betray his place with the cigarette's glow. Darkness had never, in his life, caused him worry. Often he had thought, when he hunted or when he fished for the big trout in the river, that the darkness was an ally, that he was more familiar with the darkness than with the deer and the boar or the big trout. But the quiet in the valley had been hard on him.

It had broken. The battle had restarted. Husein Bekir, an old farmer but a shrewd man, had imagination. It would have been hand-to-hand fighting at first, but he could see nothing of it, only hear the sound of it, and then Serb soldiers had driven the Muslim troops back down the hill. He had not needed to see it to understand what had happened.

They were in a straggling confused formation, a rabble.

They were soaked from swimming, their eyes shone and were wide, and Husein saw madness in their faces. There were more wounded with them and he saw again the work of the mines. The sight of the injuries troubled him because he had not said what he knew.

At dawn there was always, in the autumn cold, a mist low over the river and the fields, and the troops emerged from it. They seemed to bless the cover it gave them, and some turned to fire their rifles uselessly through it, back towards the village they had taken, and lost. They came past him, and their madness made them shout obscenities towards the unseen enemy. He saw a knife in a corporal's belt. Dark blood stained the blade, and more blood had dripped from it on to the upper trouser of the man's camouflage uniform.

Husein Bekir began to look at each man who passed him – the dead carried over the shoulders, the wounded brought back on litters, and the men who were not dead and not maimed.

The officer came last.

Husein Bekir sat on his log, lit another cigarette. He could see, as the mist cleared, a pall of smoke over Ljut, the old gold of the trees behind the village, the fallen yellow grass of the fields he had not ploughed that spring and the sagging weeds in his vineyard, the house of his friend, Dragan Kovac.

He asked, 'Did it go hard for you?'

The officer stumbled. He would have fallen from exhaustion but was able to collapse on to the log, and his breath came in great heaving pants. 'It was the mines – because we did not know where they were. I don't know, I have to check, I think I have twenty men, not more, killed or wounded, and the mines would have been fifteen, or fourteen.'

'What has happened to the people of Ljut?'

'The village is cleaned. It is no longer a threat to you,' the officer said.

Husein thought of the blood he had seen on the knives, and of the people of the village across the valley whom he had known.

'Did any escape?'

'A few ran away because we were held up some minutes by the bunkers. Most stayed in their homes, in their cellars.'

'And you had time to find them before you were pushed back?' Husein asked grimly.

'We are a platoon and they were a company. When the reinforcements came it was one man against three. . . Yes, we found them in the cellars before that. If I had wanted to stop the men I could not, not after they had seen what the mines did.'

Husein gabbled his question: 'Was there a big man there – a boar of a man – he is a retired policeman – big shoulders, big stomach, big moustache – a leader? Did he escape? Is he alive?'

'If he ran away, he is alive. If not . . .' The officer shrugged, and struggled to his feet. 'I don't know. I didn't see him – there were many I did not see, did not care to see.'

When his wife came with coffee and a slim glass of brandy, the old farmer told her that in the night the life of the valley had died. She steadied his shaking hand so that he did not spill the coffee, and he gulped the brandy. He did not have to tell her, because she knew it, that it would have been the old people who had hidden in the cellars. They knew it because on other mornings they had stared, together, across the valley and the river, and seen the distant figures going about their lives.

The sun rose and threw clear long shadows from the trees on the far side of the valley. He watched as the Serb soldiers emerged from the smoke of the village with a wheelbarrow and heavy sacks. He saw them fan out then gather in little groups and kneel. More mines were sown in his fields to replace those detonated during the night, and he tried to shut out the screams, and the whimper of a young trooper who had held his stomach and asked for his mother.

Dougie Gough would go a long way for a good funeral, if it were up on the Ardnamurchan peninsula. Many times he'd helped to carry the coffin from the Free Presbyterian chapel at Kilchoan to the cemetery that was neatly cut out from a grazing field. He liked to stand in that cemetery, high over the sea that stretched across to Mull, and ponder on the life of a friend and fellow worshipper, to feel the wind, the rain or the sun on his face. It was the best of places for a temporary parting, and he always looked to the cliffs to see if an eagle hunted or over the water for a glimpse of a seal or a porpoise. His faith gave him a sense of fatality and a feeling of inevitability that did not frighten him. He had no fear of death, or of hardship. The lack of fear toughened him.

This, though, was a pathetic funeral, he thought.

There was no dignity, no love, no respect at the crematorium.

The coffin carrying the stitched remains of Duncan Dubbs, whom he now knew as the Cruncher, was wheeled into the chapel by strangers. He stood at the back. The coffin was followed by a couple in their seventies and he thought they understood nothing of their son's adult life. Only four women had taken places in front of Gough, the same age as the parents, and two young men in loose gaudy shirts without jackets. The vicar, another stranger, hurried through the service of committal. Gough thought the churchman knew little more of the dead man than his name and therefore fell back on to familiar ground. 'Duncan was, above all, a private man, whose loyalties were primarily directed towards his beloved parents, to whom he accorded all the love of which he was capable. He was a popular and well-liked member of his community and will be sorely missed by his many friends.' A reedy hymn was sung as the curtains closed, and without the vicar's strength of voice the words would have been drowned out by the power playing of the female organist.

Outside, in light rain, his waxed coat heavy over his tweed jacket, he stood back and kept his distance as the mourners paused beside the show of flowers. The parents, Gough reflected, would now be millionaires from their son's last will and testament, and the rentboys would be hoping that the suddenness of the Cruncher's death had not precluded generous bequests. But he had come to see others, and he was disappointed. No Packer and his wife, no acolytes or enforcers. An official gently, but firmly, hurried them on. Behind a low wall with a trellis above it supporting climbing roses, a new funeral party was forming up. The vicar, sheltered under an umbrella, was pleading urgent business elsewhere, and shaking hands. They'd stayed away. In the car park the parents climbed into and were lost inside the big black limousine, and the young men left by scooter. He stayed put until a car on the far side of the car park had driven away. He'd seen the camera lens. It would have been routine for the Crime Squad to send along a police photographer, and he had no wish to be pictured and identified by them.

It was interesting to him that Packer had stayed away. It told him something of the coldness of the man, and something of the care taken by him not to display himself. He had learned from the funeral.

'He said that?'

'That's what the little shit said, Mister.'

'Tell me again what he said.'

'He said, I can quote it because I heard it, "Mister's gone, washed up, history." Then he said, "Mister's not hands-on any longer. You don't have to worry about Mister. Anyone who pays him is chucking money at a has-been. You just ignore Mister." It's all gospel. I heard Georgie Riley say it.'

In *Intrusive Surveillance – Code of Practice*, section 2 paragraph 3 states

> Any person giving an authorization (for intrusive surveillance) should first satisfy him/herself that the degree of intrusion into the privacy of those affected by the surveillance is commensurate with the seriousness of the offence ... no intrusion should be authorized which is out of proportion to the crime committed or planned. This is especially the case where the subjects of the case might reasonably assume a high degree of privacy or where there are special sensitivities such as where the intrusion might affect communications between a Minister of any religion or faith and an individual

relating to that individual's spiritual welfare.

Safer than the Eagle's office was the sacristy of a turn-of-the-century brick-built church in Hackney.

Along with the vicar, two churchwardens, and a cleaner, Mister was a keyholder to the rear door of the church and the sacristy. He had never worshipped there but his contributions to the upkeep of the grounds surrounding the building, and the generosity of his donation to the roof fund, ensured him access to a building where there was no possibility of bugs and taps.

'I appreciate what you've told me.'

In an east London pub, a medium-scale importer, dealing primarily in amphetamines ferried over the Channel from Holland, with drink taken, had shot off his mouth. That man, Riley, stood on a rung far below the one occupied by Mister. At that time, he represented no threat to Mister's commercial dealings. Mister knew the way it worked because he had climbed that ladder himself and pitched off it men who had believed themselves superior. It would start with talk, then there would be the elbowing in on Mister's territory, then he would similarly be thrown off the step. To hold his place at the top, he must act at the first sign of talk – Cruncher would have understood, but maybe not the Eagle. He knew Riley, thought he was clever and careful, except when drink was taken.

The informant scurried away, perhaps believing that he had ingratiated himself and that Mister was now indebted to him. It would be the informer's error if he acted on that conviction.

Alone in the sacristy, Mister made several short, pithy calls on his mobile, using an always-changing code to cover names and locations. He had just switched it off when the vicar, half drowned, came in behind him.

'Hello, Reverend, how did it go?'

'Well, we could have done with a few more there. But I think those who did attend valued the occasion.'

'I regret not being with you.'

'Difficult times, Mr Packer. There was a wretched photographer hiding in a car – looking for you, I suppose, no sense of decency or occasion – and one man I didn't recognize who neither the family nor the boys acknowledged.'

The funeral's stranger was described, and the vicar said he had not been dressed like a policeman, but as if from the country: he had had the appearance of a rural vet. Then he dropped his voice and grimaced. 'A miserable-looking vet, the sort who'd put down a family dog and not console you. But he sang well, knew all the words of the hymns I'd chosen, never looked at the hymnal.' If the Eagle's court strategy had not accomplished the halting of Mister's trial, the vicar had been lined up, ready to take his place in the witness box and swear firmly to 'tell the truth, the whole truth, and nothing but the truth', and say that on the night Mister was alleged to have been in the car he had in fact been in the sacristy discussing further fund-raising for the repair of the rotting roof.

'I'll be away for a bit,' Mister said casually.

'Somewhere nice?' The vicar was discarding his vestments, darkened at the hem by the rain.

'Doubt it's nice, don't know whether it's warm. I've a bit of business in Sarajevo.'

'Where poor Mr Dubbs died.'

'He was setting up a deal – too good a deal to let go. That's the trouble with business, these days, you've got to run fast just to stand still.'

'I wouldn't know . . . but I read that Sarajevo is an unhappy place, quite brutalized by that awful war. I'll be concerned for you, Mr Packer.'

Mister stood up and wrapped his coat around him. 'Don't worry about me. I can look after myself.'

David Jennings had taken home the carriage clock two years ago. He'd have preferred his farewell from the Custom House, from the Sierra Quebec Golf team, to have been marked with a crystal decanter, but they'd given him a clock. It didn't work now and the jeweller he'd taken it to had said repairs would cost more than it was worth.

Enforced retirement had been a bitter blow to him: one day an experienced executive officer working on heroin importation then targeting Albert Packer, the next thumbing through conservatory leaflets and estimating what a new back patio would cost. At first his wife had said that it was wonderful to have him home and around to help with the shopping, but that had palled. An increasingly testy marriage was kept alive by off-peak sunshine holidays.

All the girls in the travel agency were busy, so Jennings settled himself on the bench by the window, ready to book a pre-summer break in Tenerife. He didn't have to see the Fixer's face to know him. Most times he'd seen him from the back, on buses and tube carriages and pavements. He knew him well. He'd been close up in pubs with him, close enough to count hairs on the back of his neck, trying to get 'overheards'. His last year before retirement, when the team had been expanded to a branch, kitted with body microphones, with an eyeball on the Fixer, hoping to hear him talking dirty rather than talking social, he'd spent hours, nights, weeks, months on the Fixer, who was Target Six. God, and he missed it. The old life was still a microbe in his bloodstream.

When the Fixer was finished and had left with his tickets, three of them, Jennings slotted into the empty chair in front of the girl. Former habits died hard. He was a good pump man, always had been. He asked casually where his pub friend was going, and not taking the darts team, was he, not with the quarter-final coming up.

'Funny old booking,' she said, grinning. 'Takes all sorts, but . . . ferry to Calais, hire car, then Amsterdam to Zagreb on KLM, and on to Sarajevo. First time I've ever booked for there.'

'He's not taking Brennie and Pete – we won't ever win anything without Brennie, please tell me it's not Brennie and Pete.'

'A Mr Packer, a Mr Arbuthnot, and a Mr James – that's the passengers' names.'

'That's not George James, surely? He's not as tasty as Brennie, but he's useful – in our second pair.'

'Bruce James.'

'When are they going, then?'

'Travelling Thursday, arriving Friday. Now do you want some help or do you want to talk about your darts team?'

He laughed, she giggled. He started to explain the hotel details of the last trip to Tenerife, and how they wanted a back room because the front rooms were too noisy, and as high up as possible because of the row from the discothèque. By the time he had finished explaining about the hotel the girl had forgotten her breach of customer confidentiality. David Jennings hadn't forgotten when the old Target One was travelling, with his Eagle and his Atkins, or when he was arriving. As he always used to tell the few who were close to him, and who put up with his former-life anecdotes, it had never been flushed out of the system. Nursing his small morsel of information he went home, his sunshine break reserved, and made a telephone call to an old chum at the Custom House.

'It's probably nothing, but I thought you'd like to know . . .'

A message was sent from a *spieler*, a Turkish café, in Green Lanes. The café was sandwiched between a *halal* butcher and a greengrocer specializing in Near Eastern vegetables. From the long street in London that represented the heart of the immigrant Turkish population, it went by digital phone to the Bascarsija district of Sarajevo. The Turkish community in Green Lanes, and in Sarajevo, understood the value of strategic alliances.

At any time, day or night, there were in that drab street, with renovation and refurbishment yet to arrive, the parked cars and vans in which sat surveillance experts of the Church, the Crime Squad, Criminal Intelligence and the spooks.

Any of those men and women, idling away the hours, waiting for the next greasy burger and fries, watching, recording and photographing, would have known the statistic that dominated their work.

Of every ten wraps of heroin imported into the United Kingdom, nine passed through Turkish hands, and most of those hands were in Green Lanes.

The trail started in the poppy fields of fundamentalist Afghanistan. A train of camels would carry a tonne of raw produce over the porous Iranian frontier. From Iran the cargo moved by lorry, passage eased by back-handers, across the Turkish border. In Turkey the opium was refined to high-grade heroin, too strong for the human body to accept by swallowing or inhalation, and the tonne was divided into one-hundred-kilo loads, each with a final street value of eight million pounds sterling. Hidden in long-distance transport lorries the loads were moved through the Balkans, Germany and France, and up to the choke points of the Channel ports, where the danger of discovery was greatest for the Turkish importers. Once inside the United Kingdom, the Turks sold it on to the major dealers.

Mister bought in Green Lanes.

For all of the efforts, and the quality of the surveillance equipment, the clan communities of the street of dingy shops and paint-scraped homes were almost impossible to penetrate. The culture of secrecy could not be broken into. Informers were unknown. The *spielers* were regularly scanned with high-grade equipment to detect bugs and probes, and entry into a café by an executive officer of the Church or a detective sergeant of the Crime Squad would be noticed immediately. They sat in their vehicles and watched and waited for Lady Luck, but she called rarely.

The same routing, from the café to the apartment in Sarajevo's Old Quarter, had warned of the visit of Duncan Dubbs Esquire, the Cruncher, and had vouched for him.

In the early evening, a transmitted message to a mobile phone in an elegantly furnished apartment in Bosnia's capital announced the imminent arrival of Albert William Packer, with two companions, and urged that they be treated with the respect due to important players.

The entry into the terraced house was fast and brutal.

The man, Riley, was taken by men wearing balaclavas from the kitchen table where he was eating with his partner and their children and dragged out through the sagging door.

He was driven in the back of a van, chicken trussed. He wet himself. A length of sticky tape blindfolded him.

He was taken from the van, his feet scraping the ground helplessly, and into a great echoing vault that he thought was a disused warehouse.

There seemed to him to be several men in the room.

A chair scraped, as if the man sitting on it leaned forward.

A whispered voice, and his hope died: 'People tell me, Georgie, that you've been talking about me . . .'

'It'll have to be the youngster,' Gough said.

'Isn't there a way round it?' A bead of sweat rolled down the chief investigation officer's cheek.

'I've a room full of people who don't know each other, let alone the target.'

'Is he up to that sort of work?'

'Have to wait and see, won't we?'

'You're a bundle of encouragement, Mr Gough. I can arrange for a surveillance expert to accompany him.'

'That'll be useful, providing they're decent.'

The CIO scribbled briskly on his pad, and passed a name and a telephone number. 'If he's flying tomorrow, he should meet this fellow tonight. We wouldn't be endangering him, would we?'

'Don't know – don't know anything about the place.'

'Because he'll be close up to Packer, that animal,' the CIO breathed heavily.

'Not very close – it'll be surveillance, watching from a distance. Shouldn't be dangerous if he's sensible.'

'What you've got to understand, Mr Cann, is that it is a remarkable corner of Europe – you could say that it is unique in its diversity and richness of culture.'

Cann hadn't been to university. He had left the comprehensive school in his small Somerset town, applied to join the police, and been rejected on the grounds of eyesight and physique. If the school had possessed more ambitions for higher education he might have made it, but it hadn't. He'd been mooning around the estate where his father was the factor, undecided, getting in his parents' way, a sharp stone in their lives, when a Customs & Excise VAT team had come to look over the estate's books. He'd seen the way the new-money owner, a bullying, blustering man, had cringed before their power; his mother, who helped with the books, had talked after their departure of the reach of their authority. Slightly built, relying on heavy spectacles, a disappointment to his father and a worry to his mother, it had seemed to Cann like some sort of answer. He'd applied and been accepted. The man who talked to him was a lecturer at the School of East European and Slavonic Studies, part of London University.

'It was created by the great empires, those of Greece, then Rome, then that of Charlemagne, and after that the Ottomans and the Austro-Hungarians, and finally Communism. With the empires came the religion – western Christianity, the eastern Church, Judaism and Islam, then political atheism. Throw those origins together and you have a bed for artistic brilliance to breed in, and also ethnic hatred.

'Of course, each new regime interbred with what they found, but the Bosnian heritage is having a foreign power sitting on the territory, and hating it. There was a little window of independence, while they were at war and being carved up, but now – as you'll find – a new foreign power sits on them. Just don't expect to be welcomed as a liberator.'

It was past ten o'clock. In Tooting Bec Jen would be waiting for him at the bed-sit, and his bag would need packing. He had been told by Gough that it was an instruction from the chief investigation officer, that he should ring the number and beg an appointment, whatever the hour. He had beaten a retreat from the first meeting of the new Sierra Quebec Golf team and had done as he was told. The meeting had been bizarre and hurtful. He'd felt himself regarded as an intruder, the only survivor from the old disbanded and disgraced unit. The team, assembled that afternoon, arriving with small bags off trains and in their cars, had been recruited from the north-west of England, the west, the Midlands, the north-east, from Scotland, and one was from Belfast. Gough had told them that incompetence, intimidation and corruption had combined to win Albert William Packer his freedom. They were all older than him, the nine men and one woman, and Gough had said that each had been selected for their skills, their lack of fear and their integrity; then the eyes had fixed on him, as if he were the least solid of the chain's links, to be treated with suspicion, tolerated because he was the archivist. After the preamble, Gough had made him get up, talk through the cart-wheel, and give a detailed biography of Mister. At the end the eyes fastened on him seemed to wonder if he was the weak link. When he'd finished his stumbling address, Gough had taken him out into the corridor and told him in clipped, sparse sentences where he was going that evening, and where he was travelling to in the morning . . . He listened and wondered what was the relevance of it.

'Take a map, look at it. The geography is of spines of mountains and valleys cut by impassable rivers. The common phrase of today would be "bandit country". That's not something they've learned recently. Back in the reign of King Stephen Tvrtko they'd achieved a semblance of discipline, but after he'd died, 1391, and things slid, a French pilgrim wrote: "They live purely on wild beasts, fish from the rivers, figs and honey, of which they have sufficient supply, and they go in gangs from forest to forest to rob people travelling through their country."

'And right from those days, honour and sticking to one's word were seldom important. A Turkish janissary serving in Sultan Mehmet's invasion army, that's 1463, wrote of the flight of King Stephen Tomasevic to a fortress at Kljuc, in central Bosnia, where he did a deal and surrendered on the promise of safe passage: "When the king's servants who were in the fortress saw that their lord had surrendered, they gave themselves up. The Sultan took possession of the fortress, and ordered that the king and all his companions should be beheaded. And he took the entire country into his possession." Be wary of criminals, Cann, and be doubly wary of promises.

'Oh, and be most wary of the women. Two thousand years ago silver was mined by the Romans at Srebrenica. The Roman garrison's barracks have long disappeared, but you can still find there a medieval castle, in ruins, on a high hill south of the town. It was built by Jerina, a warlord's widow, with slave labour. When she'd occupied the castle it was her habit to have a slave brought up to her bedroom each night, and every following morning an exhausted slave was precipitated to his death from the castle walls ... Summary: a history of oppression, violence, plague and thieving, ruthless cruelty and utter dishonesty.'

They were seated in a hot little room in a Gower Street second-floor flat. The only light shone on the desk where the lecturer sat. A baby was crying in another room and a woman's voice tried to soothe it. The coffee he'd been given was too bitter for him and was now cold. The light shone on the map. The lecturer chain-smoked.

'So you're telling me that a major figure in organized crime in the UK is going to Bosnia, and you don't know why. Let's begin with a tasty quote. The present-day foreign occupying power, operating under various names that add up to United Nations, was headed a couple of years back by Elisabeth Rehn, UN Special Representative of the Secretary General. She said: "If we fail to do something, this country will become an Eldorado for criminals." Normally, that wouldn't matter. Take a look at that map again. Look at Bosnia's position. It used to be called "the Balkans route". It is a crossroads, a junction. It is the natural meeting-point for the roads linking the Middle East, the Mediterranean, Central Europe and the northern countries of the continent. People using that crossroads were rather inconvenienced by forty-five months of fighting, but that's over now and the lorries are rolling again. Whatever it is that you want to bring into Bosnia, once you have brought it there you have many options as to where you ship it to. Nothing was done, and it's now Eldorado . . . Do I need to say more?'

Joey assumed that the chief investigation officer – God to him, a distant figure he had never met and only seen in a presentation speech – had activated a contact from his former home, the Secret Intelligence Service. He stirred.

'You don't need to say any more. You'll excuse me, I've got to pack, an early start.'

'Do you not have a feel, Mr Cann, for the worth of academic history?'

'I'm only an executive officer, five years' service with the Investigation crowd, and I'm going away – forty-eight hours or seventy-two hours – to watch a man, write reports and come home. They're sending me on sufferance . . . I'm grateful for your time.'

'I apologize for delaying you, Mr Cann. Forgive me, but having time to pack is the least of your problems. I've tried to give you three or four snapshots, postcards, from Bosnia. Violence and treachery, a hatred of foreigners and a culture of smuggling are as ingrained in that society as mineral iron in granite rock. Don't forget that. Bosnia is not Bognor, it is not Birmingham, not Brighton. Watch your back, Mr Cann.'

He felt the shiver in his body and ground his fingernails into his palms to halt it. He stood up and said weakly, 'It's nothing serious. If it were a big deal then it wouldn't be me they'd have sent.'

Chapter Five

'You call me each day – I need to hear from you every evening.'

Gough was awake, alert. Joey reckoned him the sort of man who didn't need sleep.

'I want a total log of where he goes and who he sees. They don't protect themselves away like they do at home. They get sloppy. I've a team put together that has to be fed, got to have something to bite on. I want everything and anything.'

Himself, he was dead to the world, and the last thing he needed was Gough nannying him at Heathrow, with the unlit pipe in his mouth and the smell of it on his breath.

'It's in the balance, Joey. If you find us material to work off I can hold the team together, can't if you don't. The Church is like any organization in these sad days – results, fast and furious, justify the balance sheet. If it's taking too long, if it's going to be too expensive, if there isn't a knock in sight and handcuffs, then we'll be wound up.'

Joey had come by mini-cab but Gough, the first thing he was told, had caught two buses to reach the airport. With his rank, Gough was entitled to a car and a driver. Joey realized it was Gough's way of telling him, fiercely, that the journey and the work were not holiday. Joey didn't know of another senior investigation officer who would have come out to Heathrow at ten to seven to see off a junior on a flight. His bag was checked in. He thought that soon, if not already, the new men and women of Sierra Quebec Golf would be drifting into the Custom House. They were a miserable crowd, not like the old team. What he'd seen of them, there was no wit among them. They looked puritanical in their serenity. Pulled in from around the country so there was no possibility that they were tainted by association, they were all hard and humourless, and suspicion of him had blazed in their eyes. They would be drifting into a room where the door's locks had been changed, and where new lockers would be installed later that morning with new keys, and there was already a spyhole set in the door and a voicebox for visitors to announce themselves. Within days, the room would stink because no cleaners were to be allowed inside during the night.

'But, and this is *but* and big, you do not put yourself at risk. At all times you are professional, and you are there to collect evidence. If what you do is illegal, can't be used, then you will get no praise from me. I don't want a bag full of material that a lawyer can pick holes in. You are legal at all times, and that is not negotiable.'

He had told Jen that it was just two or three days. She'd been waiting for him and his clothes had been laid out on the bed. She'd washed all the shirts, put them through the dryer, then ironed them. She'd brought him, said sweetly, shyly, that he might want to take it with him, a strip of four photographs of herself from a supermarket booth; she smiled in one, frowned in another, pulled a solemn face in a third, and stuck her tongue out in the last. She'd stayed the night. They'd both been half awake, half asleep, after the alarm had gone off; he'd have forgotten the strip of pictures if she hadn't pointed to them, and they were in his wallet against his backside. She hadn't cried as he'd left but she might have done when he'd closed the front door and run to the mini-cab in the street.

'That's her – the lady's privilege, tardiness . . .' Gough's voice dropped. 'I want his head. I want the blood running on the plate, like it's gravy . . . but legal. Don't dare forget that.'

Following Gough's eyeline, Joey saw her. He'd expected one of the style of women he worked with in the Custom House. The style was flat shoes, square hips, small chests, chucked-back shoulders, no makeup, bobbed hair. He'd said to Jen often enough – and it mattered nothing to him – that femininity in the Church was the endangered species. They swore with the men, drank with the men, had failed marriages with the men, and pissed in the bucket with the men when they were cooped up in the vans on surveillance. He was staring because it was not what he had expected or was used to. She looked like Kensington or Knightsbridge woman. She was looking around her as she headed for the check-in of Croatian Airways. As she wafted into the queue, Gough removed the pipestem from his mouth and advanced on her. Joey trailed after him.

He heard Gough say, 'You're Miss Bolton? Good to meet you. I'm Gough, glad you made it . . .'

Joey reckoned that lateness, in Gough's book, was a cardinal, capital offence. It was a sparsely veiled rebuff, and she ignored it.

Her accent was class. 'No point hanging around this bloody shed. Yes, I'm Maggie Bolton. Who's he?'

She jerked with her thumb towards Joey. He didn't wait for Gough. He said, 'I'm Joey Cann. We're travelling together.'

'With the kindergarten, am I? Not to worry, I expect we'll manage.'

The queue moved forward. Joey, feeling himself the hired hand, reached to push forward the heavy metal-sided case that she had brought along with a lightweight one.

'Don't touch it,' she said sharply. 'I'm quite capable. Touch it and I'll kick you, bloody hard.'

She heaved the heavy case forward, then delicately toed the lighter one up against the check-in conveyor. She told the girl, as an instruction, not for debate, that the heavy case would be going in the cabin with her, and slapped her ticket down on the counter with her passport. She had the weary look of a frequent traveller, as if life was a chore. He wondered how her job description was listed in the passport. There was stamping and the tearing out of the ticket's flimsies, and she was given her boarding card.

'Come on, then,' she said. 'Let's go.'

She'd been very pretty, as she'd approached them, small, elegant and finely made, like a detailed little figurine. Close-up, leaving the check-in, Joey saw the depth of her makeup. Her alarm must have gone an age before his because her face was a minor work of art. She might have been ten years older than him, but he couldn't have said so because the makeup blanked out crow's feet and mouth lines.

Her hair, gathered into a short ponytail, was soft gold, but he didn't know whether it was real or from a bottle. She wore a loud blue-green blouse, silk, and a dark skirt suit with a knee showing above neat ankles and lightweight half-height shoes. There was an old necklace, supporting a gold pendant, at her throat, and her fingers flashed small diamonds, but no wedding-ring. He'd been told she was a technician, expert, and had not expected a businesswoman. She lugged her bags towards the departure doors, not hurrying as the third and final flight call was made. She stopped, turned.

'Right, Mr Gough, now don't worry yourself. I'll look after him, make sure he changes his socks, and bring him back safely. 'Bye – oh, how's Porky?'

'I don't think,' Gough answered stiffly, 'I know anyone of that name.'

'I thought you worked for him. Your boss, isn't he? Porky Cork – Dennis Cork. He wasn't going anywhere with us so he transferred to run your crowd. How is he?'

Gough growled, 'He's well. He's happy in his work because he is now doing a job that is worthwhile. The job is worthwhile because it affects people's lives.'

''Bye, Mr Gough,' and she was moving.

They went through the gate. He saw the passport as it was opened and handed over for cursory examination. She was a personal assistant.

They walked towards the plane's pier. She was struggling with the metal-sided bag but Joey was damned if he was going to offer help; there was a small sweat rivulet on her brow about to carve a little canyon through the blanket of makeup. On the pier, at the aircraft door, she slipped the bag down and flexed her fingers.

Joey said, 'Why were you so rude, Miss Bolton, about me, and to Mr Gough?'

'Call me Maggie – it's not the sort of work I'm used to, and you're not the sort of people I'm used to working with, and it's hardly a target that excites me.'

He had overseen the burning of his clothes, and those of the Cards who had held the man down, in a metal-worker's coke oven. Then he had gone home.

Mister showered.

He was a long time under the scalding spray and he used a heavy soap to wash every inch of his skin, and every orifice of his body.

He sang quietly to himself in the bathroom. He felt elation. The Princess had been asleep when he'd come home, and would still be sleeping when he went out again. The exhilaration coursed in him, powered by the water's heat, and the days ahead would challenge him. It was what he wanted, what he had dreamed of.

The wife wouldn't speak. Nobody would speak. Not the family, not the neighbours, and not Georgie Riley.

And the name would not be written down of the man responsible for the injuries inflicted on Georgie Riley. His name and his fate were not spoken of in the pub where thirty-six hours earlier he had slagged off *Mister* Albert William Packer. The neighbours of his terraced home had seen nothing, heard nothing and knew nothing. The wife, crouched over the hospital bed, had laughed into the face of the detective sergeant, then snarled that he should 'fuck off' and 'get lost'. The victim, Georgie Riley, had he wished to, could not have named his attacker because his tongue had been cut out with a Stanley knife. He could not have written down that name because the four fingers on each of his hands had been taken off with an industrial stone-cutter's circular blade.

He might live, a white-faced physician told the detective sergeant out of the hearing of the wife, for twenty-four hours, and it was possible that he would linger for forty-eight, but he would not survive. The damage was in the trauma and in the loss of blood. Georgie Riley had lain unconscious in a ditch at the edge of a quiet road leading into Epping Forest for an estimated seven hours before a telephone-kiosk call, when a voice disguised by a handkerchief or clothing over the receiver, had given the location and summoned an ambulance.

'How do you get the creature responsible?' the physician asked.

'I don't know why it was done, and I couldn't on oath say for certain who is responsible,' the detective sergeant said. 'It's about fear. Riley is a medium-scale villain, more time in gaol as an adult than out of it, but he's done something that's caused offence. He wasn't killed outright because the point of the exercise is to create terror and to have that talked about. Men like Riley think themselves big shots, and brave with it. A shoot-out death is acceptable, top-of-the-range funeral and buckets of flowers, that's all fine, and they think they'll go into history . . . What's happened is that he has been humiliated and made to scream and he'll have wet himself and shat himself and begged for his life. There's nothing noble about the way he's going, a piece of dismembered meat.'

'Won't somebody, eventually, inform?'

'Probably – when the man who ordered it, maybe did it, no longer has power. That's what we live for, when the power dries up. You see, sir, for that sort of man, there is no retirement. There's no day that the birthday comes and he goes down to the post office and draws a pension, or heads off to a decent little villa outside Marbella to live off the interest. They can't walk away and protect what they have and live out their old age. When they're hands-off they're finished, and the information flows. The man who did this is not hands-off, he is up and running and wants his dirty world to know it.'

'And until then nobody will inform, people won't stand up?'

'Take you, sir . . .'

'Me? Where could I possibly fit into it?'

'Riley has never in his life passed the time of day with a policeman, but he'd trust you, wouldn't he, sir? What about this for a scenario? I make available a video camera with microphone attached. You come in here in the dead of night, when his wife's asleep next door. You've cut down the sedation dose, and he can hear you and see you. You hold a photograph in front of him, a photograph of the man most likely to have inflicted these injuries on him. You ask him if that's the man who did it, and you tell him to nod or shake his head . . . Let's say, wonder of wonders, he nods, and it's on the tape. Are you with me, sir?'

The physician blanched. 'I really don't know, I'd have to think . . . There's ethics . . .'

'Very sensible, sir,' the detective sergeant said gravely. 'Let's say it all happened. Of course, we'd offer you and your family protection – wife down the supermarket with a Heckler & Koch machine-gun for company, kids at school with a Glock pistol alongside. For how long? Try the day after the trial finished, then you're on your own, and scared witless every time the wife and the kids are out of your sight, and looking under the car each morning with a mirror. Much better, sir, not to get involved and cross over to the far side of the street and hurry on, like everybody does.'

'You make me feel ashamed.'

'I don't intend to, sir. Take me. Let's say a low-level plodder like me turns up the dirt on this man and my evidence is going to send him down. He can pay me and not notice it, what I'll work for twenty years to earn, or he can have my family blown away.'

'Do you know who he is?'

'A very fair idea. It's not a level playing-field, sir. I go into an interview room to confront him and I've a camera on me and a tape recording me, and a lawyer there to make sure my questions aren't oppressive, and because society demands it I've a book full of regulations tying my hands. When he goes into an interview room to talk to Georgie Riley all he has to worry about is whether the Stanley knife blade is decently sharp and whether the motor on the concrete-cutter works.'

'Well, you'll understand that I've a ward full of patients to see.'

'You called him a creature, sir. That's selling him short. If he's who I think then he's a very clever, very cunning man – stands to reason, he's at the top.'

The physician was at the anteroom door, and flustered. 'How do you nail him?'

'By getting lucky, sir.'

'Who's going to get lucky?'

'Not me, sir. It's someone who can look him in the face, straight in his eyes, and show he can't be bought, can't be frightened. Don't know where you'll find him.'

Late by ninety-five minutes into Zagreb, they had missed the connecting flight to Sarajevo, and been told that the following flight in the afternoon was cancelled.

They had to be in Sarajevo that night, Joey had said. Then he should go and hire a car, she'd replied tartly. He'd done it. He'd picked her up outside the terminal in a small Ford. She'd gone and bought a road map of Croatia, and the look on her face said this was Mickey Mouse and more of what she was not used to. They'd driven away from Zagreb, caught the Sisak road and gone through the ghost town of Petrinja. She'd had the wheel and he'd navigated off the map. It was only when he'd missed a turning that he realized an apology wasn't necessary because she'd caught it. She knew the road. Then he'd sulked and tossed the map over his shoulder so that it fell on to her metal-sided case on the back seat. Two miles after the first signpost to Dvor, she had swung the car abruptly off the road, bumped up a track into a wood and not stopped before they were hidden from other motorists' view. He'd watched. His help was neither asked for nor offered. She stripped out the back seat, with the metalwork under it and the door panels, then opened the heavy case. There were probes, terminals, a variety of light sockets, power units and gear he could not recognize. He'd thought he'd seen everything of surveillance equipment in the room used by Sierra Quebec Golf, but some of what he now looked at was smaller and more compact, and the rest he had never seen before. It all went into the door handle and under the back seat, then she rebuilt the car. Last, she took half of her clothes from the soft bag and casually dumped them into the case. He saw, before the case was closed and locked, a couple of cocktail dresses, items of underwear, and a pair of heavy walking boots, and they'd driven on. He carried only his camera, with the 300mm lens, and that could be explained. He had no paperwork with him.

The border was a line in the river between Dvor and Bosanski Novi. The bridge over it was military, an iron frame and rattling planks. The old bridge was collapsed and unrepaired from the precision of a USAF strike five years earlier. They crossed and were waved down. As she braked she asked for his passport.

She snapped out of the vehicle. She took charge. She flourished the passport and a packet of cigarettes had emerged from her handbag, then another, as if they were loaves and fishes. The Customs men, who had been bored and lounging and smoking, were around her. She was their honeypot. She flashed smiles, and the cigarettes slipped into clawing hands. She spoke their language and they laughed with her. She marched a man with sergeant's stripes back to the car, flicked open the case and her bag, then Joey's bag, and there was more laughter as she rolled her eyes when her underwear was exposed. She went into a dismal wood-plank shack. He wondered how many languages she spoke and where she had been, and he knew, in truth, that he had just not thought through the question of going into a Customs check. When she came out, holding the passports, she offered her hand to the sergeant. He took it formally, slobbered a kiss on the back, and they were gone.

'Well done,' Joey said gruffly.

'Thrilled, I'm sure, to be honoured with praise.'

'You've been here before?' It seemed a pointless question.

'Where do you know best?' she asked.

'Nowhere, not abroad . . .' He thought his answer confirmed that he was low grade. 'Workwise? Well, bits of London. On my team it would be Green Lanes, but the last three years I've hardly been out of the Custom House. Yes, it would be Green Lanes, that's north from Stoke Newington and south from—'

'Yes, yes . . . There's a dozen places I know best. Here's one, and you don't need to know the others.'

She drove fast. Twice he closed his eyes as, late, she swerved out of a lorry's path. She'd have seen that he flinched, and that hurt. She seemed not to care about the pot-holes in the tarmac.

It was dismal country, pocked with isolated farmhouses, and he saw women doing the subsistence work and digging in fields. His mind raced. Serb territory, and the atmosphere was of poverty from which there was no recall and helplessness. They went past gaudy, ghastly roadside bars, painted to grate on the eyes, and lonely little fuel stations. He thought he was in the land of the abandoned where the people paid a collective price for their crimes. Coming towards Prijedor they skirted villages where weeds grew inside roofless houses and rake-thin dogs chased the car's wheels. No living person moved in these villages, which were being overwhelmed by undergrowth. He had seen these places on television, when it had happened, but he had not seen them since they were destroyed. Brambles and thicket bush survived where people had not.

She said quietly, 'The north-west and the south-east were the worst for cleansing. That's their word, used in their army manuals. The word is *ciscenje*, to clean – as in minefields, barricades, enemy positions. They merely transferred it to people. They surrounded these villages, one at a time, and told the Muslims they were leaving. First they made them sign away their property rights and took all evidence of property possession from them, then they separated them. The women and children went into UN camps over the Croat border. The men were taken to camps close to here. They killed as many of the men as they could, by beheading, beating, disembowelling – you name it – and they bulldozed the cemeteries, poisoned the wells and blew up the mosques. They involved a lot of people in the cleansing and the killing so that the guilt was shared round. The guilt's collective, that was the skill of the leaders. The other part of the skill was the destruction of the heritage of those forced out. But remember, always remember, there were no saints among the warlords, whatever side we're talking about, only sinners. I don't suppose you feel hungry. You can go off food here, easily.'

'I'm not hungry,' Joey said.

She told him that outside Prijedor had been the worst of the camps, source of the skeletal human images on the television, where there had been the worst of the killings.

'Could we have done that?' Joey blurted. 'Could we have done those things in the camps, you and me?'

'Of course we could,' she drawled. 'It's about environment, a sense of survival and propaganda. And it's about wanting to humiliate an enemy. Scratch anyone's skin and you'll find an abscess of beastliness hidden away. Where there's an obsession of hatred, where the loathing is targeted, where there's a desire to prove supremacy, any of us can get to act like that. Go to Germany, stand in a queue with the pensioners, dear old folks, and ask them.'

He felt the growing sensation of an awesome helplessness, more acute than when they had first driven through the ravaged villages. On the road near to Banja Luka, high above the town, he saw a great metal-fabricated complex, which she said had been an old steel works. He could make out the tanks, armoured personnel carriers and troop-carrying twin-rotor helicopters, and she told him it was the headquarters of the British army contingent attached to SFOR in Bosnia, and explained that was Stabilization Force. She drove hard. Beyond Banja Luka the road deteriorated. It was hairpin and cut out of a rock wall beside a fast river. There were stones in the road that she swung the wheel to avoid, and crashed vehicles that teetered on the cliffs above the water torrent. He had thought there might be pride in rebuilding a country after war, but he saw none of that.

There was a lake where the river was dammed and men fished among a debris of floating bottles and rubbish bags. He must have shaken his head, must have shown his bewilderment.

'You don't just pack up after a war, Joey, like nothing's happened. Nobody escapes, everyone is scarred. Because you don't read about it any more, that doesn't mean the scars have gone. All it means is that the rest of the world, which once cared, has got bloody bored . . . Can't actually say that I blame it. God helps those who help themselves, if you're with me. They don't know how to help themselves.'

The light was slipping as they skirted Jajce. They bypassed the town, which was dominated by a medieval fortress perched on a rock crag, and she said – with the casualness of a tour guide handing down morsels – that the place had been a Second World War headquarters for Tito's partisans, where the German forces had not been able to reach him. More history, as if she too thought history as important as the academic had the night before. They had the heater on in the car but the cold was creeping in. He had started to shiver, through tiredness, hunger and a bright sliver of fear. Headlights speared them. Out of the Serb territory, into Croat and Muslim-controlled land, the road climbed. It was a better surface, but there was ice on it. There were oases of light, which they sped through – Donji Vakuf, Travnik and Vitez, with shadow figures walking nowhere on dull pavements, the blocks of old socialist architecture and closed-down factories.

When she stopped at a roadside café there were foul toilets round the back. They were the only customers, but the atmosphere made them feel intruders. Three men and a woman lolled on the café counter, eyed them and never spoke or moved other than to agree the order, then bring them coffee and a Coca-Cola chaser. There was a broken ceiling fan above them, short of a spoke, and around them were faded pictures of Grand Prix cars. He noted that she didn't speak their language to them, but English. Their eyes never left her. She smoked a long, dark-wrapped cigarette, and he muttered that she could have lit up in the car had she wanted and she said that it was to cut down that she hadn't smoked, not out of consideration to him. Did she want him to drive, and she'd laid her small precise hand on his and told him it was better for her to drive . . . The road away from the café ran towards a mountain pass. The ice glistened on it and there were snow heaps at the side. Four times he saw places where the crash-barriers had been pierced by skidding vehicles. Each time the wheels slipped momentarily on the ice he felt the further fraying of his nerves. They came round a corner, low gear and struggling, and ahead of them and far below a long finger was illuminated and laid out. She pulled into the side of the road, opened her door and stepped out. The blast of cold air jolted him and he followed her, his feet crunching in the drift.

'That's it,' she said. 'That's Sarajevo.'

The cold settled on his nose and lips, and the wind hit him. He felt far from home, ignorant and uncertain. She must have read him. She tucked her hand into his arm. 'I hope he's worth it, your man.'

He was tired, stressed, and the hand on his arm irritated him. 'Can I just say something? Please, and I'm asking you pleasantly, don't patronize me ... I've never worked with your crowd, I don't know whether you're good or bad or indifferent at what you do, I have to take you on trust. Why did they send me? Because they assess me as being inside the target's skin. I hope that's enough of an explanation.'

She squeezed his arm. 'I stand chastized. What's the immediate priority?'

'We work inside a legal system. I don't know about you, what you normally do, but for us the legal system is the Bible. As a Customs officer I can't just swan in here, without local authority, and poke about at what is called "intrusive surveillance". I need permission. If I don't have that permission then anything I discover – sorry, we discover – on Target One would be ruled as inadmissible in court, as would anything that leads from initial information gathered here. Without authority, I would be bounced so hard when I get back that my feet won't touch before I'm standing at Dover, in uniform, poking into holiday suitcases. In addition, if I – that's we – show out and get lifted by the local police, and there's not a signature on a piece of paper, we're dead in the water.'

'Who's the "local authority"? Who signs?'

'A local judge, a magistrate ...'

She was laughing at him, mocking. 'Don't you know anything about this place?'

'Bugger all,' Joey said.

'It's bent, corrupt. You're not telling me you believe judges and magistrates, here, are independent. They're owned.'

He gazed down at the myriad dancing lights around which, confining them, were the darker expanses of towering snow-covered mountains.

'Then I have to find one who isn't. It's all I need – just one . . . You asked if the target was worth it?' He could see the first photograph he had filed of Mister. Mister wore brown shoes, fawn slacks and a blue polo shirt. He could hear the first tape he had transcribed of Mister's voice. Mister had been on his doorstep and had been going over, item for item, the shopping list for the supermarket given him by the Princess. And, the cruellest cut, the rest of them in the old Sierra Quebec Golf hadn't even thought to warn him that the case was going down and Mister would walk. 'He is – maybe not to you, but to me, yes, well worth it.'

Cruncher was cremated, gone. By now the few flowers would have been dumped or taken to a hospital. A hole had appeared and needed filling. Would Abie Wilkes's boy slot into it? It was a big decision to make, but young Solomon was well spoken of. Even Cruncher had said good things of Sol Wilkes, and had used him.

A different man from Mister would have floundered at the disruption of his business life. Men at the fringes had been discarded. But the inner circle had lasted the course. They were either family or from the estate where Mister had grown up, or they were trusted contacts from the Pentonville experience. They were all long-term on the team.

Before he went to a rendezvous with young Sol Wilkes, Mister travelled alone into central London to open up the safety deposit boxes, the contents of which had been known only to him and to Cruncher. There were four locations for him to visit. Since he had heard of Cruncher's death, Mister had ordered a surveillance operation mounted on the four buildings where his boxes were lodged. He had been assured that none of the locations was watched, and he had also had the streets in which the buildings stood scanned for the type of radio communications watchers would have used. He was now convinced that Cruncher had left nothing behind in the home that investigators could find. The other set of keys, not

Mister's, would have been placed in the care of a solicitor, not in the Eagle's safe.

It was a simple procedure. He visited each building, opened the boxes and cleared them, loaded the contents into his attaché case, handed in the keys and discontinued the contracts.

He walked to a West End of London hotel, no reservation made, and booked into a room. He emptied out on to the bed coverlet the legal proof of his great wealth. There were bank statements, bonds, title deeds for five hotels and three aircraft, more deeds for residential property in France, Greece, the Bahamas, the Caymans and Gibraltar, and a stack of computer disks. He could not, in the hotel room, enter the disks, but he speed-read the documents as if he needed to remind himself of the resources available to him. The fact that he did not spend the wealth on himself and the Princess, that he hoarded it and seldom released it other than to underwrite further ventures, did not in any way detract from the pleasure he took in glancing over the figures and the property descriptions with the income generated. Wealth was power – power, although he would not have recognized this, was the drug that sustained him.

He used the hotel room for fifteen minutes, then checked out. He paid two hundred and sixty-five pounds for it, cash to the cashier, and slipped anonymously into the street.

He walked across central London. It was his city. His wealth gave him the power he craved. Hundreds of people, the huge majority of whom had never heard of him, worked in that city to multiply his wealth. In the evenings and at night, thousands of the city's seething, moving, stirring population bought the product that he purchased after importation and sidled away into dark, private, hidden corners to inject themselves or to inhale. He was buffeted by the home-going office workers, shop women and the tourists, and he felt contempt for them because they would never, none of them, approach the power and wealth that were his.

He saw the young man sitting at the back of the café in the new piazza square of Covent Garden.

Sol Wilkes stood up as he approached. Mister wove a way between the tables. He'd checked outside for watchers and not seen any. Inside he took a zigzag route to the table in the rear recess of the café. It gave him the chance to observe most of its clients, and look into their ears. Any of the Church watchers, men or women, would have moulded clear plastic earpieces. It was an old routine, but useful. He liked the cut of the young man. The suit was good, new and quiet, the shirt was a gentle cream, the tie wasn't loud, and the haircut was tidy. The *Financial Times* on the table was folded beside the half-empty glass of orange juice; it was a good first impression.

'Evening, *Mister* Packer.'

'Evening, Sol – you don't mind if I call you that?'

'Not at all, what can I get you?'

'Cappuccino, please.'

The coffee was ordered. There was an attraction in going for new blood. Mister thought it spoke of his personal virility if he went after youth. Wouldn't have considered it, of course not, if the Cruncher hadn't ended up in the river. But he had ... And maybe, as the operation into the Balkans expanded and came alive, it was the right time to think the unthinkable. The Eagle was old. The Fixer might just be past his best years. New people and new ideas, it was something to chew and think on, but carefully. Everything must be done carefully.

'I've known your family a long time, Sol.'

'So my father told me.'

'Trusted your family, Sol, for many years.'

'As my father's trusted you.'

'Always had respect for your father.'

'And him for you.'

'And now I'm short of someone I can trust and respect, and who'll show the same to me, and who will handle various of my affairs.'

'Look after your investments, Mr Packer, and see them grow.'

'That sort of thing, Sol.'

'Move in where the Cruncher was.'

'With discretion.'

'My father would walk on hot coals for you, Mr Packer. I'd work for someone, with someone, if I knew I'd have the same loyalty back that my father's shown you.'

'Of course.'

'But my father was surprised that you weren't at the Cruncher's funeral.'

There had been no change of inflection in Sol Wilkes's quiet conversational tone, but the statement smacked the air separating them. Mister would have gone, and taken the clan, but the Eagle had counselled against it. The Eagle had said it would be a photographic jamboree for the Crime Squad and the Church, and he'd taken the advice. He thought the young man had balls – questioned whether it demonstrated due loyalty to an old and trusted colleague if a cold shoulder was turned at the end, the funeral. He was jolted . . . The young man wasn't frightened of him, not in the way the Eagle was. He couldn't say to Sol Wilkes that he'd stayed away because the Eagle had told him to, that he wasn't his own man when it came to a last farewell to a friend. Perhaps he should not have listened to the Eagle, but he had . . . There was no fear in the young face as there had been terror last night in an older face. His reputation created fear, but Sol Wilkes was holding his eye, not wavering, and waiting for an answer.

'If you worked for me, Sol, you'd get to see the bigger picture. You'd know more. You'd find it easier to make judgements.' He smiled. 'Whether that's good enough for you or not, that's what you're getting.'

'What are you offering me, Mr Packer?'

'To come on the payroll.'

'With a percentage of profits, as the Cruncher was?'

'Are we running before we can walk?' There was menace in his voice. He was not in control of the talk. His fist was clenched on the table as if in threat.

'If I'm inside, Mr Packer, then there's no going back. I understand that. It's not short-term, it's as far as I can see, for ever . . . Five per cent comes with my guarantee of loyalty, of respect.'

Their hands met. Mister took the smaller fist of Sol Wilkes in his and the deal was sealed. He squeezed the hand until the blood had drained from it and he heard the crack of the bone knuckles, but the young man did not flinch.

He took the papers and the disks from the attaché case and passed them across the table. They were read fast, and there was no expression of either surprise or admiration on Sol's face, just as there had been no fear. A twenty-eight-year-old, trained investment broker, the son of a friend of forty years, was invited into the inner circle. When the papers were read they were returned, with the disks, to the case. Rules of engagement were discussed, then Mister launched into his description of the future and of trade through Bosnia. He didn't think it necessary to spell out that, should he be double-crossed, ripped-off, then all of the Wilkes family would suffer, wish they had never been born, the father and mother, the sisters and brothers, and especially young Solomon; it wasn't necessary to say it because Albie would have made it clear in one-syllable words to his favourite boy. The arrangements were agreed for new safety-deposit boxes. They would meet again when Mister was back from abroad.

He walked out into the evening crowds. He felt good, lifted by Sol's youth – and he knew that the attraction of the Eagle's worried fussiness was waning: he was the big man, and supreme.

Pitching up there had not been Joey's idea. The crush of bodies was all round him, and the smoke and the loud laughter, and the big voice boomed at him, 'You're Joey? That right, Joey?'

'I'm Joey Cann, yes.'

'With Maggie? You're Maggie's bag-carrier?'

'Something like that . . . and you are?'

'Francis. We weren't introduced. Francis. I'm your host here, this is my pad, I'm HM's man in Sarajevo. She's a great girl. Why'd you make her drive the whole way? She says she's driven from Zagreb. Couldn't you have done a bit at the wheel?'

'It's what she seemed to want.'

'Terrific girl, wheelbarrows of fun. Your first time here, Joey?'

'Yes.'

'Let me mark your card, explain the ground you're on.'

'I'd be very grateful.'

He would have preferred his bed. Something to eat, a slow bath, and bed. The message at the hotel had been for her. The party at the Residence was to celebrate Commonwealth Day. He thought she would have despised him if he'd pleaded exhaustion and the need of food, a bath and bed. She'd driven for eight hours, and she was still up for a party. He could see her on the far side of the room. She must have sluiced herself under a shower, slipped into that little black dress and done her face. She had a cluster of older men round her, was honeypotting again as she had done at the Customs post at

Bosanski Novi. It was a brief little black dress. The men leered at her, and Joey thought each of them believed himself to be the centre of her attention, in with a chance. She must have told the Ambassador – cheerful, noisy Francis – that Joey Cann was her burden of the day and wasn't up to driving across Bosnia. He readied himself for the lecture, and snatched a drink off the waiter's tray.

'I'm not going to ask what you're doing here, because I don't want to know. What I usually do when Maggie's people are in town is take the phone off the hook and head off up country. Do not embarrass me, there's a good fellow. What I mean is, don't step on any toes. Last thing I want is muddy water ... We may, that's the foreign community, run this horrible little place and bankroll it, but they are extraordinarily sensitive to overt interference ... The local talent is for obstruction. We tell them how to live, we send them our best and our brightest, we shovel money at them, but it isn't working, nothing's moving. Right now they're seeing the signs of what we tell them is "attention fatigue", we're running down. They've decided all they have to do is sit tight and wait till we're off their backs. Nobody listens in London when I tell them that it's all been a very considerable failure. Truth is that you cannot make people live together when they actually hate each other, then hate us nearly as much ... Can I top you up?'

Joey shook his head.

'Even me, Joey, and I'm an old hand – I was here during the war, where I met Maggie – I'm quite astonished at the viciousness of the place. We haven't even started, haven't begun to start, getting rid of this brutality. Do you know, in the Brčko region the Serbs held Muslim civilians in a furniture factory. They had shredders there to make wood chips out of raw timber – for chipboard, you know. They fed Muslims into the shredding machines, got human chips out of raw bodies, then spread the chopped-up stuff on the fields ... Just to give you an idea of what we're up against ... I'd better circulate. Anyway, nice to have met you. Have a good stay, and please don't cause me any problems, you know what I mean. Have another drink.'

Joey stood alone against the wall.

He watched her. There was a little bag in her hand, leather and delicate.

One moment she was in the group, the next she was gone and the knot of older men were peering around, over their shoulders. He looked to see which appeared the most bereft. Then she was beside him.

'Come on, time to go.'

Joey said sourly, 'Only if you've finished enjoying yourself.'

'I was working.'

'Looked as if you were working hard.'

'Don't be so bloody pompous.'

They left. She didn't bother to wait in the queue and thank her host. Moments later, they were out in the cold air, walking down a winding cobbled street, the party's noise behind them. Her hand was back in his arm and he could smell her scent. The little shops they passed were shuttered with steel and wooden grilles. The street was empty.

'What was the work?'

'You wanted a name.'

'I'm sorry, I'm not focusing – what was the name I wanted?'

'A judge's name. You know, the needle in the haystack . . .'

'Come again?'

'The name of a judge to trust – God, you didn't think I was talking to those deadbeats for the good of my health? Cop on, Cann. Here, the judges co-operate with politicians and Mafia, drive a big car, live in a big apartment and their kids get university places. Or the judges don't co-operate and they listen to all the horseshit the foreigners give them about the sanctity of the rule of law, and they're machine-gunned or car-bombed, and they're dead. Least likely, they're marginalized, and don't get involved, not noticed – actually it's not "they", it's only one . . . He's straight, but the problem is – if you want to stay legal – he's useless. He stays alive and lives like a pauper. If you want "straight", then Zenjil Delic's your man.'

'Thanks.' They walked fast. 'What is this place?'

'It's the old market, the heart of the old city . . . The Serbs hit it with a mortar, the final straw that brought in the Americans. Thirty-eight dead and eighty-five wounded.'

He gazed over the gaunt frames of the market stands, now cleared for the night. A floodlit mosque minaret reached up towards the low cloud, the spit of snowflakes cavorting in the beam. 'Were you here? Did you see it?'

'You never ask for war stories in Sarajevo, Joey. You get enough without asking.'

'How near was the front line?'

'A few hundred yards, maybe four hundred.'

'How was the line held?'

'It was held because there was nowhere else to go.'

'Weren't they heroes, the commanders who held the line, saved the city?'

'Bad luck, Joey. Nothing here is as it seems. One day they held the line, the next day they did deals across it for the supply of black-market food, cooking oil and bullets. They weren't heroes, they were thugs.'

In the folklore of the city, he was the man who had preserved its name, identity, its heartbeat.

He had the title of *legenda*. He could strut the streets of the old quarter, walk at liberty on the Mula Mustafe Baseskija, the Branilaca Sarajeva, the Obala Kulina Bana, and the old and the young would recognize and make space for him. Some of the oldest would wish to touch his hand as their saviour and some of the young would dream of working for him.

A message reached him from London, passed by cut-out figures from the Turkish community there to the Turkish community in Sarajevo, that Albert William Packer travelled to his city the next day, and that he and his colleagues should be shown respect. In his apartment, richly furnished and luxuriously fitted, he talked of this matter with the deputy commander of the Agency for Investigation and Documentation, and with the nephew of the ruling party's politician controlling the Ministry of Justice. The latest message came by the same route as that which, two weeks before, had introduced the first visitor – now dead, taken from the river and freighted back whence he had come.

The *legenda* called himself Serif. He was Ismet Mujic. Old police files had listed him as born in 1963, reared in an orphanage following the disappearance of his father and the committal of his mother to a psychiatric ward after a nervous collapse, but the files had long since been taken from the shelves and destroyed. After running from the orphanage, a few days after his fourteenth birthday, he had joined the street kids roaming loose in the city and had begun a life of thieving. His early career had had two sides: he had also gained rich rewards from informing the police about other kids who followed the same trade. Then, and it had not seemed unnatural to him, he had become a policeman . . . He could remember very clearly the man who had come, and he could roll his tongue over the strange-sounding name of Duncan Dubbs. By 1984, Olympic year and a year of prime pickings, he had been a police bodyguard to the same official who was now paramount in the Ministry of the Interior and had mixed his duties with the lucrative provision of 'protection' to those traders, club-owners and restaurateurs who made fat killings from the Winter Games. When the war had started and chaos had gripped the undefended city, the legend of Serif had taken flight. The city had been about to collapse under the onslaught of the Serb forces, and its Muslim community had neither the men nor the munitions to prevent its fall. The scale of the impending catastrophe had thrown up, spewed out, a fighting leader. He had gone to the old prison, cleared out the hardest of the convicts, driven them in two lorries to the Central Bank and rifled the cash tills, then gone on to the Marshal Tito barracks on Zmaja od Bosne and thrown the bank-notes at the officer commanding the regular troops' armoury then taken out all the small arms that could be loaded on to two lorries, and they had gone into the line. On those first days, the greatest threat to the city's survival had been the Serb infantry push from Grbavica towards the former Olympic complex of Skenderija. In fighting of primitive ferocity, the line had held. It had been rifle against rifle, grenade against grenade, knife against knife, fist against fist. He became a fire brigade. First he deployed in Grbavica, then on assaults up the hill between the gravestones of the Jewish cemetery, then in Dobrinja to protect the tunnel linking the besieged city to the outside world – and his wealth had grown. By the end of the war his power over the city had been absolute.

Serif discussed again with the intelligence officer and a politician's nephew the proposal that had been made by Duncan Dubbs two weeks before, as they had discussed it before the visitor's death and after it, sipping good imported whisky. It was a natural arrangement in that city that a 'businessman' and an official sworn to defend the security of the state and the young relation of a principal politician should meet to talk over the merits of a contract offered by an outsider.

'What does he know?'

'Nothing,' the intelligence officer said.

'A list of witnesses has been given to the idiot judge, Delic, who will sing the same song, and the pathology report is in place – there is nothing he can know,' the politician's nephew said.

'And because he knows nothing, he comes with the promise of gifts,' Serif mused.

The intelligence officer murmured, 'Gifts should always be accepted, and after they have been given, the decisions can be made.'

They left the apartment as his boy, Enver, his sweet boy, returned from walking his Rottweiler dogs. They went out on to the street where the guards had machine pistols hidden under their coats. They walked with a cordon of guards around them. Serif had physical presence: he was short, broad-shouldered, with a clean-shaven head, and dressed always only in black. In Bascarsija's narrow lanes he owned the DiscoNite and the Platinum City where those few with money came and filled the tables, but in each a private room was always kept for him. The Platinum City was near to the river and they headed for it. It was where he had entertained Duncan Dubbs on the night of his death. At the door he paused. 'The man who came, Dubbs, he understood nothing of us. The man who is travelling with gifts, who looks to buy us, whom we are urged to treat with respect, I doubt that he understands more of us . . .'

His mobile phone rang. It sounded sharp in the night air. He answered it. 'Yes? . . . Yes, yes, this is that number . . . Who is that? . . . Who is it? . . . Do you have a wrong number? Who are you? Go fuck your father . . .' He closed the call and pocketed the phone. He shrugged. 'Just some woman, she asks me if she has the right number and reads off the digits, then says nothing – some crazy bitch.'

They went down the stairs and into the throb of the dance music.

New Year's Day 1993

The radio said that the war went badly. They did not need to be told. The tanks had come to the far side of the valley on the day before the enemy's Christmas festival. They had not fired on the day of the festival, but the shells had hit Vraca each day afterwards. The troops at Vraca had no tanks, no artillery and no heavy mortars for retaliation. Led by Husein Bekir, those villagers who had stayed in their homes spent the nights in their cellars and the days cowering in the outhouses at the rear of the houses, or they had gone to live in tents in the cover of the trees that climbed above the village. In the daylight hours it was assumed that the tank crews slept or drank themselves stupid, but it was still not safe to walk between the houses because two snipers operated from close to the river and the bullets from their long-barrelled rifles could reach Vraca.

And it had rained ever since the enemy's festival.

The day the tanks had arrived across the valley the low clouds had scattered a fine carpet of snow over the two villages and the valley between them. From Vraca, Husein had been able to see the track trails they left as they nudged into the hiding-places chosen in the wreckage of Ljut. He had seen the lorries arrive and the unloading of the bright brass shell cases. Then the rain had started. Snow was seen only rarely in the valley, but the rain came down with a particular and cruel intensity, battering the roofs of the damaged buildings and through windows and doors that had been blasted off their frames. And with the rain came the cold.

Smoke from the fires the villagers lit to warm themselves was a beacon to the tank gunners. Even when it had been safe to light fires, the kindling and split logs were too damp. There was no heating-oil left in the village; it had been finished a month before the snowfall and the arrival of the tanks. They lived, like animals, day and night, in darkness, wrapped in wet blankets; their food and the troops' rations were near to exhaustion. At dawn, on the enemy's New Year's Day, the officer came to Husein Bekir's home. He was panting because he had sprinted from the village, across open ground, to the house and then down into the cellar.

There was no coffee, if she could have heated it, that Lila could offer to the commander of the troops. 'I have bad news – and then perhaps worse.' The officer grimaced.

Over the weeks since the troops had come to Vraca, they had almost become friends. Husein thought the officer a good man, and did not believe him responsible for what had happened across the valley, in Ljut, on the autumn night of the attack over the river. They could never be close friends, but he respected the man's honour, and in return was always treated with courtesy. He was the first of the village's civilians to be told of military plans. The officer was from the east, and the town where his family lived, his wife and two children, had been purged of Muslims, and he did not know whether his family had fled successfully or been killed. The officer talked with them, Husein and Lila, as if they were his own parents.

'Brigade does not believe that Vraca is of sufficient strategic importance.'

'What does that mean?'

'That we will pull out, retreat to a more defensible position.'

'And . . . ?'

'We have information from behind the lines on the other side that the tanks have come to soften our defence before an attack on the village. When it comes, it will not be from soldiers but from the scum of the White Eagles. They are the same as Arkan's criminals or Seselj's. When they come, esteemed friend, they will kill every male, old or young. They will violate every woman, old or young, and they will destroy the village and flatten the cemetery where your people are buried, and mine. They will make the men watch the violation of their women, their daughters, their sisters and their mothers, and then they will kill them. As the chief man of the village, you would be selected for torture in front of all the men, women and children. It is what they have done all over the country. The military do the fighting, then the scum come to scavenge, and kill.'

'Because of what your men did in Ljut.'

'I cannot justify that madness – but we did not begin the barbarism.'

'And you will abandon us?'

'We will escort you from a place that is no longer defensible – I am taking casualties for no gain. Our position does not make military sense.'

'Can you not put down mines, as they have done?'

'We have no mines, we do not have the factories as they do – we have to go, Husein, and we will take you with us.'

The old farmer pulled himself to his full height, the crown of his balding scalp brushing against the beams and the sodden plaster of the cellar ceiling. Emotion broke his voice. 'It is my home. They are my fields.'

'We all have homes,' the officer said grimly. 'We all have families, and we all have cemeteries where our people are buried. My orders are to evacuate you.'

'Where will we go?'

'I don't know . . . to a camp, or abroad.'

'What can we take?'

'What you can carry – no more.'

'When do we go?'

'Tonight.'

The officer climbed out of the cellar. Husein's wife held him, and the tears streamed down his cheeks. He smelt the damp of her clothes. Without speaking they clung to each other for several minutes, near to a quarter of an hour. The village was their lives, and had been their parents' lives and their grandparents' and, until the madness came, they had assumed it would be their grandchildren's lives. She took a grimy handkerchief from the pocket of her apron, under a heavy coat, and defiantly wiped his eyes; she had not wept. He climbed the steps, treacherous from the damp, from the cellar. She would pack. She would know better than him what they, old people, could carry.

He went out of the back, then tried to run to the outbuildings. He could not go quickly and his best effort was a slow, crabbed short stride and he bent his spine to make a smaller target. The one shot was high. He reached the buildings where the cattle bellowed in protest. They were hungry: no fresh fodder had been brought to them for three days.

He went to the main double door of nailed planks, and threw it open. The rain spat on to him.

Husein Bekir looked out over the valley, peered through the driving rain. Past his rusting tractor, and his fields that had died from inattention, past his vineyard where the weeds sprouted and the posts sagged, grey streams of water ran down the hill from the village of Ljut and from the high ground that flanked it. The track from the far village was a watercourse, but many more streams were pounding in torrents from the hills and pressing past the bare trees to the flooded river, which had already broken its banks. Although he was not stupid, with a deep-set experience of agriculture, and cunning where money and commerce were concerned, Husein Bekir did not have the intelligence to consider that a minefield was, in effect, a living organism with the power of movement. His eyes roved over those places where he had witnessed the mines being laid, and he did not know that some of the PMA2 anti-personnel mines were now being buried deep under silt that would provide a protective layer over them, and that others would be lifted by the flood's force and carried metres from where they had been sown. Neither did he know that the wooden stakes holding in place the PMA3s and the PROMs could be pushed from the ground by the streams, as the stakes holding the trip-wires had been dislodged. He did not know that some of the points he believed to be poisoned with the mines were now free of them, and some of the places where he had thought the ground safe were now lethal.

As he looked across the valley there was nothing to see of this secret movement.

The whole of the afternoon, he stayed in the outbuildings and talked quietly with his cattle, the beef calves and the sheep. He told them what he would do and, in his simple way, he wished them well, and said that he would return. He would come again, he said, and they nuzzled against him. At last light, the main door to the outbuildings left open, he went back to his home where Lila had filled two small bags.

He shouted at his dog. His voice was sufficiently angry to ensure that it ran from him and hid. He could not take it, or bring himself to shoot it.

His animals were already out and foraging for food when Husein Bekir, Lila, the villagers and the troops, in the growing darkness, trudged slowly away from the village. He found only minimal comfort in the knowledge that when he came back he would remember where the mines had been laid.

Bent over his desk, her father had not noticed.

For a long time after the call had ended, Jasmina Delic sat with the phone in her hand. She had been helping her father to clear his desk. She had to nag him to keep control of the paper mountain that covered it. There were no resources to employ the staff who should have worked for a judge. She had taken one file from the pile in the corner where they were stacked, and casually opened it. At the top had been the note from the IPTF policeman, Williams, concerning the drowned Englishman, and the telephone number retrieved from a bedside notepad. Idly, she had rung the number. She had heard the voice, she had asked if the number was correct, and it was confirmed. She had recognized the voice, had listened to it until the call was cut.

She put down the phone, closed the file, wheeled herself to the corner and dropped it on to the floor. Her father noticed nothing. She would tell him in the morning.

Always the busy man, without time to waste, Mister had three more meetings between the time he left the Covent Garden café and his arrival home. At one meeting he authorized the payment on delivery at Felixstowe harbour for a container, now at Rotterdam docks, that held a fraction under a million pounds' worth of heroin, street value, bedded in made-in-China ornamental garden tubs; at another he rubber-stamped an agreement for him to be paid a little more than a thousand pounds a year by a novelty-stall holder operating in Trafalgar Square, up from the previous rate by seven per cent; at the final meeting he talked over with an architect a development project for four hectares of Mediterranean coastal land west of Cap d'Antibes. Whether the profit margin was measured in millions or hundreds was immaterial to him. He despised laziness. He kept the same close eye on all his deals. That night the negotiation that gave the greatest satisfaction was the one with Lennie Perks for the safety of the stall in Trafalgar Square, because he had taken Lennie Perks's money for twenty-nine years, and the job went at a loss. But he never gave up on a customer, would never accept that he was now too grand to deal with the bottom end of trade. He spoke on his mobile phone with Albie Wilkes, as he walked the night streets, to confirm what they both already knew because it had been well worked out before he had cast an eye over young Sol; he spoke also to a detective chief inspector in the National Crime Squad and was told that investigators were without leads in the matter of Georgie Riley, who was not expected to last the week; then he took a taxi home.

There were aspects of his life on which he would not have dreamed of acting without the approval of the Princess. His dress was one of them. He had not, as she had not, ever been to Bosnia-Herzegovina. She would have checked on the TV's text earlier in the evening for local-weather advice, and that would have decided her on what clothes he should take. On his return, they packed the case together.

Then they drank together, champagne but only one glass each, and she toasted him and wished the venture well. He knew she looked at him, over the glass, and he thought he saw in the sparkle of her eyes a sense of triumph for him because he was on the road he wanted to travel, and also of apprehension. But he knew there was no cause for fear, not for her and not for him. Nothing frightened him, nothing ever had. He kissed her eyes. His lips brushed them and when he looked again he thought he'd chucked out the anxiety. He was fine, he said, had never felt better. It was good days ahead.

Back at the hotel, Joey rang Jen. He told her about the plane delay and the drive. She said she loved him and he rang off. He was too tired to work out in his mind whether he loved her or not.

In the hotel's car park, underneath his window, the light fall of snow caked on Maggie Bolton's coat as she stripped down the hire car, retrieved her equipment, then rebuilt the car's interior – and Joey didn't know that her work was not yet finished.

He slept. Small pieces of a mosaic were falling into place, and he was dead to them, unaware of their importance.

Chapter Six

'I'm not coming,' she'd said.

'Please yourself.' He must have sounded crestfallen.

'I don't trail around after you. I've my job to do.'

'Which is?'

'Dock in the hire car, rent a van – and finish my breakfast.'

Joey had said when he would meet her, and what time the flight was due in, and hesitated . . . 'I don't suppose I take anyone from the embassy with me.'

'I don't suppose you do. Just make sure you're wearing your charm boots.'

She'd gone back to her breakfast. Joey had left her there, surrounded by rolls, jam, cheese and coffee. She hadn't even wished him luck.

He'd never worked alone before.

But what little Joey Cann knew of judges was that you didn't make appointments – you pitched up early in the morning. The room was high in the Ministry of Justice building. The lift was occupied, groaning slowly above him. He hadn't waited, but had gone up ever-narrowing flights of stairs to the floor under the roof. The building was damaged. Damp ran on the walls, and the ceiling above him had been crudely plastered. The floor at either side of the judge's door was piled high with cardboard file folders that were held tight with string and elastic bands. He steadied himself. If he were thrown out on his neck, had the door shut in his face, then he was in trouble, deep. He needed the legality of authorization. He rapped on the door and breathed hard. Maggie had said, dismissively, that she wasn't an interpreter, and that any judge spoke English. He heard a light squealing sound, metal on metal without oil, before the door was opened.

Inside, the room was chaos. It was a disaster area of failed organization, a home for lost files. A dull single bulb, without a shade, hung from a ceiling that was a trellis of cracks. What he could see of the walls, above the piled files, showed more cracks but wider ones. There was a desk at the far end and, half hidden by more files that formed a barricade to mask his chest, a small man peered at him over half-moon spectacles. Above the man, behind him, was a faded framed photograph, spider's web lines in the glass, showing the man in younger days, a handsome woman and a girl child, with pretty hair and in a party frock, holding flowers. Near to the photograph, hanging from a nail, was a calendar with last year's date on it, now being recycled because there were fresh ink notes in the days' boxes. At the side of the room, under a narrow window that was smeared on the inside where failed attempts had been made to clean it, and opaque on the outside, was a smaller desk dominated by an old computer screen, something from the Ark or a museum. From the ceiling to the floor, from the crack lines and the dim light to the worn apology for a carpet, the boards that needed staining and the electric fire where a single bar glowed dismally, he took in the scene. The man wore an overcoat and the smell of damp and dirt clogged in Joey's nostrils.

'*Zdravo . . . Da?*'

Maggie had told him what to say. '*Zovem se* Joey Cann. *Gavorite li engleski, molim?*'

'Yes, I speak English, a little. My daughter speaks it better.'

Joey heard the squealing sound. He turned his head sharply. The young woman had been hidden by the open door. It was the wheelchair that needed oil. He would not have recognized her but he knew instinctively that it was her face in the photograph. Her complexion was so very pale and there was a desperate tiredness in her eyes. He felt ashamed of staring at her. Her thin blonde hair was tied loosely behind her head, and he saw the power of her shoulders, which would have strengthened to compensate for her disability. The smile was radiant.

'I am Jasmina. You have come to see my father, Judge Delic. We do not have much time before court. How may we help, Mr Cann?'

'I'll try not to waste your time.' He remembered what he had been told. 'I'm an executive officer of British Customs and Excise. I work in the section that's called the National Investigation Service. Our work deals with the most serious cases of organized crime involving the importation into Great Britain of class A drugs. When we go abroad, in order that any evidence we obtain should be legally admissible in our court, we must have the appropriate permission from a local person in authority, who can be a judge.'

He breathed out, tried to relax.

'I was given your name. I need your help. In the UK we have a Target One, Albert William Packer. He is first among equals for trafficking in class A narcotics. He would regard himself as an untouchable. We are clutching at straws, having most recently failed to convict him. He arrives in Sarajevo this afternoon. We don't know why he is coming here, what he is attempting to set up, or who he will meet. Our experience has shown us that when our major criminals are abroad they behave with greater confidence. It's when they make mistakes. I have to say that Packer makes mistakes rarely. He may open a small window for us, and he may not. We need the authorization for what we call "intrusive surveillance". I'm asking you for that authorization.'

Maggie Bolton had told him that a judge who co-operated with the Mafia drove a big car and lived in a big apartment – and that a judge who did not co-operate was machine-gunned or car-bombed.

'He's a bad man, sir. His place is in prison with the key thrown away. His wealth, from the drugs trade, is estimated at around one hundred and fifty million American dollars. We regard him as a prime enemy of our society. If I had done this properly, by the book, the Justice Ministry of Bosnia-Herzegovina would have been contacted by our embassy and – being frank with you, sir – the probability is that I would have been shuffled into the office of a senior civil servant, given cups of coffee, and put off while bureaucracy slowly turned over, and there would have been requests for more information, and I'd have kicked my heels and our Target One would have done his business and gone home. I accept, sir, that we have taken a liberty in involving you. I am in your hands.'

And Maggie had also told him that one judge was useless, insignificant, did not get involved, lived in squalor, and was a judge to trust.

'Last week, the day that our case against Target One failed, the body of his financial associate was taken from the river in Sarajevo. He would have been preparing the ground for his chief man. At the time the associate flew here, Target One was on trial, but his network of intimidation and corruption in Britain guaranteed that he would be freed. This is, possibly, a considerable opportunity for us.'

The voice of the judge growled at him. 'What was the name of the associate?'

'Duncan Dubbs. If you refuse me, then I quite understand. I'm poorly informed on Sarajevo but informed enough to appreciate the difficulties I'm creating for you. There is no threat to me in the UK. I have never felt in personal danger. You will not see me standing in judgement if you tell me that you cannot help and do not wish to be implicated in an investigation of this sort. I have to assume that our Target One will meet, deal with, a principal figure in this city's organized-crime network. That makes for involvement. I'll be going home. I won't be here if there are consequences.'

'An authorization for surveillance from me?'

'That's what I'm asking for, sir.'

Joey didn't know whether he had won through or whether he had failed. He felt the silence in the room press around him. If a judge had come to London from Sarajevo or Zagreb, Budapest or Bucharest, Sofia or Prague, he would have been passed round the Foreign and Commonwealth or the Home Office, pushed into obscure corners of New Scotland Yard or the Custom House, would have been treated with the dignity accorded to an unwelcome blow-in. Judge Delic, wearing the deep frown of a troubled man, ferreted among the papers on his desk. Then came the persistent and rhythm-less tapping of his pencil point on the desk top. He looked at his daughter. Joey heard the scrape of the wheels behind where he stood. Then she propelled herself to her father and handed him a file. Joey did not dare to hope. The judge's face was expressionless as he opened the file, but Joey saw her face and the way her jaw jutted out as if in a demonstration of defiance. The piece of paper in the judge's hand was small enough to have been torn from a notepad, and it was encased in a cellophane sachet. He looked at the piece of paper for a long time.

She asked, '*Da?* . . . *Ne?*'

Joey had said that he would be going home and would not be there to see the consequences. He thought he had asked too much.

Judge Delic nodded. '*Da.*'

She said, 'My father says yes. I will type it for you, Mr Cann, and my father will sign it, the authorization.'

'Thank you.'

She wheeled herself to the small desk by the window, switched on the computer. After an age while it warmed, the machine clattered under her fingers. Joey had nothing to say. The judge never raised his eyes, but he shivered under his overcoat. Joey stared at the floor, following the lines of the carpet's trodden-down threads, and thought of the man due to arrive in Sarajevo, who reckoned himself an untouchable.

She worked the printer and brought the pages to him. He leaned over the desk and wrote his and Maggie Bolton's names in the spaces provided, then she gave them to her father and he signed each sheet briskly, before pushing them away as if they were a nagging dream that might wound him. She put the stamp on the document of authorization.

'Thank you, sir.'

'To be used with discretion.'

'Of course, sir.'

Joey Cann's promise of discretion was worth nothing. If evidence were found, if Target One were held, then the authorization would be in the public domain in open court. There were telephone lines, fax lines, e-mail lines between London and Sarajevo. With his scrawled signature, Judge Delic had compromised himself, and would have known it. The promise was empty. The judge had turned away and was staring up at the photograph of a family. Jasmina told Joey of the telephone number on the pad beside Duncan Dubbs's hotel bed, that the number had been answered by Ismet Mujic, and she gave him the list of three eyewitnesses and copies of their statements to the local police. He felt he was a stormcloud settling on their lives.

At the door, Joey said, 'I'm grateful to you, sir – and to you, miss – very grateful for involving yourselves.'

The judge said, flat-voiced, 'I have broken a rule of my life. The rule says that to survive here you must remain unnoticed. The rule was given me by my mother, because of my father's death. I was one and a half years old when my father died. My father, in the difficult times of the world war and the German occupation, thought it right to involve himself in the fight against the Tito *partizans*. He was recruited into the Handzar, which was the 13th SS Division, all Muslims – the word is the Turkish one for the curved dagger of our people. He was proud of his involvement and the uniform they gave him. He was trained in Germany and France. A little later, Tito formed the 16th Muslim Brigade. My father had joined the wrong side; it would have been better for him to remain unnoticed. He was shot after the war.'

'Then why, sir, did you break your rule?'

'From the claim of blood, because of blood that was spilled – from stupidity. Not a story to be told to a stranger. Be satisfied with what you have.'

She opened the door for him. Joey ran down the flights of stairs, through the cavern of the hallway and out into the street. If he had not checked himself, he would have punched the fume-filled air in triumph.

The aircraft bucked. Mister wondered whether the Eagle was going to throw up. Sitting beside him, clutching the seat's arms, choking and coughing, the lawyer's face was green-white. On the other side of him, Atkins was looking out on the dense grey mass of cloud. They were in powerful cross-winds and the plane was thrown sideways, forced down, climbed again, then plunged down further. The Eagle's discomfiture made Mister feel good and took away any anxiety he might have felt.

'Is this the way you used to come in?' What he liked about Atkins was that the former soldier never spoke unless it was required of him.

'In all weathers, Mister, and the rougher the better. This isn't bad. Worst was good weather, no cloud. We're on approach now. We used to call the RAF flights, C130 transports, "Maybe Airlines". Over the mountains and then the "Khe Sanh drop-down" – Khe Sanh was an American fire base in Vietnam where they had to come in against Triple A, anti-aircraft artillery. The pilots' technique was to corkscrew from twenty thousand feet, a little disturbing on the bowels. In good weather they'd shoot, particularly if they were pissed. In bad weather they couldn't see you.'

'Wasn't there any response?'

'Blue beret time, Mister, take it on the chin. One day I'll tell you about United Nations soldiering.'

They hit a bigger pocket. The Eagle gasped. Mister felt better than good. 'Do you know what we're doing here, Atkins?'

'I don't, but you'll tell me when you're ready to.'

His voice was faint against the thunder of the engines. 'Right now, I'm ready. I can't suffer boredom, Atkins, can't abide it. I was going nowhere, I was doing what I'd done three years before. What I needed was challenges – new scene, new drills, new business. The Cruncher put up the idea. The Afghans produce the stuff, and the Cruncher said they'd get X amount, and that wasn't negotiable. The Turks pick it up and ship it across Europe then get it over to the UK and they charge Y. I sell it on and that's Z. Three factors in the street price. X is beyond my reach, and Z is my money anyway, so it's Y that I'm going after. The Turks ship it through here. My proposition – Cruncher's – is that I buy for delivery into Bosnia for Y minus forty per cent, or Y minus fifty per cent, then I ship onwards. I run the transport organization from Bosnia. I go into an international league . . . and that, Atkins, is big bucks. We'd have been here earlier if I'd not been *away*. Got any cold water?'

The aircraft kicked a last time, then broke through the cloud ceiling. Light flooded into the cabin. He steadied the tray as they banked sharply. He had a clear view of the mountains and the snow streaks between the pine-forest plantations.

'Not for me, Mister, to pour cold water on anything you put up . . . The Triple A was up there and this was when they'd hit you, the bastards, when you were helpless and steadying to come in . . . If you can get the Turks on board you've done well, if you can get the Bosnian low-life on board then you've done better than well. But you know that.'

'I pay you to tell me what I should know.'

'Who are we dealing with, from the low-life?'

'He's called Serif . . .'

The undercarriage slipped down. The aircraft yawed. Atkins was pointing through the porthole window. Apartment blocks slipped by. It took Mister a moment to realize why they had been pointed out. He squinted to see better. The buildings were empty carcasses: they had been devastated by artillery, great holes punched in the walls; they had been ravaged by fire, scorched patches around the gaping windows; they had been pocked by small-arms bullets and shrapnel, disease-ridden and spotted from the volume of it.

Atkins said to him, 'There was a tunnel under the runway from Butmir on the far side to Dobrinja, where we're looking. It was the Muslim lifeline and the Serbs couldn't break in to close it. Serif was instrumental in defending the link. The army brought their supplies in through the tunnel, and Serif brought in the black-market stuff. He made serious money out of it, and he sealed his deals with government. Don't ever forget, Mister, Serif is protected from the top of government down. He's hard – and if the Cruncher was around that's what he'd tell you. He's a dangerous man, not to be taken lightly.'

They hit the runway hard.

Mister laid one hand over the Eagle's fist clenching the armrest and with the other he punched Atkins. He said, against the thunder of the reverse thrust, 'We'll eat him. You see if we don't.'

An old blue Japanese-made van was at the back of the airport car park. From where it was parked the driver and his passenger had a clear view through the wiped windscreen of the two black Mercedes saloons that had stopped directly in front of the outer arrivals door. Joey was behind the wheel. Maggie talked in terse code into the microphone clipped to her blouse.

'They're in place,' Cork said.

'You're lucky to have her.' Endicott's smile was superior. 'She's bloodstock.'

Dennis Cork, chief investigation officer, had stalled the meeting to answer his mobile call in the Home Office minister's private room. Giles Endicott had been his desk chief at the Secret Intelligence Service before the transfer to Customs & Excise. The transfer had brought Cork a substantial increment in salary and in civil-service grading so that he now ranked as equal to his former master, but old habits died hard: he remained, in Endicott's book, a junior.

Cork responded tetchily, 'I am merely reporting that my man is in place.'

'And I am merely observing that he has a first-class operator up alongside him.'

The minister intervened: 'I made a speech last week – you may or may not have picked it up – in which I spoke of the devastation caused by the drugs trade. I said: "In every city, town and village children are in danger of being ensnared by drugs and crime." You both know that an election's looming. An essential part of this government's battle plan is our determination to break the link between drugs and crime. I went on to say, "Addicts ruin more than just their own lives, they mug, burgle and steal to pay for their next fix. Every year heroin users criminally take more than a thousand million pounds to feed that disgusting habit – the equivalent of sixty pounds from every household in the country." We want action, gentlemen, we need visible action. Bickering over minor scraps of turf is not the action I'm looking for. I, the government, demand results – require arrests and convictions so that these foul narcotics are cleaned from our streets. In the case of Packer, what's happening?'

'We've sent a man –'

'– with a first-class operator alongside him.'

The minister, the supplicant, clasped his hands together in a prayer of frustration. 'Don't you see, dammit, what I'm trying to say? A criminal waltzes from the Old Bailey a free man. The response of the law-abiding community is to send a man after him who you tell me is twenty-seven years old, therefore inexperienced, earning the rate paid to people at the bottom of the ladder, the minimum response because you plead the strictures of expense and the un-certainty of success. You send, along with him, a woman with a box of tricks. I want results that are high-profile, I want people to read in their morning newspapers – all of those people who are scared witless that their children and grandchildren will be caught up in this ghastly life-threatening trafficking, and who vote for us – that we are doing something.'

Endicott asked coolly, 'Doing something worthwhile, Minister, or doing *anything*?'

Cork said, a little sadness in his voice, 'If, when Packer has sealed whatever business deal he's gone to make, he were to return and fall happily under the wheels of a number seventy-three bus the effect on the availability of heroin on the streets of London would be less than negligible . . . That is a fact.'

'That's not good enough.'

Endicott said, 'We are not, Minister, soldiers in a holy war.'

Cork said, 'We deal with the real, and unpleasant, world.'

'I need, require, success.'

Cork said, 'It's not the way things work, I'm sorry to say. It's slow, tedious and undramatic. He's called Joey Cann. He may, with considerable luck, put one building brick in place and that's only one – but it's ridiculous to assume he can win you those headlines, bring Packer down.'

The meeting broke up.

They went together from the minister's room out on to the pavement and into brittle spring sunshine. They paused before parting.

'Even for a politician, that fellow's not the full shilling,' Endicott said.

'If I thought Cann and Bolton were going for Packer's jugular with a hacksaw, were going to endanger themselves in that snake-pit, they'd be on the first plane home.'

Joey's eyes were on the arrivals door, fastened on it.

He saw Mister between the Eagle and Atkins. He edged the gear from neutral.

'That them?' she asked.

'That's Target One and the fat one's Target Two. The younger one's Target Three.'

'Happy days,' she said, and her camera's shutter clicked beside his ear.

The photographs he'd seen, scores of them, were good: he had recognized Mister immediately and watched him with fascination. For the first time the man was in front of him, flesh where before there had been only monochrome images. The greeting party lounged against the two waiting cars. He saw Mister's head incline towards the Eagle's and saw his lips move. It was a private moment of exhilaration. He could not have explained it to Jen. There might have been an opportunity the previous summer, when Finch had put together the arrest team, for him to have piped up and asked to be included. He'd hesitated – the team might have laughed at him, he might have had to stutter why it was important to him, their archivist and the bottom of the tree, to be there when the handcuffs went on to Mister's wrists – and the moment of opportunity had gone. That night, alone in his room and knowing what was to happen at a quarter to six in the morning, he had beaten his pillow in frustration. Yet those who might have refused him or laughed at him were all gone. He had survived. The moment was his.

'He needs to know, this Serif, who's the boss. Polite and firm, but it's understood from the start. We are big players, he's a small player, that's what he should be learning now.'

He was about to start forward but Atkins's hand was on his arm. 'They're big on pride, Mister. They think they won their war – they didn't, it was won for them, but it's what they like to believe.'

'I hear you.'

The Cruncher should have been back to London to brief him and should have been with him for the return, not the Eagle. Across the paving from them were four men, their weight against the doors and bonnets of the cars, in a uniform of black windcheaters, shaven heads, black shirts, tattoos on their necks, black jeans, gold chains at their throats, black boots, cigarettes. Mister wore a suit and a white shirt. The Eagle carried a businessman's attaché case and was dressed in a blazer, slacks, collar and tie and a maroon-brown over-coat. Atkins was the officer boy, in brogues, chocolate corduroys, sports jacket, and was loaded with the three bags. A cigarette was thrown down, then three more. The back door of the front car was opened.

'Which one's Serif?' Mister murmured.

'He's not here,' Atkins said, 'if I remember him right.'

'Shit,' the Eagle muttered. 'That's one hell of a good start.'

A policeman, with a heavy pistol slung from a waist holster, approached the cars. Gold rank on his tunic, he slapped shoulders, gripped fists, and was given a cigarette from an American pack, as if he was meeting friends, and then he was gone. Mister wondered whether it had been arranged to send a message. The boot of the front car was opened, the bags taken from Atkins and lifted inside. A pudgy hand, with gold rings on it, gestured to the car's back seats.

'Where is he?' Mister asked Atkins.

Atkins asked. Mister saw them all, in unison, shrug.

'They're saying they don't know.'

There was a sigh from the Eagle. It was the nearest he ever came to saying there were always consequences when his advice was ignored. 'I told you so' would have been too bold for the Eagle to utter. They were pressed together on the back seat of the Mercedes, a driver and a minder in the front, the second driver and second minder in the car behind. They were jerked against the leather as the car powered away. The sign they swept past proclaimed that the airport's new terminal had been built with Dutch money. They went past the guarded entrance to a French military camp. The driver didn't slow as he approached the barrier at the perimeter but hit the horn. The bar was lifted, the car accelerated, a policeman waved a greeting. Apache gunships, American, flew over them in formation, and Mister craned to watch them before their disappearance into the cloud.

Ruined buildings confronted them as they swung on to the main road – the close-up mayhem wreckage of what he had seen in the aircraft's final approach. For a moment he was unsettled, a slight toll of his confidence taken by the absence of the man due to meet him, the closeness of the police officer to the escort, the scale of military power, the extent of the war damage. Atkins looked at him, queried with his eyes. Did he want a running commentary? He shook his head. He was absorbed.

He had never seen anything like it. Whole streets were burned, shot away, roofless. Kids played football in the roads where snow-covered debris was bulldozed to the side. And people lived there . . . In the wrecked homes, people existed, as if the houses were caves. There were sagging skewed balconies on which limp plants were stacked and from which washing-lines hung taut under the weight of sheets, shirts, skirts. It was five years since the war – why hadn't it been rebuilt? He didn't know, and didn't want Atkins to tell him. The loss of confidence had been momentary. He was here because it was what he had wanted.

At a junction stood a massive collapsed building. It looked as if it had been dynamited at the base. It was five bloody years. What did these people do? Why didn't they clear it up? But he didn't ask Atkins. They drove into the dense streets of the city. His first impressions, and Mister always thought them the best, were that the place was a grade A dump, a tip. They hit a long, straight road. On the plane, Atkins had told him they would come into the city on Buleva Mese Selimovica, eight lanes, that merged into the Zmaja od Bosne, which had been called Snipers' Alley. At high speed, they passed a building whose roof was festooned with aerials and satellite dishes, and he thought it must house the telephone headquarters. Behind it he glimpsed a dispersed mess of Portakabin huts with signs leading to them for the International Police Task Force, but he knew nothing of what they did. Then a lorry park was on the left, and another and another. He saw rows of cabs, trailers and containers, more rows, and warehouses, some intact and some destroyed. The Cruncher's last message from Sarajevo had given the address, the number of the warehouse in a lorry park in Halilovici, where the charity lorry should arrive. He wondered if it was there; it should have been there that morning, or the night before, tucked from sight in the warehouse. They hammered over a bridge. He saw the murky earth-brown water, foaming on the weirs, running fast. He'd always been fond of the Cruncher. He'd never feel for Sol Wilkes what he'd felt for the Cruncher.

'I want to know where it happened, where the Cruncher went into the river. I want to go there, I want to see it.'

Atkins spoke to the driver. There seemed to be surprise on the man's face, but Mister couldn't tell whether it was at what was asked, or that he should be told what to do. The Eagle sat bolt upright and clutched his attaché case as if he believed it might be wrenched from his grip ... Drab streets, drab people, drab shops. Kids waved to the cars as they went by, and where there was a traffic block they headed into the oncoming lane and sped past. Once, a car had to swerve on to the pavement to let them by. At a junction, a policeman held up the right-of-way vehicles and they overtook jeeps loaded with armed Italian soldiers, whose drivers seemed not to notice them. When they braked hard they were level with a restaurant whose doors and windows were surrounded by silver aluminium. The sign said it was called Platinum City. Opposite was a narrow, ancient footbridge over the river. The cars stopped, the doors were opened. Mister pushed out the Eagle, then followed him.

There was a low wall between the pavement and the riverbank, and a waist-high railing on the bridge. An old woman in black squatted beside buckets of tired flowers. He saw that men and women in threadbare clothes stepped off the pavement, risking the road traffic to stay clear of the minders. Mister pointed to the flowers. Atkins spoke to the minder from the front of their car. The man went to the old crow, dropped banknotes into her lap and her face lifted in gratitude. He took a single bunch from her buckets, and she offered more for what he had paid, but he shook his head curtly. The blooms were handed to Atkins, a half-dozen drooping smog-encrusted chrysanthemums. Atkins gave them to Mister, who walked to the centre of the bridge.

He was a man to whom sentiment came rarely. He looked down at the rushing water. He was not troubled by history. He did not know that he was close to where Gavrilo Princep had held a hidden pistol and waited for an archduke and archduchess in an open car, and what had been the consequences of the shots that he had fired. Neither did he know that the bridge on which he stood was a monument to the skill of Ottoman architects now dead for centuries. Nor did he realize that had he stood on that bridge, looking down on the water, seven years earlier, or eight or nine, a sniper's 'scope would have magnified him in the seconds before he was shot. He held the flowers. He sensed the cold and the power of the river's currents. Neither Atkins nor the Eagle had followed him. He was not aware that the space and quiet around him were not accidental and did not see that the minder from the second car had crossed to the far side of the bridge and diverted pedestrians away. His mood lightened. People died, didn't they? Cruncher had died, hadn't he? Could have been a traffic accident, could have been slipping in the shower, could have been a rent-boy's knife, could have been pissed and fallen into a river. Life goes on, isn't that right, my old friend? Life goes on, with new challenges. It was the nearest Mister could grope towards feeling sentiment at the death of a friend. He threw the flowers into the river and watched the muddy waters suck them down. There was a flash of colour, then they were gone. Had he looked around him at that moment, turned sharply, and not stared into the flow of the Miljacka, he would have seen the faces of the drivers and the minders. He would have seen amusement and the curl of contempt at their mouths.

He walked briskly back to the cars.

He was driven the reverse way along Snipers' Alley to a square block of gaudy yellow topped with the logo of the Holiday Inn.

'When do I get to see him?'

Through Atkins he discovered that Serif was busy at the moment, but when he was free he would see his respected guest.

The cars drove away. They picked up their bags and walked into the lobby.

The Eagle said, 'That, Mister, is out of order. It is plainly insulting.'

Atkins said, 'It's his patch, Mister, and he'll think crude pegging you back will make him a bigger man.'

Mister smiled cheerfully. 'He'll do it once, he'll not do it again. That's my promise to him and I'm good on my word . . . Doesn't seem too bad a place, considering the rest of it.'

Across open ground where the concrete was holed ankle deep by artillery explosions was a line of sparsely filled shops and bars where a few men and youths desultorily made their coffee last. Above the shops and bars were apartments that had been repaired with a patchwork of bricks and cement. In front of the long building a blue van, paint scraped, unremarkable, was parked in a position that gave its driver and passenger good sight of the front door of the Holiday Inn hotel.

'It may be a slow old trade,' Maggie said, 'but at least we're legal.'

'That's right,' Joey answered. 'Ink on paper.'

'I thought you had a chance, but . . .'

'He was good as gold, the judge.'

'I think it's the first time I've ever been legal – is that a cause for celebration or tears? Don't know . . . Tell you what I also don't know – why. Why did Judge Delic sign? You didn't break his legs, did you? You didn't drop him a couple of thousand dollars, did you?'

'I didn't ask. He signed, I ran with it.'

She eased back in her seat, the camera settled on her lap. Behind her, in the van's interior, the workshop of her trade was neatly laid out, cosseted with foam and bubble-wrap.

'It'll be from something out of the past – don't take too much credit for it.'

He said coldly, 'You'd know about that because you worked in dirty corners that are now history. You won't mind me saying it, but the Cold War was utter shit, irrelevant, perpetuated by spooks to keep themselves on the payroll. This is something that matters.'

'I worked with men, I was at the cutting edge, I was with real men,' she flared. 'All this business about *legal*, it's pathetic. They were real men, the best and the finest.'

'Dust in the past,' he said.

He disliked so much of her, and didn't know where to focus the beam of his dislike. There was the crimped care of her makeup and her dress, and the crispness of her accent, and the fact that she had been there before and knew it all when he knew nothing, and the academic precision of her kit in the back of the van. There was the sense of class, privilege and superiority in her every speech and movement. For Joey, being in Sarajevo and close to Target One was the sweet pinnacle of his short career. For her, as she showed him, it was a tedious spell of tacky work to be endured.

'God help your lot,' she said, 'if you're the best they've got.'

Silence cloaked them. She smoked. The evening descended around them. When she dragged hard and the tip glowed he could see her face. Utter calm contentment. She should have been, was meant to be, offended by his rudeness. He thought a test had been set for him, a provocation to make him expose himself, as if then she could calculate his value, his competence. He eased himself out of the van's cab. Before he closed the door after him, Joey asked ruefully, 'You'll be all right?'

'Course I will,' she said. 'Why not? This is Bosnia.'

Spring 1993
Two old men, though they were far away from it, dreamed of the valley. They remembered only the best times, when the first of the year's warm days heated the soil and the flowers came and they could hear the river flowing over the ford, and a friendship of more than half a century.

The new home of Husein Bekir, his wife and grandchildren was a bell-tent in a camp on the edge of the town of Tuzla, some three hundred kilometres to the north-east of the valley. She had taken the small ones to the queue for bread baked from the flour brought by the United Nations convoys. He shared his home with two other families and it was an existence that was a living hell to him. When she had stood in that queue for perhaps three hours she would bring back the bread, and then she would go away again to queue with the children to fill the plastic buckets with water from the tanker that was also provided by the United Nations. With the sun on his face, Husein sat outside the tent, too listless to move, and tried to scratch from his mind the detail of the colours and contours of the valley fields. The camp was a place of filth and in it there were early signs of epidemic disease. Increasingly frequent warnings of the risk of the spread of the typhus bacteria came from the foreign doctors. It was only by struggling to recall the valley, more blurred now than the previous month, more hazed than in the winter, that Husein stayed alive. There were others, who had come from similar valleys and been displaced, as he had, who had given up the fight to remember and were now buried or lay on the damp mattresses against the tents' walls praying for death. Husein had promised himself that he would return, with Lila and the grandchildren, to the valley. He heard nothing on the radios that blasted through the avenues between the rows of tents that gave him cause to believe his pledge could be redeemed, but his fierce, awkward determination kept him alive . . .

. . . A wind came off the Ostsee and beat at the high windows of the block.

With two other families, Dragan Kovac had been dumped in a twelfth-floor apartment on the outskirts of the town of Griefswald. All day, each day, he sat by the window and stared out. That morning he could see little because the wind carried loose flakes of snow from dark low cloud. The arthritis in his knees, worse through lack of exercise, would have made it hard for him to walk outside, but he yearned, even with the pain, to stumble forward into clean air so that he could better remember his home and the village of Ljut. He was trapped in the building. The twelfth floor was his prison. It was forbidden for him, as it was for the other refugees housed in the block, to leave it. From his vantage-point he could see the police car parked across the street from the front door. Engine fumes spewed from its exhaust. A police car was always there now. The food they needed was brought to them by earnest social workers. The imprisonment of Dragan and the other refugees in the block of the Baltic town had begun five weeks before when the crowd had gathered under cover of darkness. Rocks had been thrown to break the lower windows, then lighted petrol bombs had rained against the walls, and there had been the shouted hatred of the young men with the shaven heads, the screams of old slogans. He had thought that night – as the yelling of the skinhead *nazis* had beat in his ears – and every day since that it would have been better to have died in his village when the 'fundamentalists' had attacked, better never to have left his home. But he had not stayed: he had been one of the few who had escaped. He had lumbered as fast as his old legs would carry him, flotsam with the flight of the soldiers, away from his valley, without the time to pack and carry with him even the most basic of his possessions. He had been put with many others on to a lorry that rumbled into Croatia, then on to a train that had wound, closed and with the blinds down, across Austria and into Germany then had traversed the length of that huge country. His home was now – and he had little understanding of great distance – some three thousand kilometres to the north-west of the house with the porch and the chair, and the view to the farm of his friend. The two families who shared the apartment with him showed him no respect, and said he was lazy and a fool and that he, the former police sergeant, was responsible for what had happened in their land. Tears ran down his cheeks, as the snow melted and slithered down the glass of the window. It was so hard for him to remember the valley, but he thought – trying to see the image of it – that it would still be a place of simple beauty.

Neither of these old men, abandoned to live as statistics, sustained by grudging charity, protected from the fascist gangs, knew of the harsh realities of the valley that was their talisman of survival.

Neither remembered where the mines had been sown; neither could have imagined that those little deathly clusters of plastic and explosive would have shifted. They remembered only the good times, before the mines had been laid, when the valley felt the sun and was a bed of bright flowers, and the Bunica river was low enough to be crossed and they could meet and talk. Good times before the madness had come.

They used the hotel restaurant. Atkins had asked Mister if he wanted to go out, said Reception would recommend a restaurant, but he'd shrugged away the suggestion. It was a slow meal, poorly cooked and ineptly served, but that didn't matter to him. He'd ordered mineral water with his food and the Eagle had taken his cue from him, but Atkins had a half-bottle of Slovenian wine. He didn't have to tell them that he was tired, had no interest in talk. The restaurant was on the mezzanine, three floors below his bedroom, and close to empty. He used the meal-time to think about a riposte to the insult he had received from a man too busy to meet him. It was not in Mister's nature to turn the other cheek. Weakness was never respected. Atkins told the Eagle about the hotel's history in the war: it had been the centre for journalists and aid workers, it was continually hit by artillery fire; only the rooms at the back were safe for occupancy; for weeks at a time there was no power to heat the building, but it stayed open, staff and guests living a cave-dweller existence. Pointing out of the big plate-glass windows and down at the wide street that had been Snipers' Alley, to the dark unlit towers of apartment blocks beyond the river, Atkins told the Eagle about the marksmen who had sheltered high up there and fired down on civilians going to work or queuing at bread shops and water stand-pipes, trying to get to school or college, and the callous disregard of it. The Eagle's face showed that he wished he was anywhere other than in that restaurant, in that city.

Mister ate only what he thought was necessary for sustenance. Each plate brought to him was taken away half finished. The insult, and what he would do about it, consumed him. Out of an insult, and its answer, came strength. The insult provided an opportunity for him to demonstrate his strength. When he was twelve years old, a teacher had called him 'an evil little swine, a thief' in front of the class; he had followed that teacher home after school, put on a balaclava, punched the man to the ground and kicked him again and again; charges could not be brought, the teacher could not make an identification; he had become king, much feared, among the twelve-year-old kids. As he'd grown older he'd left a trail of the same fear behind him, in gaol and on the streets. The man running Hackney and the east when Mister was climbing the ladder's rungs had said that Mister was a 'little shite with no future' and was now walking on sticks because pistol bullets had disintegrated his kneecaps. A man in Eindhoven, a dealer who was careless with buyers' money, had fled naked during the night with his wife and two children from a house that had cost him a million and a half Dutch guilders while the fire that destroyed it blazed around him. A man who had hacked him off in a pub, who now had no tongue and no fingers, might today have died.

Mister was experienced in answering insults. He had considered his problem, decided on his response.

He didn't wait for coffee.

In his room he felt safe, in control. He knew of nothing that should make him feel otherwise. A full day awaited him in the morning. He was soon asleep. Under his room the city's late-night traffic prowled and did not disturb him.

'Is there anything more about that lorry?'

It was late evening and Monika Holberg was just back in her office in the UNIS building, Tower A, and she was tired, which was rare for her, and irritable, which was rarer. She had been on a field day out in the country, west of the city. She kicked off her muddied boots and slung her heavy anorak at the door hook. Whether she was in the city and trawling through office appointments or away in the country villages, she wore the same anorak and boots. She had no other life in Sarajevo other than her work for the United Nations High Commission for Refugees. She was tired because her driver had gone sick, there hadn't been another available so she had driven herself, and on the way back – on the mountain road from Kiseljak – the rear right tyre of the Nissan four-wheel drive had punctured, she'd had to change it herself, and the nuts had been hell to shift. She was irritated because the village she'd visited beyond Kiseljak was light years from being ready to receive and impress the visitors she would be escorting there next week. She was a driven woman. It was not in Monika's character to accept that second best was enough, whether in vehicle maintenance or visit preparation. Her secretary was on the other side of the thin partition that separated their cubicles, brewing coffee and making a sandwich.

'What lorry is that, Monika?'

'The lorry from those British people. What do they call them-selves? "Bosnia with Love"? Isn't that what they call themselves? I need that lorry.'

'Maybe Ankie took the call – when I was at the meeting or at lunch.'

Monika rolled her eyes. Her secretary was not a driven woman. Her main concerns were what she was earning in salary and living allowance from UNHCR and what a sacrifice she made, and how she hated Sarajevo. She was fat on the city's back and her hair was always freshly styled. The desk was littered with small squares of sticky yellow Post-it notes, fastened where there was space among a haphazard strewn-paper sea. She was bending over her table, skipping the secretary's messages and identifying those of Ankie, the Dutch girl, who fielded her phone when it rang unanswered.

'There isn't a message from Ankie about the lorry.'

'Perhaps there was no message – can we talk about it in the morning?'

She was brought the sandwiches and the coffee. Monika had eaten nothing since a rushed breakfast at dawn, and it was the first half-good cup of coffee. Her secretary was gone. But, she needed that lorry and its load. The village had been sullen and unresponsive. Ambassadors, functionaries and officials from the international community were coming to the village next week. Unless the mood lightened the VIPs might be whistled, jeered at or, worse, ignored and cold-shouldered. A little man, dapper and dancing in expensive shoes, had waltzed into her office two weeks previously, come in off the street, Fra Andela Zvizdovica, and had offered a lorry full of clothes, toys, basic household goods, and talked about what he called 'jumble sales' and 'coffee mornings' and 'fête collections'. Monika Holberg spoke fluent English, as well as Spanish, German and Italian, but these were words that she could not translate from her experience of an island upbringing off Norway's coast north of the Arctic Circle. She needed the lorry and its cargo to wipe the morose depression off the villagers' faces before the visit. Donors, she had learned, wanted hope, required stoic optimism, if they were to dig again into their pockets and deeper than the last time.

She had a promise of the lorry but no word of its arrival in the city.

She wolfed her sandwiches and slurped her coffee.

She had believed the promise that the lorry's contents would be hers to distribute. Thirty-three years old, tanned, weather-beaten, blonde-haired, and uncaring about her appearance, Monika Holberg was another piece of the mosaic that was falling quietly into place, and she also had no knowledge of it.

She threw the cardboard sandwich plate, and the coffee beaker, at her rubbish bin, missed, and started to rip the messages off her desk.

Joey had said on the stairs, 'We'll call him the Cruncher, Target One's accountant. He was murdered. What you suspected is proven. When I find out how he was murdered and why, the door will begin to open for me. Then I get to know what our Target One is here for.'

'I'll do my best,' the policeman had said, and had hit the door with his fist. 'Can't do more than my best.'

There was a veneer of respectability, cigarette-paper thin, about the room and its tenant. She was middle-aged going on elderly, and her face was deeply lined, but on the dressing-table were the jars and powder tins that would have helped her shed a few years. She wore an old dressing-gown that had once been flamboyant, but which was now faded, and Joey could see the careful stitches where it had been repaired. Her hair was gathered into curling rollers. Her hands betrayed her immediate past. She had seen better times: now they were scarred, reddened and swollen. She smoked as she talked, clamping a short cigarette-holder between yellowed teeth. She had only one room.

Her name had been the first typed on the page that Judge Delic had given Joey. He'd had no option but to call the only other official link to the killing, the policeman, Frank Williams. The policeman was involved because he had pulled the body from the river and written the report. It was against Joey's instincts to break Church ranks and confide in a policeman, even if the man was separated from the world of Crime Squad and Criminal Intelligence, sawing on a buried nail in a log. He'd been told the policeman had to clear involvement with a superior and, if that was achieved, get away when he could. He would not have been there without the policeman, would have had no chance of finding the attic garret room, and having gained admittance he would have had no language to hear her statement. She sat on the bed from which she had been disturbed. Frank was opposite her, at the table under the ceiling light. Beside his hand was a one-hundred Deutschmark note that was on offer but not yet handed over.

She talked.

Joey's eyes roved round the room as he listened to Frank's translation.

He was trained to notice, listen and suck in the relevance of what he heard and saw.

'. . . It is what I have already told the police who came to see me. I can only say the same because that is the truth. I can tell you what I saw and nothing more. I am truthful, I have always been truthful. You want me to repeat it, I will repeat it. It is hard in Sarajevo in these times to find work. I have no family abroad. There is no money sent to me. If I am to eat I must work. In the evenings I clean shops and offices, and then in the night I go to restaurants and wash the dishes when they have closed. My husband is dead, my children are dead, my life is dead. I work to eat. The last place I work at night, which is late because it closes late, is the Platinum City restaurant. I wash plates there and dishes there, in the kitchens, and the floor. The police showed me a photograph of a man who had drowned in the river, and I remembered him . . .'

The room's furniture, the square of carpet and the wispy curtains stank of poverty. But beside the sink and the small cooker were six unopened bottles of French wine. On her feet were new bedroom slippers, pink and fluffy. Two sets of knickers and large brassières, freshly washed, worn once he thought because they had no stains and held their shape, hung over the sink. She had turned the fire on full blast, four bars. Under the pillows on the bed Joey could see the end of a tin box. He was at the far wall, in shadow, as he had been taught to be during interviews, evaluating the truth of what was said, watching the hands, the eyes and the mouth, and whether the sweat beads came, and to see if the tongue licked the lips.

'. . . I remembered him because he walked into me. That is incorrect, he staggered into me. I came round the corner, on Obala Kulina Bana, and he bounced into me. He came from the far side of the road, not the side of the back door to the kitchens of the Platinum

City. I don't know where he came from but it was not the side of the road where is the Platinum City. When he hit into me I could see that he was completely drunk, totally drunk, he was full of drink. When he walked into me, if he had not held my shoulders, he would have fallen over. He was incapable. He smelt of the drink. He was disgusting. I thought he was going to be sick on me. Of course, I pushed him away. He went towards the river, away from the Platinum City. That was the last I saw of him, going towards the river. There is nothing more I can tell you.'

Her eyes were on the one-hundred-DM note.

Frank asked him quietly, 'Any questions that you've got, Joey?'

He had only one, and the answer would reinforce the obvious. 'Who is the owner of the Platinum City?'

'I don't need to ask her that. I can tell you – it's Ismet Mujic. He's Serif. You'll have heard of him.'

Joey came from the shadows and walked on the creaking boards to the table. He picked up the one-hundred-DM note and slipped it into his wallet. He went out through the door. Frank caught up with him on the second landing down, took hold of his arm.

'Was that necessary? She's got fuck-all.'

Joey shrugged the hand off his arm. 'She was lying, the whole thing was lies. She's been paid off. Some you pay and some you frighten, if you want lies told. She was paid. You saw what she had – wine, fluffy slippers, underwear, foreign fags, cash for the electricity bill and the rest in the tin under the pillow. There were two autopsies done. One was done here, the other in London. The one here said there was alcohol in the stomach, with food. The one at home made no mention of alcohol. It was all a lie, and well paid for. We've made a link and that's a first step – a good first step. I'm grateful.'

They went out into a dark, empty street, the gloom clinging to them. Joey said what should happen the next day. He had his street map and he thought he was only a few minutes' walk to his hotel. He was about to drift away when his shoulder was caught and he was spun round.

The lilting softness was gone from Frank's voice. 'You do understand that's a powerful man, as powerful as they come in this city.'

'What do you suggest I do? Go home?'

Chapter Seven

'A good journey?'

'No problems, Mister,' the Eel said. Jason Tyrie had driven for Mister for sixteen years, and his uncle before him. 'I did the border at Bihac. It was two fifty DMs on the Croat side and seven fifty for this side's crowd. The warehouseman is one fifty a week. You can buy anyone here.'

The Eel had been in a column of lorries bringing supermarket food over the frontier from Croatia. The sums he'd paid out to Customs, on both sides of the line, had been the going rate for avoiding inspection and duty, and getting the documents stamped. All the drivers carried wads of German notes. The lorry, 'Bosnia with Love' painted gaudily on its sides, was parked in the shadowed rear of the warehouse. The Eel had left the bonnet up, had scattered tools on the concrete floor. The inquisitive, or the prying, would have thought it was there for repairs. The warehouseman, minding his own business, was out in the cold morning air hosing vehicles clean and sweeping away the lakes of water into the drain.

'Right,' Mister said. 'Let's get to work.'

He had the Eagle, the Eel and Atkins to help him. Atkins had been up early and had been to a vehicle dealer. The Toyota four-wheel drive, smoked-glass windows, had been bought for cash. The papers that went with it, which made a pretence of a legal purchase, were economic with its history: they made no mention of its former ownership by the OSCE. The Toyota had been stolen from outside a hotel in Vitez used by the Organization for Security and Co-operation in Europe, had been resprayed and the plates had been changed – close examination would have shown the OSCE logo on the doors, but Atkins had said that didn't matter. No one was looking for such things. They made a tunnel into the back of the lorry, Mister and the Eel passing boxes down to the Eagle and Atkins. They burrowed towards the bulkhead, shifting only enough of the clothes and toys collected by the charities to give them access. Far to the back of the lorry were the heavier boxes. Mister was in charge and revelling in it. The Eagle was sweating, had taken off his coat, loosened his tie, and when he thought Mister wasn't watching him he left Atkins to take the workload. Atkins stacked the boxes. The ones they were after were bulkier, more awkward to push and lift, though the contents had been stripped down to the minimum.

The first of the bigger boxes came down, passed to the Eagle who sagged under its weight. Atkins used a penknife to slit the adhesive tape holding it shut, and lifted out the first launcher.

Mister watched him. He felt warm pride. To cut down on the weight and the bulk, the launchers had been transferred from the slatted-wood boxes and put into cardboard containers: the Eel had been told not to drive fast and to keep clear of rutted road surfaces. Atkins had it on the concrete floor, knelt beside it and threw a small switch. There was a faint humming sound, and a red light showed at its rear.

Good old Cruncher.

While Mister had been in Brixton, Cruncher – with Atkins's help – had given six months of his life to getting his hands on four of the medium-range Trigat launchers. There had been an exercise in northern Finland. While Mister had languished in his cell, Cruncher and Atkins had done the deal with a major on a Lapland range. For fifty thousand American dollars in high-denomination notes, the major responsible for driving the four launchers back from the range where they had been tested in minus 18 degrees C, not allowing for windchill, had dropped back in the convoy on the iced road. He had made easy excuses for his driver to travel in one of the lorries ahead. At a carefully chosen point, where the road between the range and the barracks wound above a sheer cliff that fell to a deep, ice-covered lake, the jeep had skidded off the road – as the official report stated – plummeted down, fractured the ice and would have come to rest among jagged rocks some two hundred metres below the frozen surface. The Cruncher and Atkins had collected the four launchers and the twenty missiles, taken from the jeep before the 'accident', and driven them away. Before they left, Atkins had beaten up the major, giving him injuries consistent with being thrown clear from the jeep as it had started its descent. The major had been abandoned in a state of theatrical shock to walk eight kilometres to the barracks. The pride of the Finnish military determined that the manufacturers – Euromissile Dynamics Group of Fontenoy-aux-Roses in France – were given an horrific picture of the road mishap. The loss was forgotten, the launchers and missiles were written off. They had been loaded on to a lorry carrying pulped timber, driven by the Eel, known to his mother as Billy Smith. They had reached a British port a week after the scarred, trembling major had shown investigators the tyre-marks on the packed snow and the scars in the ice below.

Well done, Cruncher.

Seven weeks before the start of his trial Mister had been told by the Eagle that the launchers and missiles had reached safe haven, and he'd nodded, as if he'd never doubted they would. Three of the boxes were manhandled by Atkins and the Eel into an inner room at the extreme rear of the warehouse, after a handgun had been taken from each. Before the fourth box was loaded into the Toyota, a map was spread out on it.

In magnified detail, it showed the streets of the old quarter of the city. As he outlined what would happen, Mister saw the way the Eagle craned forward over Atkins's shoulder to listen and watch his darting fingers; he noted how the Eagle hated all of it and could not help himself. The map was folded away. A small, loaded PPK Walther went into the back of his own belt and two filled magazines into his jacket pocket. Atkins drove away with the box, with a Luger pistol in the glove compartment. He told the Eagle that they would walk and find a taxi, didn't bother to offer him a firearm.

Mister left the Eel, a Makharov in his anorak pocket, to mind the lorry, and stepped out into the streets of Sarajevo to put right the matter of an insult.

'I still don't see why I have to do it.'

'You're doing it because that's what I'm telling you to do, and you'll do it just like I've told you to,' Maggie Bolton said decisively.

'It doesn't make sense.'

'Everything, just like I've told you.'

Joey shrugged and sighed so that she could read his annoyance and took the case from her hand. They did a last check on her button microphone and his earpiece, then on his microphone, clipped to his undershirt, and her earpiece. Folded in his shirt pocket was the authorization for intrusive surveillance signed by Judge Delic, typed by his daughter – if it was needed, if he showed out, at the Custom House they would feed him to the rats on the Thames mudflats. She had a copy run off on the hotel's machine. He'd argued all through breakfast, and all through their walk from their hotel to the Holiday Inn, and she'd taken not a blind bit of notice, and had carried on with her briefing detail of where in the room the bug should be placed. She was quiet, businesslike. The speech microphones were press-to-talk. If speech was not possible then the crash-out code was the repeated click on the button.

The atrium area of the hotel was empty now. The ashtrays had been filled by the delegates to a foreign-donor conference but they'd started their meeting, and the lethargic staff had not yet stirred themselves to clear up. The pot plants were dying slowly. Outside, through the plate glass of the picture windows, were the two black Mercedes saloons, and the hoods; they weren't lounging as they'd been at the airport but were agitated, smoking hard, shouting into mobiles.

'It's not my job. This isn't my area of expertise.' He knew the argument was lost.

'Can we go to work, or shall we just carry on squabbling? Be a dear boy, stop messing.'

He'd argued because he was frightened, could neither help it nor hide it.

He walked towards the lift with the bag. He turned once and looked back at her. She winked, gave him a little wave then headed for the revolving glass door. From where the van was parked, closer than last night, she'd have a clear view of the door and anyone who went through it, if they used the revolving door and not the coffee-shop entrance. The lift took Joey to the third floor. He'd stood back, when they'd arrived at the Holiday Inn, and she'd gone to Reception. She was a travel agent from London, handling business packages. She booked flights and hotels in the commercial sector. She was checking through accommodation facilities in Zagreb, Podgorica in Montenegro, Priština in Kosovo, and in Sarajevo. Could she please inspect a room? Were all the rooms the same? Businessmen, she had learned, were happiest on the third floor, not too high if they had a vertigo problem, not too low to be disturbed by a hotel's bars and the street traffic. She had been shown, Joey trailing her, unintroduced, the bag carrier, a room on the third floor and assured that the rooms were all the same, exactly the same, as was the policy of the hotel. For a few moments, Joey and the woman from Reception had been together in the bathroom and he'd made a little point of examining the bottles of shampoo and bath foam, and had seen the Polaroid's flash from behind the nearly closed door. When they'd come out Maggie had thanked the woman profusely and told her they were excellent rooms, then moved on to rates and credit-card acceptability. Over coffee in the atrium they'd studied the photographs and she'd told him what he should do, and where the bug should be placed. He went in the lift to the third floor. ﹀

She'd shown him, at their own hotel, how to open a hotel room with a plastic bank card.

Room 318. He closed the door behind him. The maid had been in and the room was clean, the bed made. Pyjamas were folded on the pillow. The wardrobe doors were closed. A suitcase was on a rack. A pair of shoes was underneath it. He felt the room was a trap. He did not know how long he had, only that the opportunity might not come again. He must hurry, but not so that he made errors. He had the photograph to guide him. The telephone was too obvious, she'd said, the first place that would be checked if the room were searched for bugs – the light and power sockets would be the next. He took a towel from the bathroom, laid it on the upright chair from the desk, carried the chair to the wardrobe and kicked off his trainers. He stood on the towel, no shoes so that he would not dirty it, and the towel so that he would not indent the chair. Maggie had identified the waste space above the wardrobe, below the ceiling, as suitable housing. With a screwdriver he prised back the wardrobe's upper fascia board. Into the space behind went the power unit, a black box the size of a paperback book. He used the fine-needled spike she'd given him and pressed it in sharply, drove it in until he could feel the pressure on the front against his finger. He made a tiny hole in the outer stained wood, threaded the microphone, a pinhead, into the hole and worked it until the head was flush with the hole. He threw a switch in the control, saw the green light glow, and held the board in his hand.

Joey whispered, 'Testing – two, three, four – testing . . .'

In his ear. 'You close up?'

'Right beside it.'

'Is it back together?'

'Not yet.'

'May need a volume tweak. Before it goes back together, try it from the window, then from beside the phone.'

'Will do.'

He put the board crudely into place and slipped down from the chair. He went to the window and looked down to the pavement a full hundred feet below. There was no balcony. He saw a taxi swing off the road and then disappear under the flat roof sheltering the main door.

Joey said, 'I'm by the window. This is normal speech level – two, three, four, testing from the window . . . Give me the OK, then I'll go to the phone position.'

Silence in his ear.

'Maggie, I'm at the window. Have you got me at the window? Come in, Maggie.'

A plaintive voice shrilled in his ear. 'Oh, Christ. He's back. I bloody missed him. Gone through the door. Get out, out, *out*. Target One is through the door. I missed him.'

He froze. His trainers were on the floor by the desk. The chair was by the wardrobe, with the towel on it. The fascia board was still loose, out of place, unfastened and cables were visible above it. In an act of will, he had to throw, almost, one leg in front of the other to get himself moving. He lurched across the room towards the door. The board was priority. Board, chair, towel . . . He was on the chair, using the heel of his hand to batter the board back into place. Maggie was screaming in his ear. He could see the pinhead hole in the board, and with his palm he made the last adjustment, looked at it, and jumped. Towel into the bathroom. He slapped it on the rail, but it slipped off. More of the precious seconds were used hanging it as neatly as a maid would have. Out of the bathroom. He ferried the chair to the desk. He turned for the door and his toe, right foot toe, stubbed the chair leg . . . No shoes, no bloody shoes. He shovelled on the shoes.

The voice in his ear, calm now, said, 'You ran out of time, Joey. He's on the landing outside the room.'

There were voices in the corridor. He knew the one voice from the hours of the tapes and the earphones. The door was the only way out. The bed was too low on the floor to slide under. He heard the room card go into the door lock. He went to the window where there was the drop that would kill him and insinuated himself behind the curtain. There was silence in his ear, as if there was nothing more she could tell him, no more help she could offer. The door opened, then the inner bathroom door. He heard Mister urinate, then the flush. The creak of the wardrobe door being pulled open. Mister was whistling. Joey found himself trying to recognize the tune, and couldn't. Mister belched. Looking down at his feet Joey saw that one of the untied laces would be protruding from behind the curtain, would be in view . . . From the files, he knew of every killing attributed to Mister, knew the details of every death. All the killings featured pain before death, were never quick. He was bursting to wet his trousers.

He heard the door close and the footsteps retreat.

Joey counted to fifty, tied his laces, then let himself out.

Down the corridor, into the lift, down in the lift, into the atrium. He thought she'd have been there, waiting, but she wasn't.

The two black Mercedes cars were pulling out of the hotel parking area and into the traffic flow of Zmaja od Bosne. There was a piercing horn blast. He ran towards the blue van, which had been driven on to the forecourt. He fell into the passenger seat.

'Did you hear him whistling?' he asked.

'Like a nightingale,' Maggie said. She drove fast towards the road.

'What was the tune? What was its name? I couldn't remember its bloody name,' Joey said flatly.

'It was Elvis, come on – or are you too young? "Wooden Heart", recorded during his army service – weren't you born then? It was clear as a bell. Are you all right?'

'I was actually about to piss in my trousers. I suppose you're too important to put your own bugs in place. Give the job to the boy.'

'Who would have checked the gear, seen it was working? You?'

It was icily said; he hadn't thought of it. He subsided. She was in touch, just, with the second Mercedes. He was thinking dully of the fear he had felt, and he had not even seen the man. He had feared the whistling closeness, and did not know how to confront the fear.

He let the anger burst. 'You were bloody damn late on the warning. I could have been killed because you were late. I had fuck-all time to get the room back in place because of you. He *kills* people, do you know that? He *hurts* people before he kills them. This isn't some bloody game with diplomatic bloody immunity. You said it yourself, "I bloody missed him." You couldn't have given me less warning if you'd bloody tried. Miss fucking Superior, who the fuck do you think you are?'

Maggie Bolton had a soul but precious few could find it. Her father hadn't. A Ministry of Defence quality-control engineer at the aerospace factory at Preston in Lancashire would admit to colleagues and relations that he could not reach close enough to touch the emotions of his daughter, christened Margaret Emily. Eight years back he had gone to the crematorium, two months after being declared redundant, still not knowing her. Proud of her, yes, but not understanding. Her mother, too, was kept at arm's length, had been there through Maggie's childhood, young womanhood, and was there still as her daughter drifted into middle age, was phoned once a week if it was convenient, was sent postcards if Maggie was away and it did not breach security, but was not confided in. There had been no schoolfriends who had lasted into adult life. A bachelor uncle had taught at a minor public school in the West Country, and since the school was short of girl entrants had arranged a bursary for her. She had taken no interest in sport as the other girls had, and had devoted her time to the physics and electronics laboratories. She had won a place at Sussex University to study electronic engineering, the only female in that year's intake on the course. At the end of three years her exam results had disappointed her lecturers: she had taken only a lower-second degree. She had spent too much of her last academic year working on a programme of research and development hived out to her department by technicians from the Secret Intelligence Service – routinely such organizations looked to the universities to upgrade their equipment into state-of-the-art standards. Afterwards, regardless of her poor degree, the SIS managers had snapped her up. The secrecy of intelligence work suited her: it was a wall behind which she could live. She could even justify her lack of communication with her parents: they were not on the 'need-to-know' list.

As a new recruit, she was in the basement workshops of the building they called Ceauşescu Towers, below the waterline level of the Thames. In the evenings she spent hours with the master technicians of Imperial College's laboratories after the lecturers and students had gone home. No one in her life was allowed close to her. At parties, home or away, her prettiness, laughter, trim figure and ringless finger ensured that she was a central attraction, but although she flirted shamelessly in public, she was alone in bed. Her fingernails were the giveaway to her skill, clipped back to the quick. The fingers were small and firmly boned, perfect for the precision of her work with microphones, infinity transmitters, tracking beacons, and fish-eye pinhead cameras. In the basement workshops and in the university's laboratories she was admired. A foreman at Imperial had once said, 'She could get a probe bug up a crocodile's bum and he wouldn't even know his sphincter was being tickled.' Her research was focused on two specific areas, both equally critical for SIS operations: the downsizing of equipment and the clarity of reception.

It was not on her file, but she had only loved two men in her forty-seven years.

In the summer of '88, she had gone to Warsaw, travelling on a diplomatic passport and with her gear in a diplomatic bag. The contact, introduced to her by the station officer, was a young male clerk working in the Polish Ministry of Defence, with access to the permanent secretary's office. She had provided the bug, he'd put it in place. She was then thirty-four and a virgin, and he was eleven years younger, frightened witless at what he had agreed to do. It had been a sort of love, more in the mind than in the muscle, furtive kisses and hands held briefly in the clandestine night meetings. The bug was the best she had ever made; its low transmission of power signals ensured it defeated the monthly scanning of the permanent secretary's office, and intelligence flowed to the antennae on the roof of the British embassy. Six months later, long after she had gone home, she was told that the clerk had been arrested, tried *in camera*, for treason, and hanged in the central prison. When she was told – she had been offered, and had accepted – a pink gin. Her composure had not flickered.

In '94, she had manufactured the tiny microphone bug to be fitted into the mobile phone of an Iraqi official of the Mukhabarat who travelled to meet fellow secret intelligence officers in Tripoli, Libya. The beauty of the device was that it could be activated to monitor both telephone transmissions and voice conversations that did not involve the phone. She had spent five days in Malta with the Libyan police bodyguard who had been turned and had the task of inserting the bug in the target's phone. It had worked, she was told, like 'a dream'. And she was told, also, two months later that the bodyguard – sweet, charming, courteous, vulnerable, and loving on evenings on the hotel veranda overlooking the sea – had been held, tortured and shot. Again the gin had been offered her, again her composure had held. If she cried, it was only in the silence of her tiny flat.

She was a part of the old world, a Cold War warrior.

She had protested viciously when her line-manager had assigned her to Sarajevo, told that her annual assessment interview would be postponed, given to understand that the latest rate of *per diem* expenses should not be exceeded unless she was prepared to stump up the excess herself. Yes, she had been to Sarajevo in the war, but with her own people, and in a time before the line-managers had taken control of Ceaucescu Towers, a time before assessments were *de rigueur* for experienced experts, when expenses were passed without quibble. There had been bugs in the President's office, and in the UN general's operations centre, and nearly – if there had been another week to work on it – in Ratko Mladic's headquarters. As far as she was concerned this assignment was vulgar plod work, a waste of her time.

She was damned if she would easily give a sight of her soul to Joey Cann.

*

'Forget it,' Maggie said. 'It's in the past.'

'Is that all you've got to say?'

'Too right, that's all you're getting.'

He'd subsided into silence and let her drive. She'd been on the courses run from Fort Monkton at Gosport. From the old strong-point built to deter Napoleonic ideas of invasion, on the Hampshire coast overlooking the English Channel, she'd learned to drive surveillance cars through the close Portsmouth city streets, in country lanes, and up the motorway towards London. She knew what she was doing, but it was hard in the clogged traffic to hold the link with the Mercedes, and she didn't need his righteous scared anger.

'You don't know as much as you think, do you?' she said.

'What . . . ?'

'You say you know everything about the target, but you don't – you didn't know he liked Presley for starters. It's only small, but it's the small things that matter. In my experience, the better people in this game have humility.'

He brooded. She didn't regret chipping away at his arrogance.

She braked. They were in the old quarter. The cars were parked half on the pavement a hundred yards ahead. She saw Packer, Target One, and the gang of the hoods, and Targets Two and Three, and then she saw Serif.

Mister said, 'You've been kept waiting, I do apologize. I had business to attend to – it's so annoying, isn't it, when business holds things up?'

Mobile to mobile, Sarajevo to London, Cruncher had reported to the Eagle that Serif spoke good English.

Serif said, 'And I should apologize to you, Mr Packer, because my business prevented me from meeting you at the airport yesterday.'

'That's fine, no offence – and that's the apologies out of the way. Good.' Other than to his mother, who was dead, and to his father in Cripps House, Mister never apologized and meant it.

'I am happy, and I welcome you – as I welcomed your associate, Mr Dubbs.'

'Very sad, what happened to Mr Dubbs. He was a trusted friend.'

'A great loss to you, and a great hurt to me that such a tragic accident should happen in my city.'

'We'll talk about it . . . First, I'm going to ask a favour of you, Serif – if I may call you that? I'd be gratified if you'd accompany me. Something of a bit of a surprise for you.' Mister never asked favours and seldom expressed gratitude.

Predictably, Serif hesitated. Mister smiled guilelessly at him. They were standing on the pavement outside the guarded staircase that led to Serif's apartment in a district of narrow streets and alleyways of traditional jewellery stores, little restaurants, coffee-houses and bookshops, all dominated by a slender mosque tower. Mister's smile, calculated, and the gentle way he took the sleeve of Serif's jacket made it difficult for the man to refuse. It was as he had intended.

They rode in the two Mercedes. He shared the back seat with Serif, and the Eagle was sandwiched between them, his shoulder in Serif's armpit, and the impression of the holstered weapon digging into him. Mister saw the nervous flutter on the Eagle's face. Mister's PPK Walther was against his buttocks.

It was fourteen years since he had fired a handgun in anger, across a street and into the upper thigh of Chrissie Dimmock; it was eleven years since he had fired in vengeance, point blank into the back of the skull of the Yardie, Ivanhoe Pilton. Chrissie Dimmock and Ivanhoe Pilton had disputed territory with him. If the roles had been reversed, if the Bosnian had come on to his turf, he would have shot him, and left the Mixer to dispose of him, washed himself down and gone to have a good lunch or dinner . . . The road climbed past the crumpled-down pylon of a ski-lift. They stopped on a piece of wasteground. At its furthest edge he saw the tall, upright Atkins. There were kids, who watched over a few skinny goats, looking at the cars.

Mister stepped from the car, the Eagle at his side, sealed to him as if they were Siamese. He waved for Serif to catch him up and walked towards Atkins. Behind him, a voice at the kids and they ran. At a sharp pace, he crossed the wasteground to where the medium-range Trigat launcher squatted on the ground, its tripod legs set in the earth, a sheet of plastic behind it, beside Atkins's feet. It was aimed back over the city, into the indistinct mass of roofs and windows. Atkins nodded to him briskly. Mister thought Atkins brought class with him.

156

Mister said, 'A little present, Serif, something that expresses my goodwill. You got a mobile?'

'I have a mobile.'

'You got someone in your address?'

'I have a friend there.'

'You should ring your friend and tell him to open the front window, the big one, then stand there. Please, could you do that for me?'

The call was made.

Mister said, 'Since this is going to be yours, Serif, I expect you'd like to know about it. Mr Atkins is your man.'

Atkins said, as if he was an instructor at a class, 'This is the Trigat, a multi-mission medium-range system for infantry. It's designed for use against tanks, helicopters and reinforced bunkers. The range is two hundred to two and a half thousand metres, and at two thousand metres the missile flight time is under twelve seconds, when it will have reached a speed of one hundred and fifty kilometres per hour. The aim point is the hit point, and cannot be affected by counter-measures, with a double charge for maximum penetration. It will come into full service production next year. It will work equally well at minus thirty-five degrees or plus forty degrees. It's the best . . . Would you like to see what it can do?'

'What, here? In the city?' Serif giggled.

Mister said, 'Perhaps you'd like to see, Serif, what Mr Atkins chose as a target. Take a look through the sight.'

He thought it would have been obvious to Serif, but the man knelt and then lay on the plastic sheet, his eye to the aperture. The view through the sight, times ten magnification, would carry Serif over the rooftops, over the river and the bridges, over more roofs, to an open window where the curtains blew in the wind, where a man in a black shirt and black jeans stood, and behind him the most prized possessions of Serif, low-life hood. If the missile were fired, its bright flame exhaust fizzing across the city, it would explode inside that room.

Mister flicked his eyebrow, the slightest movement, but it was picked up by Atkins – a good man, alert. Atkins crouched beside Serif and depressed the main system switch. There was the sound of a bee's drone.

He said easily, without malice, 'It's live, Serif, just press the tit and you'll see how good it is. Only destroys the target, everything around the target's OK. You up for it?'

Serif wriggled back on the plastic sheet as if he were frightened that any slip, any clumsy movement against the launcher might trigger its firing.

Mister grinned. The detective chief inspector he owned, in the Crime Squad, had once quoted to him the remark of the detective superintendent then leading the hunt for evidence against him: 'Always watch his eyes. The rest of his face can be all sparkling and laughing. Never his eyes, they're fucking evil eyes.' He'd stood, the night he was told that, in front of the mirror, and had stared into his reflection. He'd not told the Princess how the detective superintendent had described his eyes. He reached out with his hand to help Serif up, and Atkins switched off the Trigat.

He held Serif's hand, and with the other he slapped the man's back. 'You'll find me a good friend, Serif. I'm not the sort of little man who takes offence when I'm stood up at the airport by a guy who has more important business than meeting me. It's yours, because you're my friend, and there's four warheads to go with it. And there's more where it's come from for you, for when we've done trading. And there's different presents as well. When you're with me, you'll feel like it's your birthday every day. Let's meet tomorrow, and I'll see that nice apartment of yours. It'll be my pleasure.'

'What is it?'

'It's an anti-tank launcher,' Maggie said, as she took the binoculars back from him. She slung their strap around her neck, against the gold chain and the hanging St Christopher. Half a roll of film had been exposed in her camera.

'Bloody hell,' Joey mouthed.

He thought he could see, without the binoculars, the launcher being loaded into the boot of the second Mercedes. She had turned the van round so that it faced down the hill and away from the wasteground.

She said softly, 'I wonder if our friend Ismet knows the expression, "Beware of strangers bearing gifts." There's going to be tears if his mother never told him that.'

They left. As the second Mercedes boot was closed down, they drove away. They were too exposed where they had parked.

'What would that thing do?' Joey asked.

She was thoughtful. 'It's not about what it can do. Possession of it gives a man power, but not as much power as goes to the man who provides it. That's a big play, for serious business . . .'

'Am I not obliged to report that, tell the authorities, the International Police Task Force? Shouldn't I?'

'Don't be ridiculous,' Maggie said. 'Don't make me wish you'd stayed in your pram.'

They went back to the Holiday Inn, parked within sight of the main door, and Maggie crawled into the back of the van and settled with her earphones and tape decks while Joey went to look for sandwiches.

Summer 1994

He was called 'Rado'. The new men stationed in the village of Ljut called him by that name because the previous unit had, and the unit before them. Each morning, they had watched him wander purposefully from the ruins of the village opposite, down the track to the ford across the river, which was now low, and wade across, then seen his stride quicken as he stampeded out of the water and settled for his day's feeding in the overgrown grasslands of the grazing meadows. In the evening, when the sun dipped, he reversed his route and went back to a lonely sleep in the byre near the well of Vraca village.

During long days, Rado was the men's only sight of movement in the fields to the front of them, their only source of interest. They bet on his survival as had the unit before them and the unit before that. The soldiers were little more than boys, from villages where their parents had farms and, far from home, they took comfort from the sight of Rado each day because he represented something familiar. His story was handed down on the day each unit was relieved . . .

On New Year's Day, nineteen months before, the fundamentalists had abandoned the village across the river and the livestock had been turned out to fend for themselves. Rado, then unnamed, was a recently castrated bull calf of Limousin stock. The dairy cows had died in trumpeting agony because they were not milked. The sheep had been scattered by a wolf pack. Some had been hunted down and some had fled to the high woods behind the village. The chickens and geese had been the prey of foxes. The heifers, dominated by the one bull calf among them, had come down to the ford in the spring fifteen months before, when the river's pace slackened and its depth dropped. They would have scented the good new grass ahead of them and had crossed; each, in sporadic and haphazard turn, had stepped on, disturbed or shifted a mine. Last summer all but three had been killed. They went back, these survivors, each evening to the byre over the river where a dog waited for them. The autumn had come, the river had risen, and the three heifers and the bull calf had been blocked from coming over. Then it was spring again, and they were back. They had returned for their daily feeding in the grass meadow in the first week in April. By the third week of April, after two dulled smoke-rising explosions, there had been only one heifer to walk beside the bull calf; lost, sad, mooning lovers. On the last day of April the ground had erupted in a mess of noise and upthrown turf sods, and the bull calf had been alone.

The story handed down to each successive unit occupying the bunkers flanking Ljut village was that the bull calf had stayed with the maimed heifer all that day, that it had steadily licked the heifer's head, hour after hour, had quietened her screams of agony, had stayed with her until death and release. Then, as the evening had come on, he had gone back to the ford and crossed to sleep alone.

Through May, June and July, into August, the daily return of Rado was watched by the troops, and he was given his name.

It was the familiar abbreviation of Radovan, the given name of their leader, Karadzic, to confer respect and admiration.

The sector was at peace, there was no fighting in the valley. On the orders of their sergeant, the soldiers manned the two bunkers every morning for the hour before and after dawn, and every evening from the hour before and after dusk. Then they had no duties other than cleaning the bunkers, their sleeping quarters and their weapons. Rado was the attraction.

The betting started at the time he was named.

In the grazing fields, among the weeds of the unploughed arable fields and between the fallen posts and sagging wires of the vineyard, lay the skeletal outlines of the heifers. Rado seemed not to notice the upturned weather-whitened ribcages. Occasionally, not more than once a day, he would raise his massive neck, throw his huge head high and bellow for company. He was doomed, all the soldiers knew it, and they bet on which hour, which day, which week, his great hoofs would wrench the trip-wire of a PROM mine, or brush the post holding a PMR3 mine, or drop his weight on to the squat antenna points of a PMA2 mine. He seemed immune, invulnerable, so they watched him, fascinated, from the high ground, and the bets were laid.

The sergeant was their bank and issued the betting slips. A thoughtful man, he had realized that unpayable debts between his soldiers would increase tension among them. He had ordered that all bets should be of not a *pfennig* more than a single German mark, the only currency they valued, and that no soldier could wager more than twice a day. He set the odds, collected the money, and left enough in a plastic sack to pay out a winner, using the profit margin to buy little luxuries in the market in the town – cigarettes, vegetables, cooking utensils, blankets. Long, hot, fly-blown days followed one another. While the soldiers slept, ate, smoked, read magazines or wrote to their homes, one man was always deputed as sentry, but his real job was to watch Rado.

There was a full-canopied ash tree between the grazing fields and the arable fields. It was ten minutes to two o'clock. The sentry in the bunker saw Rado rise from the tree's shade, first by extending his rear legs, then kneeling on his front legs before straightening them. His tail flicked his back to clear the flies.

He looked around him and sniffed. Perhaps he needed water from the river or to eat. Rado went slowly. The long grass was pushed aside by his lowered muscled belly, and flattened by his hoofs. Each step he took, pressing with such weight on the ground, seemed deliberate and purposeful. The sentry watched, and the sound of the flies droned in his ears. Through the shimmer of the heat, Rado's progress, proud, strong and tall, was the only movement in the valley.

There was a flash of firelight . . . then a puff of grey chemical smoke . . . then the rush of the explosion . . . The fire was gone, the grass and earth fell back . . . the smoke started to drift . . . then quiet and stillness.

The great beast keeled over. For a moment its four legs were upright, visible above the tall grass, then they were thrashing. The cry of the castrated bull rang out across the valley. The sentry was leaning against the hot metal of his machine-gun, his hands covering his eyes so that he could not see, but he could not shut out Rado's call for help. The tears flooded his face.

The others had heard the explosion, had broken from their meal or their siesta. The bunker filled with soldiers. He was pulled aside. From the earth floor of the bunker he saw the sergeant lock the butt of the machine-gun against his shoulder. In the sentry's mind was the desperate kicking of Rado's legs. A single shot for aiming, then the burst of fire and the bunker was filled with cordite stench and with the rattle of the ejected bullet cases. The weapon was made safe. The sentry dared to stand and look through the firing port.

There was nothing to see, no movement in the grass near the river.

He did not know it, none of them could have, but the bullets that ended the pain of the animal would be the last fired in the war over the fields of the valley.

'Hello, didn't expect to see you in here . . . I went for a walk. My room's too hot . . . will you have a drink?'

Atkins had come in from the street, had gone to the atrium bar, bought a beer, and had seen him. It was still short of eleven o'clock and Mister was in his room. The bar of the eight-storey hotel was deserted except for them and a bored waiter. The Eagle sat, disconsolate as a reformed alcoholic, with a half-consumed orange juice in front of him. He was lonely, sad, and had been thinking of home, wrapped in the thoughts of the Chiddingfold house and the stables, of Mo and the girls.

'Fine as I am, thank you.'

'May I join you?'

'Be my guest.'

He knew little of Atkins, except that Mister valued him. It was the way of Mister that life and business should be boxed, kept apart. A policeman, over lunch, had once told him that the Irish terrorists used a cell system to cut off an information leak if one cell should be arrested. It was the same principle. He knew as little of Atkins as he did of the Mixer or the Eels or the Cards. The only one he knew, because he drew up the legal contracts for the deals, was the Cruncher – who was dead. Atkins ripped off an anorak and a fleece then dumped them beside the chair. Low music played through loudspeakers.

Atkins looked directly at him. 'If you don't mind my saying so, and I don't mean to be impertinent, but you don't seem totally on board.'

'Is it that obvious?' He was too tired for denials.

'Funny thing, when I was here before, twice, at this time of year we lived like Eskimos. We were wrapped up in every coat we could fit on, Tuzla and Sarajevo. There wasn't the heating-oil. Your nose was half frozen when you woke up, you could get frostbite, or damn near it, in bed. Doesn't seem right to be here and cooked. I've turned the thermostat down and opened the window – seems pretty obvious to me.'

'I do what I'm asked to do and when I have a role to play I'll play it,' he said wearily.

Atkins pressed. 'What's wrong with the concept?'

The Eagle was careful. 'That's a leading question – I might rule it inadmissible.'

'I'm not a blagger – I suppose that's the vernacular of your clients. I hold my drink, my water and my secrets. You're an educated, intelligent man, a professional . . .'

He interrupted sharply. 'Don't ever underestimate him because he hasn't a conventional career training. He is a very clever man.'

After a lifetime of living with it, the Eagle understood every facet of questioning and interrogation. He could recognize when he was being pumped for opinions and those questions that came from personal confusion.

'But you're not on board. It's there for anyone to see that you don't approve. Does anyone ever stand up to him?'

'It's not that simple. I give advice when it's asked for. I keep my mouth shut when it's not asked for.'

The question was asked again. 'But does anyone stand up to him?'

'A few have. They're either dead, maimed or living their lives behind locked doors. Do you need to know?'

'That was high risk today. It was *fun* but it was taking a hell of a chance. I wouldn't have done it, but – I'm not ashamed to say it – I hadn't the balls to tell him. He doesn't know this place, has no idea about these people.'

'I told him that, and my opinion wasn't asked a second time. The grave took the only person who I've known to stand up to him – his mother.' The Eagle would not have said that in his office, in his home, wouldn't have said it anywhere that was familiar. In the great cave of the atrium bar, he felt, in truth, so goddam lonely. He spoke quietly and Atkins had to hunch forward to hear him. 'We're in this together, you and me. If we ever get out of this bloody place, Cruncher didn't, and get home and I thought that you'd repeated this conversation, then I'd see to it that you needed crutches to walk on . . .'

'His mother?'

'She stood up to him.'

Incredulity splashed Atkins's face.

'He idolizes the memory of the woman.' He should have stopped and talked about the weather. But he was drawn forward, did not stop. 'She was a good, decent, salt-of-the-earth working-class woman. I am not patronizing. It all came out when she died. The only time he's been maudlin. I had to endure an hour of self-pitying shit. It was the usual grubby little story. 1981 was the year. He'd just started to buy heroin in Green Lanes, off the Turks, and he was pushing into an existing dealer's territory to sell it on. There are few surprises in this life, and that dealer was not a happy man. He came looking for our lord and master. He was shot in the stomach. The only thing the dealer said to the detectives at his bedside was "No comment", said it again and again. I was down at Caledonian Road with Mister. He's very good when being interrogated, a legal adviser could not ask more of a client. Nine questions out of ten he would say nothing and stare at the ceiling, but at the tenth he would speak. "On the advice of my solicitor I cannot answer your question at this stage." It can't be used in court then that he refused to co-operate, the blame for it shifts to me. He doesn't answer questions because he'd have to lie, and lies are caught out. The detectives hear a lie and move on, then jump back to it twenty minutes later from a different line of questions. Lies don't work. The police knew he was responsible for the shooting, but they hadn't forensics, hadn't a victim's accusation, and hadn't a lie. It was two years before he was married and moved out of Cripps House. The police searched the flat. It was, my words at the time, "a vindictive and destructive search". They wrecked the place. Anything that could be broken was broken. It was an act of frustrated vandalism. He came back from the police station, cocky and free. His father was at work, but not his mother.

'She turned on him, laid into him, that's what he told me. And he hit her across the face with his fist. Blacked her eye and split her forehead. She wouldn't go to the surgery for stitches, she told his father that she'd walked into a door. She carried the scar on her eyebrow, the hair never grew on it again, for the rest of her life. His father isn't a fool – he'd have known a door didn't make that sort of injury. It was never referred to again. He tried to buy his way out of the guilt, but they didn't want a retirement home at Peacehaven or Brightlingsea. They stayed in Cripps House, maybe as a reminder. They could have lived like millionaires, but they wouldn't have it. There's a pretence in his life that his mother and father always supported him, never criticized him, that they took the line that "the Old Bill just got lucky" and it was the "bad company that led him on", and "deep down, he's a decent boy", the usual old crap. That's not true. His mind is compartmentalized, and hitting his mother is ringfenced and excised from memory. It was only the shock of her death that brought it back, for an hour, on my bloody shoulder. He pumps money into the hospice where she died and into the church where they had the funeral, but that's as far as it goes. No one else ever stood up to him.'

'Why are you here?'

'Try *greed*, young man. Try that for a reason.'

'That's two of us, I suppose,' Atkins said softly. He gathered up his anorak and fleece and wandered to the lift.

The Eagle had a house in the country with horses, all paid for; Atkins had a two-bedroom flat in Fulham that could go on the market for half a million. The Eagle had a 7-series BMW coupé in the drive and a top-of-the-price-list Range Rover for Mo to drag the horsebox; Atkins had a Lotus sports, soft top. Without Mister, the Eagle would have been a struggling lawyer dependent on legal aid pickings; without Mister, Atkins would have been another failed ex-soldier struggling on the consultancy circuit, bullshitting for a living. Of course it was greed, for them both . . . If the gravy train hit the buffers it would be here, because Mister was off his territory. Did Atkins know that, or was Atkins a fool? Too tired to make an answer, the Eagle went to his room. He was guilty for having talked, but Atkins, too, was guilty, for having listened. God, he wished he could drink, but he dared not.

'I just want to hear the statement, not the story, and then I want to get out,' Joey said.

The story, translated in full by Frank, no edit, was of the daily life in Sarajevo under siege. 'It's better you hear it. You won't understand the truth unless you hear the story,' Frank answered him from the side of his mouth, a murmur on his lips. 'I think you should let me handle it, my way.'

They were close to what Frank called the Jewish cemetery. He said it was where there had been the worst fighting, where the Muslim infantry had sustained the worst casualties. Frank told him that the cemetery was still stuffed with mines, ordnance, unexploded grenades and bodies, and hadn't yet been cleared, but there wasn't too much of a hurry because all the Jews had gone to the death camps sixty years earlier. From the layout of the windows, there would have been eight apartments in the building. Only two of the windows had lights on. The rest of the building, Joey thought, was too damaged to be lived in. It was a bare room. The largest feature in it, more dominating than the bed, the cooker, the washbasin and the plastic garden table, was a metal bookcase. It could have held more than five hundred hardbacked books, and it was empty. A small, thin man with cavernous cheeks and bad, gapped teeth sat on the bed. His hair was wispy thin, and his hands were locked together as if to stop them shaking. The fingers were gentle and thin.

'It was a living death. We had no electricity, no water except from the river, no sewage system, no food, no transport, no work. To look forward to, we had only the escape of death. We existed alongside death for month after month. There were some in my block who for three years did not go outside their front door, never went out. There were some who put on a tie each day and a filthy shirt, then walked into the city, never running, as if it were normal. There were others who ran everywhere . . . The ones who stayed in, they could as easily have been killed by a tank shell. The dogs did well. If you were killed and not picked up, if it was too dangerous to retrieve you, the dogs had you, would feast on you. They ate better than us. In the winter, when there was snow and rain we had enough water. We would boil it up and put in grass or nettles or leaves, and that we would call a Sarajevo soup. To heat the water, we burned books. I had many books, I could make many fires. I am a musician. To make a better fire one day, to heat my soup more quickly, I burned my violin.'

The man unlocked his hands and reached for a glass of water, which slopped to the floor on its journey from the table to his lips and back.

'I was lucky. A restaurant opened in a basement, a safe building, and I was taken on to play for the diners. There were restaurants open, for foreigners to eat in, where the food had come through the tunnel under the runway at the airport. I was lucky to be chosen as a musician there because the kitchen allowed me to eat what was left on the plates, but that was in the last year of the war.'

Joey listened, stone-faced. He could remember nothing of the war. If it was on television at home his father had broken off from whatever he was talking about and muttered his contempt for people of such savagery. If his mother had the remote, she flipped channels. The war had not registered with him. It had been far away and someone else's problem.

'They were not interested in hearing me play a violin even if I could have found another one. I played the electric guitar. I did not complain. I would have preferred to play Mozart, the violin concerto, K216, *Allegro*, but I preferred more to eat, so I was the backing to the *chanteuse* singing Elton John and Eric Clapton. It was survival . . . In war, sacrifices must be made.'

Joey asked of Frank, 'Where did he play?'

The question was put and answered. Frank said, 'He says he played at the DiscoNite, and he still plays there.'

'Ask him what he saw.'

Frank recited. 'I have been shown a photograph of the face of the dead man. He was drunk. He was alone and staggering. I saw him cross the Obala Kulina Bana and then he went to the wall above the river. He was leaning on it and swaying. I had the impression he might have been vomiting over the wall. The last thing I saw of him, he was heading towards the bridge. That is all I can tell you.'

167

Even across the barriers of language, Joey could recognize a rehearsed speech; there was no attempt at disguise.

Frank said ruefully, 'It is the same, verbatim, as his statement.'

'Who owns the DiscoNite restaurant?'

'Same man as the Platinum City.'

Joey shrugged. Yes, he knew, but he had needed to hear it. There was no banknote for the violinist who did not bother to hide a lie. They went out, closed the outer door after them.

Joey said, 'If I were to threaten to break his hands, to smash his fingers, so that he would not play again a violin or an electric guitar . . .'

Frank looked at him, shook his head. 'Forget the illegality, right? They have been through the war. They are hardened to any cruelty that you or I are capable of inflicting. You wouldn't be able to do it, nor me.'

Joey was a farm boy. His father was the factor of a landowner's estate. He had seen rabbits dying in snares, and enmeshed in nets when fleeing from ferrets. He had seen huntsmen dig out vixens and their cubs from the dens and toss them to the hounds. He had seen badgers choked in sealed setts. He had seen, when beating for the owner's shoot, the fluttering fall of winged pheasants before the dogs caught and shook them to death. He had hated what he had seen. 'I know.'

'You said last night, "When I find out how he was murdered and why he was murdered then the door begins to open for me." You said that.' Frank's voice was hoarse as if he realized he walked on an unmapped road. 'If it's that important, *if* – and your hands and mine would stay, sort of, clean – then their own people could do it.'

Chapter Eight

Frank showed Joey in. The building was at the heart of a little empire of white prefabricated boxes. The room was reached down a hushed corridor covered with lifeless green synthetic carpet that stifled the sound of shoes. Policemen and women, in a polyglot of laundered uniforms, their national flags sewn to their upper sleeves, busily carried papers from office to office, laid them beside colleagues who laboured at computer screens. The corridor smelt of fresh ground coffee and fresh heated croissants. There were no raised voices. Here, speech was as muted as the murmur of the computers.

A quiet voice responded to Frank's knock. Joey was shown inside.

It was a tiny workspace shoe-horned between walls that were little more than screens.

The walls were pincushions for leave charts, maps, duty rosters, and photographs of children, and the shield insignias of police forces from all over the world, from the Czech Republic and South Australia to Mexico. It represented a brotherhood he felt no part of.

'You're Mr Cann, Customs and Excise of the United Kingdom. Frank's told me about you. How can I help?'

Joey had no insignia to offer. The office co-ordinated the training of the Bosnian police to deal with the threat of organized crime. It was the start of their fourth day in Sarajevo, the third of Mister, the Eagle and Atkins, and a routine had been established. For both Joey and Maggie a routine was important. They came from structured employment and an ordered division of responsibilities suited them. Maggie Bolton was up early and had driven the blue van to the parking area close to the Holiday Inn hotel, to tune the audio equipment monitoring room 318. Joey would follow later and join her, after his visit to the headquarters of the International Police Task Force. When their Target One left the hotel they would both follow, as best they could, and share the surveillance through the day and the evening. When Target One returned to the hotel, Maggie would resume her watch with the earphones, and Joey was free to roam.

'I don't have much time . . .'

'That's not a Sarajevo habit. God, a man in a hurry, it's almost worth a diary entry. Shoot.'

Frank didn't intervene, leaving Joey to explain what was wanted and to emphasize the requirement for security, secrecy.

The man, relentlessly chewing gum, wore the badge of the Royal Canadian Mounted Police on his upper sleeve. He listened without comment. He had small, darting eyes that stayed locked on Joey's spectacles. The smartness of the Canadian's uniform and the high polish of his boots unsettled Joey in his faded jeans, sweatshirt, sweater and windcheater. He heard Joey out.

'Let me tell you, Mr Cann, about my day. I am from a town in Manitoba, you wouldn't know its name, with a population of around fifteen thousand who are mostly Aboriginals. Right now, there, it's late evening, the temperature is around minus thirty-five degrees, and it's my home. I was shipped out of there six months ago, and I'll be shipped back in three months, and I can't wait . . . My day starts each morning at five and I leave my little room out in Ilidza – for which I pay five hundred German marks a month – and I go to work out in a gymnasium that's equipped by the SFOR military. I shower, and at seven I ring my wife, then I get my breakfast in the American camp at Butmir where it's familiar food and cheap. I am in my office by eight o'clock and until five o'clock in the afternoon I put papers from my in-tray into my out-tray, and when the out-tray is full I put them back in the empty in-tray. I break that up with a couple of meetings, most of which are taken up by translation time, and a sandwich for lunch. After five o'clock I go back to my room and cook myself a meal in the kitchen I share with two Swedish dog-handlers, and I might gossip a little with them. After my meal I watch a video or read a book and I'm in bed by nine o'clock. That way the nights go faster. My regret is that I cannot make the days go quicker. I am wasting my time here. I know that and my government knows it. As each RCMP officer goes home he will not be replaced. It's not about the cost but about the lack of achievement. Put brutally, Mr Cann, we are kicking soft excreta.

'The place is a crossroads. Every form of criminal trafficking is coming through here. Women from the Ukraine, Romania and Russia, either to work in brothels here or for transit into western Europe. Asylum seekers from China, Afghanistan, Iran, anywhere you want, are stacked here before being moved on. Tobacco is shipped in from Italy and resold in bulk. A luxury car is stolen in the street in the morning in Hamburg or Stuttgart, the next morning it's here and in a workshop where the numbers are filed off, and the morning after it's on its way via Slovakia to Moscow. The Balkan trail of the drugs route has reopened after the war; it's not being moved in kilos but in tonnes. I want to go home, back to that balls-freezing cold in Manitoba, because I can't do a damn thing here.

'The country is held in a web of corruption. I cannot fight it. People like me are in place, and people more important than me, and we're all just pissing in the wind. Everyone's on the take. At the moment, we keep the corruption under the surface and nearly out of sight, but the Canadians are leaving and everyone else will be quitting, and then a whole country in the heart of Europe will be handed over to serious gangsters – the Turks, Russians, Albanians, Italians, and the local men. Have you heard of Serif? You have, OK. There isn't a senior politician here, or a senior official with any power, who is fighting the culture of corruption.

'We were supposed to do some good by coming here, remember? We were going to teach a society that had endured the rape of war how to put that experience behind them. We came with a noble sentiment and generosity. About the tenth time you get your shin kicked you start to get the message. Little people are too frightened to come to us. The big people see us as being in the way and obstructing their snouts from going deeper into the swill troughs. Today I'm dealing with three million American dollars' worth of tractors, trailers, balers, plus a hundred tonnes of agricultural fertilizer, plus eighty tonnes of seed potatoes – donated by the UN, which is your tax-payers and mine – found upcountry in a warehouse owned by a politician. He'd have sold part of the loot on, and the rest he'd have distributed as largesse. That was a chance find by a bloody-minded patrol of Finns, who haven't been here long enough to have given up on the place. We are not even scratching the surface.

'There's a bigger problem, Mr Cann, and it worries me a whole lot more. Who am I to stand in judgement? Where I come from in Manitoba we are getting into a culture of criminality. The Aboriginal kids are on dope, LSD and lighter fuel. They're drinking aftershave lotion, and the adults are smashed out of their minds on class A stuff. A city like Winnipeg, where your senior-citizen tourists come to start their coach trips of the Rockies, has what we classify as a "serious heroin problem". In British Columbia they now grow better marijuana than the Mexicans. On the US border, we're stopping perhaps one load out of twenty, five per cent, of hard drugs. It's not that we're losing, the war is already lost. We're in a sewer at home. So, who am I to tell these people that it's wrong for them to be in a cesspit? Perhaps thinking never helped a law-enforcement officer.

'You said you were a busy man, Mr Cann. That's good, and I hope you can keep hold of your enthusiasm. I am prepared to authorize Frank Williams to continue liaison with you . . . I am also prepared to authorize the four officers, named by Frank, to be available to be with you as a part of a training exercise. You understand me, Mr Cann, *a training exercise* – and I wish to know nothing more. Good luck.'

'Thank you, sir.'

Joey made a mental note to send him a pin or a tie when he was back, when he had finished. He ran from the stifling heat of the Portakabin city and hoped he was not late to link with Maggie.

Mister said, 'I want a warehouse, full time and permanent.'

'What you want, Packer, is protection.'

They were around a circular glass table, Mister, the Eagle and himself on one side, and facing them were Ismet Mujic and two men. Atkins thought the older one, heavy-built, big-fisted, square-faced and crop-haired, might be an intelligence officer or senior in the police, but he was not introduced and he had not spoken. The other man, younger, without a name or a voice, had lank black hair with gel in it and the air of privileged connection. Atkins presumed the conversation was recorded, just as the Eagle had their device built into the base of his attaché case. Laid on a side table at the back of the room, not hidden, was a loaded Kalashnikov assault rifle with two magazines taped together, and at the side of the table and positioned like a favourite new toy was the launcher still holding the missile tube. The Rottweilers were beside the door, stretched out and sleeping, occasionally pawing each other, then yawning to show their teeth. Sometimes, through the door, came the grating cough of one of the guards. The ambience – guns, dogs, guards – was intended to intimidate. Mister had left his PPK Walther in the Toyota, and said the Luger given to Atkins should be with it. It was the first time Atkins had been with Mister for a major negotiation, seen the style. Mister, the Eagle and he had countered the intention to intimidate by hooking their jackets on to the chair behind them, showing they were not armed.

'It is not "Packer" it is "Mister". I don't need protection, I want co-operation.'

'Can you be so sure, after so few hours here, Mister Packer, that you will not need protection?'

'I have never needed protection in my life, but always try to find co-operation.'

Before they'd left the Toyota Mister had said that it was all about body language. The body must never show fear. On the road into and out of Tuzla, when Atkins had worn the blue beret and been on food-convoy escort, he'd known that noise and determination, and an absence of fear, were the currency for getting through the road-blocks manned by drunk Serb, Muslim or Croat thugs. At the road-blocks were *papaks*, oafs, and they were bullies. He had learned it was a crime to show fear to the road-block kids. He thought the body language of Mister was a master class in itself. It was all about bluff and presence.

'Mr Dubbs used that word many times. He spoke of co-operation.'

'We'll talk of him when we have agreed on co-operation.'

'You bring a lawyer with you – what is the value of a lawyer?'

'My colleague is here to draw up a document of co-operation. I co-operate with you and you co-operate with me. It is put down on paper and we sign it, we both sign it. The document is our bond. You have a copy and I have a copy.'

Around the table from him, at Mister's left shoulder, the Eagle had nodded decisively at the mention of his part in the matter. Atkins remembered the lonely outpouring of the previous evening in the atrium bar. He thought the Eagle's dependence on Mister out-weighed a fear of the guns, the dogs and the guards. He thought also that Mister's quiet answers confused Ismet Mujic, and there were moments when he hesitated and glanced to either side of him before throwing his next question.

'And if, Mister Packer, you should break the bond?'

'It's just "Mister" – then you've lost nothing.'

'And if I should break the bond, Mister?'

'I'm not making threats, Serif. The launcher aimed at your lovely apartment was only my idea of a little joke. If you were to break the bond, go back on your word, you would lose more money than you can dream of. I pay well for co-operation.'

Mister's voice was pitched low. To hear him they all had to lean across the table, which gave gravity to him. The Eagle had said that Mister was 'a very clever man'. The agenda was his, and Ismet Mujic followed.

'Mr Dubbs did not say what you would pay.'

'For me to decide, when we have discussed co-operation.'

'The problem, Mister . . .'

'There are no problems. When two men of business both seek to do a deal then there isn't a need for problems.'

'If you do not have protection then it is *possible* that you have a difficulty with the police.'

Each point made by Ismet Mujic was countered immediately by Mister, sometimes with a small off-hand gesture of his arm, and diminished.

'A part of the reward for your co-operation is that I don't have such a difficulty.'

'Without protection, a foreigner here, you could face more diffi-culties with the political leadership.'

'You would see to it, Serif, that I had no difficulties with the police or with politicians. It is how you would co-operate.'

'Would I be your partner?'

It was slyly put. Atkins thought Ismet Mujic expected rejection, which would give him cause to bluster and take the high ground. Mister's smile was supreme, as if he dealt with an old friend.

'I think that's the direction we're going.'

'I have other partners to consider.'

'A businessman such as yourself, Serif, would have many partners.'

'There is a Russian gentleman. And an Italian gentleman from Sicily – I am told that is a most beautiful island. I have partnerships with the Turks – they are very serious with business. It would be most expensive to satisfy all of my partners.'

'Let's deal with yourself first, Serif, and others later.'

Atkins saw the Eagle's eyes flit to the ceiling. It was a killer blow. A new strain was introduced. When he had been told on the aircraft what Mister planned, it had seemed easy, reasonable. The scale of the operation now being pursued by Mister hit him, slugged him, as it had the Eagle, but Mister's reply was gentle, as if nothing ambushed or surprised him.

'Co-operation or protection, whatever you want to call it, how much do you pay?'

'I pay for what I get.' Mister's voice was softly reasonable.

'For no difficulties with the police, no investigations by government, for transport over the border without delays from Customs, for warehousing space rental, for the service of vehicle mechanics who are reliable, and guards to ride with the drivers because this is a country of many bandits, how much do you pay?'

'I could pay a flat cash figure, or I could pay for each vehicle movement, or I could pay a percentage of profit.'

'A percentage of profit?' A smear of derision from Ismet Mujic.

Mister never hesitated. 'You'd have my word on it, Serif. We say in England, "My word is my bond." You've never been to England, to London. If you'd been there, met the people I do business with, then you'd hear that my word is good enough for anybody. In business I'm a good friend, but if I'm ripped off then I make a bad enemy.'

'What is flat cash?'

'A million American dollars for the first year, payable quarterly, the first payment on signature of the document, and I would suggest a Cyprus bank would be the most convenient. I'm not bargaining at this stage. At the end of the first year we renegotiate, but my guarantee is that the first year's payments will be less than the second year's. That's my offer.'

They broke.

Mister, the Eagle and Atkins were left in the room, watched by the Rottweilers. Atkins moved from the chair and stood casually near the low table on which the Kalashnikov lay. It was what he was paid to do. The Eagle wiped sweat from his forehead. He didn't say anything because Mister had closed his eyes, tipped himself back and catnapped, slept, as if there were no problems and no difficulties, only co-operation.

From the coffee-house they could watch the building's street door. They had been there an hour and Joey had started to fidget. They were on the second cup of coffee. Every ten minutes one of the men in black, with the tattoos, the shaven head and the hanging belly, would walk to the end of the block and back, and each time would look into the shops, bars and the café window. They had to be beside the glass to have a clear view of the street door. They were the only foreigners in there.

It was three years since Joey had done regular surveillance duties. On a good day, in London, the whole of Sierra Quebec Golf – twelve of them – would have been used for such a stake-out, and three cars; on a bad day there would have been eight, and still three cars. Now, there were the two of them and the van was parked up the street. The last two times when the man in black had examined them through the café window, Maggie had held his hand and looked Labrador-like into his eyes, as if they were lovers. It was called Jack and Jill at home, a male executive officer and a female executive officer attracted less attention than two men, and sometimes it went from handholding to kissing, and sometimes from kissing to groping, and sometimes to bed at the end of the shift. She had his hand again. The shadow of the man passed the window. It was not often that Joey looked into Jen's eyes and searched her face. The eyes and the face opposite him were lined, older. There was a coldness in them. He thought he didn't matter to her – they had no small-talk and no confidences. In the Sierra Quebec Golf vans and cars, and on the pavements when they did Jack and Jill, and in the pubs, in the office afterwards, they all learned about and prodded into each other's lives. The shadow passed again, and her hand slipped out of his. The touch of her fingers on his hand meant nothing to her, and they both watched the street door. He stared fiercely out through the window and sensed her amusement.

Joey snatched her hand back, and gripped it. He thought she'd cry out, but she did not. 'In his life, Mister has won every time. I am Joey Cann and I have never won, not a bloody thing. Mister is a winner and Joey Cann is a loser. At home it would be no contest. We are not at home . . . Don't sell me short. If he's off his own ground, I *think*, I might just be a winner.'

'I want to consider what you offer.'

'Reasonable.'

'Concern myself with details and then talk more.'

'Accepted.'

They should never have come, the Eagle had convinced himself. He should have been hosting a long-arranged meal, choosing the wines from the cellar, pottering in an apron behind Mo in the kitchen, pouring drinks for the president of the county's Law Society, a recently retired Home Office civil servant, a consultant surgeon, a land-rich farmer and their wives. Now, there would be an empty place at the end of the table. He was not there because without Mister there would be no gardener, no country house, no complacent fat bastards as guests. Mister called and the Eagle jumped . . .

For ten minutes there had been whispered voices in the hall, then Serif had led his people back in, and Mister had jerked awake.

'And I suggest that we meet tonight for dinner, to talk of the details.'

'Serif, I'm afraid I can't do that.'

'I am offering you dinner at my restaurant, where the best food in Sarajevo is served, and the best wine.'

'I never mix eating with business.'

The dogs were whining at the door. They'd slept until the meeting had broken but had roused themselves the moment Serif had left the room. The Eagle listened but his eyes never left the dogs and their jaws. The Rottweilers showed their teeth as they whined, and the air in the room and the carpets stank of them. Serif turned to the door, clapped his hands then shouted a name. The young man who came in was not in the uniform of the guards. The Eagle thought the name shouted was 'Enver'. He was pale, smooth-skinned and not tattooed; his shirt was burgundy silk and blond hair rested on its collar; his trousers were tight and white. Little escaped the Eagle. The young man, Enver, sauntered into the room, while the guards' every movement was abrupt. He carried two short, woven leashes, crooned softly to the dogs, clipped the leashes to the studded collars, and took the strain as they bounded ahead of him through the door. Down in the country, at dinner with his friends, the Eagle would have used the word faggot, but never in Mister's hearing. Ismet Mujic's heavy eyes were watching him and could not have failed to notice his relief that the brutes were gone from the room.

'You don't like dogs? Do dogs make you nervous? I tell you they are very gentle. They are strong but they are soft. I call them Michael and Rupert. They were generals here from the British army, leading the UN forces. Like your generals, they make a show of aggression but will not use their teeth. They left us to do the fighting while they hid behind their sandbags. It was Celo, Caco and I who held the city. Without us it would have fallen.'

The withering eyes turned back to face Mister. 'You do not wish to have dinner with me?'

'Always best to do business with a clear head and an empty stomach.'

'Tomorrow at the same time, is that acceptable?'

'The same time tomorrow, and after the business is finished, I would be delighted to eat with you . . .' Mister paused. Then said, as if it were an afterthought, 'What happened to my friend?'

A study of concern slipped on to Serif's face. 'It was very sad . . . I am still sad to this day . . . I feel a responsibility.'

'Why do you feel a responsibility?'

He had been with Mister since 1972. In twenty-nine years he had learned to read each inflection of Mister's voice. The question was put so softly, without malice. What he knew of Mister, a question was never asked for the sake of him hearing his own voice. His questions either searched for information or set a trap.

'He was my guest, I was his host. We had eaten in my restaurant. He was very happy. He drank freely. He left us. I had offered him a driver to take him to the hotel, he refused. He said he would prefer to walk. I think he wanted the air.'

The Cruncher never walked when he could ride. He'd take a taxi to go the length of a street. The Cruncher was a barrow-boy at heart and his delight was to be driven. In the back of a chauffeured limousine he was the kid from Attlee House who had made it good . . . The Eagle thought, for dinner with Ismet Mujic and the rest of the low-life scrotes, the Cruncher would have spent a full half-hour dressing himself. The best clothes for the best impression. On a mission for Mister, the child of his own brain, it was inconceivable that the Cruncher would have taken to the sauce.

'I have friends in the police. There was a most thorough investigation, and an autopsy was done. You have friends in the police? As a businessman it is necessary, you understand. I have copies of the autopsy report, and the statements of the witnesses who saw him going towards the river. If you would like them . . . ?'

'I think I would. That's very thoughtful of you.'

A chair was spun, a cabinet of antique rosewood was opened to reveal a safe. Ismet Mujic's hips hid the combinations he turned to unlock it, and hid them again as it was relocked. The papers were passed to Mister, who handed them on to him. He dropped the four sheets into his attaché case.

'But they are not translated.'

'Not to worry, Serif. I'll pass them to his family, and add your condolences. I expect his family will find someone to translate for them. Tomorrow, then, at the same time – and it will be my pleasure.'

It was the time for smiles, handshakes and slapped backs, and then they were down and on to the street.

They walked, three abreast on the narrow pavement, towards the parked Toyota with the smoked windows. Mister said to them that he'd walk, walk and think, and he told the Eagle that he should start to work on the draft of an agreement of co-operation. He told Atkins that by the evening he wanted a working translation of the papers. Ahead of them was a small square of grass where the Rottweilers meandered and sniffed, and beside it men in thin coats watched a chess game played on black and white pavings with knee-high pieces, as if it were the best show in town. The young man, Enver, followed the chess and let the dogs wander free.

Mister said, 'If it's what I think then the river's calling for fucking pretty-boy.' Hands in his pockets, he walked away. It was the moment at which the Eagle knew for double damn certain that they should never have come.

'What do I do?'

'It's your shout, Joey, you do whatever you think right.'

The Toyota had powered past Mister and gone off up Mula Mustafe Baseskija. He walked and seemed to have no care.

'Do we split?'

'That's fairly obvious.'

'But you can't track one on one.'

'As we say at Box Eight Fifty, if it gets tough, "you'll just have to pedal a bit harder". Try that for advice.'

She climbed into the van and drove away.

Joey strode past the chess game and the dogs. He'd seen them come out of the street door and knew they were Ismet Mujic's dogs. He twisted his head away so that the young man with the dogs wouldn't see his face. He closed the gap. Mister had stopped, so Joey stopped. Mister was gazing into a shop window. What they said on the surveillance training courses, always to be remembered, was that ninety-five per cent of targets' days were entirely innocent and legal. Mister was window-shopping. He was gazing at jewellery in a window. Maybe Mister was thinking of the Princess . . . He was walking back. He was coming closer . . . Joey was frozen. Didn't know what to do. On a training exercise, or in Green Lanes for real, the target would have been in a box and covered by eight, ten or twelve personnel; Joey would have gone out of the cordon. He could not back off, not when he was one on one. The pavement space closed between them. He had been taught, had it dinned into him, that the worst crime was to show out . . . Mister was three paces from him. Joey could see how well he'd shaved, and that his tie was loose by a slight tug, and the hairs on his head were caught by the wind . . . Mister had stopped in front of another window where there was a display of Italian and French silk scarves. Brilliant, big decision of the day – a Cartier bloody watch or a Givenchy bloody scarf, a high-carat gold bracelet or an Yves St Laurent shoulder wrap. Then Mister turned and walked on, like any other bloody tourist who'd put off buying the presents until the last day. What Joey had learned lifted him. Mister wasn't doing figure eights, and wasn't doing doorway cut-outs, and wasn't doing double-backs. He was the Untouchable, far from home, and wasn't using the anti-surveillance techniques that would have been his second nature to burn out a 'footman'. That was the bastard's confidence, why it wasn't 'no contest'.

Joey followed him, and clung to the sight of the rolling shoulders of his target.

December 1995
Spanish troops brought them the last leg of the journey back to Vraca. The young men of the unit that had been recruited from the Andalucía region easily lifted Husein Bekir's frail frame down from the back of the three-tonne lorry. He accepted their help but would not let them take the small case from him. His clawed veined hands hung to it. Then they lifted down Lila, his wife, and the grandchildren.

He stared out over the valley and soaked up the sight of what was familiar and remembered. It was three years less two weeks since the day he had left. He gazed at the river and the fields, the ruined village above them and the mountains beyond, and all the time he clutched his case because it contained everything he owned. Lila was beside him and held his arm; the grandchildren stood around them.

It had been a long journey.

The television sets, thirty days before, in the tent camp at Tuzla, had shown the signing of the agreement at a military camp in far-away America, at a place called Dayton in the state of Ohio. It had taken place under the wing of a huge bomber in a museum hangar. He did not know how difficult it had been for the American negotiators to win that agreement, and could not comprehend the detail of the maps and computer graphics used to fix the new boundaries that would decide who should live where, but the map on the television showed a line of red running through his valley, and he had known he could go home. Going home had been all that concerned him.

The morning after the announcement from Dayton, Husein had led his tiny tribe out of the tent camp. In deep winter weather they had walked, hitched, ridden on carts pulled by slipping horses, been taken by military lorries, begged rides on buses when they had no money to buy tickets and they had crossed the ravaged country. They had slept in snow-covered woods, huddling together for warmth, and in ruined homes and in the wrecked outbuildings of farms and among cattle and pigs and in the hall wells of apartment blocks in the towns. They had eaten grass and rotting cabbages that were scraped from ice-locked earth, and they had begged for food. A week before they had sold Lila's ring, given her on their marriage day, the last thing they owned of value, and had bought smoked ham and potato broth, enough to fill a bucket.

Eight kilometres short of Vraca, at the café where in the old days they had stopped for coffee and brandy on the way to the cattle-market, they had found a building without a roof and a platoon of Spanish troops. Lila had said to him that, last night, it was only because of the grandchildren that the foreigners gave them shelter and blankets and promised to take them on in the morning.

Every muscle in his body was stiffened from the journey. He stood and gazed as the pain dribbled through him, and she clung to his arm. It was a bright, sunny winter morning, and long shadows thrown from the bare roof beams of the village houses caught his face, and his wife's and the grandchildren's faces, to accentuate the thin skin covering their bones, and the sunken eyes. If Lila had not been holding his arm he would have stumbled forward and fallen through exhaustion and hunger. It was all as he remembered it.

The officer, with an interpreter, hovered behind him.

The baker's, the blacksmith's and the engineer's houses were all as he had last seen them, gutted by fire from the artillery, open to the skies, displaying the wallpaper and the carpets in the upper rooms where the outer walls had been holed. The minaret was down, felled by a direct hit from a tank shell, just as it had been. The weeds grew on the cobbled village street. He tottered a few short steps forward, past the end of the building that had been the village meeting-hall and the school for the smallest children before they were old enough to go on the bus, and he saw his own home. A tree, without a leaf to decorate its branches, grew through the missing tiles of the roof . . . There was a piteous crying. His hearing was poorer now and he heard the sound faintly, and with the crying was a cringing whine. The cat came. He heard Lila's gasp, then the excited screams of his grandchildren; for three years he had not heard them scream in happiness. The cat broke from shadow, white, black and brown markings, and slunk in a belly scrape through the weeds towards them. The grandchildren ran to it and it stopped, its back arched, nuzzled their legs before they swept it up in their arms, held it close and passed it between them. The tears ran in his face and through his stubble beard. Then he saw the dog. He could not have taken it with him. Each morning or evening, in the hellish heat of the tent or in the numbing cold, he had thought about the dog and said silent words of apology; he remembered the stones he had thrown at it to stop it following them out of the village. The dog was so thin and it crawled near to him, cowed. He had thrown stones at the dog and shouted at it to be gone and he had heard it yelp when a stone had caught its stomach, but to the last it had obeyed him and gone back to the deserted home. He shook with weeping and bent down awkwardly, rubbed his hand on its ribcage and saw the fleas scampering on his fingers.

Through the interpreter, the officer said, 'It is what we are supposed to do, to escort people back to their homes. It will be difficult for you to live here. It is against my judgement to let you stay.'

'I will not leave. Are you prepared to shoot me?'

'We will do what we can for you. We will leave bread and milk, and a little meat. We will come again with more.'

'I say to your God that he should look after you.'

'My great-uncle fought in a civil war in my country. I understand that people have to go home, and start again, and forget.'

'It will be hard to forget.'

'If you do not forget, it is what my great-uncle told me – and forgive – then no sort of life is possible.'

Husein looked past his house, and the well, and down to the track to the ford, and over the river. He saw his flattened yellowed fields, topped by black dead thistles and brown dead cow parsley and grey dead ragwort, and he saw the toppled posts in the vineyard. He looked for coils of new barbed wire.

'It is my land, they put mines in my land. Do you know where they put them? Are they marked?'

'They left two weeks ago. The Serbs told me the track was safe. The commander said he did not have a record of where the mines were laid, so they are not fenced. Even if they were fenced it would be difficult to know their position. Mines *swim* in the ground. It is a strange word to use, but it is what happens. They can move many metres. The commander would give me no information.'

'Do I forget that? Do I forgive them for it?'

'If you do not then you have no life – I can give you some heating-oil and some blankets.'

'And I will need matches. To light fires I will need many boxes of matches.'

'You will have matches. Also I can give you candles.'

'When did it last rain?'

'We have had no rain for a month, so the river is low. Use the river for water, but boil it. I do not know if those people came across and sabotaged the well. The graveyard is desecrated. It would be wise to assume the well cannot be used.'

'May your God watch over you.'

Husein stood at the top of the track with the pile of blankets and the cardboard box of food and milk, and the plastic bag of match cartons with the candles and the jerry-can of heating-oil. The wind on his face was from the west. The ground under his feet was rock dry. The dog licked his hand when he bent, creaking joints, and felt the grass and found no moisture there.

He went back to his land, down the track, and waded across the river at the ford. The water flowed above his knees and the stones under his shoes were slippery as glass, but his will helped him make the crossing. In his hands were the jerry-can of oil, the bag of matches and the candles, kept dry and held high even when he stumbled. On the far side of the ford he looked up at his friend's house and wondered how he did and where he was, whether he was dead and in an unmarked grave, whether he was in a distant camp and still dreaming of the valley. On the track, near to the home of Dragan Kovac, the water sloshing in his shoes, he reached to snatch up handfuls of dry grass, made little heaps of it then spilled heating-oil on them. The wind came harder on his back and he welcomed it. He could see, ahead of him, the ribcages of his animals, and a hawk circled above him. When he had made a dozen small mounds of dried grass, buried halves of the candles in them and splashed them with the oil, he lit the candles' wicks.

The fires raged then guttered, then took. He had heard in the camp at Tuzla that fire destroyed mines.

A crackling wall of flames slowly advanced across his grazing fields and moved towards the ground which, in years gone, he had ploughed to grow vegetables and maize. A great smoke pall hung over his valley and was carried on the wind beyond the line of fire. He believed what he had been told in the tent camp. The proof was there in the explosions. Seven times the ground broke and was thrown upwards by detonations; and the shrapnel sang over his head. The wind lifted burning grass tufts and wafted them beyond the extent of the line, spreading the fire. To his right, far out towards the line of the fire, there was a grass island circled by black scorched ground. The flames moved on and left the island behind.

Husein Bekir had heard in the camp that fire exploded mines. He had not been told, by experts, that only the mines nearest the surface would be affected; others would smoulder but would not explode; some would have their stakes burned through and would fall over but would not explode; some would have their nylon trip-wires melted but would stay in place with their antennae still lethal; and some had metal wire that the fire would not sever. Each time a mine detonated he felt a wild sense of excitement, as if his youth returned to him.

A young boar broke in a panic run from the grass island. It ran back over the ground that the fire had covered and headed for the track where Husein stood. Its stampede had covered twenty-five metres when it was lifted high by the flash of light and the crest of smoke. He saw the blood spurt while it was in the air and its right leg flying free as it fell.

Husein Bekir turned away. He thought he had wasted half of the heating-oil, half of the candles, and two cartons of matches. He went back across the ford.

Joey had lost himself in the late-evening darkness, had gone to his rendezvous.

When she was out on the street, or in the van and trailing, Maggie dressed up-market. When she was parked in the van, in the back of it, with her earphones for company, and her book, she was dressed down. Neat skirts, blouses, cardigans and sensible shoes were left behind in the hotel wardrobe. She was in black jeans and wore a loose black roll-neck sweater and a black headscarf over her hair. She had been a small, darting shadow when she had gone to the Toyota four-wheel drive, had ducked down and levered herself underneath it on her back. With a small penknife, she had scraped mud sludge, crusted salt and the paintwork off the bottom of the vehicle. She had made a square of clean metal that was large enough to take the magnet of the device. She called the device, in her own jargon, an OTTER. It would send a beacon signal for two kilometres in a built-up area, and up to three kilometres in countryside. It was One Time – Throw Away equipment, not meant to be retrieved. When the assignment was completed, she would have to pick up the probe bug in room 318 of the building towering above her, but the beacon would be abandoned.

Already she had learned from her earphones that Target One did not use his hotel telephone, nor did he hold meetings in the room.

She heard him shower, dress, whistle to himself, and she heard him snore when he catnapped on his bed. The only time she had heard his voice was when he thanked, and tipped, the maid for the return of his laundry. She was wasting her time and wished she were at home, with colleagues who mattered to her and with work that had a grain of importance. She thought that Joey Cann – slight, intense, his pebble spectacles hiding half of his face – would not have moved past the first-interview stage for recruitment into her world.

She heard Target One cough to clear his throat, then the room's door closing, then the silence.

First, Mister read the document prepared by the Eagle and printed out on his laptop. 'That'll do,' he said.

He passed it back, and the waiter came to take their order. He had again refused Atkins's offer to go out and find a restaurant away from the hotel. He gave his order, let the others tell the waiter what they'd have, then flicked his fingers impatiently at Atkins, ready for the papers to be passed him. He scanned the translated witness statements and reflected that they were conveniently tidy.

'You got your street map?'

Atkins unfolded his large-scale map of the city and spread it over their laid places. Mister pointed to the third witness statement, and the address of the discharged and disabled soldier. Atkins turned over the map and ran his finger down the street index; he said that the street, Hamdije Kaprazica, was in the Dobrinja district. 'It's about where I showed you from the plane when we came in. That's the old front line.'

'Could you find it for me?' Mister asked.

'Yes – what, in the morning?'

'Tonight. According to his statement, he was the last man to see Cruncher alive.'

The Eagle spluttered on his bread roll.

'You got a problem?'

'No problem, Mister, if that's what you want.'

'I'd like to see him and hear how it was with Cruncher just before he went into the river. He was a good friend.'

The waiter carried the tray to their table.

'I lost my leg in the war. It is taken off at the knee. The amputation was not done well. It was the circumstances of the operation. I cannot have an artificial one. The stump does not allow it. We were fighting here to hold the tunnel entrance at the airport. Do you have money for me?'

The room was a pit of filth. There was no electricity, no fire. In the brutal light of Frank's torch beam he could have been thirty or fifty. The face was sunken and pale, the hair was thinned through, and the hands shook perpetually. He was propped up on a bed of sacking, newspapers, and pillows that had no covers and leaked feathers. There was a stink of old faeces and urine. When the torch beam had roved across the room, searched for him, it had skipped over three syringes. Joey watched him and Frank translated: 'I have to have money. You want to know what I saw? I say nothing without money.'

He held a crutch across his chest, as if to protect himself. His eyes were dulled in their sockets. His sleeves, both arms, were pulled up. Joey thought, from what he knew of pincushion arms, that the man would be finding it hard by now to get a fix on the veins. Joey pulled money from his pocket and handed it to Frank. The little wad of notes was tossed into the torchlight and on to the man's lap, above the stump. Joey saw the money counted and there was a flash of what he thought was cunning in the lustreless eyes. The notes were slipped under the bed of sacks and newspapers.

'Sometimes I go into town to buy. If I buy here, because I cannot defend myself, because I have a stump, sometimes I am attacked, for my money. I go to the old quarter. It is more expensive there, but I am not attacked. Also in the old quarter I can ask for money from foreigners. There are many foreigners there and sometimes they are kind . . . You want to know what I saw? And more money when I have told you . . . ? You are gentlemen, I think you will be kind. I told the police what I saw. He was on the bridge. He was leaning over the rail, and sick. I thought it was alcohol that made him sick. He could hardly stand, and when his grip on the rail failed he nearly fell over it. The river was very high that night. I looked away. Someone came and I went to them to ask for money. I was refused. I looked again for him, I didn't see him. He must have gone into the river. Someone else came and they gave me money. I went to buy. It was two days later, when I was back at the bridge that the police stopped me and asked if I had seen anything, and they showed me the photograph of the man.'

The hands shook harder on the crutch.

Joey said icily, 'Will you ask him, please, what unit he was with when he lost his leg?'

The reply came through Frank. 'I was with the fighters led by Ismet Mujic. We had to hold Dobrinja, we—'

Joey swung on his heel. There had been a teacher at school who had tried to reintroduce Latin into the curriculum. Joey had been in the small class. Little of it remained with him. Julius Caesar had crossed the Rubicon river and had said: '*Iacta alea est.*' And they had translated Suetonius, who had quoted Caesar: 'Let us go whither the omens of the gods and the iniquity of our enemies call us. The die is now cast.' The step was taken and there was no drawing back from its consequences. And in English classes they had read Shakespeare's *Richard III*: 'I have set my life upon a cast, / And I will stand the hazard of the die.' He went down the staircase.

There was light snow falling, but not heavily enough to settle.

Frank passed him and went to the back of the small truck. Its windows were painted over. His hand was on the door's handle.

'It's what you want?'

'It's what I want.'

'It breaks every rule in my life . . .'

'And mine,' Joey said. 'Just get on with it.'

Frank opened the door. Four men scrambled out. They wore drab blue overalls and their faces were masked by balaclavas. Frank talked to them briefly. None seemed to look at Joey, as if he were unimportant. They went towards the block's entrance, with purpose. He had not been introduced to them, dark, silent, smoking shapes in the back of the van, when Frank had collected him and they had driven into Dobrinja.

Frank had said they were on an unmarked frontier. The blocks on the far side of the street were rebuilt, holes plugged, had new plastic windows and street-lights. The lights didn't carry the width of the street but died in the central grassy reservation. They stood in dank darkness. Frank told him that when they had drawn the map lines at Dayton that ended the war and provided the new ethnic boundaries, they had used a blunt pencil. The pencil's marking, on the map, was fifty metres wide: the east side of Hamdije Kaprozice was left in a no man's land, unclaimed by either the Muslim authorities or by the Serbs. Small gangs of men floated past them. In Britain, Joey never had as much as a truncheon when he was out on surveillance late in the night, only a long-handled torch. He thought the no man's land was the territory of dealers and pushers. The only thing he had believed that the disabled soldier had said was that here, in the darkness, he might be attacked and stripped of the money he needed for heroin. He wondered how long, doing what he himself could not do, the men would be. He said, 'They won't hang around will they – God, what a place – your thugs?'

'Not thugs, Joey. I call them the Sreb Four. If you don't know a man's story you don't call him a thug. When you're not burdened with facts it's best to keep the judgements short. I met them in Sanski Most, that's the extreme west of the country. When people like me first arrive we're sent somewhere for a month's acclimatization before the permanent posting starts. They were about as far from home as is possible, because home was the east. Then I met up with them again in Sarajevo. They are cousins, and they are all from the village of Bibici, which is south of the town. It was an extended family. All the houses in the village were lived in by the family. They were all policemen. When the war started Srebrenica was besieged and they, as policemen, were at the front, in the trenches. The population in the town had gone from nine thousand pre-war to fifty thousand during the siege. Then it fell . . . That's a long story, why it fell. I'm telling you this because you will never see these people again, and it'll be good for you to think of them when you're snuggled up warm in your bed at home and your biggest problem is remembering whether you've done a new lot of fucking lottery numbers for the weekend . . . The women and kids, they reckoned, would be shipped out under UN supervision because Srebrenica was designated as a "safe haven". Nobody at that time – least of all UN generals and the politicians who directed them – had enough of a sense of honour to guarantee the haven, but the duplicity wasn't known then. The women and children would be protected. The men would fight their way out over the mountains, through forests. The NATO planes, it was thought, would put down carpet bombing on the Serbs so that the men had a chance in the break-out. The fittest of the men, the best fighters and the best armed, were at the front of the column – the Sreb Four were at the front of the front, because they were the best. What they didn't know was that, behind them, their fathers, uncles, nephews, grandfathers, had been either rounded up in Srebrenica and butchered or were being killed, trapped and ambushed. They reckon they were betrayed, and I couldn't argue with it, not just by the UN and NATO but by their own people. What they think, the town was allowed to fall as a part of the end-game peace deal, they weren't given the guns and the reinforcements to hold it. The men of the family, all except the Sreb Four, were killed. Some of their women hanged themselves so that they wouldn't be raped, and some strangled their daughters so it didn't happen to them. They got out, and they're inseparable. They hate the Serbs for what was done to their families, and they hate the Muslim leaders for betraying them. They have been through hell, have walked through it, and come out the far side of it. You'll want to know what I did that makes them indebted to me – not much, in truth. There's IPTF in Srebrenica, and I arranged for myself to have a day there. I took flowers and laid them in a warehouse where some of the women killed themselves, and in the factory at Potocari where the older men were shot, and in the woods where the younger men were caught and had their throats slit. I took photographs of where I'd put the flowers. That's all I did. What they are doing in there won't trouble them, after what they've seen, not an iota . . . So, don't go fucking soft on me.'

They came out. Joey thought that if he had been able to see their faces they would have been expressionless. There was no tension in their bodies and no laughter in their voices. They huddled round Frank, and told him quietly what they had learned. Then one of them wiped his hands on the seat of his overalls, felt in his pocket and passed Frank the clean banknotes. He gave them back to Joey.

Joey had crossed a river.

'Turn him over,' Mister said.

A little spear of light from the pencil torch followed Atkins's boot as it tipped the man over from his stomach to his back.

The Eagle, behind Mister, gasped. Mister could see the eyes through swollen lids and the mouth through split lips, but the rest of the facial features were lost in a sea of blood. Mister knew a great deal about beatings – fists, cosh-sticks, boots – it was what he had done in the past, and he felt cheated because he would have done it again, there, that night.

'Is he gone?'

Atkins knelt beside the man and felt the pulse at his neck. As he straightened, he shook his head.

'If he's not gone now then he will be soon,' Mister said.

'We should get out of here, Mister,' the Eagle hissed.

'It's not a healthy place.' Atkins's pistol had been in his hand from the moment they had left the Toyota, and it had been between his legs as soon as they had driven into Dobrinja.

'In our own time. You never know when you're watched, so you never run. You never let anyone see you run. Gives us something to think about – eh, Eagle – who'd have done a fancy job like that . . . A druggies' fight, or my friend with the puppy dogs and the pretty boy? Let's go, let's go to bed.'

It was past midnight when the chief investigation officer took a call from Gough, received a peremptory apology for the lateness of the hour, and was alerted to a fax sent to him. The CIO apologized to his wife, slipped into a dressing-gown and went down to his home cubicle office.

He read:

From: SQG12/Sarajevo, B-H
To: SQG1/London
Timed: 00.18 15.03.01
Message Starts:
Para One – Target One in contact with Ismet Mujic, a.k.a. Serif.
Sweetener supplied is anti-tank missile launcher (make and
origin unknown). Box 850 have hotel bug in place for Target One,
as yet no result – also location beacon on Target One's vehicle.
Target One is accompanied at all times by Target Two (Eagle) and
Target Three (Atkins). Believe (not confirmed) a-tml brought to
B-H in overland charity shipment from Bosnia with Love.
Para Two – From information received, I learn that Dubbs, a.k.a.
the Cruncher, was murdered by Ismet Mujic, plus associates. It's
choice, exclaimer. Cruncher was taken to niteclub/restaurant,
the Platinum City, owned by IM. In the party was Enver – toy-
boy partner of IM. I learn that, during dinner, Cruncher's sexual
preferences were made obvious: he reached under the table and
squeezed Enver's testicles – to demonstrate, I presume, his availability. His host, no doubt used to providing said demonstration
himself, took offence. Eyewitness was begging outside Platinum
City, regular pitch, heard the accusations made in the street as
Cruncher was taken out, saw a chop-hand blow to back of
Cruncher's neck by IM, saw goons put Cruncher from bridge
into Miljacka river. Regret that eyewitness declined to provide
sworn/signed statement of above.
Para Three – Full permission for intrusive surveillance from
Judge Zenjil Delic, signed and stamped. God knows why,
haven't got round to asking Him.
Para Four – My observation: Target One is unaware of current
surveillance. Opinion is shared by Box 850.
Message Ends

He minuted a little note for himself. He would speak to Gough in
the morning. Past experience told him that danger beckoned when
footmen were confident that their trailing presence was not
observed.

Chapter Nine

It was the spring day, in Sarajevo, when nothing much happened. There was a fast snow blizzard at dawn that hurried down the Igman slopes to envelop the city, then a bright, cold morning, then a bright, warm afternoon, then an overcast dusk, and rain in the evening.

The longest queue in the city, from dawn to dusk, was outside the high, guarded gates of the German embassy on Mejtas Buka. Every day on which it was open the queue was there. In the hunt for visas and escape it stretched down the street and round the corner. A few at a time were admitted to the hidden buildings behind the wall. Many of those who queued would fail to reach the front of the line before the offices closed. Few of those allowed inside would be given entry to a Promised Land. Down by the Miljacka river, a shorter queue of men jostled at the door of the Slovenian embassy, also looking for a route out of a doomed country.

There were no queues waiting for the shops to open on Mula Mustafe Baseskije and Saraci and Bravadziluk Halaci. The windows displaying designer clothes brought in from outside were looked into, but the tills did not ring and the fitting rooms stayed empty. The boutiques gave an impression of vibrant wealth, but it was bogus.

No one could afford the dresses, blouses, skirts and lingerie; most items would have cost a civil servant a year's salary.

The street markets were full from early morning when the stalls were set up to late afternoon when they were taken down and little pick-up trucks drove away with what had not been sold. The produce – cabbage, potatoes, carrots, beans, onions, peas – came from across the southern frontiers, because the country was still locked in winter's frosts. On other stalls there were clothes that had been smuggled in, no duty paid; they were cheap and thin, would not have kept out the morning's cold or the evening's rain. Everything in the markets came from abroad because the small factories, five years after the war's end, had not been rebuilt.

On the steps of the buildings appropriated for the use of the international community, foreign men and foreign women gathered to smoke their cigarettes, most of which had been bought on the black market. Marlboro, Winston and Camel cigarettes, brought by high-speed launches from Italy or driven in from Serbia, were smoked on the steps of the buildings used by the Commission of Property Claims of Displaced Persons, the European Bank for Reconstruction, the International Committee of the Red Cross, the International Labour Office and the International Monetary Fund ... and the Office of the High Representative, the Office of the Human Rights Ombudsman and the Organization for Security and Co-operation in Europe ... and the United Nations Children's Fund, the International Criminal Tribunal for the Former Yugoslavia and the World Food Programme ... and the United States Agency for International Development and the International Crisis Group. Men and women snatched short breaks, then ground out their cigarettes and went back to administering the country's every heartbeat. Roads, bus timetables, postage rates, sewage disposal, the design of banknotes, television programme schedules – the life of the city was in the hands of those foreigners, this day and every day.

Romany beggars haunted the streets and crouched on corners beside war-maimed veterans who let their amputated limbs be seen, but their upturned caps and little cardboard boxes went unfilled. The city had no time for charity.

Government ministers swept between their homes and offices in bomb-proof cars. The black Mercedes of the gangsters raced on the narrow streets. Italian troops, bored near to sleep, patrolled as a show but had no power of arrest and had orders to avoid provocation.

In the street cafés, young men made a thimble of espresso or a can of Coca-Cola last an hour and swapped gossip on the best ways to gain admission to an Austrian, German or Scandinavian university.

Nothing much happened.

The Eel drove Mister along the Zmaja od Bosne, past the Holiday Inn, to Tower A of the UNIS building complex on Fra Andela Zvizdovica.

Compartments again ruled his mind. Stacked at the back of his thoughts, and ignored, were the matters involving Serif and the deal, the death of his friend and the blood-laced face of an addict. As they came down what Atkins had called Snipers' Alley, past ruins and shell-holed blocks, Mister was pondering what lorries from Bosnia with Love could bring into the city, and what they could take out. He was rested and sleeping well, but he had slept well in his cell in Brixton. He slept well because the shadow of failure did not exist in Mister's mind.

From the Cruncher's calls to London, he had a name.

He dropped down from the lorry cab. It had been the Cruncher's idea to paint the slogan 'Bosnia with Love' on the trailer's sides. When the trade was up and running, the lorry, and others, needed to be recognized, known. He saw three towers. Two were still fire-gutted and open to the weather. Tower A had lights burning in the bottom half of its floors and above he saw men working precariously. He went into a cavernous hallway, gave the name at a reception desk and was told which floor he should go to, also that he should take the stairs as the lift wasn't operating. Before Cruncher had reported on it, Mister had never heard of the United Nations High Commission for Refugees. After five flights of concrete steps he came to a landing. He straightened his quiet tie and smoothed his hair. He felt good. He asked for her at the security desk, and said what he'd brought.

She came out through an inner door, and her smile of welcome and relief hit him – a bright light in darkness. 'I'm Monika Holberg, a field officer but based in Sarajevo canton, and you are my white knight. Your name is?'

'I'm Packer. Mister Packer.'

'I am so delighted to see you because you have the lorry, you have what I need.'

'I have a lorry, Miss Holberg, and it is filled to overflowing with clothes, toys, everything that people at home thought would be wanted in Bosnia by those less fortunate than themselves.'

It was only a small untruth. The lorry was not 'overflowing'. Against the bulkhead at the back of the trailer was the empty space where the launchers and missiles, the handguns and the communications sets had been. She gripped his hand. In business he dealt with few women ... only the Princess, in whom he confided everything. He went to his sisters, with the Eagle, when their signatures were needed for property contracts and bond purchases. At an associate's house he made it crystal plain that the women should be out of the room. He was never sure about women, except the Princess – never certain that they felt the same ties of loyalty as men, and that in interview rooms, late at night, battered by the questions of detectives in relays, they would stare at the ceiling and stay quiet.

She dropped his hand and her enthusiasm gushed. 'I am so grateful, so happy – it is what your friend, Mr Dubbs, said you would bring?'

'Just what he said. Would you like to come and look?'

She bounded down the stairs. Her blonde hair bounced on her anorak's collar. He had to scramble to keep up with her. She wore no makeup. His sisters, all past their fiftieth birthdays, and the brat girls they'd produced, all carried handbags full of powders and scent squeezers and mascara brushes. They tripped along on heels. She went down the stairs, two steps at a time, on muddied old walking-boots. He struggled to keep up. She was waiting for him at the bottom of the last flight, grinning and arching her eyebrows and he was laughing. He didn't laugh often, but the droll grin and the eyebrows forced it from him. They crossed the hall. On the outside steps he whistled for the Eel's attention in the lorry cab, and pointed to the rear doors of the trailer. When the Eel opened them for her, she scrambled up athletically, and began to rip the adhesive binding tape off the first cardboard box. Sweaters, jackets, knitted woollen socks, coats, trousers, all were thrown up, then stuffed back. She

196

looked into the depth of the trailer and her gaze hovered on the stacked boxes.

'They are all like this one?'

'Best as I know it, they are – but there's everything. It's not just clothes, it's toys too.'

'Fantastic – it is marvellous!'

Her eyes were alight. Mister lived in a world where enthusiasm was forbidden, and gratitude made debts.

Mister shrugged. 'I'm glad it's all going to help.'

'It is what I needed.'

She dropped down from the trailer. He didn't offer his hand to steady her – she wouldn't have needed it.

Mister said, 'I'm pleased it's wanted. I honestly thought you'd have more of this sort of stuff than you could handle—'

She interrupted him, seemed to think nothing of cutting him short. 'Once, yes, but not now. It is "donor fatigue". People are tired, abroad, of giving to Bosnia. They see no benefit and hear nothing good. They give to East Timor and Kosovo, and a little to Chechnya. There was a window for Bosnia and people looked in, were sympathetic and gave, but the window is now closed. The refugees suffer as much now as when the window was open. The need is as great, but the goodwill does not exist.'

'I'm glad to be—'

'I used to have warehouses filled by the generosity of people in Europe, even in America, but they are empty now. There is a village near Kiseljak. We have brought DPs – displaced persons – back to live in their old homes. They are complaining, they say they have nothing. They say it is worse than the refugee camp.'

'I'm happy that—'

'In three days we are taking ambassadors, administrators and generals to this village to see the achievement of bringing these people home. We need money for them, for all the DPs. Many more than two million people fled their homes in the war. We have to have money to get them home. We need the international pledges, and each month it is harder. If the people seen by the VIPs are unhappy, complaining, the visitors will not write memoranda urging their governments to pledge more. It is a very little village, but it is very important . . .' The torrent of words subsided. There was innocence and a wide grin of apology on her face. 'I am sorry, I interrupted you – twice.'

Very few men, and fewer women, interrupted Mister. 'It's nothing. I'm glad to be of help – happy to have done something worthwhile.'

'I need the lorry for this afternoon, to deliver.'

'Probably better you use your own driver, someone who knows the roads.'

'Of course. Where do you stay in Sarajevo, Mister Packer?'

He evaded the question effortlessly. 'I'd like you to know that I intend this should not be a one-off. There's plenty more where this load came from. I'm looking to offer regular deliveries. There must be a load of other people needing the same help as those in your village. Jason, give the lady the keys. I don't know how often I'll be able to get over here myself, but I promise you haven't seen the last of Bosnia with Love. It's been my pleasure meeting you, Miss Holberg. Just leave the keys at Reception when you're back and Jason'll collect them tonight. You'll have to excuse me, I've a few things to attend to – and, good luck.'

He sauntered away. Every week a lorry would arrive in Sarajevo, under cover of the bright-painted Bosnia with Love logo and filled with any kind of junk and chuck-out that the Mixer could lay his hands on. And every week an apparently empty lorry would leave from Sarajevo with a hidden class A load that would not be measured in grams and low kilos, but high kilos to a tonne. At ferry ports, frontier crossings and at border Customs posts, Bosnia with Love, doing good works, would be a familiar sight. No bastard in uniform would stop a charity vehicle, going in or coming out . . . The Cruncher's plan was in motion.

He hadn't given her the name of the hotel where he stayed.

She was on the fifth floor, dialling on her telephone for the drivers' pool, Ankie was bringing her coffee and she was gazing idly from the window, when she saw him.

There were only a few generous people, in Monika Holberg's experience, who did good work and slipped away from the lime-light, who did not want medals, official congratulations and invitations to international receptions, who shunned flashbulbs. She thought Mr Packer was one of them.

From her vantage-point, she watched as he went into the rear entrance of the Holiday Inn.

'He cannot do the meeting this morning,' the young man, Enver, said. 'He is sorry if that makes an inconvenience for you.'

The Eagle's response was curt. 'Mister Packer is not only an important man, he is a busy man.'

'The meeting will be in the afternoon, at four o'clock. I think he has interesting news for Mister Packer.'

'I speak for him – he'll be there.'

They'd been on a final cup in the coffee shop. The young man had found them there, bringing the dogs with him. The Eagle reckoned that in any other coffee shop, in any other city, the boy and his dogs would have been thrown out. One of the dogs had lunged at the cake trolley. It was disgusting, unhygienic. The Eagle had left Mister and Atkins at their window table, had gone to intercept Enver. He'd had a bad feeling about it the previous night, and the meeting's postponement had ratcheted it up. He never saw the enforcement side of Mister's business, was insulated from it, but the sight of the addict's pulped face had unsettled him. Between three and five years back, Mister had run a small side-show of enforcement business. A middle-rank figure was in debt to another middle-ranker who did not have the muscle strength to get himself paid. Mister bought out the debt, less twenty per cent, and sent the Cards round. The debt was paid – before or after the fists, coshes or a shotgun was used – and Mister's profit margin was one pound in five, or ten thousand in fifty thousand. The Cruncher had liked to call it 'diversification', but Mister didn't do it any longer because ten thousand pounds was chickenshit. The druggie's bloodied face had been the Eagle's sleeping companion, and his temper was on a short fuse.

'They've put you off again, Mister, they're giving you the runaround. Do we sit much longer in this hole? That's what I'm asking myself. Personally . . .'

Mister asked softly, 'Are they suggesting another time?'

'Four o'clock in the afternoon.'

'That's not a problem, then. That's when it is, fine.'

'So, we've a day to kick our heels.' The Eagle snorted, and sat down, confused. He had expected, been damned certain he'd see,

Mister's snarled anger at the slight . . . but everything was *fine*. He did not understand. Earlier, the Eagle had been explaining cash-flow and the notice required to move substantial money orders, then the need for decisions on the conversion of a Caymans account from dollars into euros, and the further movement of funds into an Israeli bank . . . and he'd given up because he hadn't had Mister's attention.

Mister said to Atkins, 'You know this place. We've half the morning and half the afternoon. Show me round. We'll do the sights.'

The Eagle was left worse than confused. He was bewildered.

'You want me to drive?'

'I'm quite capable – don't mind me saying it, you're a right misery today.'

'Is that so?'

'Lighten up, you're piss poor company. About last night?'

'Forget it . . . It's not your business.'

She ripped through the gears. The transmission from the Toyota's beacon was a continuous strong bleep. A light flashed, with constant reassurance, on the screen she'd bolted under the dash. He'd spelled it out last night, after he'd returned to the hotel and sent his signal. He'd come to her room and she'd had to clear a chair of her under-clothes so that he could sit down. He'd told it in a monologue of fifteen minutes. All the time he'd talked he'd never looked at her or her underclothes as she'd sat on the bed with her robe round her shoulders. He'd stared at the drawn curtain. She'd sent him to his own room after telling him that everything, always, seemed better in the morning. There had been a man in Ceauşescu Towers, old guard, who'd clung with his fingernails to employment because there was nothing else in his life, who had been a rookie youngster on the team running Oleg Penkovsky, the best source ever out of Moscow. She'd been with him in Beirut and she'd asked him how it was in the Century House building, home before the Towers, when they heard first that the Russian had been arrested, and then when they'd heard he'd been executed. He'd said, over king prawns and a bottle from the Beka'a, 'It's like when you've a good dog. As long as it's able to retrieve for the guns it's special. When it can't pick up birds you tell the keeper to get on with it. You hear the shot behind the stables, and you don't even blink. Hard things happen, and that's recognized by any man worth half a peck of salt.' She'd heard that the old warrior had died six months after they'd finally burned him out of the building . . . She'd taken what he said as a mantra ever since.

He was white-faced, had been since they'd met. All the time they'd watched and followed the lorry to Tower A, his fingers had been knotted tightly together.

'I can see my room from here.' Mister was crouched close to the firing position, and Atkins heard the tremor in his voice.

'They used the fort for artillery spotting,' Atkins said. 'They couldn't have hit your room, not at this range, with a sniper rifle, but they could have put a tank shell through it.'

He had brought Mister and the Eagle to the strongpoint, high and south of the city, past a modern memorial of slate-coloured marble that was set into snow-spattered flagstones then walked into the old fortress. He didn't think the Eagle cared a damn for it, but Mister's fascination was obvious. In front of a two-storey barracks building of off-white hewn stone blocks was a small parade area, closed in by the lower wall with the gun slits. The slits each had two shutters that closed on rollers. They were made of intimidating black-painted metal and were bullet- and shrapnel-proof. All the time Atkins had been in Sarajevo serving on the general's staff and wearing the blue beret, he had cursed the strongpoint and its view down on to Snipers' Alley, the Holiday Inn and every damn building that mattered. The city was laid out as a peaceful tableau and made benevolent by the snow. He remembered ruefully what he had thought then, that the spotters for the guns had the power of life and death, could see the panicked groups at the water stand-pipes, the groups round market stalls, and the schoolchildren, and could decide on which to call down the shells of the heavy guns.

'You couldn't hide from it, could you?' Mister said.

'Only if you'd done a deal, Mister.' Atkins remembered how much the blue beret men had hated the warlords – Caco, Celo and Serif. 'Some could, because they did deals. Serif, yes, he'd fight one day a week, and six days a week he'd be trading across the front line, particularly before the tunnel was dug. Drugs, ammunition, jewellery if they could steal it, food, alcohol, they all went back and forth across the front line. That was the other side of the war . . .'

'Am I hearing you right, Atkins, *ammunition*?'

'The Serb warlords sold the Muslim warlords – the likes of Serif – ordnance that was fired back on their own men. They achieved power by holding the line, and made themselves rich by trading.'

Mister had straightened up and he stared hard at Atkins. 'You're telling me not to trust him?'

'Not as far as you can kick him, Mister. Here, you trust nobody.'

'Ink on paper?'

'Worthless . . . Nobody.'

Atkins saw, first time he'd seen it, a pensive scowl cutting Mister's face. He had engineered the occasion. They could have gone to monuments in the city to the Ottoman time of greatness and seen mosques and galleries that were half a millennium old. They could have gone to the Imperial coffee-house, the interior unchanged since Austro-Hungarian rule. Instead, he had taken them to see the front line and had prepared the message he wanted to pass on. Mister was thinking.

They were walking back from the barracks' parade-ground, away from the gun slits and the view of Mister's bedroom far below. The Eagle wandered ahead of them then veered off the flagstones, his shoes sinking in the snow as he went to examine the marble of the memorial. Atkins had told them when they'd arrived that the memorial was for Tito's fighters killed in the world war.

Atkins shouted, a pressing, ruthless yell, 'Stop right there. Now, come back. Retrace your steps. Exactly . . .'

For a moment the Eagle stood statue still. Then he turned, fear on his face.

'Put your feet precisely where you walked, and move.'

The Eagle came back to them. In the bright sunlight, in the crisp wind, the sweat dribbled on his forehead. Step by step, through the snow, until he reached the flagstones.

Atkins said, 'This was a military position, it would have been mined. You were walking on snow. You didn't know what was under it – could have been flags, concrete or earth. If it had been earth there could have been mines. You never walk off-road here, or off the hard core – not if you want to keep your legs. Of course it's been "cleared", but there's no such thing as guaranteed clearance, and won't be for a hundred years. Just don't go walkabout.'

They went in silence to the Toyota.

He drove them along a winding road, away from the memorial, that cut down into a valley. The traffic signs were now in Cyrillic script; he told them they were in Sérb territory. They went past old women sitting on collapsible stools with big plastic bags by their knees. He said it was where they sold smuggled cigarettes from Italy, at eighty British pence a packet. They went left and climbed, came to the crest of the hill. The road hugged the rim. Below them, again, was another view of the city. He drove on another hundred and fifty metres then pulled into what had once been a car park for a bunga-low restaurant, but the building was wrecked and bullet-pocked, and its roof timbers were charred.

He slipped out of his seat and walked away from the Toyota. Mister and the Eagle followed him. He remembered watching, with image-intensifier binoculars handed him by French troops, a night attack up through the Jewish cemetery towards the trenches that were now in front of his feet. He stood on a narrow strip of cracked concrete. He had willed on, that night, those Muslim troops, civilians in ill-fitting uniforms and with outdated weapons, scrambling up the hill and advancing into the machine-gun fire from these trenches. He had shouted his support to them into the darkness, and they wouldn't have heard even the whisper of what he screamed over the volume and intensity of the gunfire. He thought of who he was now, and what he did now, and he spat the bile from his throat. He had not planned that memory or that thought.

'I can see the hotel, but I can't see my room,' Mister said.

The trenches were a metre wide and a metre and a half deep. Where the machine-guns had been sited, which had driven off that night attack, with the grenades and the bayonets, there were still heavy logs of pine laid flat to protect the Serb soldiers. The water in the pit of the trenches was frozen, and caught in the ice were dulled rusty cartridge cases. Further along, going east and in front of what had been the restaurant's conservatory dining area, the trench was reinforced by a twenty-metre length of half-moon concrete section. He could have told them, because it was what he had been told years back, that the section came from the Olympic Winter Games bob-sleigh run, but he didn't bother.

Atkins said, 'The gunfire would have broken up their little kitchen gardens. Both sides grew cannabis plants right in front of their forward positions. The warlords, that's Serif and those on the Serb side, encouraged the planting of cannabis. They reckoned that stoned guys wouldn't think too much about the war, and they also reckoned they'd fight harder because they wouldn't want to abandon their crop. Can you think what it was like up here in winter if you weren't drunk or stoned out of your mind? The little men fought, stoned, pissed and half dead with cold, and the big men – like Serif – got fat on their backs and their bodies. He's scum.'

'I do business anywhere I can find it, if the price is right.'

'I thought it might help you, Mister, to know where your new partner is coming from. I thought it might help you to know what sort of man he is, and what's his power base. He danced on graves . . .' Atkins let his words die.

He turned. Neither of them had listened to him. They were already walking back to the Toyota.

Didn't he know it? He was a fly in the spider's skein. He trotted after them to the vehicle.

'You all right, Atkins?'

'Never been better, Mister.'

'You know what? I reckon it's the tourist trail. They're doing the battlefield tour . . . It's not Utah or Gold Beach, or the Passchendaele Ridge or that farmhouse at Waterloo, but he's getting the Sarajevo scene. Don't you think?'

'How the hell do I know?'

'Just making conversation, sunshine . . . You'd be doing me a favour if you spat it,' Maggie said.

They were a clear quarter of a mile from where the Toyota was parked. Joey watched it through the binoculars.

He said, a recitation without feeling, 'I crossed a line. I broke every rule I'm supposed to abide by. I knew the illegality of what I asked for, and had other men who'd no scruples do what I was incapable of. I wanted it to happen.'

She shrugged. 'So that's all right, then – stop moaning.'

'What I did, and justified to myself, meant I walked outside my team.'

'Are you one of these "enthusiasts"? We weed them out at our

204

place. Even if they've fooled the recruitment board, we spot them and chuck them. Their feet don't touch the ground. Don't, please, tell me you're an *enthusiast*.'

'You've a good sneer . . . No, I don't think I am.'

'But it's justified, the nasty work? Right, right – you've a sister who died of drugs, overdosed?'

'No, I haven't.'

'What's the other hackneyed drop of tripe – oh, yes. "My best friend got to be a pusher. That's why I'm a crusader against drugs." Is that it?'

'I didn't have a best friend on Sierra Quebec Golf,' Joey said simply. 'My best friend at school teaches maths in a comprehensive in Birmingham.'

'So, what justified last night?'

'Are you listening?' Joey breathed in hard. His mind was a tangle of snipped string, no knots. 'It's about him, who he is – and about me, about who I am.'

'A winner and a loser is what you told me.'

'He's the highest mountain. Why climb a mountain? Because it's there. It's *there* in front of you. It's in front of you, indestructible, and laughing at you because you are so small – pygmy fucking small. The whole team of Sierra Quebec Golf spent three bloody years and they fell off the bloody mountain, they're history. I want to climb the mountain, beat the bastard, sit with my arse on his nose, because it's there . . . because *he*'s there. They say he's no fear, I want to see him scared. They say he's in control, I want to hear him scream and beg. I want – little, small me, and it's the only thing in my life that I want – to bring down the mountain. Is that an answer?'

Maggie touched his hand. 'I think it's better than most could give.'

She thought that the clerk in Warsaw, in the shadows when he kissed her, would have said something like that, about mountains, if she'd asked him, and the Libyan boy on the veranda in Valetta's moonlight. She'd wept for them both. God, was that her future, growing old and sad because young men fell off the crags on bloody mountains?

They were climbing back into the Toyota, made huge by the binocular lenses, and she eased the van forward.

*

There were others in her organization, and in every one of the foreign communities camped in the city, who didn't care. She loathed their company.

With the lorry driver, Monika headed for the village beyond Kiseljak.

She cared. If she had not then she might as well, as she often told herself, have stayed at Njusford, sheltered by the mountains and overlooking a bay that was classified by UNESCO as a 'preservation-worthy environment'. The bay was on Flakstodoya island, one of the Lofoten archipelago. It was the home she had rejected. Because she had needed to care she had left Njusford, turned her back on the little coral-painted house that had been her home. She had seen in Bosnia everything that brutality had to offer. She was toughened to suffering. She would not have acknowledged it of herself – she despised introverted self-examination – but part of her character that was remarkable was the absence of cynicism, and she did not know despair. The reward she found was in the gratitude of simple people – women who had nothing laughed with her and touched her arm or her clothes, children without a future chirped as they chanted her name. All the hours of sitting in officials' rooms and hearing excuses for procrastination were forgotten when she witnessed the gratitude and heard the chanting.

Bumping along in the lorry as it wove between sheets of ice on the road, she was cheerful, happy.

The man who had brought her the lorry had caused the lift in her mood. Most, if they had come with a lorry across Europe, would have wanted a photo-call and publicity for their generosity. She thought him the best of men because he had wanted nothing of her. She sang cheerily in the lorry cab, not looking at the snow-capped peaks because they would have reminded her of home at Njusford. Thinking of home would have destroyed her mood. In that month, on that day, if the seas were not too fierce, her father would have been out in his boat with her elder brother, and her mother and sister would have been left to gut and behead the previous day's cod catch. And all of them, when the boat came in, would have gone in the afternoon darkness to the grave of her younger brother. The black hours of winter, the harshness of the seas, the remoteness of the island and the agony of her brother's suicide had driven her away from Njusford. If she looked at mountains, she remembered. She sang with all of her ingrained enthusiasm.

They turned off the metalled road and lurched on a stone track towards the village with the charity load brought to her by a modest, caring stranger.

They were back from the court. For the midday recess, to save money, they avoided the canteen in the basement of the court building and went to his office to eat the sandwiches she always prepared at home.

While her father ate and concerned himself with the case papers, Jasmina threw her eyes cursorily over the overnight list of police reports. She would not normally have interrupted his concentration on a difficult case, which taxed both his humanity and his legal obligations. The case was murder. The defendant was a woman of twenty-two, already the mother of four children. The victim was a fellow gypsy, the father of two of the children. The weapon was an axe. The defence was that the victim had beaten the defendant and she had acted to save her own life. The accusation was that the defendant had bludgeoned the victim nine times because he had found a younger lover. Self-defence or premeditated murder. Freedom or imprisonment. In the old days, before the war, her father would have been assisted in room 118 of the Ministry of Justice by a jury of professionals, but there was no longer the money for that luxury; he sat alone. He must decide on guilt or innocence. It was typical of the cases thrown at him, without political overtones but laden with dilemma.

The fifth item on the police report of last night's incidents bounced back at her from the page.

She wheeled herself from her desk to the corner of the room, lifted a file and slid the rubber band from it. She riffled among the top papers, selected one, then moved to his desk. He looked up irritably as she laid the report in front of him and pointed to the fifth item. She waited until he had read it and when he looked up at her in annoyance she placed the page from the file on top of it.

A cloud seemed to shadow his face. He read the two pages a second time.

A drug addict, a disabled war veteran, had been savagely attacked in the Dobrinja district. Neighbours had seen nothing, had heard nothing, knew nothing except his name . . . A man of the same name and from the same address in Dobrinja had made a statement to the police on the death of the foreigner, Duncan Dubbs, in the Miljacka river . . . and the statement had been passed to the young British investigator, with permission for intrusive surveillance . . . and the IPTF had made the link with Ismet Mujic, who was the prime crime baron of Sarajevo, and Ismet Mujic was at the heart of his and his daughter's history.

'Better if I had never been involved,' he said. 'But I am, and I cannot step back from involvement . . . There is an English expression – what do they say in English?'

'I think it is "You reap what you sow." '

Frank, and all of the team, sat in on the briefing for the new man attached to the Kula station. He was introduced as a senior detective from Dakar, Senegal. The briefing was by the station commander, an intelligence officer from the Public Security Department of Jordan, who used a pointer and a blackboard to emphasize his message. 'We are not colonialists, we do not give out instructions and orders, we are here to advise and help the local police forces. Above all else, we must show them that we believe totally in the importance of the law . . .'

Frank heard the briefing with wavering attention, distracted by a nagging shame. He had tossed through the night, failed to sleep, and had felt his self-imposed reputation of dedication to policing slip through his fingers. He had no friends in Bosnia; he went about his work, struggled with it, without the support of comrades. The only men who greeted him with warmth, on the rare times they saw him, were the cousins who made up the Sreb Four – Salko, Ante, Fahro and Muhsin. He had welcomed the liaison opportunity and had hoped he would grow to like Joey Cann, out from London. But Cann was now the source of his shame.

The Jordanian droned on . . . Frank had come to Bosnia for many reasons, most to do with the split from Megan, but among them had been a heartfelt desire to help a war-weary community. He detested the crime that ravaged the city but, like his international colleagues, could see no way to fight it . . . He had been dragged down, with his fine ideals, by Joey Cann . . . He didn't want to see him, hear from him, again.

He began to dream – the Irish bar at the weekend at the top of Patriotske lige, fried breakfast-lunch, wearing the red shirt and the dragon, the pint of Guinness, and the satellite relay of the international match from home, and the shame gone . . . but only if Joey Cann didn't ring him.

November 1996

Headlights speared against the plastic that covered the windows and interrupted the feast and the celebration. Alija, the son-in-law of Husein and Lila Bekir, had come to Vraca for his week's leave from army duties.

Their daughter now lived with the old couple. For ten months she had been with them and taken off them the weight of caring for their grandchildren, but it was good that the little ones' father was there. He had come the night before, dropped off by an army truck, and he would be with them for a week.

The family, reunited, sat in the candlelight around the table in the one room of the house that was dry and sealed against the cold, and they ate, laughed, sang and put aside the disasters of the past years. In their own bed, the night before, cuddling each other against the chill, Husein and Lila had heard the heave of the rusted springs in the next room, through a wall weakened by old shell fire. They had chuckled and predicted the arrival of another grandchild, and they had each, in their own way, prayed that they would be there to see its birth. There was little enough for them to look forward to, and much for them to forget.

Half of the population of Vraca had now returned. Each day there was the beating of hammers, the scrape of saws and the crack of chisels reshaping the old, scorched stones. For that year, it was their aim that the returned families should have at least one room that was proof against the weather. No electricity, no water other than from the river, but protection against the elements. As patriarch of the community it was the role of Husein Bekir to decide who was next in the queue for help with the necessary repairs, and to assign the labour. It was slow work. Those who had come back were the elderly; the young men would not return. If the young did not come back he doubted their community could ever achieve vibrant life – but that was for another day's thoughts, not for an evening of celebration, with a feast before the family.

Under the terms of what the foreigners called the quick-support grant, Husein had been given a pregnant cow, which would give birth in February of next year, and through the income-generation grant they had been given tools, nails and sacks of cement. The foreigners brought them food, heating-oil, plastic sheeting for the roofing not yet repaired, and packets of vegetable seed. Without the gifts they would have starved. There was a little sour milk to be taken each day from the goats but, in truth, they had nothing. They were dependent on the foreigners' charity. They had hoed strips of ground near the village to plant the vegetable seed but the crop had been minimal.

The good ground was across the ford over the river. There was no sign left of the fire that Husein had lit to clear the grass, the weeds and the mines. He could not look across the valley from inside his house: he had no glass for the windows, which were screened with heavy nailed-on plastic sheeting. Each time he had stepped out of his house – through the successive seasons of the last year – he had thought that his fields beyond the river mocked him. The ground on his side of the river made poor grazing for the few sheep and goats his dog had rounded up from the woods, and the pregnant cow, and he had no fertilizer for the ground where he had sown the seeds.

They had gone out that morning, at first light.

Pelted by rain Husein – in the old overcoat that he lived in, tied with bale twine – and his son-in-law had gone down to the river-bank. Husein had started to explain where he thought mines had been buried, scratching in his memory, but Alija had gestured with his hand that Husein should not speak but let him concentrate. Unless it had been pointed out to him, Husein would not have seen the small round grey-green plastic shape lying in a run of silt in the arable field a dozen paces from the far bank. Directly opposite the point where the PMA2 mine had surfaced, Alija stripped off his boots and clothes, shed everything except his undershirt and underpants. Then, not seeming to feel the cold, he unknotted the twine from Husein's waist. He unravelled it, then tied the strands together to make a long thin length of more than thirty metres. He said he knew about mines from his army training. The strands that made a slender rope were all he took with him when he went down the bank and swam the width of the dark pool. Husein had stood very still and watched. Alija crawled up the far bank and slithered through old grass and dead nettles towards the mine. Husein had thought it bravado, and madness. He would be blamed by Lila and his daughter, by the tears of his grandchildren, if the mine exploded because he had complained they had no food worthy of a feast and a celebration. Very carefully, Alija scraped away with his fingers the silt earth in which the mine lay, then lifted it clear of the ground. Husein had gasped. It was so small. Alija tied the end of the strand of twine to the mine's narrow neck, between its body and the little stubbed antenna, and had called softly to Husein to lie flat and put his hands over his ears. He had been on the ground, pressing down into wet grass, when Alija had tossed the mine casually into the river pool. There had been a thunderous roar reaching deep into his covered ears, then water had rained down on him.

They had returned to the house with two pike, the largest more than five kilos in weight, and three trout, all heavier than a kilo. Poached in an old dish, with rich flesh to be handpicked from the bones, the trout and the pike made a feast for a celebration.

The headlights against the plastic were cut, and the growling engine of the jeep died. There was a rapped fist at the timber door.

They always welcomed the young Spanish officer. They stood around the table long enough to embarrass him. He was introduced as their benefactor to Alija, and Husein's daughter offered him a chair at the table, but he refused it and sat on an upturned wooden box. The officer apologized for his lateness, but the supplies were now being unloaded at the building that had been a schoolhouse. They had no alcohol to offer him, but Lila sluiced the plate in the bucket of river water, wiped her hand on her apron, picked the last of the trout and pike flesh from the carcasses and set it before the officer.

'I congratulate you,' he said. 'You are successful fishermen.'

They had no lines in the village, no hooks, and no money to buy them. He was told how it had been done.

The frown cut his forehead. 'That is very dangerous. I cannot encourage that. Until it is cleared I very much advise that you do not go across again.'

Husein squirmed. He would have been responsible. He challenged, 'We are trapped here. The valley was our life. Without going across the river, how can we live, what life do we have?'

The officer said, as if he believed none of it, 'A committee has been set up in Sarajevo, a mine-action centre, and they are now examining the places where it is known mines were laid. They are drawing up a list for the priority of clearance.'

'Where would I be in that priority?' Husein persisted doggedly.

'I would lie if I said you were high on it. The cities come first. Sarajevo is at the top, then Goražde, then Tuzla. There is Travnik and Zenica, and the whole of Bihac province. It is said there are a million mines laid in Bosnia . . . but you are on the list, I promise you.'

'At the bottom of it?'

'Not high on it.'

'How long before we are high on the list?'

'At an estimate, there are thirty thousand places where mines were put. I think it is a very long time before you are high on the list.'

Husein knew he had destroyed the pleasure of the evening, but could not stop. 'How many mines do you believe are in my fields?'

'I don't know. You ask me questions that I cannot answer . . . It could be ten, it could be a hundred, it could be the last one that went into the river to kill the fish . . . I don't know.'

Husein clutched the straw. 'It might have been the last one?'

'I cannot promise it – it is a *possibility*, not more.'

'You are blessed with the privilege of education, you are an intelligent man. If you were me, what would you do? How would you live?'

'It is my duty to urge you to be patient . . . I have some interesting news for you. The first from across the valley is coming back next week, to the other side. We have to escort him.'

'Who is that?'

'An old man, a retired policeman. He has the house over the river that is nearest to your house. He has been in Germany, but the Germans are pushing out the refugees. He will be the first of them.'

Husein thought it was said to cheer them. The officer had eaten none of the fish laid in front of him. The wooden box scraped back, and he stood. He was apologizing for his intrusion. Husein thought momentarily of the return of his friend, of the chance again to argue, bicker and dispute, to play chess in the shade of his friend's mulberry tree – if he crossed the ford when the river was slow in the next summer, and if the track to Dragan Kovac's house was clear, clean, safe. The officer was at the door.

'It is a possibility that was the last mine?' He said it so quietly that the officer did not hear his question and was gone out into the night.

'How are you settling in, Mr Gough?'

'Not badly.'

'That's good news. I don't suppose you're fond of London.'

'I'll survive it.'

In the late afternoon Dougie Gough and the chief investigation officer, Dennis Cork, slipped out of the Custom House and on to the embankment path beside the river. Ostensibly they left the building so that Gough could light his pipe. Unspoken was the desire of each man to be clear of the building, away from the eyes and ears that might watch or listen to them. Gough, face wreathed in pipesmoke, wore his old raincoat and a thick knitted scarf over the tweed suit. Cork was wrapped in a dark camel coat with a spatter of dandruff showing on the collar. The small-talk, conversational, was for the corridor and the knot of smokers on the outside step. Yes, Gough was settling, surviving; it was what he had told his wife in a phone call to Glasgow. She hadn't commented, seldom queried his work duties. He'd said the same thing to his son, Rory, and to his daughter-in-law, Emma, whose back bedroom in their south-west London terrace home he now occupied. He hated London and yearned for escape to Ardnamurchan, but that was behind him. They walked briskly.

'I wouldn't want you to misconstrue, Mr Gough, but I don't see the signs of great progress. I'm not complaining at your telephoning me in the dead of night – Cann's last report – but I'm not getting an impression of action. Can we liven it up a bit?'

'I was never one to rush things.'

'Create a frisson of excitement. Put them off balance. Isn't that the road to mistakes?'

'It's a two-sided game. Hurry when you should be walking and it's not just them that can make mistakes. *We* can make mistakes.'

'I want Packer and his crowd to feel pressured. I've a minister sitting on me. We've taken prime position in this investigation. I've elbowed aside both the Crime Squad and Criminal Intelligence, I've refused to share with them. Without a result, and a quick one, I may not survive.'

'That's the way of the game.'

'The young man we have there, Cann – it's interesting what he's turned up but it doesn't move us forward. Frankly, I'd have thought he'd have done better by now. It's all fat we've learned, not meat. I shouldn't, but I lie awake at night and think of that man, Packer, and he seems to turn to me, in the street, wherever, and laugh at me.'

'I sleep well at night.'

'Where I used to work we believed in the gospel of proaction. Leading and dominating, not merely reacting.' Cork remembered that he had minuted himself to refer to the dangers of over-confidence in surveillance, but he erased the minute.

'It's your bad luck you don't still work there, sir.'

'Dammit, Gough – Mr Gough – if Packer isn't nailed to a courtroom bench, I'll go down as a failure. You tell me what Cann has unearthed, what has been in his communications that has been important.'

'Learn to be patient. You have to sit for hours, days, to see a fine dog-otter off the rocks at Kilchoan or on the beaches under Ben Hiant. No patience, no reward . . . "Target One is unaware of current surveillance." That's important.'

The minute was forgotten. 'I'd better be getting back.'

Gough leaned on the rail above the river, smoked his pipe and pondered. The camel coat was disappearing among the pedestrians. Dougie Gough had plans, of course he had, for 'jarring' and 'pressuring' Mister and Mister's clan, but they would not be discussed and negotiated with a man who had dandruff on his shoulders and who worried about the future of his career. It was about patience, and crucial to the fruits of patience was Joey Cann, a shadow, unseen, tracking Mister on Sarajevo's streets.

'Hello, dear. Just popped round, have you?'

'Thought I'd tidy up, and make sure everything's all right.'

The girlfriend, Jennifer, was rather pretty, Violet Robinson thought, and a decent girl, attentive and dutiful. Violet was fond of her. As freehold owner of the house in Tooting Bec, and the landlady, she made it her business to know all of the comings and goings in the building. She had two young women in the basement, both City professionals, and she rather hoped – for their benefit – they'd get themselves married off and find places of their own. Joey, she'd always had a soft spot for him, had the top-floor room under the eaves. When the girls in the basement moved out, it was her idea that Joey and his girlfriend could take it over. She'd be comfortable with them in her house. She thought young Jennifer was strained, tense . . . She'd checked the room after Joey had gone in that early-morning rush for his plane and thought it puritanically tidy. But perhaps there was ironing that was needed, or somesuch excuse, but more likely this little soul was lonely and had come over from Wimbledon simply to be in his single room.

'That's lovely, dear. Have you heard from him?'

'He rang to say he'd arrived. Didn't tell me much. He hasn't rung since.'

'You know you can always use the phone here.'

'He didn't give me the number.'

Violet Robinson had been a widow for eight years. Her late husband had been with the diplomatic corps and had been taken from her by a rare strain of fever with an unpronounceable name and beyond the skills of the American hospital's doctors in Asunción. Perry had been acting ambassador to Paraguay, had gone down overnight and been too ill to be flown out to better facilities in Buenos Aires. With the degree of independence expected from a seasoned Foreign Office wife she had set to and divided up their home in Tooting Bec. The ground and first floor she had kept for herself, but the basement and attic were converted to rented accommodation. Joey had been with her for five years. Until young Jennifer came into his life, she'd thought that he would still be there when she was carried out by an ambulance crew or an undertaker, had been almost at the point of despair of him meeting the right sort of girl – and then Jennifer had arrived.

'Well, ring his work, ask them for it.'

'They wouldn't give it me, it's against the regulations.'

'Of course they would, in an emergency. Not to worry, I'm sure he's all right there.'

'Yes . . . I keep expecting him to ring from the airport. It's only a few days.'

It was her opinion, a little of it from vanity, that Joey confided in her more than he did in his girlfriend, Jennifer. At least once a week, when he came back late at night from work, she would invite him into her sitting room off the ground-floor hall, and sit him down in Perry's old chair. She'd make him strong coffee, cook him Welsh rarebit or an omelette, pour him a stiff whisky and let him talk. She was used to discretion. She knew everything about the working days of what he called Sierra Quebec Golf, and everything about the life of Albert William Packer. To pass long days and long evenings she watched the soap operas, but there was nothing on television that was remotely as interesting as the work of SQG and the life of Mister. Joey had told her that he only gave the barest skeleton of it all to Jennifer. It gave her pride, and some little purpose, to know the heart of the story.

'And we're missing him, aren't we?'

''Fraid so – anyway, I'll get on.'

'He's a sensible young man and, what you should remember, they wouldn't have sent him if he wouldn't be all right there.'

'Of course you're right – and thanks for saying it.'

Young Jennifer's back was to her, going up the stairs, and she wouldn't have seen Violet's shiver. Perry had told her often enough that when diplomats, soldiers or intelligence officers were sent abroad, were far from home, they lost their sense of self-preserving caution. It had been a theme of his. Men and women, on duty and overseas, shed the ability to recognize the moment to step back. It was about the isolation, Perry had said. They felt invulnerable, discarded the armour of carefulness, and walked close to cliff edges – he often talked about it.

She called up the stairs, 'Don't you worry yourself.'

The answer came down to her, and the surprise: 'Why do you say that, Mrs Robinson? I'm not worried.'

'Of course you're not, and you've no cause to be.'

'I won't be long – just get it shipshape. I've got to get back for the cat . . .'

When she'd checked the room after he'd gone, Violet had noted that the photograph was no longer on the wall. As she'd put her own rubbish sack in the outside bin for the refuse men, she'd found it ripped to small pieces. It had been an ugly picture of an ugly man, like an odour in her house. She went back into her room. She hoped Joey, spare, slight, with his big spectacles, was not drawn close to a cliff edge. High above her, carried down the staircase, she could hear the whine of a vacuum cleaner.

'Is that so?'

To another man, a lesser man, what Mister was told by Serif would have been a pickaxe into the stomach. Beside him the Eagle had gasped and he had heard a little whistle of shock hiss from between Atkins's teeth. Serif's signature was on the document, drawn up by the Eagle, after two hours of dispute and amendments. There had been brittle politeness in the haggling and twice Serif had gone out with his people into the corridor. Mister was satisfied. The figure agreed, to be paid quarterly, was for a million and a half sterling, converted to American dollars, paid into Nicosia. Under Atkins's supervision, Serif's men had carried two more of the boxed medium-range Trigat launchers from the Toyota into the apartment, and the missiles. The communications systems had been handed over and Serif had leaned intently over Atkins's shoulder as the workings were explained. It should have been the moment for a popping cork, but Mister – still smiling – had asked with a laser's directness whether Serif was responsible for the beating given to the eyewitness from Dobrinja, the last person to see the Cruncher alive. Serif had denied it. Then Serif had rolled the hand-grenade across the table, and it had fallen into Mister's lap, and the Eagle had gasped, Atkins had whistled, but Mister had not blinked.

'You have my promise, Mister Packer, of the truth of it. You are followed.'

'I hear you.'

'A young man, foreign – I assume from your country. He is small, with big spectacles and dressed without any style. His coat is green. He followed you yesterday, Enver saw him. You stopped to look in a window, and he stopped. You walked back towards him and stood very close to him, and he looked away from you. You went away, and

217

he followed. You are under surveillance. It is not a situation that I welcome ... I know nothing of the beating of the addict in Dobrinja. Look elsewhere for those responsible, look to a man who follows you.'

No panic flicked in Mister's eyes. His calm dripped off him. 'I am grateful to you.'

'I do not tolerate investigation of my business. You bring good trade to me, but also embarrassment.'

Mister's fingers rapped the table. 'I'll deal with it.'

'But you will need help. It is better we take responsibility.'

'Thank you, no help.'

'It is my city.'

Mister said decisively, burgeoning his authority. 'I help myself. I need no assistance. If I have a problem, then *I* finish it. Thank you, but I don't ask for help.'

He detested providing the opportunity for a smirk to play at Serif's mouth. Hands were shaken and then, at the last, he let Serif take him in his broad arms and brush-kiss his cheeks. He himself dealt with every problem that faced him, had ever challenged him, and would do so until he dropped. They were out in the street and heading for the Toyota. The Eagle was a lawyer and good on contracts. Atkins was a soldier and understood war weapons. Atkins knew nothing of counter-surveillance, and the Eagle knew less. He told them to drive back to the hotel and wait for him. He left them by the vehicle and started to walk slowly, with his eyes on the shop fronts, along Mula Mustafe Baseskija.

He wandered at his own pace, never looked behind him, never doubled back, and turned at the big junction on to Kosevo, and climbed the hill.

It was the day that nothing much happened, and everything changed.

Chapter Ten

Joey Cann trudged up the steep street. For the life of him, he could not understand why Mister had walked out of the inner city and taken the street up the hill. It was a lesson learned long ago by Joey, heard at the feet of experts, that where a target went a footman followed. The task of the footman was merely to stay in touch, stay unseen, but to hold the link.

At first, going up the street, past small guest-houses and smaller shops with barely filled shelves, he thought of himself as a predator and Mister as his prey. As a child, on the estate where his father was the factor, he had been taught a stalker's arts by the gamekeeper. The keeper had been young, just out of agricultural college, from the Exmoor countryside, and had been – so his father said – the best that the estate owner had ever employed. Joey, a teenager, and the keeper, early twenties, in late summer mornings had stalked fallow deer, and he'd watched the keeper shoot them with a rifle. At different times of the year, when killing was not the priority, their game had been to creep close, and Joey had known that flushing excitement from being so near and unobserved. Then he had felt himself the predator and thought of the deer as his prey. The man ahead of him took the prey's role, showed no awareness and no fear, and strolled. The keeper had gone when the new owner had taken the estate, too expensive for the new money. A syndicate from Bristol had bought the shooting rights and employed a part-time man who had neither the time nor the inclination to take a youngster out with him. Joey's stalking talent had lain dormant until now.

He had said he was the loser and Mister was the winner. But the loser tracked the winner. Elation surged in him. He felt the power of the predator.

His mind was focused on the roll of the shoulders in front of him and the bob of the curly uncombed hair. He did not think of Jen, or of Dougie Gough who had given him the chance, or of *why* Mister wandered towards the outskirts of the city. He had a bounce in his stride.

Ahead of him, the sunshine of the afternoon was slipping to dull dusk, but low light snatched at the stunted little concrete posts of vivid white that rose from the dirt earth. Why would Mister come to a place of the dead? On the hill above Patriotske lige, and on the slope below, were the densely packed white graveposts, not in ordered lines, not set with geometric precision, but squeezed in, forced together too close for decency.

Where Mister led him, he followed. Above the railings and below them, women and men and children moved with sad duty and carried little bunches of posies, a gift to the graves. Joey had not comprehended the scale of the Sarajevo slaughter. He remembered, fleetingly, the stories of the radio and in newspapers, of night-time funerals so that mourners would not have inflicted on them the shell and mortar fire of their enemies. Snuggled against the lower side of the twin cemeteries was an earth and shale soccer pitch, not blessed with a blade of grass, and he remembered, too, hearing and reading that a sports field had been used as an overspill graveyard. Looking through the railings on the upper side of the cemetery, flush to the pavement as if the corpses had been squashed short to fit the space given them, were five white stones, same family name and same date of death.

The pavement ahead of him was empty.

Joey cursed for allowing a graveyard, the war dead, to break his concentration.

His eyes raked the desolation around him.

He saw Mister, and breathed hard. The moment's tension slipped

220

from his muscles. Mister walked among the dead's marker posts. They reached to his hips. Some had fresh-cut flowers resting against them, some had sealed glass bowls protecting artificial flowers, some had flowers long dead, some were abandoned. He should have asked why, and did not. Mister went slowly towards a great grey stone monument that sprouted above the posts, dark against light and dominating. He seemed to have time, not to be worrying. Mister did not look at his watch, as any man would have done if he had made a rendezvous there.

Mister walked past the monument and out of Joey's view.

'I'll deal with it,' he'd said.

Mister was wearing his best suit and good, lightweight shoes. Mud and snow slush clung to the knees of his trousers, was caked on his shoes. He knelt. He was behind haphazard rows of white posts and away to the right of the monument. It was the first time he'd seen him.

He would deal with it because that was his way. At stake was respect. To have been in debt and under obligation to Ismet Mujic was unthinkable to Mister.

The young man was near the monument. He had stopped and hesitated, and looked around him. The circling glance was supposed to be casual . . . The tracker had lost his target. The monument was a fallen lion, or a sleeping one, and the inscription that was hard to read was in German. The tracker eyed the monument, as if to display his innocence, and kept his head movement minimal but his eyes traversed the posts and the graves. Mister watched.

He looked like a student. Mister had never travelled abroad on work before, but he had been to Spain often enough with the Princess for sunshine breaks and he'd have prided himself that he could spot the stereotypical characteristics of foreigners. He thought the tracker was British. The spectacles were the give-away. They weren't a fashion accessory, styled, they were functional: he could see the big lenses that flashed in the last light as the head was gently twisted . . . A policeman wouldn't have passed Hendon with eyesight needing such assistance. Low on the wet dirt earth and puddles of slush water around his knees, his viewpoint gave him the narrowest of corridors between the posts.

All the way up the hill, a route chosen at random, he had never looked back. He had not doubled on himself or used the reflection of shop doorways. Ahead of him had been the cemeteries, the locked-up sports stadium, and the hospital high on the furthest hill. The upper sloping cemetery had seemed to give him the best opportunity. He waited and watched ... He searched for more of them. Down the slope, beyond the monument, were the railings, the pavement and the road. He looked for men in raincoats or leather jackets, for women who had no purpose in being there. All he saw was old women, old men and a few children walking slowly to graves, or sitting on seats and reflecting, or hurrying away because the evening closed on the city. He did not identify a team.

The realization came quickly. They had sent one man. That was lack of *respect*. He knew all the women and men from the police Crime Squad, from the police intelligence, from Customs' Investigation Service who were prominent in tracking, trailing, following him. He knew their rank, their addresses and their families' names. He knew about their kids, their cars and their holidays. With the Eagle he had walked past them at the Old Bailey on his way to the side door, had gone past their misery and their sourness. He did not know this one young man who now stood confused close to the monument.

A heavy rain had begun to fall.

He saw only the whiteness of the stones, the little clumps of flowers and the dark grey slabs of the monument. The lion, shrapnel-pocked, slept. It was a memorial to the German soldiers killed in a long-ago war. Joey felt the chill of the place, and the rain that was carried in the growing wind beat on his back and against his trousers. In some of the stones, set in shallow recesses, nested photographs of the dead – young men, from the carved dates of their lives. He did not know whether they were soldiers or civilians, whether they had died in combat or been killed by shell splinters or by snipers. Some would now have been his age, or younger. Dreaming ... and the wrong place to dream.

Joey Cann was the loser. While he had stood near to the monument around him the cemetery had emptied. Joey, the footman, had lost the eyeball.

He turned away. The rain ran on his spectacles and he dragged them off and wiped them hard; without them the white posts were jagged blurs. He did not know whether he had shown out or whether he had fouled up. He could not say that he had been seen, or whether the bulk of the monument – the sleeping artillery-shredded lion – had masked Mister as he'd walked out of the cemetery's far side and disappeared into the network of small streets above it. There was a story written into the history of the Church of the day when twenty executive officers and higher executive officers had been deployed to follow a Colombian from a bank meeting in the City of London. Five lost the target in the first Underground station. More had been scattered as the target had changed trains on his journey. Three out of twenty had reached Heathrow with him. No one in authority could blame him for being dropped by his target, but he blamed himself. He left the cemetery. The rain was sprayed in headlights, spattered off the glistening road, and soaked his trousers.

Going down the hill, first on Patriotske liga and then on Kosevo, he walked fast. Then, abruptly, he crossed a small park that separated Kosevo from Alipasino. He went past the fortress of the guarded American embassy, could see only the roofs of the buildings behind the high walls. The flag above them was limp and the floodlights burned brightly. Guards eyed him, a camera swivelled to train on him. Joey was trained in footman surveillance, not in the counterculture. He had passed the tests, flying colours and praise from the instructors, in following, not in being followed. The sense of failure overwhelmed him. The failure, an itch in his mind, shut out a cooler response. Tears smarting in his eyes, he did not wave down taxis, didn't jump on buses. His nightly report would list Mister's movements, the tourist trail around old trenches above Sarajevo and lunch in a fish restaurant above Pale, and his drive to the meeting with Ismet Mujic and the unloading of more boxes that had been taken into the apartment. It would not speak of failure. He remembered how it had been in the room occupied by the new men and women recruited to Sierra Quebec Golf; Gough's harsh, staccato introduction, the hostile suspicion of the eyes that had glared at him, the interloper.

With the rainwater dripping off him, he stamped into the hall of his hotel, didn't respond to the friendly inquiry from the reception clerk as to whether he'd had a good day, and hurried for the stairs, his room and dry clothes. He never looked back, never saw the reaction of the snubbed clerk.

A hand palmed a banknote across the table to the value of one hundred German marks. It represented a quarter of the monthly wage paid to a hotel reception clerk, and won an answer. 'Joey Cann, room 239, from London.'

Another banknote, another hundred marks, slipped into the clerk's hip pocket and the name was fed into the hotel computer. A bill was printed out then passed over the desk. It was scanned. A name, a passport number, no address beyond London SW17, no occupation given, itemized food and coffee, one call made on the room's telephone.

A final question, and another banknote: was Mr Cann alone? He was travelling with a woman, separate rooms, a very smart woman – a lady. Hands were shaken, smiles were exchanged.

Mister walked out into the rain and the falling darkness.

The number of the mobile telephone was known only to its owner and its owner's paymaster. Three calls were made from it that evening.

The trigger for the calls was a simple request for information. As soon as the bleep and vibration heralding the call had cut into the conversation in the crowded Italian restaurant in Victoria, its owner had left the table and gone to the toilets. He was never without that phone, pay-as-you-go. He had listened to the brief message left against a rumble of background traffic.

His first call was to the night duty officer at the National Investigation Service of Customs & Excise. He identified himself as the father of Joey Cann, and asked to speak to him. He was patched through to an extension number, and repeated himself. He was told, curtly, that Cann was abroad and apologized with humility. Buried in the workings of the mobile was an attachment that scrambled its number, preventing it being traced, placed there by a three-man electronics company from the east of London.

His second call was to a British Telecom engineer's home. The engineer worked in a building in central Bristol considered sufficiently sensitive to be unpublicized. From the building, telephone taps and the inquiries of covert law-enforcement organizations were handled. Among its many prized facilities was the ability to feed a number into a computerized system and receive back the name and address of the subscriber.

He waited in the toilet, left his wife and three colleagues, and their wives, at the table.

He was a detective chief inspector, on attachment to the National Crime Squad. A recent paper that he had read, 'Police Corruption Vulnerability Profiling', had offered a solid description of him, but he went unidentified and trusted because it was not the nature of the squad actively to search for culprits. He had known Mister since 1973 when he had been a probationer beat constable out of Caledonian Road and had taken the first small 'donation'. Now he was three years from retirement and had a record, with commendations, of distinguished service and a high detection rate. He was well regarded by colleagues and had successfully served in drugs, serious crime and robbery teams; he seemed to have a nose for guilt. He was regarded by those alongside him as arrogant and brash, with justification. The woman at the table, waiting for his return, represented his third venture into marriage; his income from the Crime Squad, paid monthly, was divided between what he kept and what he paid to the two women from the failed relationships. He was secretive about his policing methods, seldom shared, rejoiced in the title of 'a copper's copper'. It was whispered of him that he bent regulations, but that had never been proven. He should have made detective superintendent but promotion had been denied him for no articulated reason. It was likely that it had been blocked because he seldom hid an overweening contempt of his superiors and their dogma of political, sexual, ethnic and legal correctness; he was a 'thief-taker' and what the bosses wanted was a 'socialist pedagogue who was black and had a law degree in criminal sociology' – this was his familiar refrain when he bought the big drinks rounds for the juniors. Without the money Mister paid him he would have been as impoverished as a stray dog. He had no fear of being unmasked. His seasoned experience meant that he knew the system of internal investigation and covered his tracks with care. Most recently for Mister he had identified the location of a prison's Protected Witness

Unit, and the PWU number given to a prisoner, and had named a technician at a Home Office Forensic Laboratory to which incriminating fingerprints had been sent. For a quarter of a century, his arrangement with Mister had been mutually beneficial; he had received information on Mister's rivals and lifted them, always with evidence to convict. He had earned the right to promotion by his successes. Its denial had added a hatred of the system he served, he had no qualms about what he did – and the money kept coming.

His telephone bleeped, tickling the palm of his hand. He listened and wrote down what he was told, for the sake of accuracy.

He made his third call. He heard the distant traffic.

'Joey Cann works at NIS, the Church – he's abroad right now. The subscriber on that number is Jennifer Martin, address is Ground Floor Flat, 219A Lavenham Road, London SW18. Got it?' The connection cut in his ear.

The piece of paper, torn into many pieces, was flushed down the pan. He returned to the table to resume as its life and soul.

He looked around, saw nobody who he thought watched him, and lightly rapped the door at the back of the van. 'Me,' Joey said.

He was let in. He scrambled into her territory. There was a dull light inside, like a photographer's dark room. Maggie was squatting on her stool in front of her console. He avoided the bucket, saw that it was a quarter full. Beside it were her sandwich wrappings, two apple cores and an empty Pepsi tin. He looked at the screen. The camera, trained on the hotel main door, was bolted on to the dashboard top and was covered in yesterday's newspapers.

She grimaced. 'God, you smell nice – going somewhere I don't know about?'

'Got soaked, had a shower, changed.'

'Bloody marvellous – I'd give an arm right now for a shower and clean tights.'

The log, written in her neat copperplate hand, recorded that Target Two and Target Three had returned one hundred and eighty-five minutes earlier, that seventy minutes earlier Target Three had exited and driven away in the Toyota, that sixty-six minutes earlier the beacon signal had been lost, that fourteen minutes earlier Target

Three had been dropped back at the hotel by a taxi.

'Is he back?'

'I thought you were supposed to know.'

'What I'm asking – is he back?'

'Steady down – yes, he's back. Didn't I log it? His door was unlocked eighty-four minutes ago.'

'Do I have to ask twice every time? Make something complicated where it should be bloody simple. "Is he back?" "Yes, he's back." Thank you. Now we've established he's back, please tell me what he's doing.'

'Who bit you this evening?'

'Second time – what's he doing?'

'Don't know – so you don't have to ask twice, I don't know what he's doing.'

'God . . . What do you *think* he's doing?'

'I'm never a pessimist – if you were to ask me to tell you, not on oath, I'd say he's moving the furniture round. Before that he was tapping the walls and the ceiling.'

'Shit.' Joey mouthed it.

'Take a listen for yourself . . .'

She passed him the earphones. It might have been a chair dragged across the carpet, or drawers pulled out from the chest and dropped, or wood being torn from its holding glue.

Maggie wrenched the earphones off his head. 'You lost him, didn't you?'

He said, tried to summon defiance, 'Contact was broken, yes.'

'You bloody showed out, didn't you?'

After a little more than an hour and a half of searching, Mister found the bug. He had gently tapped his way round the walls of the room, and stood on a chair to tap the ceiling. It had been a methodical, close search. He had taken all the pictures off the wall and had unscrewed the ventilation grilles and the power points. He had satisfied himself that the walls, ceilings, grilles and electric fittings were clear, then he had taken the back off the TV set, stripped down the bedside radio, prised the cover off the telephone and had unplugged it at the wall socket to break the link of an infinity transmitter using the receiver's microphone.

He had turfed the sheets, blankets, pillows and coverlet off the bed, then heaved off the mattress and minutely examined the legs, headboard and base. He had taken the drawers out of the desk supports, stripped his clothes from them. He had gone through the bathroom with the same precision, looked under the bath, looked at the shaving and hair-dryer plug points, had removed the bath's side cover, stretched his hand into the space and lit it with his pencil torch. He had turned his attention to the wardrobe. His suits and best shirts were on the floor, and his shoes. He worked from the bottom of the wardrobe to the top.

In the east of London, at Romford, was a three-man business with whom Mister had an association. Thoughtfully, and with an eye for the future, he had provided start-up funds for their business, but Mister's connection with them was well buried and did not appear on their company paperwork. His small initial investment had paid handsomely, but he had never called in the debt. The business, run from a shabby and unprepossessing industrial park, supplied state-of-the-art bugs, cameras, homing beacons, scanners and recording equipment to a smartly appointed shop in the West End's Bond Street. It sold its goods mainly on the Middle Eastern Gulf market; the best money-spinner was the lightweight beacons attached by princes, sheikhs and emirs to the ankles of their hunting falcons. The shop gathered in the money, and the three men in the industrial park each worked seventy-hour weeks to satisfy demand. Mister had never asked to be repaid his investment: what he demanded was to be kept up to date on the latest, most sophisticated devices that could be used against him. From his continuing contact he knew of most of the equipment available to the Secret Intelligence Service, the Security Service, GCHQ, the National Crime Squad, the National Criminal Intelligence Service and the Church ... what was on offer, and where it could be hidden.

Because he stood on the chair and was close to the woodwork at the top of the wardrobe, because his torch beam played on the joins at the angles of the wood screen, he saw the faint scrape where the join had been loosened. The wood creaked and small splinters fell from it as Mister dragged it apart.

It was smaller than anything the men in the industrial park at Romford had shown him. He grinned to himself. The bug, he thought, was the most recently developed and most miniaturized,

228

and it had been used against him. The grin was because he felt that *respect* was being shown him. His anger slackened. He looked at the box, the wires and the listening probe slotted into the wood, and he considered . . . There were options open to him. He could leave it where it was and feed false information into it, get the Eagle in and talk riddles, discuss bogus travel movements, but no message would then be sent. He could go down the third-floor corridor, take Atkins's radio, put the volume to full, hold the radio beside the probe's microphone, throw the on switch, and blast the ears that would be listening under headphones, but that would not send the message he wanted. He could swear down the link, blasphemies and obscenities, and laugh raucously, but that would lessen the message.

He left it in place.

He put his room back together, undid the chaos of his search.

He stripped out of the suit with the mud wet on his knees, scraped the caked clay off his shoes, then took a long shower and dressed for dinner.

Standing on the chair, he took down the box, the wires and the probe, then used the flat of his hand to hammer the joins on the wood screen back into place. He took the bug out of his room and walked briskly down the corridor, down three flights of stairs, across the atrium hall, through the swing doors and out into the spitting night. He hurried because he did not want his clean suit and clean shoes to get wet from the rain.

They watched the screen. The bright lights of the hotel's porch roof flared the picture and burned out the face of Target One, but as he came forward the picture compensated. He was whistling to himself, amplified and tinny over the van's speaker.

Maggie tilted the joystick control and the camera tracked with him.

Joey breathed hard. He was against her back, could feel the warmth of her, peered over her shoulder.

He went into the centre of the car park. A taxi flashed him with its headlights, but he smiled and gestured that he didn't need it. Mister looked around him and saw what he wanted. The camera followed him towards a rubbish bin at the edge of the car park. He never looked around or hunted for them, as if they weren't important, as if he knew they were there. He was beside the bin, his arm moved, and the box, the wires and the fine probe dropped at his feet. The speaker carried its clatter. The box had bounced on the gravel but was still now and the twisted wires lay on it. A polished shoe was raised. Mister stamped twice on the box. The speaker reverberated once, then the silence was around them. Mister bent, picked up the pieces of the box and the wires that had detached from it. He snapped the probe in half, and dropped it into the rubbish bin. He wiped his hands, rubbed the rain off his hair, turned for the hotel's door, and disappeared inside.

'Well, go on . . .' she said.

Joey looked blankly at her.

'Didn't your mother ever tell you, "Waste not, want not"? I can rebuild it, so go and get it.'

He thought she enjoyed the moment.

'You were the one who showed out, remember – so just get it.'

Joey said feebly, 'I don't know where or when. I just don't understand at what moment I showed out.'

"Winners and losers", as I recall. It's quite simple. You weren't good enough. You overvalued your capability. Please, just go and get it.'

Joey slipped out of the back of the van and went towards the rubbish bin. He had never felt so miserable, so worthless – not when the letter had dropped into the box of his parents' tied cottage to tell him his exam results had been inadequate for a college place, not when the Sierra Quebec Golf team had drifted in from the Old Bailey. Always, before, he could have blamed others. This time, only he carried the blame . . . He retrieved the pieces from the rubbish bin and carried them back. In the van she examined them.

He had not brought everything: he had missed the snapped-off head of the probe. He was told what he had missed. He went a second time to the rubbish bin, groped in it and couldn't find the length of the broken probe. He pulled the wire frame out of the bin, shook it out and crawled among the debris until he found it. He brought the piece back to her, and left the rubbish scattered.

She smiled, winked at him, and put it into a bag with the box and the wires. She closed down the camera, switched off the audio console and climbed into the van's driving seat. She offered no explanation as they drove along Zmaje od Bosne then on to the Bulevar Mese Selimovica.

They sat in silence, and he nursed the hurt. The rain had lifted a shallow mist off the road, the warehouses and darkened factories. At first the beacon was faint. The light on the screen and the bleep drew them. They reached the junction for the turning to the airport. The building on the corner had had a massive tower that was collapsed now in huge concrete shapes. The beacon was stronger. The van's headlights found an encampment of caravans, lorries and bell-tents. They drove off the road and on to a mud track. The wheels spun, but she had control and edged past the camp. The light on the screen and the bleep intensified. He saw the fire engine, men with hoses and a crowd of dancing, leaping urchin kids. The smoke from the burned-out skeleton of the Toyota sagged in the wind. She gazed at the scene.

'Not bad, eh? Still working.'

He tried to summon the pith of sarcasm: 'I suppose you want me to go and retrieve it?'

'It's OTTER, didn't I tell you? That's One Time – Throw Away. What a star, still going after that sort of fire.'

'Are we on a test-to-destruction exercise?'

'We are merely confirming that you showed out, that the targets know of our surveillance – cheer up, look on the bright side.'

'Does it get worse?'

'Doubt it. You showing out should make it all the more challenging. It could be, at last, interesting.'

February 1997
He already wore his heavy calf-length underpants under his pyjamas, a vest and thick woollen socks. He crawled from his bed on to the floor. The bed legs had been unscrewed and burned for warmth. He reached the solid old table that he would never chop up for the fire, heaved himself upright, went to the door and lifted down his heavy coat. Dragan Kovac would never be parted from that coat, which was twenty-five years old and a symbol of his past. Most of its front buttons were still in place; they were dulled but still, if he squinted at them, he could see the rampant eagle head embossed on them. The coat reminded him of the days when he had been a man of importance, the police sergeant, just as the table

reminded him of the blessed days before his wife had been taken from him.

There had been an explosion in the night.

Without the help of the Spanish soldiers it would not have been possible for him to move back into his house. They had strung a great canvas sheet over the roof tiles that kept out the rain but not the damp. They had sealed the windows with planks, had replaced the broken chimney stack with a tube of silvery metal, but it smoked if the winter gales came from the east or the south. They brought him the basics of food, and paraffin oil for his lamp, and nagged that it was not a fit place for an elderly man to live on his own. But, he was back, and he would not shift before his Maker took him. Then he would be buried in the graveyard above Ljut beside his wife, below a rough-chiselled stone cross. The family with whom he had been force-lodged in Griefswald had packed his bags for him a full forty-eight hours before the mini-bus had come to collect him.

The crisp sun lit the valley.

From the door, looking down, he saw Husein Bekir with his fundamentalist son-in-law. Dragan Kovac spat a gob of mucus on to the concrete path that led from his front door. If they wore that uniform, camouflage markings and forage cap, they were fundamentalists and war criminals. He had no doubt of it. It was his surprise that a decent man like Husein Bekir – avaricious for land and money, but decent – allowed the man his daughter had married to flaunt that killers' uniform. He would speak to Husein about it when the fundamentalist criminal had returned to his unit . . . The uniforms, he had been told in the transit camp before he had returned to Ljut, were the cast-off clothes of the American army, and the weapons with which they were issued were American; their instructors were American, and they would have American advisers when, finally, they attacked the defenceless Serb people and drove them from their homes. It was what he had been told and he believed it. He believed, also, that this criminal soldier would have killed Serb babies and Serb women without mercy; he had been told it.

Husein and his son-in-law were at the far riverbank, away from the ford.

Since he had come back, Dragan Kovac had spoken twice to his neighbour. The Spanish soldiers had told him, repeated it, drilled it into him as though he were an idiot, that he should not step off the track that went down to the ford or up to the village. They had asked him where the mines were laid, but his memory was hazy and he could not remember what type had been sown, in what quantities, or where. Dragan had walked twice down to the ford, on the hard track, and they had shouted across the river to each other. How was Husein? He was fine. How was Lila? She was fine. How was the house? It was fine . . . That was the first time. The second time they had shouted over the water about the weather, about the volume of the rainfall and that it was worse than any year since 1989, and about small things, and about his friend's hope of being given a new tractor . . . No politics, and nothing about the mines. When the water level fell, when it was possible for Husein Bekir to cross the ford, he would come and they would play chess, and Dragan had promised to cook for Husein and fill him with brandy while they played.

The previous day, the son-in-law had slung a rope with a grapple-hook tied to its end over the river and dragged it tight till the claws caught fast in a withy clump then knotted his own end to an alder's roots.

Perhaps Husein's memory was better than his own, or perhaps the son-in-law was merely lucky and had the arrogance of youth. Hanging from the rope, the young man had hauled himself over the river. Even at that long distance, Dragan had observed the fretted anxiety of Husein as the son-in-law searched for the mines. They were the ones on stakes that were fired with trip-wires. Much of the grass was still thin from the fire Husein had lit before Dragan's return. The son-in-law found four of what the Spanish soldiers called the PMR3 fragmentation mines, which they said were the most dangerous. The fire would have burned the nylon wires, but the mines had survived the fire. Dragan had thought it crass stupidity, but the son-in-law with the four mines had gone along the bank of the river and he'd lost sight of him where the wood came down to the water. An hour later he had come back without the mines . . . He watched the young man cross the river on the rope then walk along the riverbank towards the tree-line.

There had been the detonation in the night, then silence.

He put on his boots, tied them loosely, and stamped off down the track. He shouted for Husein to join him and wove towards the ford.

He kept to the centre of the track. He felt good now, but he thought Husein walked less steadily than he remembered, and Husein was a year and seven months younger than him. He waited until Husein reached the ford and felt satisfaction that he walked less well than himself. And Husein, also, had poorer hearing, so Dragan had to shout above the tumble of the water to be heard.

'What's *he* . . .' Dragan spat into the river and saw his phlegm bobble before being carried away '. . . what's he doing?'

'Yesterday he picked up four of the mines and moved them.'

'That's the job of a fool.'

'He said we should eat meat – that we eat too much of the soya and pasta shit that the military brings.'

'I heard a mine in the night,' Dragan replied sourly. 'The soya and pasta is good enough for me.'

'But not for my son-in-law. He took four mines from the field to the trees and looked for the tracks of deer. He moved the mines to kill a deer.'

'Has he killed a deer?'

'He's gone to see what he has killed. If it's a young deer it's good. It is God's gift. If it is a fox then the risk he took was wasted – he says we should eat meat.'

Dragan, with the pomposity given him by his police overcoat, said, 'It is better to have a life and limbs than to have meat.'

'He says he knows about mines.'

'Then he's a fool – you should eat pasta and soya.'

'Only once have we had fish since we came back. We need more than pasta and soya, the children must have meat if they are to grow . . . It is because of your people that we have the mines in my fields.'

'The mines were put in the ground to protect us from barbarian criminals – like your son-in-law. Our officer called them "defensive mines".'

Husein Bekir had spread his arms, waved them as if to call on God as a witness, and raged, 'You shelled us, you fired on our homes.'

'You came and slit our throats in the night. You would have killed me.' The veins bulged in Dragan Kovac's throat as he bellowed his riposte.

'You fired shells on us, on our women and our children.'

'Enough, Husein Bekir, enough – can you not recognize that it is over, the war is finished?'

'How is the war over when your mines are still in my fields?'

Dragan laughed. 'I know the war is over when you are at my house and we play chess, and the brandy is on the table – and I will beat you on the table, and I will still be sitting when you are on the ground, drunk.'

'You have no skill at chess, you cannot hold liquor. Never had . . . never could . . . never will.' The laughter cackled across the water. And over the laughter was the crack of the explosion.

His friend, Husein, with the poorer hearing did not hear the blast. He still laughed. Dragan Kovac, the powerful man who had been in authority, cringed. The only time in his life he had ever run from the responsibilities of his position in Ljut was during the attack, and he had suffered – his God knew he had suffered – been imprisoned in the tower block in Griefswald as punishment for running. He had vowed then, many times, he would never flee his obligation again. He pointed to the wood. He stabbed at the wood with his finger. Husein Bekir's eyes followed the jabbing hand, laughter gone.

A narrow column of dark, chemical smoke rose from the heart of the trees, and above the smoke, crows circled and screamed.

Dragan saw Husein crumple. He said hoarsely, 'You cannot go there, friend. You have the children to look after, and Lila. You must not go.'

He had to strain to hear the voice. 'What if he is not dead? You said yourself . . .'

'Believe he is dead.' It was the nearest, spoken with gruffness, that Dragan could get to kindness. 'Believe it was quick.'

He watched as Husein turned and started up the track for his home. In the far distance he could see Husein's wife, daughter and grandchildren at the door of their ruined house, and others in the village were running to them.

The minefield was active, spawning, and its reach had spread because four mines had been moved by his friend's son-in-law, and two had exploded, but two more were now placed in new ground, where none had been before.

He thought the valley, cut by the river between the villages of Vraca and Ljut, was damned.

The wind caught the trees in Lavenham Road.

Jen heard the cat-flap go, snapping in the kitchen door.

She couldn't sleep. She missed him, that was God's honest truth. She hadn't needed the landlady, Violet, to tell her that she missed him. If she hadn't needed to get back to her two-room flat to feed the cat she would have slept in his bed. It would have been better to have been alone in his bed than alone in her own. Her cat, Walter, was a big black long-haired neutered male. He was a tie, demanding, and precious little affection from him repaid what she spent on his food. The cat never slept on her bed. He'd have been welcome enough but with the independence of his species he never took up the invitation.

Jen's flat was the whole of the ground floor of a narrow terraced house; she shared the front door with a couple with a baby who rented the floor above, but they were away and there wasn't the crying of the child to disturb her. Jen would have liked the reassurance of the cat on her bed and the crying from upstairs. It was the quiet of the house that disturbed her. The wind was in the trees and it sang high-pitched in the telephone wire from the pole to the house, and it scudded a carton down Lavenham Road that bounced erratically, noisily.

Cleaning Joey's room had been a waste of her time, but being there had been a comfort. Of course he'd be 'all right' . . . She heard the creak of the fence at the back of the house, loud enough to carry through the length of the building, and then there was a sharp, shrill cry, but very brief, as if Walter fought with a rival. She hadn't thought the wind fierce enough to shift the back fence. She snuggled further down in the bed. She had responsibility for the fence. She used the garden. A fencepost or a section of paling would cost a fortune. She started the big debate that usually ended in sleep. Would he ask her to marry him? Would she accept if he asked? If he didn't ask, by next Christmas, or in a year's time, would she ask him to marry her? Her mother sniped about it, talked about her neighbours' joy in their grandchildren, said she'd soon be too old, said it was wrong for babies to be born out of wedlock. The wind had come on harder. She heard the singing, creaking. The front bell rang, persistent and loud. The hands of her watch told her it was half past midnight. The finger stayed on the bell button. She staggered from the bed. Could it be

Joey? Could he be back, silly beggar, and not carrying his mobile? Could he have gone to Tooting Bec, then come on here, for her? She was out of bed and into her dressing-gown. The bell was a siren. It couldn't be Joey, he'd have rung her from Tooting Bec, from the telephone in the downstairs hall. She was into the hall, switched on the ceiling light. Through the frosted glass on the upper half of the door was the outline of a figure. The bell yelled for her. Then the silence, and the figure was gone from the far side of the door.

The door was on the chain. She opened it. She heard, didn't see it, a car driving away. There was a cardboard box on the mat.

Jen took the chain off, opened the door and lifted the top flap of the box. Then she screamed, howled at the wind.

Dougie Gough wondered whether he had expected too much of a young man without the necessary bedrock of experience. Another couple of days and he might, probably would, pitch Cann home. He read the report a second time.

> From: SQG12/Sarajevo, B-H
> To: SQG1/London
> Timed: 00.10 16.03.01
> Message Starts:
> Para One – Observed, with Box 850, Target One/Two/Three on drive round former city battlefields, presumably time-killing.
> Para Two – Observed, with Box 850, Target One/Two/Three visit apartment of IM. Boxes were carried into the apartment but cannot say what they contained.
> Para Three – Target One visited Lion cemetery, then returned to hotel.
> Message Ends

He thought it pretty damn thin. He rocked with tiredness. He had stayed on alone in the Sierra Quebec Golf room for two full hours after the last of the rest of the team had gone home, stayed for nothing.

He started for his bed in south-west London. He did not know, because he hadn't been told, that a call had come through that evening for Cann and that Cann's father had been informed that his son was abroad. He marched with a good stride for the bus-stop on the all-night route. Nor did he know, had no reason to, that Jennifer Martin lived a dozen streets, across two main roads, from where he would sleep.

At the bus-stop, Dougie Gough lit his pipe and waited – and wondered what in Sarajevo's day had been kept from him.

The guests at the City livery-hall dinner – black tie and stag – finished the last of their brandy and their port and hurried for their chauffeurs and taxis.

Cork had lost count of the times the minister had tried to catch his eye from the top table. He'd thought himself safe as the dinner broke up because the minister was surrounded by well-wishers. On the step, looking for a taxi, he was trapped.

'A lift anywhere, can I drop you?'

'Out of your way, I'm afraid – a taxi'll be along.'

The minister's car waited, the door open.

'I don't wish to press but the Secretary of State's taken an interest. Billy wanted to know where we were with Packer—'

'We never use *names* on the pavement, Minister.'

'So I told him you had assured me this creature was getting maximum effort – Billy's own constituency, two days ago, came out two from the top of the country's worst heroin-addiction areas, of course he's concerned, he has voters' complaints littering his surgeries – with maximum resources.'

'About spot on. I think I also warned you against high hopes of quick fixes. If I didn't, I should have.'

'I may call him "this creature", yes? Billy sees him as an affront to the government's whole law-and-order policy. Is he still in Sarajevo?'

'Not *locations* on the pavement, please.'

'Billy said it was intolerable that a man like – er – this creature could beat the justice system. I'm to be called in next week to say where we are, to give assurances. Don't get me wrong, I'm sure you understand the priority of this.'

'Of course . . . Sorry, must go.'

He saw the taxi's light a full hundred yards up the street. He ran. He bounced off guests who were nearer to it and waving for it. He was in the taxi. Through the window, as it pulled away, he heard the curses of those he'd queue-jumped. He'd do it in the morning, beat the ear of Gough – the privilege of rank. Had he been right to force the issue, to have the youngster, Cann, sent to Sarajevo? The clock ticked. Perhaps he'd drunk a little too much, perhaps he was too casual with the prescribed tablets for his blood pressure, but he sweated as the taxi speeded him home. Gough talked of patience . . . but that was a damned luxury.

'Do you know what he's done, what's "deal with it myself"?'

'Well, we've all changed rooms – we've lost our vehicle, or you have, and he has thrown a sophisticated listening device into a rubbish bin. That's what I know.'

Atkins needed to talk. He felt isolated. Dinner had been strained. As Mister had talked, a rambling monologue, he had also felt frightened. The Eagle had eaten his food, sipped his Perrier and, with the regularity of a metronome, every minute or so, had nodded his agreement to what was said. Going into the hotel restaurant, Mister had asked casually if the new rooms were satisfactory, and had not referred to the surveillance again.

He'd found the Eagle sitting in a corner of the atrium bar, half hidden by pot plants, alone in its late-night emptiness.

'Is that all of it?'

'I wouldn't have thought so.'

'It seemed a bit tame, what's happened at this end.'

'There's nothing tame about Mister, or haven't you learned that?'

At the Royal Military Academy, Atkins had enjoyed the classes on military history. He remembered. On the wall of one classroom was a reproduction print of the retreat from Moscow. He'd listened to the monologue, and seen the gloom and defiance of Napoleon. It had been a campaign too far, he should never have travelled. The worm ate at him . . . Sarajevo was Mister's Moscow. Von Goethe had written, and the lecturer had repeated it, of Napoleon: 'His life was the stride of a demi-god, from battle to battle, and from victory to victory.' At dinner, Mister had talked easily about the state of the aid programme going into Bosnia and the volume of charitable boxes needed, the numbers of lorries required to ferry them, the oppor- tunities provided. It was grand talk. He gave them a vision of a future where the lorries of Bosnia with Love criss-crossed the country, brought in dross and took out 'product'. Goldwin Scott had written, of Napoleon: 'If utter selfishness, if the reckless sacrifice of humanity to your own interest and passions be vileness, history has no viler name.' He seemed to have no care.

'He's under surveillance. He's targeted with an audio device. That's heavy . . . I didn't expect that – not here, anyway. You're close to him, much closer than me – surely you need to know what action he's taking.'

'I wouldn't ask and I wouldn't listen if I were told. It's called "accessory before the fact" or it's "accessory after the fact", depending – I don't need that. As a legal professional, my advice to you is to maintain a similar indifference.'

'It's not going well, is it?'

'What do you think? Good night.'

Mister had switched from the lorries and their trade to the wider horizons. He was above the small, confined world of London. He was going to an international stage. Electronically moved monies went too fast to be tracked. Commodities were needed on the global scale, and would be paid for without the petty restrictions of Value Added Tax and levied Customs duties. The vision was of a centre controlling a network of assets. The centre was Untouchable. Napoleon had said, 'The bullet that is to kill me has not yet been moulded.' Atkins had remembered the quotation, and been frightened. Mister talked of power, talked with arrogance, and neither he nor the Eagle dared contradict him. It wasn't going well and Mister didn't recognize it. He was a messiah but had only the Eagle and Atkins with him to play his disciples.

Atkins ordered another beer, swallowed it, and ordered another.

Joey said, 'She was hysterical, she couldn't put a sentence together, she was gone.'

Maggie was wiping sleep dust from her eyes. 'Start it again – start it all over again.'

'When she opened the box there was a plastic bag in it. On top of the box was a piece of paper. Written on it was my name, the room number, and the hotel's phone, even the international dialling code for Sarajevo.'

Maggie pushed herself up in her bed. She was hunched with her knees against her chest. He had been banging, frantic, at her door.

'In the plastic bag?'

'Her cat.'

'Oh, God. Tell me, come on.'

'The cat's called Walter.'

'Fuck its name – what had they done to it?'

'They must have caught it in the garden. It had only just gone out, it's a hunter. It goes out and—'

'Spare me the soundbites.'

'She loves the cat, the cat is—'

'We all love cats. Everyone loves cats, except dogs. What had they done to the cat?'

He sat on the end of the bed. She had draped a blanket over her shoulders. She noted, at that moment, a calm came to him. The choke in his throat was gone. There was no longer any emotion in his voice.

'She took the plastic bag out of the box and opened it. Her cat was in the bag. I don't know which they had done first. They had cut its head off and also sliced its stomach so its bowels were hanging out. She opened the bag and its entrails and blood went over her hall floor. The blood was still warm, and so was the cat's body. They knew who she was. She's a teacher, she's just my girlfriend, for fuck's sake. If they'd killed Jen, then I'd just have felt blind bloody anger and they'd have known – *he* would have known – that I'd have gone to the end of the earth to follow him. He enjoys inflicting pain. This is all about pain, not about elimination. She will never forget her cat was killed because of me, what I do – he'll have broken us. She was yelling for me to come back, first flight. She said that Packer wasn't worth it. It's how he destroys people . . . Jen's never been to the Custom House, she doesn't do the socials there with me, nobody's ever heard of her – how did he know about Jen?'

'Have you rung her from here?'

'On the first evening, when we'd just checked in, I—'

'On the room phone?'

Joey nodded. It hurt too much to admit the responsibility out loud. His head dropped. She didn't sneer at him, didn't hit him with sarcasm.

'Where is she now?'

He said, 'I told her to go to a friend's house, ring school in the morning, and stay away sick.'

'Has she spoken to the police? Can't she get protection?'

'I told her not to speak to the police, and not to ring the Church.'

'How did you explain that?'

'Gave her some crap about informers, touts – about leaking sieves, shit about not knowing who you can trust. She wasn't thinking straight enough to argue.'

She took his hand. 'Why did you do that, Joey? Why did you tell her not to ring the police or your people at the Custom House?'

'They'd call me home,' Joey said simply. He let her hold his hand. 'If they knew I'd showed out and that I was identified by name, they'd call me home.'

'You'd better sleep in here with me, but you're on the floor.'

She threw him a blanket and watched him settle on the carpet. She switched the light out.

Chapter Eleven

They were getting out of the car, off the main road, in front of steel-shuttered gates, when the klaxon sounded behind them. The lorry had slowed but kept going.

Mister turned, saw Bosnia with Love on the side, and the Eel in the cab waving to him, before the lorry accelerated away down Bulevar Mese Selimovica, going away from the city. He waved back. It was the last time that the lorry would return to London empty. The next time the lorry rolled for the frontier it would be carrying 'product'; this time it carried, in a pouch fastened to the base of the driver's seat, a short, affectionate letter to the Princess, and instructions to young Sol for the transfer of monies from a Cayman account to a Cypriot bank in Nicosia.

For a moment, deep inside himself and hidden from the Eagle and from Serif, he felt a small sensation of loneliness. For that moment he almost wished himself into the cab beside the Eel and going home to what was familiar.

They walked to the gate and one of Serif's men produced the keys that unfastened a rusting padlock. The heavy chain was freed, and the gates scraped open. It would be his Sarajevo base, the site from which he would launch his new career. It was the heart of Mister's grand design. He was told that it had once been the transport head-quarters of the nationalized electricity company. He stepped through the gate after Serif, followed by the Eagle, then looked around him. The compound was enclosed by high walls that were concrete rendered except where shell fire had hit them. The holes were filled with crudely placed cement blocks or sheets of old corrugated iron. The walls were topped with weathered coils of barbed wire. They were high enough, and the surrounding buildings low enough, to prevent the compound being overlooked. There were three steel-sided warehouses at the far end, and a small brick shed. The ware-houses had been burned out and were charred black, but the shed had survived without a direct hit. Rough repairs had been made, enough to proof the roofing against the weather and seal the sides. To the right side of the compound there was a mountain of wrecked vehicles, as if they had been bulldozed together after the artillery and the fires had destroyed them. Rubble, debris, glass shards were scattered through the compound and Mister's feet crunched as he walked towards the shed. It would be his place. There was a louder, abrasive crushing behind him, and he turned to see Atkins drive into the yard. He was at the wheel of the replacement four-wheel drive, a white Mitsubishi. It was more thousands of marks of outlay, a minor investment against what he would accrue when the lorries rolled home with the 'product' on board. Glass slivers and little showers of concrete spat from under the wheels. Atkins hurried to catch him.

He was led to the first warehouse. When the hatch door was pulled open he stared inside and blinked. As far as he could see were stacked boxes: every Japanese manufacturer's televisions, stereos and videos. The second warehouse was filled half with wheat, barley and flour sacks, and half with plastic racks of women's clothes. The third was empty. He noted the ramp for vehicle repair. It would have been the electricity company's maintenance workshop. One of the men came to Serif and whispered in his ear, pointed to the gate, and was dismissed.

The location was right, the facilities were right, but it was not Mister's way to show enthusiasm.

Serif eyed him, as if waiting for the opportunity to state something of importance, but holding back for a better moment. Fuck him, he thought. They went to the shed. Coffee was made. A radio played local music. An electric fire made a fuggy heat. He took off his jacket, and so did Atkins. Neither carried a firearm, but he noted that Serif kept his jacket on. He spoke of the arrangements he had made for the transfer of monies, because the deal was signed and the contract agreed. The statement of importance from Serif, when it came, was a question that surprised him.

'You were followed in Sarajevo, you were tracked, who . . . ?'

'I said I'd deal with it – I have dealt with it.'

'Who followed you, from what agency?'

'One man from Customs in UK. It's not a problem, I dealt with it.'

'What does "dealt with it" mean?'

'They'll pull back, ship out. You can forget it.'

'My question that concerns me: can the Customs in UK send a man to Sarajevo and track you without notifying the authorities here? Is permission not required?'

Mister turned to the Eagle. 'What's the position when they operate abroad?'

The Eagle said, 'It's quite clearly laid down. Couldn't just come in here like tourists and operate clandestinely. That would be cowboy. They would require written authorization in Sarajevo from a government minister or a senior official or a judge.'

Mister thought it was the answer Serif expected. There was a silence round them. Words moved soundlessly on Serif's lips, as if names flicked on to and off his tongue, as if his mind turned over a list. His head went up and he stared at the ceiling as he pondered. He must believe he owns, Mister thought, all the ministers in the city, all the officials with influence, and all the judges of importance – except one. Abruptly Serif cracked his fingers as if by elimination he had decided which of them he did not own . . . Then he threw the bomb.

'You said you would deal with it, had dealt – but you are still tracked, followed.'

Mister merely rolled his eyes, raised an eyebrow, queried it. Serif put down his coffee cup, went to the shed door and beckoned. Mister followed him. The Eagle and Atkins scraped back their chairs and made to go with him but he waved them back. They walked across the compound. The red mist played in his mind but he smiled, as if the matter was of no consequence. He felt rare, raw anger. They reached the closed gate. In the steel plate, at a man's eye height, was a hole the size of a large screw's head. Serif had to strain up on his toes to peer through it, then backed away. He stood aside. Mister bent his head slightly, looked through the hole and up the rutted street leading from the compound to the main road. He saw the traffic – buses, lorries, vans, cars, jeeps – on the Bulevar Mese Selimovica's eight lanes. He saw the pedestrians on both pavements going slowly against the wind. He saw tower blocks beyond the road.

He saw him . . . He saw Joey Cann.

Cann was sitting on a concrete rubbish bin where the street joined the road and seemed to shiver as the wind that funnelled down the road snatched at his anorak and his hair. Mister watched him take off his spectacles, wipe them hard on a handkerchief, then replace them . . . There should have been telephone calls from bright-lit rooms in the Custom House, in the small hours of the night, from the high men of the Church to the hotel. Calls should have been pumped through the switchboard of the hotel by the clerk who had eased money into his hip pocket. The high men should have ordered Joey Cann to pull out, quit, run. There should have been packed bags, empty rooms, and a stampede for the airport.

But Cann sat on the rubbish bin and did not even make a pretence of concealment. Mister backed away from the spyhole. He smiled again but his nails dug into his soft palms and his knuckles were white, bloodless, with the effort of it. He went back towards the shed. Among those who knew him, the few who were close enough to watch, it was unthinkable for Mister to act when his temper was shredded. Rules he lived by were seldom broken. At the shed door Serif took his arm. 'What will you do?'

'I will deal with it myself.'

'It is what you said before.'

'Myself. I don't want, need, help. Ourselves.'

Mister pulled open the shed door. He waved, a short, chopped gesture, for the Eagle and Atkins. He led them away into the yard. As he said what they would do, his finger jabbed in emphasis. The spittle from his fury bounced on Atkins's face and the Eagle's. It was personal, an insult. He would not turn the cheek to an insult, never had.

*

'Sounds to me as if that's not in your bloody precious manual,' Maggie had said.

She was parked up off the road. Except when high-sided lorries went by she could see him. He was so small. He sat on the rubbish bin and his legs were too short for his feet to rest on the pavement. He seemed to blanch in the wind that carried sheets of newspaper and empty packets up the pavement and the road around him. He had stepped over an undrawn line, and she'd told him that. He hadn't listened, but had slipped away from the van when she'd parked and walked back to the junction of the road and the street leading down to a warehouse complex, and he'd jerked himself up on to the rubbish bin. She had the camera on him, at that range a tiny blurred figure, and she had the tape running on a loop . . . She saw Joey ease himself off his perch. He walked away from it carelessly, back towards her. When he looked behind him, every dozen strides, the wind lifted his hair, pulled it up to the roots, which made him look younger, and without protection. She'd seen the Mitsubishi turn into the street, driven by the former soldier, as Joey would have done. He'd been loitering then, but almost immediately afterwards he had taken to the perch on the rubbish bin. He'd have moved because the gates were opening and started his walk away up the pavement towards her. But it wasn't the Mitsubishi that appeared from the street and waited to join the traffic, it was Target One. To her, he seemed a small, insignificant figure, hunched in his overcoat. He came out of the street on to the pavement, turned and walked towards Sarajevo's centre. Why walk? Why go alone? Why not ride? Joey was following, a hundred yards behind, and matched the quick stride of Target One. She did not know the manner of it, but she recognized that a man-trap was set.

Atkins thought he tramped a treadmill, and did not know how to get off.

'This isn't a discussion,' Mister had said, and stabbed his finger into Atkins's chest. 'I'm not asking for advice, I am telling you how it is. It's not for talking round, it's for doing, doing the way I say it.'

By driving the new Mitsubishi, he walked the treadmill. He'd bought the Toyota outright, but the Mitsubishi was cash up front for rental. The vehicle had been stolen, four days before, from the parking area outside the apartments occupied by the International Committee of the Red Cross, and the ICRC logo had been spray-painted off the doors, new number plates fitted and an additional set, with different numbers, lay on the floor behind him. It handled easily and well. He took it out into the traffic flow. Mister was a full three hundred yards ahead of him, and the tail – as the man had been described to him – was a hundred yards behind Mister. He idled the engine and scanned the road ahead. The Eagle had said nothing, hadn't protested, hadn't joined in when Atkins had queried his instructions and been slapped down. Ahead of him were the fruits of an effort to brighten the route into the city. New trees had been planted in the grass between the road and the pavement, supported to give them stability by tripods of wooden stakes, and interspersed between them were high street-lamps. He eased the vehicle forward. The Eagle's eyes were closed and he was breathing hard. Atkins held the slow lane. He should have had notice of this, should have planned and rehearsed it, but it was on the hoof and he hadn't dared dispute it further with Mister. From the slow lane he would accelerate towards the tail and Mister, then pick the moment, swing at increased speed between the new trees and the street-lamps, hit the pavement, straighten, take the target square on the radiator grille, pull back between the obstacles, bump over the kerb, and swerve into the fast lane. The way Mister had said it, it had seemed so easy. It was beyond anything Atkins had ever done in his life – and the sweat ran on his back and across the pit of his gut. Each gap between the new trees and the street-lamps was as good as the last, as good as the next.

'Do it in your own time,' Mister had said. 'Just do it when you're ready.'

He recognized that Mister kept the pace steady, so that the tail's pace and position could be estimated, and the timing of the surge through the gap could be more exact. It couldn't fail, if he had the will . . . it was murder. In the army he had never killed, never fired a weapon in anger. Bosnia, with the blue beret force, the source of his casually told war stories, had seen him in the ditches and crouched behind the sandbags, trembling and close to wetting himself, just like all the other guys. Mister would have done it, wouldn't have hesitated, but Mister played the decoy, wasn't there to stiffen him, and the Eagle shook, uncontrolled, beside him. He was alone. Atkins edged up through the gears, speed surging, and picked out a gap between the new trees and the street-lamps, his eyes tunnel-focusing on the head and shoulders, back, hips and striding legs of the tail.

'No need to be scared. Just imagine I'm holding your hand,' Mister had said.

It seemed to unfold so slowly in front of Maggie.

She started to shout into the microphone clipped to her blouse, incoherent. She'd said to him that if he insisted on going through with this ludicrous, unprofessional surveillance procedure, she'd only be a part of it if he listened, and bloody close, all the time to his earpiece. She yelled, and the white Mitsubishi was going faster and closing on him, but his stride speed never altered. A young woman with a pram and her shopping in plastic bags balanced on it had passed Mister and walked towards Joey. Maggie could see through which gap the Mitsubishi would go. It was going too fast for it to be a shooting hit. The distance between her van and Joey, for the earpiece to pick up her screamed warnings, was too great. He should back off, take cover, dive. He should ... She hit the van horn, smashed her clenched fist down on it, again and again, beat a tattoo with it. The woman with the pram and the shopping was near him. The Mitsubishi lurched as the nearside wheels bounced on the kerb, skidded on the grass, found grip, then aimed for the gap. The cacophony of the horn dinned in her cab, and Joey stopped, turned. Beside him, frozen, petrified, was the woman with the pram. Maggie saw Joey throw himself at the woman and she fell away from him, the pram toppling over, her shopping scattering.

The edge of the Mitsubishi's fender caught him.

No pain, but he felt himself tossed upwards, and he thought he floated. No sound, as the flank of the vehicle swept past him. He fell. The breath was driven out of his body, and everything around him was blurred.

Joey lay on the wet grass, the damp from it seeping into his clothes, and he gasped.

The woman picked herself up, righted her pram, and scooped up the shopping strewn around him. She never looked at him. When he squinted, screwed his eyes together, he thought he could make out the shock on her face. She said not a word, merely scurried away, pushing the pram along the pavement. He thought he had saved her life, and her baby's life, and her shopping, but she had nothing to say to him – then the pain spilled in him.

A man came past him, going towards the city, and didn't look down at him. Two youths, smoking, went by him, going away from the city, and seemed not to see him. Was he *invisible* to them as they hurried on their different ways? Fuck you, he mouthed. He groped on the grass for his spectacles, found them – bent arms but the lenses intact. He put them on, wedged them at a clown's angle on his nose. The pain ran through his leg and hip. Far down the road, the Mitsubishi slowed to a stop and Mister disappeared into it. Then it was gone, lost in the speed of the traffic. Only tyremarks on the grass showed what had happened. He crawled to a tripod of stakes holding erect a young tree and tried to pull himself up, but couldn't.

The van swept over the kerb and on to the grass.

From the windows of two black Mercedes, faces peered at him, shallow outlines against the smoked glass of the windows, and ducked away when he caught their gaze.

Maggie ran from the van, came to him and knelt. He thought, irrationally, that she didn't have to get her knees wet and her tights dirty on the mud in the grass.

'Are you all right?'

'I think I am – my leg hurts.'

'You tried to climb up, I saw you, against the tree.'

'I couldn't.'

'If you'd really hurt yourself you wouldn't have been able to get half-way up the tree, not if you'd done a bone.'

'You've a great bedside way. He tried to kill me.'

'But he didn't, that's the point.'

She reached over him and put her hand into the tear rip of his jeans that ran from the faded knee to the hip. Her fingers gripped at his bone and the flesh covering it. She'd the sensitivity, he thought, of one of those old, seen-it-all veterinary surgeons who had come to the estate and were taken by his father to see a lame heifer or a limping ewe.

She straightened. 'I don't think anything's broken – you were lucky. I expect it'll bruise up quite prettily.'

Joey flared. 'You were supposed to be watching my bloody back. I wouldn't have had to be *lucky* if you'd been awake. What about the goddam radio?'

He saw a small blood smear on her hand as she wiped it with her handkerchief.

'Didn't you hear me?'

He shook his head. She looked around. A frown settled on the delicacy of her forehead. Her gaze fastened on the PTT building back up the road and the antenna forest on the roof, the tilted mushroom dishes.

Joey said, 'Oh, that's good. Radio interference, too many spikes and bowls. Useful for you to know that when you get back. Be able to do something about that in the lab, won't you? It's very pleasing to know I've contributed to pushing along the frontiers of science. So, when did you cut your hand?'

A Discovery four-wheel drive pulled on to the kerb and the grass behind her. A man peered at her as if seeking confirmation.

She said, quietly, 'Must have done it on the wheel when I was hitting the horn.'

The man was angular, sallow, and his suit hung loosely off him. 'Isn't that Maggie? Isn't that the lovely Maggie Bolton, pride of the probe, terror of the bug technicians? You got a problem, darling?'

'Pardon my French, Mr Cann, but people like you are just a fucking nuisance here, and interfere.' He introduced himself as Benjamin Curwin. She called him Benjie.

Joey recognized him as one of the group of optimists around her at the ambassador's Commonwealth Day drinks session, when she'd worn the little black dress. Benjie had invited them in, insisted on it. He worked from the United Nations Mission for Bosnia-Herzegovina building two hundred yards up the road from where it had happened. Black coffee and a whisky generously poured into a crystal tumbler for Joey and a seat on a sofa where he could examine the rent in his trousers and feel the start of an aching stiffness, and an opportunity for them first to flirt-talk then slide to nostalgia. It was good-old-days time. Ignored and with bitterness rising, Joey thought that he was in the heartland of the men drafted in to run a country, and it was all so bloody smug. They'd gone through an outer office where secretaries had swooned with respect for a fat-cat hero. Benjie – Benjamin – wiped the mud off Maggie's knees, his hand hovering over her thigh, and they gossiped about times when the Secret Intelligence Service was run by officers, not bloody accountants, the brilliant days when the enemy was behind a curtain of minefields and fences, armed guards and dogs. He'd said, and she'd agreed, that present management's idea of a good day was lopping fifteen per cent off the Lisbon desk head's entertainment budget – what a bloody scandal. Joey had finished his coffee, swilled down his Scotch, and coughed hard, like he had work on his plate. Maggie had told Benjie – Benjamin – what had happened on the road, and why.

'I'm sure it's useful for me to have your opinion,' Joey said.

'You can have it, for free. We don't need you here, stirring the pot. We like it nice and quiet, the lid on tight. We want it so that we can control it. We came here – we were sent here – every man jack on this corridor, to achieve the impossible, the rebuilding of Bosnia-Herzegovina as a democratic multi-ethnic state, at a time when the international community fairly gushed with sympathy. We are resigned to failure. Criminality and corruption have beaten us. Our present brief is to fail without it being noticed. We do not want noisy killings on the streets, and the spotlight on us. We want to creep away unseen.'

'Sorry if that's inconvenient, but Sarajevo happens to be the centre of major investigation.'

'Bollocks, nothing important happens here. I tell you what I think. This is a boring, sleazy little provincial town. They believe they're somebody, they're not. They want to be recognized as the Anne Frank of the Balkans, so that everybody weeps for them. Save your tears. It's without romance here, you couldn't fill an egg-cup with drama in Sarajevo. The rest of the world has lost patience with them, is trying its damnedest to forget them. The place lives on a myth and the sooner they recognize that the better. As for you, go home.'

Joey said doggedly, like a stubborn kid, 'I am involved in a major investigation, as is Miss Bolton.'

'You want some excitement, young man, go down to Montenegro, that's where you'll find it by the bucketful. Serif? He's like every-thing else here, minor league. We may not like the way Sarajevo ticks, but at least we have the measure of it. Then in comes a little joker –

you, Mr Cann – and maybe upsets the cart and that makes my life harder. Walk away. Do your investigation some place else.'

'I have the full authority for intrusive surveillance, by Miss Bolton and myself, in this city from Judge Zenjil Delic. I'm legal, and—'

At the name, Benjie – Benjamin – seemed to jerk up on the sofa seat where he sat close to Maggie. It was as if everything said before had been for amusement. His glance stabbed at Maggie. 'Is that why you wanted that bloody name? It was all games, wasn't it, you clever little bitch?' He mimicked her voice. ' "Bet there's not one straight judge in this city, bet there isn't, bet each last one of them's bent." And I gave it you . . .' He stared at Joey. 'And you've conned him into signing on the dotted line. Jesus. He is gold dust. He's for a rainy day when something actually matters, he's not for some piffling fucking drugs inquiry. Have you compromised him? I'll wring your bloody head off your bloody shoulders if you have. You haven't, have you, compromised him?'

Joey walked heavily to the door.

The grated voice followed him. 'Get out of this city. You understand nothing.'

'The Eagle says you bottled out,' Mister said calmly.

He'd had an hour to prepare his response. Atkins had taken Mister and the Eagle back to the Holiday Inn, had dropped them there, then followed the new procedure. He'd driven the Mitsubishi, with the slight dent on the front nearside fender, to the warehouse compound, had been let inside and left it there, then walked up to the road and waved down a taxi to return him to the hotel. He'd thought his job was to escort the missile launchers and the communications equipment into the city, demonstrate their capabilities, and act as the trusted interpreter. Killing had not been in the brief. At the hotel he joined Mister and the Eagle in the coffee-shop. The Eagle gazed ahead of him, past Atkins's shoulder.

Atkins blurted, 'I don't know how he can give an opinion. He was crapping himself and had his eyes closed.'

'He was only telling me what he thought. I pay him to tell me what he thinks.'

'I did not bottle out.'

'Very pleased to hear that, Atkins.'

Atkins couldn't read the man. There was no menace in the voice, no inflection that would create fear. Mister spoke as if in gentle conversation. He thought of himself as being in an interview room alone with two detectives, and a tape-recorder's spools turning. The detective who led would have said, 'It was an attempt at murder, an attempt to kill a member of Her Majesty's Customs and Excise. If you didn't like the idea, weren't on board, why didn't you refuse?' The detective at the back would have slapped a fist into a hand for emphasis and said, 'Don't give us bullshit about coercion.' Maybe those detectives, maybe everybody else, had never heard Mister speak quietly . . . Mister's eyes were mesmeric. He could not escape them. He said feebly, 'I did the best I could.'

'Wasn't a very good *best*, was it?'

He blustered, 'I had him all lined up, I was going for him. Then beside him was this woman with a pram. He dived towards her. The cowardly shit used her to cover himself. I don't kill women or babies. If I'd gone after him I'd have hit the woman and the pram with the baby.'

'Did she come out of a manhole – push the cover up and lift the pram through it? Was there a manhole in the pavement? She popped up?'

'I didn't see her coming. I was just looking for him. I didn't have any help from Eagle. If his eyes had been open – and he hadn't been busy wetting himself – he could have called the woman and the pram for me. I hit the target, just a glance but a hit, if it had been a full hit, head on, then I would have taken out the woman and the pram. I'm not having killing women and babies on my conscience.'

'I'll look after your conscience, Atkins. I look after a lot of people's consciences.'

'It's the way it was.' Atkins's voice was a shrill whine.

'Do I criticize you? Calm down. Have a biscuit.'

He didn't want a biscuit, but he took one, held it in his hand and trembled. It cracked in his grip. He didn't want to look into Mister's eyes, but he couldn't look away. There was no light in the eyes; they had the quality of death. He knew that one day he would stumble through an explanation to two detectives in an interview room, and they would not believe him, and they would ask, again and again, why he had not walked away. He was Mister's toy, and toys could be thrown away ... He was expendable. Napoleon had said, to Metternich, in 1810: 'You can't stop me. I spend thirty thousand men a month.'

'I'm sorry,' Atkins said, and despised himself.

'You sent that?'

'Two things, and you'd better remember them, Joey. I don't work for your crowd, and it's not my intention to go home in a box.'

'You said it would be "interesting". Do I quote correctly?'

Maggie bridled. 'And I was wrong. I'm not so arrogant that I can't admit when I'm wrong.'

She switched off the small screen. He felt betrayed. She wound back the tape. The picture on the screen – she'd marched him from his room to the van and made him squat in the back, beside the bucket, and watch it – was good quality. It was now, he believed her, in London. It would be watched, each second of it. The white Mitsubishi, reduced to monochrome, veering out of the slow lane, heaving on to the grass, cutting a line towards Joey, a woman and a pram, him throwing himself at her, and ...

She said, 'You shouldn't worry. They'll all say you're a proper little hero.'

She asked him for Frank Williams's number and he gave it to her, didn't question why she wanted it.

'I'm going to find a bar.'

'That is being utterly pathetic,' Maggie accused.

He slammed the van door shut on her.

A biker couriered the tape across the Thames and along the Embankment, from Ceauşescu Towers to the Custom House. The package was delivered into the hands of the PA to the chief investigation officer. The instruction was given that there should be no interruptions, and the cassette was fed into Cork's VCR.

He settled in a comfortable chair and watched the screen.

Gough had been called from the Sierra Quebec Golf room. The meeting into which the summons had broken had reached the detailed stage where personnel were allocated to the raids he planned. Search warrants had been drafted in preparation for submission to a magistrate for approval. Large-scale Ordnance Survey maps, fastened with tacks to the walls, reproduced the streets of the Fulham district of west London, an area of the Surrey country-side and a section of roads immediately to the south of the capital's North Circular. But the call had come from on high, and the meeting was suspended.

He'd stood behind the comfortable chair. Cork said he had already seen the relevant part of the tape twice, but had not told him what it showed. Gough had his pipe, unlit, in his mouth.

Watching the picture gave him a curious sensation of non-involvement, of distance. It was a feeling Dougie Gough always experienced when he viewed surveillance tapes. He was not a foot-man, never had been. He was an organizer, an administrator, a decision-taker and a strategist. His skills were considered by his superiors too great for him to pound pavements or idle in cars. He sent men and women out, and he listened to and read through their reports when they came back from the field, and he felt – would never have shown it – envy . . . He peered hard at the screen. The tape was mute. Far from the camera, Joey Cann sat on a rubbish bin and his heels kicked its concrete sides. He remembered the young man, hesitant yet defiant, but committed. The camera's eye pitched Gough half-way across the mass of Europe to a wide road that ran between tower buildings and walled warehouses. He had no concept of Sarajevo but he was carried there by the lens and it seemed to him that he stood now within hailing distance of Cann. Men, women and children passed the camera, front on and back on, and Dougie Gough could have reached out and tapped their shoulders. He was trans-ported there.

No attempt at concealment, Cann sat in full view, then dropped off the rubbish bin and walked towards the camera eye. The lens zoomed on him. Dougie Gough saw tight lips, the muscles clenched hard in his cheeks, the jutting chin, and recognized the tension in him. Twice Cann glanced behind him, but kept walking. The third time he turned, Cann spun his body and retraced his walk. The camera panned wide. Dougie Gough had watched surveillance tapes of Albert William Packer and seen enough telephoto stills of his Target One. The two men walked away, separated by a distance of around a hundred yards. He never saw the face of Target One.

Dougie Gough felt a little winnow of excitement: everything he had read, been told, was that his Target One employed cunning and great care to avoid surveillance ... The camera jerked, the picture wavered, as the vehicle in which it was mounted edged forward. Basic precautions had been discarded on both sides, but Gough did not understand why.

Cann kept to the same stride, the same pace as the man ahead. A vehicle came by the camera, a white four-wheel drive, he saw it and forgot it. He had lost the two men, Packer and Cann, behind three lorries in convoy. He started to look at the tower blocks and was matching them to those on the outskirts of Glasgow beside the M8 motorway. As the lorries cleared the view of Target One and SQG12, he realized that the platform for the camera had sped forward, gone frantic. He felt his teeth tighten on the pipe's stem. He wanted to shout out, yell a warning. The white four-wheel drive came off the road – Cann turned – Dougie Gough saw the woman and the pram – Cann was the target. It happened quickly, the camera lost focus, the vehicle masked Cann, the woman and the pram before it was wrenched away. He saw the woman on the ground, Cann close to her, and the pram overturned. He said a little prayer, a begging plea. He could have shouted in relief as he saw Cann roll over, and the woman was pushing herself up then righting the pram. The focus on the camera was regained as Maggie Bolton ran into picture and knelt beside Cann ... Dougie Gough had never lost an executive officer, killed or injured, in three decades with the Church. He had never thought it remotely likely he would lose a man. It had been so fast.

Cork cut the picture and the screen went to snowstorm.

Gough took out his matches and lit his pipe. The smoke cloud hid the screen.

Cork passed him a single sheet of paper. He read.

To: Endicott, Room 709, VBX
From: Bolton (Technical Support), Sarajevo
Subject: Organized Crime/AWP
Timed: 14.19 (local) 17.03.01
Security Classification: Secret
Message Starts:
See enclosed tape – my C&E comrade survived unhurt a murder

attempt organized this a.m. by Target One. Vehicle used driven by Target Three.

Yesterday, unreported to C&E, my comrade showed out on surveillance of Target One, and a subsequent telephone call from his girlfriend, Jennifer Martin (address not known), reported her cat killed, disembowelled and dumped on her doorstep. Comrade's concern is that he will be called home!

Following the 'show out' my bug in Target One's hotel room was removed, and the vehicle fitted with my beacon was destroyed. I am exposed and without basic security. I request immediate pull out.

Luv, Maggie

Message Ends

Gough handed back the sheet of paper.

'I can't say I'm pleased at this development,' Cork intoned. 'They're going to bring her home. It's not a matter for discussion, it's their decision and they've taken it. Haven't you anything to say?'

Dougie Gough, acid in his voice, said, 'Beyond reminding you it was your order that he travelled, not a lot.'

'He should come home, shouldn't he, before it's – you know – too late?'

'If that's what you want . . .'

'I want your advice!' Cork railed at him, 'What's the alternative? Put in a team of half a dozen, drop a Special Forces section alongside them for close protection? Hack into a budget I don't have? God – I've a minister on my back. What do I do, Mr Gough?'

'You do not offer knee-jerk interference.'

Cork ignored the impertinence – wouldn't have if it had been offered by any other man or woman in the building. 'The buck stops on my desk.'

'You leave running the operation to me.'

'If anything happens to him, I'll be crucified.'

'If my Maker will excuse a vile blasphemy, Mr Cork, I'll expect to be on the cross next to you. I'd like to think about it.'

He already had. Gough left the room and his feet stamped hard down the corridor, down the stairs and down another corridor. He lit his pipe, sucked hard on it, and the smoke clouds billowed behind him. There was that look on Dougie Gough's face that warned off any of the senior, higher or executive officers who passed him in the corridors or on the stairs from telling him that the Custom House was a protected no-smoking zone. He made his way back to the room used by the Sierra Quebec Golf team. Had there been mirrors on those corridors, had he looked at them, he would have seen a reflected image, older of course, of the face on the tape: Cann's – lips, cheek muscles, chin, tension and commitment. He tapped the numbers into the pad and went into the room. They all looked at him, ten of them, and awaited the explanation as to why he had been called away.

'Right, gentlemen, ladies – where were we?'

December 1997

The rain fell hard, had done so each day that week. He did not know it, but again the mines moved, carried in the rivulets that ran from the slopes above his fields. Some were buried deeper in the silt brought down, but others had been washed out of the ground, and were exposed. Husein Bekir would not have known that he was responsible for the shifting life of the mines. By setting fire to the fields two years back, he had killed the grass roots that held the soil; he had released the ground from the binding roots and facilitated the movement.

His fatherless grandchildren walked with him down the track towards the swollen ford, with the Englishman who had come from Mostar.

They, he reflected between shouts towards the house across the Bunica river, were the strong ones. It was nine months since their father's death, but they had seemed to mourn him for only a day, not for weeks as he and Lila had, not for months as his daughter had. He called for his friend, Dragan Kovac, and the children echoed his shouts as if it were a game, skipped and ran ahead of him and the Englishman. The foreigner said his name was Barnaby and he spoke Husein's language, but nothing of what he said was welcome. The children were strong and did not act out roles as victims. Husein Bekir hoped that, one day, his grandchildren would know nothing of a war and would farm his fields in the valley.

The Englishman had arrived unannounced, had come to Vraca with his driver.

His grandchildren were like all those in the village of their age. They were thin, weedy, skinny. They had no muscle on them, and no sinew in their arms. The strength was not in their bodies but in their minds. They could dismiss the memory of their father, but they could not lift a hay bale. When Husein had been the age of his grandson, he could work outside all day and every day of the school holidays, and during termtime before school and after it finished in the afternoons. The sight of them steeled the determination of Husein Bekir that he must fight – in whatever time was left to him – to have the valley cleared so that good meat was produced and good vegetables, to build the bodies of his grandchildren. If their bodies were not built then they could never farm the land. If they did not farm the land it would be sold off. What generations of the family had achieved, put together with sweat, would be sold in an hour to a stranger, perhaps to a Serb.

There had been a meeting that week in Sarajevo.

It was more than twenty years since Husein Bekir had been in Sarajevo. Then, it had been a long journey by bus for him to travel to the distant city for the wedding of the son of a blood cousin of Lila. He had not enjoyed it and he'd thanked his God when the bus had pulled clear of the city. And the day before, and in the evening, at the wedding feast, he had been treated by Lila's cousins as a peasant. None of them owned land. They worked in the state's factories. He had thirty hectares, paid for, on his own side of the Bunica river and nineteen hectares of the finest fields on the far side, and two hectares of vineyard, also paid for. He had no debts. They had regarded him as a person without value. When it had left Sarajevo, the bus had gone past the Marshal Tito barracks, and he could recall them. Barnaby said that the meeting had taken place at the mine-action centre in the barracks.

He called to Dragan Kovac as a last resort, in the hope that his friend's argument might change the message brought from Sarajevo.

The rain spat down on him and plastered the hair of his grandchildren to their scalps. He saw Dragan Kovac at his door, sheltering under his porch, and he heard a muffled answering shout. He waved for him to come to the ford. They had played chess in the summer five times. Dragan Kovac would never come down the track, cross the ford and walk to Husein Bekir's home. Always Husein had to go to his house, to wade through the ford, and back again in the dark with the brandy swilling in his belly. And five times the fool – or the cheat – had beaten Husein Bekir. He saw Dragan Kovac emerge from the porch, and he was wearing his old coat, the Cetniks' coat, and he had on his old cap, with the eagle over the peak. The fool, the old fool, stomped down the track towards them. The country had been ruined by war, the valley was filled with mines, and he wore his uniform as if it still gave him importance. They waited. Dragan Kovac came slowly, stopped twice and leaned on his stick before starting again. Husein Bekir did not need a stick to help him walk.

'This is Barnaby. He is an Englishman from Sarajevo. He is from the mine-action centre. He wants to know about the mines you put in my ground.'

'Put because we were attacked – is your memory slipping, old man?'

'We did not put in any mines. Because you put mines down I cannot farm my fields.'

'To keep criminals away.'

'I told him that Dragan Kovac was senile, and would remember nothing.'

They both spat at the ground in front of their boots, it was their ritual. The grandchildren were throwing stones into the river. The Englishman was laughing. He was a big man, dwarfed Husein Bekir, and he had a fine bearing, a good stature, and the appearance of a military man. Heavy binoculars hung from his neck. He saw the old fool stiffen to attention and heard him bark a greeting.

'I am Dragan Kovac, sir, I am Retired Police Sergeant Kovac. May I be of help?'

'Maybe, maybe not, Mr Kovac. I was explaining to Mr Bekir that we had a meeting yesterday at the mine-action centre at which a number of mine-clearance proposals were considered. Right from the start I do not wish to raise false hopes. We have a list of thirteen thousand six hundred minefields in the country, of which one-tenth are in Neretva canton, here. But we try to look most closely at locations where direct hardship is caused by polluted ground, where a farmer cannot work, or where there have been casualties. Because you had a death here you are on that list. Today I was in Mostar, and

261

it wasn't a long journey to come up here, just to see the ground. I was hoping you might remember where the mines were laid.'

'And don't bluster,' Husein interjected. 'Give the gentleman facts.'

'I laid no mines.' Dragan Kovac jutted his jaw.

'The war is over. We're not talking about blame,' Barnaby said. 'I work with Muslims, Serbs and Croats as the consultant to both governments. I don't recognize flags – but neither do mines recognize the difference between soldiers and children. I have to know how many mines were laid and over how wide an area. If I have that information I can estimate, only roughly, how many de-miners will be needed, how long it will take, and how much it will cost. Do you remember?'

Dragan Kovac shook his head, looked up at the rainclouds, scratched his ear. 'It is very hard. I was not here all the time, after they attacked and tried to kill us.'

Husein Bekir said, 'You see? I told you the old fool remembers nothing.'

The Englishman had his binoculars up and gazed over the fields. 'I can see the bones of cattle out there. Extraordinary how long bones survive before they rot down, and they're in the middle of the fields. It's not surprising but it's a bad indication. The middle of the fields is not where the mines would have been buried. It means they've moved. Rain like this shifts them. People shift them. Foxes, it's hard to believe, will pick up a small anti-personnel device that's exposed, carry it off and put it down a hundred metres away. Then there's more rain and it's covered over. Even where there were correctly made maps, they cannot be relied upon. The minefield is an organism, it breathes, it has a pulse. There could be ten, there could be a hundred. It's a big area, it would take many men and much money, and the difficulties of one farmer are not a priority.'

'I don't know, I want to help but . . .' Dragan Kovac shrugged.

'When will you come?' Husein Bekir tugged the Englishman's sleeve.

'Not soon. I apologize for dragging you out on a filthy day. It certainly will not be next year.'

Husein Bekir stood at his full height and gazed at the Englishman's face. 'If I and my wife, my daughter and my grandchildren, all my neighbours, my animals and my dog make a line, walk across my fields, if we all step on a mine and we are all killed, would you come then, more quickly? Would that make you come?'

'We will come, I promise it to both of you, when we can. We can only do so much . . .'

Joey pushed himself up from behind the wall of beer bottles that stretched across his table. His legs were rubber soft and gave as he lurched from the table. He grabbed the leather-jacket shoulder of a youth, was cursed and shoved away. He set his sights on the door to the street and swayed as he moved towards his target. The last time he had been drunk, incapable, and it was hard with a fuddled mind to remember it, had been on his fifteenth birthday, which had clashed on the estate with the final afternoon of the harvest. The tractor men and the baling men had seen the fun of it and had poured rough cider down his throat, which they could handle but he could not. They'd brought him home to his mother then driven away, abandoning him to her piercing anger, and she'd not let him in the house before he'd thrown up into the silage pit. He'd wrecked what should have been a special dinner. He'd been alone, spinning in his bed, while his mother and father had eaten the dinner with his empty chair for company. He stood in the doorway, propped against the jamb, and saw a shrunken, bowed man go past the glass front, disappear beyond it. The man pushed a wheelchair. A young woman was in the wheelchair.

It wasn't the night cold that sobered him.

A man had said, 'You haven't, have you, compromised him?'

Joey ran after Judge Delic and Jasmina. Ran until he caught them.

Chapter Twelve

He heard the knock on the door over the noise of the shower. It was the time the laundry usually came back. He shouted from the bathroom that he would be a moment. He was towelling himself dry. He could have asked the maid to leave the laundry outside the door, but he'd also given her his shoes for cleaning, and he wanted to thank her and tip her when she returned them. Mister fastened one towel around his waist and looped a second over his shoulders, picked up loose change from the desk and went to the door. He opened it and reached out his hand with the fist of coins.

'I surprise you . . .' She rolled her eyes. 'I apologize.'

'Miss Holberg – I thought you were the maid.' He blushed. 'Forgive me.'

He saw the sparkle in her face, its cleanness, and the fun in her. 'I'm not in a state to receive a distinguished visitor.'

'It is wrong of me not to have telephoned from Reception. I did not because I am devious, and I thought it would provide you with an opportunity to refuse me.'

She said that the next morning the VIP visitors would go to the village of Visnjica. It was a one-hour drive from the city. She would be honoured if he would agree to accompany her. She understood that he was shy of personal publicity and that she both respected and admired this. His name would not be given to the visitors or to the villagers, but he would have the opportunity to see for himself the value of his generosity in bringing the Bosnia with Love lorry to Sarajevo. It was to be an important day for her and it would be further fulfilled if he would accompany her – assuming, of course, that he did not have more important business in the city. She hoped very much that he could accept.

'I'd like that,' Mister said. 'I'm flattered. I'm delighted to accept.'

She said she would pick him up in the morning, told him what he should wear – not towels, her laughter gently mocking him – and wished him a good evening.

A minute after she'd gone, the maid brought his laundry and his dried, polished shoes. He whistled as he dressed. It was all compartments. He forgot the Princess, his wife, and in a compartment further recessed in his mind was the man who should have been killed on the grass beside the pavement.

'You no longer have the mentality of a Customs officer.'

'I wonder if I ever had it.'

'You have become a competitor,' the judge said drily.

'I am Joey Cann, the competitor who loses.'

They had brought him to their home. He had helped to push the chair across the bridge and up the steep hill between lines of apartment buildings wrecked by artillery, fire-gutted and covered by a rash of bullet holes. The narrow width of the road would have been the front line. There were no lights above them or in the open windows. They made their way by torch beam, shining it down in front of the chair's wheels so that they did not hit debris and jolt her, and he'd wondered how the judge pushed his daughter up that hill each evening. They had turned into a narrower street and he had seen a heavy concrete mass, what had been the front of the third floor of a block, hanging threateningly over them, but she hadn't looked up at it and neither had the judge. The beam had been aimed at a house. It was half a building, one storey, and half a ruin. A door and a window were intact. The left side of the house had fallen away. Joey saw the snipped-off rafters, and wallpaper was exposed, still showing a pattern of pink flowers. The beam flickered on to three old pallets covered by a length of sheet metal to make a ramp for the chair. When the door was opened he had stayed outside and emptied the beer from his bladder. He had gone inside. He had to talk and purge himself.

The room was lit with an oil lamp. The walls were dark with damp stains and cracks ran in the plaster. There was a cooker attached by a pipe to a liquid-gas barrel, and a sink with clean plates on a draining-board. They had no refrigerator, and no electric fire. There were worn rugs on bare boards. It was a place of penury. They gave him wine from an opened bottle and he sipped it sparingly because it tasted foul, because he did not need to drink more, because he thought it all they had to offer a guest. She never interrupted her father, but wheeled herself round the table to a cupboard and back, and filled a sandwich for him. He had been given a place on a sofa that was covered by a blanket and propped up by old books. He thought the judge's need to speak was greater than his own.

The judge sat on a low bed. 'We live, Mr Cann, in an Olympic city. *Citius, Altius, Fortius*. But there was another motto of the Games. We read about it as we prepared ourselves to welcome the world. In 1908 London was the host. There was a service at your great cathedral, St Paul's, and the Bishop of Pennsylvania was invited to preach to the congregation. Sitting there, listening to the bishop, was the founder of the modern Olympics, Pierre de Coubertin. We are told that what de Coubertin heard thrilled him: "The important thing in the Olympic Games is not so much to have been victorious as to have taken part." Not every man can win.'

'I have been a loser enough times,' Joey said. He felt the cold around him, but it would have been rude for him, the guest, to shiver or pity himself. Till the summer, he thought, they would live in the house in their coats. 'I call him, I told you, Target One. He has been too many times a winner.'

'Am I a loser?'

Joey said simply, believed it, 'You are a man of dignity, you are not a loser.'

'And Jasmina, with a broken back? She has no mother. She has no carer but me. It is uncertain what is her future when I am dead. Is she a loser?'

'She has self-respect, she is not a loser.'

'May I tell you a story about what obsesses you, Mr Cann, a story of a winner and a loser?'

'I am in your home. You may tell me what you want.'

Jasmina gave him the sandwich. He did not know whether she wanted the story told or not. Her pale cheeks, sunken set eyes and her mouth, no lipstick, were without expression.

'The story has many characters, but at the end of it there was one winner and one loser . . .'

'Is it the story that is not to be told to a stranger – about blood?'

'That story, Mr Cann. I broke my rule on involvement, and you have told me that because of you my involvement may be known, and I should take precautions. Very frankly, few are possible . . . You should know why I became involved, helped you.'

'Please.' He strained to listen and to hold concentration against the waves of nausea.

'My wife, Maria, Jasmina's mother, was dead. She had a backroom administration post at the Bosnia Hotel, but when she was killed she was another mother and wife out in the streets and parks, scavenging. It had rained in the morning and she had come to the Jewish cemetery, near to here, to add to the snails she had collected. If you can find enough snails and take them out of their shells, and you can boil water, you can make soup. She was killed by a sniper's bullet. We had been married for twenty-one years. Jasmina was nineteen. My wife, Maria, was buried in the football pitch of the stadium. I could have left the city, but to turn your back on your wife's grave is, I promise you, difficult. I went on with my work as a teacher in law at the university. Jasmina, the only jewel left in my life, was my student. We managed. She had a boyfriend, Mirko, another of my students. A Serb, what we Muslims call a *Cetnik*. In the war, at first, it was possible for Serb men to remain in Sarajevo, but later it became hard, and soon it was impossible. There was hysteria, they were thought to be spies for the enemy. Jasmina and Mirko were in love, as I and her mother had been. They had pledged to spend their lives together, as we had. I blessed them. I said they should go, escape the madness.

'There was a telephone engineer who, before the war, I defended on a charge of killing while driving. My defence was successful. He went free. He was a rogue, he should have gone to prison. He said that if he could ever repay me he would. The telephone link from the main PTT building was cut when the fighting started, but the engineer kept one line open to Grbavica. It was possible if you waited, and if you paid, to use the line. First you called and asked the Serb operator to pass a message, for the person you would speak with to come to the sub-exchange in Grbavica at a certain time on a certain day. The day came, the time, you spoke to them. The engineer is now a wealthy man, he does not have to work. Mirko, with my money, made the calls and asked relatives on that side to help him, if he came over, to leave the country. The guarantee was given. But how to go over?

'There was the tunnel at the airport. It was impossible to use it. The military had it, the government, and they rented it to the gangsters – to Caco, Celo and Serif. They paid two thousand DMs an hour to use it. They brought in sugar, coffee, cigarettes, alcohol, everything for the black market, but between the military and the gangsters there was a stranglehold on the use of the tunnel. I heard there was one other way.

'I went to see Serif. It was an agony to me to go to see such a man. I have to say it was because I loved my child, and she loved her boy. He named the price. Of course we did not have such money. The price was five thousand American dollars, for him, and three thousand American dollars for the gangsters on the other side. I sold everything I had that was of material and sentimental value, my wife's jewellery, the ring I had given her, and the ring she had given me, even the watch on my wrist that had been my father's, and a loan from relatives, and I mortgaged my pension. Everything went to pay the thug for Jasmina's and Mirko's freedom.

'I remember the evening. I will never forget it. She took a small sports bag and Mirko had a little rucksack. It was all they owned. They had such confidence in a new world, their new life, away from the killing. When we came near to the bridge I was told to stay back. I kissed them both. I saw Serif. She had the money, all we could raise, and she gave it him, and he seemed to sneer because it was so little to him, and so much to us. I heard him say to her that all the arrangements were made. They went away into the darkness. They were to cross the Miljacka river at the Vrbanja bridge, it was the no man's land between the front lines. They were desperate, as I was, so we took on trust what we were told. I imagined every stride they took towards the bridge.

'I heard the shots. There were two long bursts of automatic gunfire, as if one for each of them. First it was Serif's men who held me back, then the police came, and they prevented me from going to the bridge. French troops came to the ends of the bridge but they would not go forward because, I heard it a week later, they considered it too dangerous. They were on the bridge, Jasmina and Mirko, through the night. At dawn, a Ukrainian army corporal drove by, and saw them. He walked on to the bridge. The French told him to stop but he refused. The Serbs on the other side told him to go back but he would not. He brought them back, carried them one under each of his arms. I never learned his name, was never able to thank him. Their lives were saved in the Kosevo hospital. Mirko had stomach wounds, his shoulder was damaged and he cannot run. My Jasmina, my jewel, was paralysed . . . A year afterwards there was another shooting on the Vrbanja bridge, what the foreign pressmen called the Romeo and Juliet shooting when two similar lovers paid to cross, and they both died, were betrayed, but their bodies were on the bridge for many days, exposed to the elements and to the foreign TV. Everybody knows about them, but Jasmina and Mirko were only another statistic of the injured. You will want to know what happened to their romance . . . Mirko is now in Vienna and has studied to be an architect. We have no jewellery and my pension belongs to the bank.

'I took part, as the bishop said in London that I should. I lost, and Jasmina lost. Yes, Mr Cann, while she was in the hospital, while I did not know whether she would live or die, I went to visit Ismet Mujic – Serif. He refused to return the money and refused to take responsibility for the betrayal. He said that if I came near him again or made trouble for him he would set his dogs on me, and that he would see to it I never worked again. He had that power. It is the symptom of the loser, you might find it hard to believe it of me, but for nine years I have cultivated a wish to be avenged. There is something in our faith that tells us, one day – however long in the future – the chance of vengeance comes. You walked, in your innocence, through my door. I told you that the man found in the river . . .'

'He was murdered,' Joey said, through the last mouthful of the sandwich. 'He was hit, then thrown over the bridge.'

'... was linked to Ismet Mujic – Serif. It was when I thought, for the first time in long years, that I could be the winner ... *Citius, Altius, Fortius* ... could run faster than him, jump higher, be stronger – could crush him. I discarded the mentality of a judge.'

'Threw off the uniform.' Joey drained the last of the wine in his glass.

'Became the competitor. Demanded to win.'

'It is very human, it is the way we are.'

'To gain respect for myself.'

'At the expense of charity – it is not a time for mercy.'

'It is a passion to me.'

Joey said, 'We learned about it at school. Shylock, the Jewish money-lender in *The Merchant of Venice*, said: "The villainy you teach me I will execute, and it shall go hard but I will better the instruction." I promise nothing but my best – that, at the end, it is we who are standing.'

Joey Cann left them, stumbled away down the street. He thought that a father would be helping a crippled daughter to prepare for bed. He fell twice but picked himself up and went on into the night. He was humbled. He crossed the bridge, where she had been shot and the dream had been lost, and headed towards the hotel. He heard his own words and wondered if they were just the beer's brave talk. He wore no uniform, the ID in his wallet he thought was worthless. If he was the loser he would not be left standing, for their sakes.

They ate off bone china. Mister was their honoured guest. His reputation had travelled with him from Green Lanes to Sarajevo.

The villa was on a hillside and faced west over the city. The introductions had been made in front of a blazing log fire. Serif and the men who had sat with him at the negotiations were there: the older man with his superior, announced as a brigadier in the intelligence agency, the younger man showing deference to his uncle, the politician. The villa was the politician's. If it had been damaged by war, repairs had been made: there was no sign of the war, only of the affluence, and the influence. Mister was not interested in the display of wealth, but while the talk eddied around him, he glanced at the photographs on one wall showing the politician, always wearing a quiet suit, meeting visitors to the city on the outside steps of buildings, cocooned in flak jackets and with military helmets on their heads. Serif did not speak but lounged in a carver chair at the end of a long oak table on which bounced reflections from the candles' flames. The politician and the brigadier spoke rarely, and conversation was maintained by the nephew and the junior officer. There was no small-talk. Mister listened, which was his talent, and he watched and learned, which was his skill. While he listened he looked to understand the relationship between Serif and the politician: if Serif were the subordinate he would have spoken, Mister thought. He assumed everything around him, the luxury of the furniture, the drapes, the paintings, the glasses on the table, the food served, came to the politician from Serif. He was told of a meeting that would take place in four or five days, where he would meet partners, and that invitations to them had been sent. He replied with a shrug that if the business were important he had the time to give. And he was told of a problem, and his help was asked, and he said that he was always anxious to help a friend in difficulty. He drank nothing . . . They would all have known of the death of the Cruncher, and he wondered which of them had sanctioned it, and which of them would suffer. When they talked of the meeting he smiled at them, and smiled again when they told him of their problem. He thought he was at the top table, a player in the league where he wanted to be. He was alert, on guard, but he felt himself wallowing in self-induced satisfaction. He had arrived where he wanted to be.

The Eagle would be with him for the meeting, and Atkins could solve their problem.

He was treated with due respect, and that was precious to him.

Atkins came into the restaurant, which was empty but for the table where the Eagle sat. 'I thought I was late, but I've beaten him in.'

'Not joining us.'

'Where is he?'

'Been whisked away to dine with the great and the good.' The Eagle grimaced. 'I, thankfully, was not included in the invitation.'

'I thought I was late . . . Do you fancy something slightly better? There are decent restaurants in Sarajevo.'

'I've already ordered. You go off if you want to.'

But Atkins sat down and a waiter sprinted forward to offer him the menu – the same as the previous night, and the night before that, and . . . He chose soup and the schnitzel, as he had the previous night, and the night before . . . He had been lying on his bed, without the light on, the curtains undrawn, in the gloom, and had been thinking, pondering, about the two or three inches by which he had missed the responsibility for the murder of a Customs officer.

'A good choice, what I'm having,' the Eagle said.

'Well . . .'

'Well what?'

'Who's going to tell him?'

'I don't follow you.'

'Who is going to tell him that it's time we quit?'

A little smile flickered on the Eagle's face. 'Quite a big speech.'

Atkins felt a reckless calm. 'Will you tell him?'

'I hadn't planned to.'

'Me? Do you leave it to me, the new boy on the block? We were guilty of attempted murder.'

The Eagle's open hands were up, as if to display the purity of innocence. 'I wasn't, *you* were. I don't recall driving the vehicle.'

'What's going to be asked of us next? How long are we stuck here? I didn't reckon on kicking my heels. In and out, that's what I thought. Christ knows what's next on his list for us.'

'Then you should tell him you've had enough.'

'Would you back me?' Atkins hissed across the table.

'That is a very difficult question.'

'Are you with me or against me?'

The Eagle's lips pursed, the answer was whispered. 'In principle, with you.'

'Damn you . . . Not fucking "principle". For me or against?'

'I would have to say that I'm beginning to feel we have overstayed the very limited welcome shown to us. Do I have work in London that would better employ me? Yes. Would I prefer to be at home and eating my dinner quietly? Yes. Would I pick a fight with Mister, rubbish his ideas, at the moment he believes he stands on the threshold of triumph? That poses a difficult question. I know how difficult.'

'Are you always this fucking spineless?'

The Eagle smiled the same sad, tired smile. 'I doubt you've seen him crossed. It is not a pleasant sight. I am told that grown men, confronted with a view of it, are prone to lose control of their bladders. It's fatuous to refer to "spine". I walk out on him, or you do, or we both do, and where do we go? Home? To our loved ones? Back to living our lives without him, and without his money? He has a long arm. Do we live in the company of a battalion of paratroops? You'd be in a gutter, I'd be down on a pavement, in blood, in pain. He always hurts first, it's the message he likes to send.'

Atkins, not play-acting, said simply, 'I'm frightened.'

'Aren't we all?'

'I'm being sucked down, so are you. Will you back me, support me? A clear answer.'

'There is rarely a right moment to gainsay Mister. If such a moment arises, yes. That moment is not now. Do you think we can try to enjoy our meal?'

The waiter brought the soup. The vegetables floating in it, carrot and celery, leek and parsnip, had all been sliced into small pieces. Atkins gazed at them and wondered at the sharpness of the knife that had cut them.

The computers had the power to dig into the registrations of births, property sales, electoral rolls, income-tax returns, council-tax lists and telephone numbers. The trace was done by SQG8 and handed to Dougie Gough.

'You can go home now,' Gough said. 'I appreciate you staying on.'

'Home' for SQG8 was a single room in a guest-house behind King's Cross terminus, far from her husband and kids in the Manchester suburbs. He dismissed her because he did not wish his call to be overheard. He trusted nobody, not even those he had picked with his own hand. He never quoted it to a second person, but Dougie Gough lived as a senior investigation officer on the maxim of an Irish judge who had said, in 1790: 'The condition upon which God hath given liberty to man is eternal vigilance.' John Philpot Curran had spoken for him.

He thought it a reasonable assumption that a young woman in terror would not have run to a work friend or a college colleague, but to her mother.

The track through the computer's records by SQG8 gave him the telephone number of the parents of Jennifer Martin. He waited until the room was empty, then dialled. The message sifting in his mind should not be shared.

'Could I speak to Miss Jennifer Martin, please? I do apologize for disturbing you at this late hour. If she's reluctant to take my call, could you tell her that it's Douglas Gough and that I run the team – Sierra Quebec Golf – for which Joey Cann works. Thank you so much.' He waited. He had had little doubt that Cann would have told his girl something of the background to his work on the Packer investigation. All the men and women, senior and junior, on the class A teams used wives, husbands and partners as crutches to lean on. A small voice answered the telephone. His reply purred, was re-assuring. 'So good of you to come to the phone – may I call you Jennifer? I may? Thank you. I heard about your pet and I want you to know that I am deeply shocked, and sincerely sympathetic. Both Joey and I work in a dark corner of our society. Most of that society ignores the darkness, doesn't feel it's their business to illuminate it, or to get involved. Go to any multi-screen complex, in any city, and you can guarantee there will be a flashy gangster apology to be seen. Those films portray a glamorous, fraudulent image of the men we target. The films do our society a disservice. The men they depict are not Jack the Lad, they are *leeches*. They are evil, foul bastards – forgive me if I sound emotional – but Joey will have told you that. I've sent him on a mission that I regard as of critical importance. The measure of his success so far, and the mission is not yet completed, is that Packer has struck back at what he thinks is Joey's weak point. You. I am taking a great liberty in asking it of you – you are not a law-enforcement officer although you are a citizen – but I want you to stay where you are. It's Shropshire, isn't it? I want you to stay there, not break cover, not use the telephone, not contact Joey. I'm asking you to be brave. I think you're up to it . . . I'm going to give you a telephone number to call if you have any suspicions that you are watched, call it night or day. You're important to me, Jennifer, and I need your co-operation. Can I rely on you?'

She sounded what his wife would call a 'decent girl'. He gave the number of his own mobile phone. He wished her well.

He switched off the room's lights and the door locked after him. Those who worked with him would not have expected a flicker of sentiment from Dougie Gough. He hadn't wanted a frightened

274

girlfriend's calls to Sarajevo to distract Joey Cann from work in hand. He had not spoken of a murder attempt, or of the withdrawal by the Secret Intelligence Service of one half of Cann's partnership.

He walked along the empty corridor and remembered the picture of Cann, from the video, kicking his heels in an act of bloody-minded defiance against the concrete of the rubbish bin. It was Cann who had said that the weakest link was Mister – Albert William Packer – and he'd liked what he'd heard ... He recognized obsession and thought it valuable if channelled, but dangerous if not. He believed, with Cann alongside him, that he stood at the threshold of success. Was the obsession compulsive enough to hold fast? He must check its strength. He felt no shame for sweet-talking the young woman, and he would lie again before the night was over.

He lay on his back on his bed, and he thought of Jasmina's face.

He had gone past Maggie's room and the dark strip under the door had told him her light was off, he'd paused and heard her tossing in her bed, and he'd gone to his room.

The note had been on the pillow.

> Joey,
> My crowd are pulling me out. They, and me, say it's not worth the candle – sorry. You should be with me. It's the 7.15 early bird for Zagreb. There are seats on it. Where were you tonight? I waited up, we should have talked about it. Pride never won anything. I'm leaving at 6.00, on the dot. Be there!
> Luv, Maggie.

He thought of her strength, and what she went through, each day, to keep that strength. He was humbled by her. What he would do was for her. He wanted to push her, in her wheelchair, in a park, among flowers, where birds sang, and share her strength.

He would go, for her, wherever the road went, wherever it led.

May 1998
The sun shone on the valley. The scene in front of Dragan Kovac was a picture of beauty. It was impossible for him, looking from the porch of his home, to recall the war. The village of Ljut was behind him and

he could not see the wreckage of the houses. Across the fields and over the river small columns of smoke rose from Vraca, but his eyesight was too weak for him to distinguish which buildings were repaired and which were abandoned as derelict. He saw the carpet blanket of the flowers that were the sign of the coming summer, specks, pockets and expanses of blue, pink, yellow. The sun fell on him and warmed his bones.

He was a meticulous man. As the police sergeant, the core of his life had been based on careful planning and thorough preparation. He had risen early. He had made his bed and swept through the room that doubled for living and sleeping, cleaned it, and then he had carried out the small table from inside and placed it on the stone flags under the porch roof. It would be hot later. He put the table where the porch shade would cover it, and then he brought out two strong wooden chairs and manoeuvred them on the uneven stone so that they were firmly set. He went back in for the chess set and the board, brought them out. He spread the board and laid out the pieces. He always felt a little shimmer of pleasure when he handled them. They had been carved by his father from oak; the legacy passed to him from his father's deathbed, given to him seven months after his father had come home from the Partizans with the festering leg wound from a German machine-gun bullet. He had been twelve years old and he had promised his father that he would value the set. King, queen, bishops, pawns, all were freshly painted each year with linseed and had been for fifty-five years. The largest pieces, those of greatest importance, were twenty centimetres high, those of least worth were ten centimetres. It was a fine set, and it was a worry to him that the future of their ownership was not yet determined. The grandson of his friend had a good child's face, intelligent, serious. Dragan Kovac had no son of his own, no nephew, no child that he could be certain would respect the chess set. He set out the pieces, then brought an old glass ashtray to the table. It had been on his desk in the police station for more than twenty years and it had disappeared from there on the evening of his retirement. He had his last two remaining, unbroken, glasses for the brandy. It was all done with exactness and pride. He looked at the river, and already the shimmer of the heat was on it. Each day of the previous week it had dropped and he could finally see the silver speckle of the ford. The old fool would make an easy crossing and they would play their first game of the summer . . . He'd had a pain in his chest that morning – more an ache than a pain – and it had worried him. He thought he would take the opportunity that day to speak with the old fool, his friend, about the grandchild and about the chess set.

He had no spectacles. It would have been hard for him to read, but he had no books. His eyesight was sufficient for his needs. He did not recognize it but, perversely, his failing vision helped him. He saw that morning only the beauty of the valley, as if the war had passed it by. The track to the ford and beyond it was empty. Was the old fool going to be late? His preparations were dictated by a schedule. He sniffed, smelt the stewing rabbit.

He hurried inside. He stoked more wood into the stove. The stove, like him, was a survivor of the war. When the Spanish soldiers had brought him back to his house, before they'd left him, they'd cleared bucketfuls of plaster rubble from its top and cleaned the hob. He went twice a week into the almost deserted village of Ljut with his bow saw and took his time to cut wood from fallen rafters, and wheeled it back in a barrow. Last week a soldier had brought an axe and had cut enough logs to supply his cooking needs for a month. The cats ran wild in the village. They moved in packs among the dried-out ruins. He had studied their hunting habits as if it were a minor paramilitary police operation, had learned where the cats took the rabbits they killed. They were creatures of routine. The eating place, a charnel house of bones, was the tool shed at the back of the church. A cat caught a fine buck rabbit, held it screaming in its jaws, and proudly strutted with it to the shed. He'd waited the previous day in the shed's shadows, heard its death scream and the cat's proud yowl. He'd thrown a stone at the cat, had missed, but the rabbit had been dropped. He had taken it home, skinned and gutted it, and had hung it from a beam above his bed. The rabbit was now in the pot, and the fire burned well in the stove. He had only the potatoes that the Spanish troops brought him and peas from packets to stew with it. It would not be a meal for an emperor, but a meal fit for a true friend, an old fool. He looked at his watch. Husein Bekir was twenty-seven minutes late.

He heard the movement outside, and the bark of the dog. He stood up, gained the stature of a retired police sergeant and went to the door, ready to chide his guest.

It was the daughter, the widow of the criminal, the mother of the child. She had come, she said, to tell him that her father had a chill. She thought he had been out too long, too late, two nights before, with a goat and a sickly kid. It was not serious but her father had taken to his bed. He saw the way she scented, in envy, the stewing rabbit. She was wan-coloured, worried.

Dragan Kovac prided himself on understanding the mentality of men, most certainly the mind of Husein Bekir. He thought it was more about the fields, and the mines that lay in them. There was, perhaps, a chill, but there would also be a reluctance to walk to the ford and wade across it, then to walk up the track past the grazing ground where there were no cattle and the arable ground that had not been ploughed and sown, and past the vineyard where the weeds overwhelmed the vines.

He gave her the steaming pot. He said, and hoped that the message would be carried back, that Husein Bekir should come as soon as he was fit enough, and that he should bring her son, and that together he and his friend should teach the child the mysteries of their game. She nodded.

Dragan Kovac put away the chess pieces, folded the board, and carried the table inside. The sun rose and shimmered on the valley, and the flowers.

'Did I wake you, Joey? Very sorry. It's Gough. Where am I? I am crossing Kingston bridge, then it's Hampton Wick, then it's Teddington and my bed. I've spoken to Jennifer, she's fine, very supportive. I have arranged round-the-clock protection for her, but discreet. She won't see it. Don't worry on her behalf . . . I'm sure you were worried but you've no cause to be. I need you there, Joey. I want you on his back. I want him squeezed. What I'm looking for, Joey, is mistakes, big ones, the ones that nail him.'

The black Mercedes dropped Mister at the door of the Holiday Inn. They were on the settee seats of the atrium bar, close to each other. He saw that they had waited up for his return.

He had drunk nothing during the evening, was cold sober. There were beer bottles in front of Atkins and soft-drink cans on the table in front of the Eagle. He walked towards them. They stood. He recognized the signs of crisis. He didn't hurry as he approached them, because that would have shown doubt or weakness. When he was close to them he smiled. The Eagle didn't meet his eye, but Atkins was flushed and his fingers tugged and pinched at the hem of his trouser pocket. Mister knew that the difficulty, wherever it lay, was with Atkins. Divide the opposition, then control it. It was what he had learned from childhood.

He grinned at the Eagle. 'All right, then? You didn't have to sit up for me.'

Through a sickly smile, 'Yes, all right, Mister. You had a good evening?'

'An acceptable evening, making bridges we can walk over . . . What's up, Atkins?'

'We were talking . . .'

The Eagle shrugged. Message clear. Atkins had been talking and the Eagle had been listening. They were already divided, he knew it.

'What were you talking about, Atkins?'

It came in a torrent. 'About being here. How long are we here? What we're doing here, that was what we were talking about. How long and what . . . And about attempted murder . . .'

'I'm listening, Atkins, but you're not making much sense to me. Where's all this leading?'

'Quit. It's time we quit.'

'Do you agree, Eagle, that it's time we quit? No? Lost your voice? Come on, Eagle, I always listen to you. Anything legal, and I'm all ears. Don't I listen to you, Eagle? Nothing to say?'

He used sharp, staccato, harsh questions to beat on the Eagle. Always worked, always made him cringe. He could bully the Eagle, like kicking a dog and knowing it always came back to whimper at his heel. He'd his beaded gaze on the Eagle, unwavering.

He turned in sweetness to Atkins. 'Things are bothering you, my friend. I don't like that. I like things in the open. Take your time.'

Mister hadn't heard it before, a croak in Atkins's voice. They'd have talked it over at dinner, wouldn't they? He twisted on the settee, gave Atkins his full attention and the Eagle was ignored, as if he was of no importance.

'I came to do a job, but you didn't say the job was murder – and those people killed Dubbs. You don't trust that sort, not an inch.'

'The point's made, Atkins. I think I know that – and I don't do job descriptions. You know that. We see an opportunity and we move. We see an obstacle and we dismantle it.'

'I didn't come for this. I want out.'

'Fair's fair. I hear you.'

'It's not my game.'

He reached out. The expression set on his face was of concern. The appearance was of a sympathy, genuine. It was a little gesture, not the thing grown men did, but he reached out his hand, took Atkins's in his, and held it gently.

'Right, it's out of the system. You won't mind if I say something?'

'My mind's made up – I'm quitting.'

'Yes, yes . . . You see, Atkins, you won't find a man in London who'd call himself bigger than me. I'm top of the heap. I'm the one they look to. Why's that? It's because I have ambition. No backwaters for me. I'm at the top, in the fast lane. How am I there? Because I choose men of quality. Plenty of people want to work for me. Silly to think about it, but if I advertised a position, working for me, then the queue would stretch round the corner. Plenty of people who could organize hardware for me. I'm only interested in the best, got me? The *best*. Only quality interests me. Looking for the best, for quality, I asked you to accept my offer of employment . . . Does everything, always, go to plan? Course it doesn't. It screws up, falls on its face. The reason, most times, it works out is that I have the best men alongside me, quality men – not gorillas, but men of intelligence. I'm not afraid to hold my hands up when I'm wrong. I think I owe you an apology, Atkins. Why? I've taken you for granted. I haven't kept you in the picture. That's remiss of me. You want out because you don't think you're valued . . . You are, sincerely you are. Who was the last person to tell you that you were quality, the best? Your father?'

He held Atkins's hand and his thumb massaged the knuckle. His voice was pitched low and Atkins had to lean forward to hear him. He knew about all the people he employed, and their families. There was a brigadier, retired, down in Wiltshire who had received from the Queen in his soldiering days a Distinguished Service Order and a Military Cross. From what Mister had learned, the brigadier thought worthless the son who had been bumped out of the army in disgrace. He knew Atkins hadn't been home last Christmas. If he skipped going home at Christmas then it was to save himself from supercilious insult. He held the hand and saw the head shaken glumly.

'It's what I'm telling you, you're quality and the best. I want you beside me. I value you, Atkins. Everything's going to be all right, I promise. Just a few hiccups, but it'll all work out. Anything you want to say?'

'No, Mister, nothing.'

'No more talk of quitting?'

'None.'

'Well said. Said by a man I can lean on, a man I'd depend on. You want to go and get some sleep. That hand . . .' Mister loosed it. '. . . I'd put my life in that hand and know it's safe.'

He watched Atkins shamble away to the lift.

He leaned further across the table. Without warning, with a short-range jab, he punched the Eagle's upper arm, aimed at the flab where it would hurt. He laughed, as if that were his idea of amusement. 'Snivelling little rat . . . Tell me it wasn't your idea, Eagle, didn't prime him to it. No, no . . .'

'You did well, Mister,' the Eagle said. 'But, then, you always do.'

He told the Eagle about his dinner, what he'd learned and what he'd agreed to. He said where he would be early in the morning, and where he would be for the day, and what he wanted from the Eagle and Atkins while he was away.

'Seems good to me, Mister.'

They ambled towards the lift and his arm draped over the Eagle's shoulder. 'I reckon we're rolling.'

Chapter Thirteen

For Mister the day started well.

There was a clear sky over him with a dipping quarter-moon. The sun wasn't yet up over the rooftops of the city but a sheen of its coming light slipped into the side-street where he stood. His position, half in the doorway of a steel-shuttered boutique, gave him a useful view of the square and its shrub bushes draped with wind-blown litter, the hotel's steps, the interior foyer and the reception desk. He had the timetable of the flights. He had risen early and expected to be rewarded for it. He saw them come into the foyer together, and go to the desk. He understood the way they worked, operated, at the Church. They backed off. It was the difference between him and them. There would have been a meeting, and fed into the meeting would have been options – to stay and reinforce or to back off. He felt supreme.

She carried a lightweight case out of the foyer and down the hotel's steps. The young man, Cann, followed her, loaded with a heavy silvery metal case and a smaller overnight sports bag. She didn't look like anyone from the Church he'd seen before – too petite, too smart – and not police either. She would have been the bug expert . . . but he'd seen her off. She turned on the pavement and walked towards the far end of the hotel building, Cann trailing behind her. Under a street-lamp, Mister saw their faces. Hers was tight, his was depressed and lowered. They disappeared from his view, went round the corner of the hotel's block. Mister waited. He had seen enough, but his innate care and sense of caution ruled him.

An old blue van came fast from the side of the hotel and accelerated past the steps to the foyer, then braked noisily at the traffic lights. She was driving. A lesser man than himself would have whistled and waved to them, or given them the finger. They were gone. He looked down at his watch to make the quick calculation. They were on schedule for the flight out.

There was a bounce in his stride when he left the side-street. It would be a good day for him.

She'd held her silence all the way down the old Snipers' Alley, past the destroyed newspaper building, past the ruins of what had been the front line protecting the airport corridor, and past the camp of the French soldiers. She'd said nothing and Joey hadn't broken into her mood.

She parked, switched off the engine, then tossed him the keys.

'Good luck,' she said.

'I'll see you in.'

'You don't have to – I'm capable of catching, on my own, an airline flight.'

'I'll carry your case.'

She pouted. 'The gentleman to the last.'

Not that Joey had seen many but he thought it was like any early-morning airport anywhere. She took her place in the check-in queue. In front and behind them were the personnel of the international community. There was a buzz and a rippling of jokes in a mess of languages. They were getting out, they were getting shot of the place for ever, or had the lesser escape of a week's leave. Policemen, soldiers, Red Cross workers, United Nations officials, they all let the staff on the check-in know how they felt about a reservation on the silver freedom bird. Maggie Bolton wasn't a part of them. She was severe, cold, as if that were her protection. The laughter rang around her, over her. When she was one place short of the front of the queue, she turned to Joey. She didn't speak but pointed to her ticket, her eyes asking the question: was he coming? He shook his head. She knew nothing of the clamour of his bedside telephone. *What I'm looking for, Joey, is mistakes, big ones, the ones that nail him.* It had been a long time, many clocks' chimes disturbing the night quiet, before he had slept again. Maggie gazed at him, as if he were far away, then jabbed her elbow into his ribcage.

'Right, that's it, that's me on board.'

Both of her bags would go with her in the cabin. She left the check-in and started to walk towards the departure doors, let him carry the heavier bug case.

'What happens when you get back?' Joey asked.

'Is that supposed to be bloody sarcastic?'

'It's merely a simple question, meant to be polite.'

She paused at the doors and stood against the flow. 'Into Heathrow about eleven thirty, if the Zagreb connection works. A car to meet me and take me into London – not because I'm important but because of the bag. A debrief – if they ask me why you didn't travel, I'll say you were waiting for the dry-cleaning to come back. Don't worry, I won't shop you.'

Joey said softly, 'My instructions are to stay, carry on without you, as best I can.'

Her composure broke. 'What? That is worse than bloody stupid.'

'And when you've had your debrief?'

'Check the bug into the workshop, see if it's past help. Go home. Look at the post, ring my mother. The usual. Then put my feet up. Then . . . We all fail, you know. We don't brood about it. Learn to accept failure.'

'Have a good flight.'

She swivelled away from him, joined the flow and went through the doors.

'It's a tip,' Atkins said.

'The right road, the right number.'

'Can't be right . . .'

'It's what Mister said,' the Eagle muttered. 'Are you going to whinge, or are you going to do what he told you to do?'

'You bastard.'

'Eating from his hand. A couple of little compliments – God, you come cheap.'

Atkins flushed.

They walked towards the half-intact, half-destroyed house. Where his parents were, down in Wiltshire, a dry cow or a useless lame gelding wouldn't have been kept in such a place. This building was lived in. Where the stumped rafters were lowest from the angle of the roof, what was left of it, a washing-line was suspended and it reached to the bottom branch of a bare tree. On the line, drying in the sunshine, were a young woman's flimsy pieces of underwear, and mixed with them was a ragged assortment of long baggy pants, thick vests, heavy check shirts and the darned socks of an old man. There had once been a garden. Over the rubble of the house end lay the tangle of sprouting rose suckers, trying to crawl towards the open, wall-papered interior. What had been an inner door was barricaded with nailed planks. Atkins thought it a pitiful place, not a judge's home, not five years after the war had ended. He saw the nearly buried roof of a car. If he hadn't been examining the building, turning it over with his trained eye, he would not have seen it. It would have been parked beside the building when the artillery shell had struck home. Part of the roof and all of the outer wall had fallen on it, along with the last of the dirtied snow of the winter. There were narrow wheelmarks making tramlines to and from a ramp leading to the main door. It was the right address, the wheelmarks confirmed it. The door, with the paint weathered off it, was firmly shut. There were no lights behind the two remaining windows, which were covered with double layers of cellophane; he could not see inside . . . He was the best, quality. Mister had said it. He turned his back on Judge Delic's home.

Over breakfast and before leaving for a vaguely explained destination, Mister had described the departure of Cann and a woman scuttling with their bags from a central hotel – without crowing – and then Atkins had been told of a 'little problem' that Mister wanted sorting out. He looked above the house. He searched the hillside for a place of elevation, where the tripod could be set up, that could be reached on tarmac.

He thought the place would be near the Jewish cemetery.

Atkins set off to find it, and the Eagle puffed after him.

'Miss Bolton? I'm Ruthin, Eddie Ruthin. I came down from Vienna.' She thought him a vacuous-looking younger man, with a quiff of hair falling on his forehead below a trilby, thin under an oversized Burberry mackintosh.

'What for?'

She had come into the airside concourse at Zagreb. She felt wretched. It was not the turbulence that had hit the flight, but the glowering thoughts in her head that affected her. She was out, Cann was still in. She had found justification for it and had walked away, abandoned him. She hadn't even pecked him on the cheek, but had given him instead a homily on failure.

'They thought, in London, after what you've been through, that a friendly face might help.'

'Did they?'

'Well, your life was in danger, wasn't it? So, how can I help?'

'How long do I have here?'

''Fraid there's three hours to kill before the London flight. I suppose, also, they didn't want you lugging all your gear round on your own. May I take the case?'

'I'm perfectly capable.'

'Well, let's find a chair, somewhere to sit you down. What about a coffee?'

Maggie sat in a chair and faced the plate-glass windows. She manoeuvred the heavy case under her thighs and behind her shins, stared out over the runways and saw a distant line of hills to the west. Beyond the hills was the border, and beyond the border was Joey Cann. The case holding the equipment that might have helped him was cold against her shins and thighs.

'I'd like, please, if you can get them to make it, a pink gin.'

Gough listened. 'So, you came down to see old Finch, to see how the old beggar's surviving, and to pick the old brains. Surviving not too bad, actually, with a bit of help from ten-year-old malt. You know the best-kept secret in the Custom House? There's a life outside. Fancy that. My life now is the garden and the newspapers, and I do the housework because Emily's still working, and I've a bit of time to think. You'll be wondering if I'm all bitter and twisted. Can answer that easily enough – I am. What makes me bitterest, twists me tightest, is that Cann still works in Sierra Quebec Golf. I used to pity him, almost feel sorry for him, now I just detest him. I go to the wall at dawn, blindfold over my face, and the rest of my people get the Church's version of Siberia, but Cann survives. You want to know what I think? He's one of those empty people, fuck-all in him. No life and therefore no balanced view, searching for a cause. The cause might have been God, might have been Chelsea bloody Football Club, might have been fuchsias in a greenhouse, but it was Packer. That sort of empty person needs a bloody cause, something to fill the hole. Bastard didn't have one iota of the ethic of law enforcement, not like I had and the rest of my people – and look where it's got us. It was more like that pitiful sort of dedication those sick creatures have who stalk celebrities, photograph them, stand outside their homes and go through their rubbish, all wrapped up in some shitty justification that he was the only one who cared about the job. I ran a good team. We worked for each other. He didn't. To the other guys, girls, he was a pain. He wanted to be alone, wasn't a part of us, he had his mission. His mission made him a big boy, gave him a reason for living. People with a mission, they come unstuck, don't know when to stop. You shouldn't have sent him there, not to Bosnia. Wouldn't that be the sort of place where you'd need to know when to stop, and back off?'

Gough left Brian Finch in his conservatory with the first glass of the day in his hand. He had heard what he wanted to hear.

'It's a neck of the world I don't know.' Mister's confession of ignorance felt like an apology.

'I promise you, there is no place more beautiful, more pure, Mr Packer, or more sad. Perhaps one day you will go there, yes?'

'Maybe. The way you tell it maybe I should – but not to see the sad part.'

Monika Holberg was like no woman he had ever known. But, then, the Lofoten Islands, north of the Arctic Circle, was a place he had never heard of. As she'd told him about her home and a life of farming small fields, and of dragging cod out of the sea, he'd thought grimly that they didn't grow poppies in their fields or coca bushes, didn't have laboratories that manufactured E tablets or amphetamines, had nothing for him to buy, nothing for him to sell. Not good fertile territory for trading. She was like no woman he'd known because she talked. From the time she'd picked him up, with her driver, sitting in the back of the UNHCR jeep she had barely drawn breath. He knew about her home village, Njusford on the island of Flakstodoya. He knew about her parents, Henrik and Helge. About her brother and sister, Johan and Hulde. He knew the names of their cows that lived eight months of the year in a heated barn, and the annual weight of the cod they caught in the nets. He knew about the brother, Knut, who had hanged himself, aged sixteen, twelve years before as an escape from the 'demon depression' of the winter's darkness. She told him everything and asked him nothing. Her life cascaded over him. It was so rare for him to be treated to such trusting, personal confidences. Then, when she had finished with the Lofoten Islands, and the hanging of her brother, she switched effortlessly to her career working with refugees in Somalia and East Timor, Mozambique and Kosovo; he knew where Kosovo was, had a vague idea of where Somalia and Mozambique were positioned on the African continent, but had never heard of East Timor. He didn't like to display his ignorance, thought it lessened him. He didn't want to be small in her eyes.

They turned off the main road and the jeep began to bump up a rough track. 'You are all right, Mr Packer?'

'I'm fine, I'm really enjoying myself.'

'I am not talking too much?'

'Not at all. You fascinate me. You make me think that I've led a very sheltered life ... Everyone calls me *Mister*. I'd like you to, please.'

She pulled a face, then she giggled. 'It is a very strange name – but if that is what you want ... We are nearly there. The village is called Visnjica. You will remember that? Visnjica in Opstina Kiseljak.'

Mister said, didn't think about it, 'They all sound the same to me, these names.'

'But you must remember the name and the district, Mister. Surely, when you go home, you will tell the charities who have made the gift where their generosity has gone. It is important, surely.'

'Yes,' Mister said. 'It is important.'

On the yellowed grass between the track and a small river, in spate, were the heavy tyremarks of the military vehicles parked up. He saw armoured personnel carriers, flying the German flag, an ambulance and jeeps. Beyond them, over the river, above the trees where snow was scattered, two heavy helicopters hovered, then descended.

'Typical of the Germans to strike completely the wrong note. We are trying to tell frightened people that it is safe to come back to their homes. The people have been the victims of war, perhaps the most savage Europe has seen, and we are telling them that the danger is over. But this is the area of responsibility of the German military, and they have VIPs coming by the helicopters and it is necessary for them to make a show. They are so clumsy, so bovine . . . In Norway we do not have a good experience of the Germans.'

She left the driver with the jeep. They walked into the village, a long ribbon of scattered buildings that stretched up the hill on both sides of the track. Behind them the helicopters disgorged generals, men in suits and women in smart dresses. Some houses showed no war damage, cattle bellowed from the barns behind them, and smoke puffed from the chimneys. But most were destroyed, their roofs sunk between the four upstanding walls, the undergrowth high around and inside them. A few had bright new tiled roofs and new walls of red brick or concrete blocks, new windows and doors, and washing draped in front of them. Men, women and children walked from them towards the track and formed a thin line of welcome.

'The village, before the war, was home to Croats and Muslims. It is easy, Mister, to believe the war was only made by Serbs. The Croats were as bad as the Serbs. They waited until the Muslims were defenceless then attacked them. Before the war there were three hundred Muslim families here, and sixty Croat families. Then there was the ethnic cleansing. The Muslims were expelled, their houses were destroyed – not in fighting but by explosives after they had gone. Most went to Germany, but they have been expelled again, so they try to return to their old homes and to live beside their old neighbours, who became their enemies. Of three hundred, we now have the first twenty families back. They find their homes have been looted, everything of value has been taken, and is now inside the houses that are not damaged – TVs, stoves, baths, bulbs, even the electric wires, and the cattle, sheep and goats. It is not easy, but my job is to help to rebuild the relations between neighbours.'

Women with small children and babies, and old men with dulled faces, stood in a knot outside a square-set building that had no roof, no glass in the tall windows, and a wide hole where the door should have been. They had their backs to the ruin as if it did not exist. The women wore old coats against the chill, and the wind snatched at their headscarves; the men wore berets and thick sweaters, had weathered faces that were expressionless, and the children stared back at Mister and held limply to toys. In the field beside the building were short, freshly painted white pegs.

'It could have been worse, Mister. If it had not been for your generosity I do not think they would have come out of their houses to see the VIPs. The coats, scarves, sweaters and toys came from Bosnia with Love. At least they are warm, and the little ones have something to amuse them. It is too much, I am sorry, to expect them to smile, but at least they have come . . . The building is their mosque. It was not a military target, it was destroyed by their neighbours as an act of vandalism, and the graveyard, all the stones were smashed with sledge-hammers and pickaxes. In such circumstances, it takes great courage and determination to come home. If I ask the Croats who live here, who today hide, who destroyed the mosque, they will tell me it was outsiders who came, criminal scum, under the control of warlords. Perhaps in Sarajevo you have heard of the Muslim scum – Caco, Celo, Serif. The Croats had Tuta and Sela. The Serbs had many criminals – Arkan and Selsjek. I am not supposed to hate, it does not fit with the principles of the UNHCR, but I loathe those scum – they've sucked the blood from good, decent, simple people.'

There was a desultory clapping behind them. She held his arm, did it naturally and without premeditation, and turned him round. The uniforms, suits and smart-styled women were glad-handing their way up the track and through the village. Women were nodded to, men's shoulders were slapped, the babies' cheeks were tweaked in the show of solidarity. He watched the cameras. It was an event. Earnest conversations started up and lasted long enough to be recorded and witnessed on film. A little scrum had developed at the front of the VIPs, and a sergeant of the German army, red-faced, attempted to push back the cameras and microphones, succeeded, then was outflanked to the right, drove the right back, and was outflanked to the left. Twice when he thought a lens was aimed towards him, that he would figure in the background of a picture, Mister did what was reflex to him and presented his back to them.

'We have to have them here because we need the publicity to go round the world. The need for money for these people has to be reinforced with the pictures and the interviews – but it is degrading. They take the dignity from people. How can people talk, with honesty, about their situation when they have a camera in one nostril and a microphone in the other? The media has no discipline. They are like frogs, slimy frogs, and you collect them in a bucket but as you put one in another slips out.'

They were both laughing. It was their own moment, and private. She took his hand. She was holding his hand as they laughed, and their faces were close, and he saw the white cleanness of her teeth and the tan of her skin. She led him further up the hill. Mister let her hold his hand.

The shutter clattered on automatic. Through the viewfinder, using the 300mm lens, Joey watched them laughing and holding hands. Eight frames, or nine, and then his view of them was obscured by the old mill building above the stream. He lay on his stomach, crushing down last autumn's fall of leaves, and huddled behind the camera.

'What other charities, Mister, do you help?'
'Well, bits and pieces.'
'You can tell me – I admire your modesty. Too many people boast. Tell me.'
'I do things for a hospice. You know what a hospice is? Yes? I help them . . . I put a roof on a church . . .'
'Is that your life, Mister? Helping in Bosnia, helping in a hospice, helping a church?'
'Well, not entirely.'
She squeezed his hand. He felt the warmth of her smile.
'Come on.'
In the distance he heard the helicopter rotors start to turn. They'd barely been on the ground half an hour. The VIPs, in a slithering column, retraced their way through the village, and the media were boarding buses. The villagers drifted from the track and meandered

in little groups towards the few rebuilt homes. He was surprised the visit had been so short, and she must have read his thoughts. She told him that it was important the visitors were not bored, were enthusiastic, went back to their offices and wrote the reports that would bring in more donations from their governments.

Children now surrounded the two of them as they walked along a mud-packed path. With one hand she held Mister's, with the other a child's. He saw the way they touched her, pinched at her coat sleeve, gripped the hem of her anorak, and he saw the love in her face for them. They went towards a narrow plank bridge spanning the stream. He felt the little tickle in his trailing hand and looked down sharply. A small boy had reached to take the trailing hand. Mister was about to reject him, snatch his own hand away. He'd never allowed his sisters' children to get close to him. His sisters always scolded their children if they came close to him and told them not to 'bother' their uncle. He knew nothing of the trust of children. He let the small boy take his trailing hand as they went across the loose-fastened planks of the bridge. A little girl came behind the boy and took his free hand for the bridge crossing, and Mister saw the upturned tag of her anorak; Marks & Spencer, a cast-off. As he came off the bridge, still holding the little boy's hand, Monika looked at him and winked. She approved. He could not remember the last time that pleasure and pride had coursed through him at such a small thing. She took him to a house.

'They have no electricity, only heating-oil for the fire and a gas can for the stove. A little paraffin is given them each month for light. If we get more people back, have more homes for them to move into, we can pressure the authorities to spend money and restore the electricity supply. There are three families living here, nineteen people. Work has been done on the ground floor, but not yet upstairs because they are waiting for more building materials to be brought. It is not possible for them to buy the materials themselves because they have no work, no money, but at least they are, again, in their homes . . . How many bedrooms do you have in your house, Mister?'

'Five.'

'How many people?'

'My wife and myself.'

They went inside. He hovered behind her, and she was greeted like a true friend. He saw in the gloom two of the boxes, unpacked, on which were scrawled Bosnia with Love. Leading to the one table were mud smears across the bare concrete floor. An old man sat in a chair near to the table and smoked; his pullover bore the woven insignia of the Edinburgh Woollen Mill and crossed golf clubs under the stitched writing, and he smoked as if that were the luxury left to him. There was a line of institution beds, with metal frames, dull blankets. The little girl careered away and bounced on to a bed, but the small boy kept hold of Mister's hand. The women were of all ages, but only old men were crowding into the room. The child wanted, Mister thought, to hold the hand of his father . . . There were four bedrooms always empty at his home by the North Circular Road. His father visited, occasionally, but would not stay over. His mother had never slept in his house. He and the Princess had no friends they would have invited, nor her father and mother. They never entertained in the dining room with the big mahogany table and the matching set of eight chairs. If it was necessary to entertain, for business, he went to a restaurant, the Mixer arranged a private room at the back, a Card sat in the kitchen and another stood at the private room's door. He had so many bedrooms. He had hotel bedrooms and service accommodation bedrooms and time-share bedrooms. He had more bedrooms in Cyprus, the South of France, on the Spanish coast and in the Caribbean and . . . He had the money to rebuild the village and bring every man, woman and child back to it and to dress all of them in Armani or Yves St Laurent, to give them electricity, plumb in the sewage, put boards and carpets under their feet and curtains at their windows, to build a factory for them, and to bring them pedigree cattle. If he had done that he would not have noticed the loss.

He was served coffee. To Mister it was bitter and the sludge at the bottom of the tiny cup caught between his teeth. It was the coffee of Green Lanes that he drank in the *spieler* cafés with the Turks, and he was practised in hiding his disgust as he drank. A dog-eared set of cards was cut. The stakes for the game were used matches, plucked from a filled ashtray and blown on to remove the tobacco dust. It wasn't easy for him to play, and twice he grimaced at Monika. The small boy held his hand, would not let go of it. He played, and the time slipped away. He made certain he was never the winner. At home, in London, he would never be a loser, and not a loser in the old city of Sarajevo when he played the high-stakes game with Serif, whom she called criminal scum. He lost the matches he had been given. She was at the far end of the room, with the women, and she glanced at him, tapped the face of her watch.

They went out into the dusk. It was only when they left that Mister realized a crowd had gathered in the room and outside the door to watch him fail at cards, and to be close to her. She kissed many cheeks, he shook the many hands pressed on him.

On the slippery path he took her fingers so that she would not fall. It was an excuse. She wore good walking-boots, he had smooth leather-soled shoes. They went across the bridge, clung to a handrail that was a slack strand of rope, and walked on the track down through the village. The shells of the burned-out houses remained in darkness. Brighter lights shone out from the undamaged homes where the generator engines thudded and where uncovered windows showed the flicker of television pictures . . . He heard the patter of the feet that followed him.

'Why don't they go back and get them, the TVs?'

'Because they are beaten people, Mister, they have no more any spirit to fight.'

'Then they've no future.'

'The other future is to start the war again, Mister. Of course you are angry – I am angry – but violence, criminal violence, solves nothing. It is the way of the barbarian. The place for the criminals is not at the head of armies of thugs and thieves, it is in gaol where there are bars and where there is no key.'

They reached her jeep. The engine was on and her driver slept in the sealed warmth. He heard a low, guttered, hacking cough behind him. He turned. For a moment the small boy cringed away, was a retreating shadow figure on the empty track. He reached out his arms and the child came to him. He lifted the little boy and hugged the thin frame to his chest. Monika was with him. Together they held the child. He kissed the child's face, and Monika kissed his. He put the small boy down and watched him go into the darkness.

'If the visitors had done what you have they would have learned ten times, a hundred times, more. I thank you.'

'For nothing.'

They climbed into the jeep, were driven away from the village. On the seat between them her hand rested on his.

June 1998

Three times Husein Bekir had conceded defeat in the past five hours. Three times the patronizing victor's satisfaction had been on Dragan Kovac's face.

Each time he lost, while the retired police sergeant poured more brandy, burped on his lunch, and called him an old fool and a man without intelligence, Husein immediately set the carved wooden pieces back on the board, and they played again. He had played the last game, and the next would be the same, with a desperate intensity that furrowed his forehead, that made his hand tremble as he lifted a piece and slapped it down in its new position. His concentration was on his own moves, and what he anticipated would be Dragan Kovac's moves, but above all he searched for a sign of his opponent's cheating. As yet he could not find such a sign and that confused him hugely. If his opponent did not cheat, the implication was clear to Husein: he, himself, was inferior ... Of course Dragan Kovac cheated. He heard a distant voice calling his name, but ignored it. The grandchild and the dog were also ignored, and had slipped out of the door to search for entertainment.

When the bottle's mouth hovered over his glass, Husein put his hand clumsily over it and succeeded only in tipping over the glass. His head was bent over the board and he saw nothing of the fields below the porch, and he did not look up to find the voice calling his name, and he did not glance at the mulberry tree beyond the sagging fence of barbed wire, and he did not see the dog chasing after the ball his grandson had thrown for it. He tried, his concentration fading, to plot the defence of his bishop, and he thought it was with un-necessary ostentation that Dragan Kovac wiped the spilled brandy off the table.

Until she reached him he had not been aware of Lila's approach up the track.

As he peered down at the board and looked for answers, he saw at the edge of his vision her river-washed rubber boots, which came to the top of her muscled shins. When was he coming home? she asked: he was coming home when the game was finished. Who was going to milk the goats? she asked: he would milk the goats when he had finished the game. What was more important, milking the goats or drinking and playing games? Where was his grandchild? He did not know. She snorted at him in derision, and he heard Dragan Kovac's chuckle. There was the cackling of her voice, and he lost the threads of his defence. He looked up. He was palpitating with anger. He looked around. The child was high in the mulberry tree beyond the fence. The dog sat under the spread of the tree with the ball in its mouth and the saliva dripped from its jaws. Did he consider it responsible to allow the child to climb a tree – from which he might fall – and not even know where he was? Did he consider it responsible to be drunk when in charge of the child, his grandson? Under his breath, holding his head in his hands, he swore.

If he wanted to get back his chill, she said, that was his business, but she was not permitting him to abandon her grandson up a dangerous tree. If he got his chill back, through his own stupidity, when he should have been milking the goats, then it would not be she who nursed him. He wriggled in annoyance, and Dragan Kovac reached, grinning, for the bottle.

Husein Bekir saw his wife, Lila, stamp away from him in her shining rubber boots. She was stout, strong for her age, heavy-built. She seemed to plough through the long uncut grass below the porch towards the drooping fence in front of the mulberry tree. She straddled the fence, caught her skirt on the wire, extricated herself, leaving a thread on the barbs when she swung over her back leg, then went into the shade under the tree's leaves. He saw the deepening lines in his friend's forehead, and his eyes were screwed to narrow slits. His mouth gaped open, as if he tried to clarify a little moment of memory from far back, and could not. Then his friend's tongue flapped idly, but no words came. She was calling the child down. Husein did not know what memory seeped back into the mind of Dragan Kovac, nor what his friend tried to say.

The child was pale, thin, like the scrawny dog gliding on the baked earth under the tree, had no meat on him and was lightweight.

His woman, Lila, was solid and heavy.

She moved under the tree so that she could better steady the child when he dropped down to her and her voice was harsh with her command as if she had no patience.

Dragan Kovac hissed, 'It's where they did it – put them – I remember, it's where—'

'Put what?'

The mine exploded under her foot.

For Joey, it had been the journey from hell.

The nightmare had begun after he had seen Mister and the woman leave the village in the UNHCR jeep. It had been hard to track them at the end, in the failed light. He had kept a distance back from them, but had seen Mister pick up a child and hug it, and then the small boy had run up the track past him. Joey had walked another mile through the long strip of the village, to where the blue van was hidden in trees beside the river. As he'd approached, stumbling over fallen branches, he'd heard the charge of their escape. They would have run when they'd heard his approach. The van's doors were open. He'd sworn. He'd reached inside, felt the dash and found the loose wires from the radio. His foot, as he'd stood by the door, had brushed against bricks. He'd sworn aloud. He'd gone round to the passenger side, found the pocket open, and the torch hadn't been there. More bricks against his hand on the passenger side – bricks to hold up the van, because there were no bloody wheels, no tyres. He'd sworn again in fury. Of course he had seen the poverty of the village, abject poverty, but he'd never thought that a little of the poverty might be removed by the acquisition of his tyres, his goddam wheels. He'd started to walk.

He dragged himself up the stairs of the hotel. A man had been sitting, smoking, an empty coffee cup in front of him, close to the reception desk, and he'd been given his key by a scowling night porter whose eyes were never off the man. He went up to his landing.

A man lounged in a chair at the top of the stairs, seemed to strip Joey with his gaze. He, too, wore the uniform of the man in the foyer – jeans, a cigarette, close-cut hair, a black leather jacket. A short-barrelled machine pistol, two magazines taped together, lay on his lap. Joey knew the face but couldn't put a place to it. It confused him, but in his exhaustion he didn't stop.

He went past the door of the room that had been Maggie's; there was a light under it and low voices, the scented fumes of cigarettes.

He let himself into his room, dumped his bag on the bed and took out the camera.

Opening up his laptop, he wrote his report, his fingers hammering on the keys.

He'd walked to the main road, then gone west along it. He'd hitched every car and lorry that had passed him, but none had stopped and some had nearly clipped him. He'd reached a village and seen a café's lights. He'd gone into it. Was there a taxi in the village? Shrugged responses, there was no taxi. Was there a tele- phone to call a taxi from Kiseljak? The telephone was broken. He'd headed off, continued walking.

The report was typed out. He was tired, so bloody tired. He was cold, he was damp, he was hungry. He snatched the wire cables from his bag. His fingers shivered. It was slow going, and his temper was fuelled – should have taken him thirty seconds but it took him minutes – and he linked the cables to his laptop and his mobile, and hit the transmission-code keys. The first time, with his clumsiness, it didn't go through, second time it did.

He had walked for an hour and a half to reach Kiseljak. No taxis, no buses. In the police station he had gone half-way down on his knees, and flagged them with his ID. A police car had taken him to Rakovica, half-way to Sarajevo, and the driver had gestured that he could go no further, that he was not allowed beyond his area. Again, he had walked. A lorry with a drunk driver had lifted him as far as Blasuj, then dropped him. He'd walked in the dark, another hour, almost crying in his frustration, towards the always distant lights of the city, his goal.

Joey wired the digital camera to his mobile, and dialled. And the camera's pictures were downloaded to London. The mobile's screen message told him they were received.

He'd walked into Ilidza. No taxis in Kiseljak, Rakovica or Blasuj, and half a hundred bloody taxis in the Ilidja suburb. He'd been driven to the hotel. He'd staggered in through the door, into the bright light, mud on his boots, his trousers and his coat.

He remembered, the recognition seeped into his mind, where he'd seen the men . . . They had been in the back of the truck. When he had been picked up in the truck, and the door had been opened for him, the interior light had come on. They had been in the back – Ante and

Muhsin. He had seen their faces – Salko and Fahro – before he had nestled down in the front seat and slammed the truck door, and the light had gone out. When they had come from the truck and had gone into the druggie's block, they had worn balaclavas and he hadn't seen their faces. He'd seen their faces when they'd come out of the block, work done, before they'd pulled their hoods back down.

'An excellent meal,' Mister said, and pushed his chair back from the table.

It had been the same meal, the Eagle reflected, that they'd eaten every night, but it was the first time Mister had praised the food. He'd talked, rambling, about his day, about war and poverty, about hatred, and the Eagle and Atkins had been his audience. If it had been hot, stinking hot, he would have diagnosed Mister as a sunstroke case, but there hadn't been any fierce sun ... *She* wasn't mentioned. The Eagle began to think the unthinkable.

Almost as an afterthought, Mister turned to Atkins. 'You did all right today?'

'Went well, Mister.'

'You got the place?'

'We did a reconnaissance on the house and we've found a position where there's a clear field of vision on to it, a clear field of fire.'

'And tarmac?'

'Tarmac and frozen ground. The ground's smooth.'

'That's great, well done.'

The Eagle thought Atkins was a bloody puppy lapping praise.

'That's what we do tomorrow – should be a bit special. I mean, seeing it actually fired, that'll be sort of exciting ... Good night, guys.'

Mister walked away from the table, left them, and his whistling echoed out of the restaurant. It was, of course, unthinkable, and he had known Mister for twenty-eight years, and the Princess for eighteen of them – *unthinkable*.

The pictures were passed by Gough round the central table, to be subjected to the team's scrutiny.

'Choice – I'd fancy a bit of it myself,' said SQG3.

'Not what I'd have expected from him, dipping his wick, not from what Boy Brilliant left us on him, out of the character Cann drew,' said SQG8.

'Silly old beggar, getting the flushes at his age, and his Princess won't like it, will not be a happy girl if she gets to see them,' said SQG5.

'She'll get to see them, in good time,' Gough growled. 'What I'd like, at both ends from tomorrow we start to build the pressure. From pressure comes mistakes – only a little diversion and can we now, please, concentrate.'

He gathered up the pictures of his Target One and an unidentified young woman, locked them in his drawer, and they applied themselves again to the first of the rummages that would be launched in the morning that would build the pressure, force the mistakes. The name of Cann, and what he did, did not deserve another mention. They were too busy, inside their own agenda, to think of him.

He closed his door behind him and went down the corridor. He waved his ID at the man on the landing, thought it was Salko, and saw that both the hands were on the machine pistol. He had left behind his coat and he swivelled to show that there was no weapon in his belt. Outside her room, the one he thought was Muhsin acknowledged him sourly, and Joey thought he was allowed with reluctance to go to the door.

He knocked and heard a scrabble of movement behind it. He said his name. The door opened on the chain, then closed again, then was fully opened.

'Come on in,' she said. 'Join the party.'

She was on the bed, dressed, a filled glass in her hand, shared with a cigarette. Frank Williams, the policeman, in uniform, was in the chair by the window. The last two of what he had called the Sreb Four were hunched on the carpet – jeans, leather jackets and cigarettes, machine pistols against their knees within fast reach – one against the foot of the bed and one against the wardrobe. Joey reckoned they were Fahro and Ante. He saw the metal case on the floor under the window, by the chair.

'It's the advantage of a transit lounge, the duty-free. I've Chivas Regal and Courvoisier.'

'You're drunk.'

'Have to be drunk or mental to come back here.'

'Why did you turn round?'

'A nice young man met me at Zagreb. He thought I was in mortal danger. He bought me three pink gins ... So, I got to think you needed wet-nursing.'

'Why don't you fuck off?'

'And needed looking after. I thought it was pretty foul to ditch you. I was three hours from home. At the debrief they'd all have bad-mouthed you, and they'd have apologized for sending me out with a kid, an amateur. The knives would have been in your back, Joey, and the sneers down the phone to where you work. I'd have gone home, alone.'

'I didn't ask you to stay.'

She spat, 'God, you make it hard!'

'I don't want you, don't need you.'

'A speech, we will have a speech. You will not, please, interrupt my speech.'

'Do you have something to eat?'

'Damn you.' She wiggled her bottom. The hem of her skirt climbed her thighs. She pulled two packets of peanuts from under her and hurled them at him. 'I was about to say—'

'I'll have the whisky.'

'You're an obstinate, arrogant sod. I am trying to help you.' She reached for the bottle and threw it at him. He caught it, then the plastic beaker that followed. Frank had his hand over his mouth, as if he was stifling laughter. The men with the guns were expressionless. 'We are all trying to help you. I tracked Frank down from the airport, he drove me here, then he called in the cavalry. We are all trying to bloody help you.'

'I don't want you, any of you. I'm doing all right.'

'I've stepped over the same line as you have. I—'

'I doubt it – isn't there anything more than peanuts?'

'Shut up, hear me – for God's sake, do me that courtesy.' The crackle slipped from her voice, and the wasp's sting. 'You showed me the line to cross and I've followed you. I told the joker who met me at Zagreb that I'd realized I'd left my best black shoes behind and was going back to get them – heh, don't look so damn pissed off, it's supposed to be funny. Your Target One, he's your enemy. At my place, we don't have enemies. We don't hate our opposition, don't despise it, we play a fucking game with it. Where are the KGB now, and the Hungarians and the Poles? They're at our seminars, or giving us lectures, and then we go off to the bar and we swap old stories, chat through the equipment we used, and we have a laugh about the poor puny bastards who believed in us, who they tortured and shot. We're dying, you're alive. You're bloody lucky to have an enemy. So I came back.'

He downed the whisky. He poured what was left of the first peanut packet into his mouth and pocketed the second.

'I'll see you in the morning.'

Chapter Fourteen

The neighbour knew Bruce James was away. He had been gone nearly a week; she'd seen him go with his bags. She had heard the footsteps tramping on the stairs, then the landing off which she lived, then going on up the last flight. Very few people called to visit him at any hour of the day or night, but she could not remember when anyone had come at a quarter to six in the morning. She thought there were four or five of them, and all men from the weight of their tread. She went to her door and listened as they walked up the final steps. Her nose wrinkled; she could smell pipe tobacco.

She liked Bruce James. She thought him courteous and well-mannered. Her own grandson was in the navy, an engineer on board a frigate, serving in the Gulf. Sometimes he brought up her post and then they'd talk, and he'd tell her of his own days in the army. She kept an eye on his small flat at the top of the stairs, under the building's eaves.

She heard a jangle of keys, then metal scrapes, and low-spoken obscenities. At the moment she realized that four or five men were attempting to unlock the door to Mr James's rooms, she heard the thud then the splintering of breaking wood.

She hurried to her telephone. Programmed into the set were the numbers she considered most important, and among them was that of Hammersmith police station. She used the phrase she'd heard on television: 'Intruders on the premises'.

She heard the dragging of furniture above her ceiling and the movement of feet. It was a thin ceiling. Mr James was exceptionally considerate and never had his music loud. She waited. She heard the siren of the approaching police car.

She met them on her landing, a young police constable and an older policewoman. She pointed up the last stairs, at the door off the hinges. The noise seeped through the doorway, and the voices. They told her to close her door and lock it, and she saw them take their truncheons off the belts, and the little gas canisters; she knew about the gas from the television programmes. She thought them very brave.

She locked her own door, bolted and chained it.

Joey slept in. When he woke his body ached, but his head was worse. There were the few seconds when he could not place where he was and he lay in the gloom of his room, but the pain in his head, his body and his feet lurched him alert. The curtains were drawn, but carelessly. A strip of gold light came between them and made a shaft on to his bed. He saw the time on his watch, swore and rolled out of the bed. He doused himself in the shower, let tepid water run over him. He was half wet, half dry, as he dressed. He pulled on the same trousers he'd worn the day before, with the same mud on the knees, and the same shirt. He couldn't find clean socks in his bag, only used pairs, and he had to go down on the floor to find those he'd worn yesterday and which he'd scattered when he had undressed with the whisky in him. He didn't shave, didn't look in the mirror. He went out of his room and stopped at her door. He knocked. There was no reply from Maggie Bolton, just the stale stink of the cigarettes, and no man on the landing. He took the stairs two at a time.

They were in the far corner of the breakfast room. It was a quarter past nine.

'Good of you to show up,' she said.

'Why didn't you wake me?'

'Wild horses wouldn't have.' She grinned. 'You young things have no stamina.'

He slouched into a chair. All of the Sreb Four were smoking. The cigarettes were as much part of their uniform as the jeans, boots and cheap leather jackets. To get to the chair he had had to step over two sports bags. He couldn't see their guns and assumed that the machine pistols were in the bags. Frank Williams was beside her and seemed to smile at Joey, without mercy. He poured himself coffee from the jug, into her cup, and turned it so that he didn't drink from the side marked with her burgundy lipstick. The coffee dispersed the ache in his head. He snatched a bread roll off a plate and broke it, crumbs scattering on the cloth as he wolfed it. She passed him a sheet of flimsy paper.

From: Endicott, Room 709, VBX
To: Bolton (Technical Support), Sarajevo
Subject: Organized Crime / AWP
Timed: 02.27GMT 19.03.01
Security Classification: Secret
Message Starts:
If you determined to play the wild goose/aka silly bugger, good LUCK. We insist you have serious protection – arrange it. You are not, repeat *not*, to put your personal safety at risk. We require your wrap-up within 48 hours, and then your immediate return UK. Remember at all times that we are the senior Service; you do not take instructions from the C&E junior.
Don't go native,
Endicott

'Am I supposed to thank you?'

'It's not compulsory. I don't mean to be personal, but actually you stink. I hope you filled a laundry-bag.'

Joey had finished the roll and the coffee. He tried to sound firm, decisive, but thought he failed. 'Can we, please, sort out the priorities of the day, and then I'll do my laundry?'

She asked, innocently, what he meant by 'priorities'.

He was too tired and too flustered to recognize the trap she laid for him. He said, 'Well, we need wheels. We need to assess the targets and recce them, decide whether we can return to intrusive sur-veillance, then how we're going to divide up areas of responsibility.'

Her small hand hovered in front of her mouth as if to mask a yawn. Williams, the bastard, straight-faced, whispered a translation into the ear of the Sreb Four man on his right side and the message was passed between them. They were impassive and told him nothing of the trap.

'Well, isn't that the professional approach to take?' Joey flared. 'Have you a better idea? I was once called an "obstinate, arrogant sod", but I don't compete. You're light years ahead.'

She turned in her chair and reached to the venetian blind covering the window. She depressed one bar and lifted another, made a slit. The window faced on to the hotel's rear car park. He leaned forward, over the cups and the plates. He saw the blue van. The sun reflected from the new hub caps and glanced on the new tyres. He settled back in his chair and wrapped his arms around his chest.

She said, 'Waste not, want not, that's what my mum always told me, still tells me. I rather liked it. The van sort of felt like home. I'm sorry you lost my bucket. Frank and two of the boys, Muhsin and Salko, went to retrieve it this morning, and borrowed the new wheels. While they were doing that, I went with the other boys to track down that Mitsubishi they tried to run you down with. There's now a beacon on it. It was easier than I thought it'd be. There were two guys asleep, pissed like you, in a shed at the side. The boys were good with the dog, made a proper friend of it – it's all in the body language, isn't it? I'm good on locks, so we checked out the warehouse, then went back the way we'd come, over the wall. Had the time of my life – big strong hands holding me where they shouldn't have, lifting me up and helping me down. Anyway, then we popped down to the old quarter. They took me up over the rooftops, to a place they knew. Bloody damn slippery the tiles were, and bloody great rough fingers on my waist, steadying me – quite a compensation. From there I had a line of sight into Ismet Mujic's apartment, and I unpacked one of my choicest little boxes of tricks. It's the infinity transmitter. Across the street from my box is his window and behind his window is his phone. My box does the leap. It uses the phone's microphone to transmit the room's conversations. We have another relay in the box and that goes to a room the boys have rented, and there's a tape-recorder turning there, voice-activated. Quite clever, yes? We didn't wake you because we thought you'd be tired. Sorry about that.'

He attempted civility. 'What do you suggest I do with my day?'

'If you don't mind me saying so, the way you look I'd reckon you're no use to man or beast. Take the rest of the day off – after you've done your laundry and shaved.'

'Thanks very bloody much.'

'Please excuse me, I've work to be getting on with. Put your feet up, Joey. Come on, boys.'

She smiled sweetly at Joey as he crumpled. They followed her out of the breakfast room, carrying their bags, and formed a phalanx around her. The big men's boots padded around the clatter of her heels. Frank Williams was last up from the table. Joey caught his arm, pulled him close. 'I didn't think you'd be part of it.'

'Part of what?'

'Humiliating me – her showing off, at my expense, in front of "her boys".'

'Take the day off. The way you are, you're useless.' He prised Joey's hand off his sleeve, and leaned closer. 'You know what she said to me? She said you'd lost the sense of fear, and without fear you'd get hurt – so she turned round. She's gone on a limb for you, and I have, and the boys. You've earned it, take the day off.'

Frank Williams ran to catch her.

Gough had taken the Underground to Tooting Bec. He sipped a good strong cup of tea, sat in the old chair, and listened.

'I wondered if someone would come to see me, but I hoped they wouldn't. I knew that if someone came and asked that question it would be to assess how well, or how badly, he would stand against the pressures of extreme stress – because he was in danger. I know him better than anyone, you see, better even than young Jennifer. He used to come in here in the evenings, late, and sit where you're sitting, in Perry's chair, and tell me about his day. Don't think me conceited, please, but I believe I'm as well briefed as anyone on that awful man, Packer. Perry was in the Diplomatic Corps and before that I was an army wife. I've seen what stress can do to young people . . . It started as dedication. There seemed to be a sense of – may I use a word that's out of vogue in these times? – duty. I thought it was keenness. I'd seen plenty of that in young officers and young second secretaries. To me, keenness, duty, dedication are all admirable. You were hunting for evidence against Packer, and Joey was working all hours, and he seemed utterly happy. He'd a girlfriend, a sweet soul, and he was making an adult life for himself, and was proud of what he did. Then it all changed. I didn't recognize it at the time, but I can see it now. He was in that chair, where you are, it was near to midnight, and he told me that a surveillance operation had identified Packer in a car with those ghastly drugs, and it was enough to warrant his arrest. It wasn't dedication any longer, it was more obsession. Give a child a toy, a favourite toy, then tell the child that at the weekend it will be taken from him. After Packer was arrested the light seemed to go from his life. He was brooding. I used to hear him in his room reading aloud the surveillance and evidence statements, and late at night he'd be playing the tapes of telephone intercepts, and I'd hear him striding around his room and asking the questions of the people interrogating Packer. Packer had become the reason for his existence. Packer had the power, even in his prison cell, the authority. Joey started to feel worthless, and that was when the dedication went and the obsession came. I don't want to speak ill of him, but I began to think of Joey as a hollow shell, as if he couldn't live without Packer. It is rather frightening, isn't it, obsession? It changes people. It brutalized Joey. It bred a sort of cruelty in his character, and I'd never seen it before, a quite unpleasant cruelty – he became savage with Jennifer, and she'd done nothing to deserve it. It is like a dark cloud on the sun – you don't often see it but when it's there it chills you. Is he still in Bosnia, still trailing Packer? He'll fight foul to win, to achieve whatever it is that drives him, he'll fight very dirty. I had a distressing thought the other night, it quite upset me. When he comes back, if he's won, if he's destroyed Packer, then he won't be the sort of young man I want to know . . . Will he stand up to the stress? He will, very well – the cruelty will sustain him.'

Gough laid down the cup and saucer, and made his excuses. It had been more of what he had hoped to hear.

The detective chief inspector wandered out of the entrance. Within sight of the front-desk security people, he lit up a cigarette. Half of the building, home of the National Crime Squad, slipped outside during a working day for a drag, cough, gasp. Round the corner, in the small length of pavement where the high cameras were blind, he reached in his pocket for the pay-as-you-go mobile. There was a clipped answer and he heard traffic in the background. He reported what he knew. He suggested what he would do next and it was sanctioned.

When the camera picked him up again, the mobile was back in his pocket and his cigarette was nearly smoked. He returned through the security check and took a lift to the fourth floor.

He stood in front of a grey-suited commander. His life was lived at the edge, walking a tightrope that was razor fine, and precarious. His bank accounts, held in customer confidentiality in the Channel Islands, proved it. He had known the commander for twenty years of police service, he was trusted and a friend, but was always correct.

'I thought you should know something, sir.'

'Cut the "sir" crap – what is it?'

'Hammersmith had a call, "intruders on premises", from a member of the public. They went to this address and found it stuffed with the Church, doing the place over, warrant and all. The property is the home of Bruce James, a security consultant and ex-military. He is also, which makes him interesting, listed as an associate of Packer. We are, as I understand it, supposed to be fully appraised of any Customs operation mounted against Packer. Wasn't that laid down, agreed? Nothing's come across my desk. It's not a situation I'm happy with, sir, if we're sharing with them but they're not sharing with us. Put frankly, it makes life bloody impossible – and it's a slur. We're not to be trusted. I can't see you, sir, taking that lying down . . . Just thought you should know.'

He pushed the wheelchair. He had changed into cleaner clothes, filled in the laundry list and dumped the bag outside his room. Then he had shaved, and walked to the Ministry of Justice, where he had searched out her father's courtroom. He had gone inside, tiptoed between the public's benches and the lawyers' desks, moved past a stenographer and the accused. He had gone to the raised desk where her father sat, walked under his nose to the side of the dais. He had slipped off the chair's wheel locks and pushed her out of the courtroom. Nobody had spoken, the case arguments had continued, nobody had intervened. He had wheeled her out into the sunshine.

On the pavement, Joey had said, 'It's my day off, that's what I'm told. I'm a stranger in need of a guide.'

Jasmina had said, 'Rules of engagement forbid discussion of the past, the war – of the present, the criminals.'

'To see the sights,' he'd said, 'which way do we go?'

It was an hour since they had set off. He protected the wheels from the broken pavements as best he could, and steered her across streets where the lights were with them but the traffic screamed to a threatening halt close to them. She showed him the locked doors of the old Orthodox church and took him inside the twin-towered cathedral; they looked across the Miljacka river to the synagogue and she told him that all the Jews were gone from the city. She waved for him to stop propelling her when she'd picked a view of the Ali-Pasina Dzamija, and she said that that mosque was the finest example of Islamic sacred architecture in Europe. There were libraries, public buildings, Olympic sites, and the bridge where an assassin had killed an archduke.

They did not speak of the war, or of the present. There was nothing she showed him, and no story she told him, that could make them laugh. What was unsaid was all around them. The broken buildings and the grinding squeal of the wheelchair were allies in his despair.

He bought her flowers.

She sat in the chair and her hands gripped the stems that made the posy.

They were in a park. She pointed to old gravestones from medieval times and said they were called *stecaks* and recited to him as if she were his tour guide. 'It is taught us that the *stecaks* are the monuments of a period of our history not penetrated by understanding, by light. They are secret-keepers to us. If you do not know the stones then you do not know us. An epitaph is carved on one: "I stood praying to God, meaning no evil, yet I was struck to death by lightning." We can be a sad people, and we live in darkness. Fortune does not shine on us, Joey. We have little to offer strangers, only our misery. You want to laugh, I want to laugh. What can we find to laugh at?'

The sun beat on them. He looked at the old stones.

'Why did you come to get me, Joey, today?'

'To be with you,' he said simply. 'Because I wanted to be with you.

I'm not meaning to patronize you. It's not that I feel sorry for you. I just wanted to be here, close to you.'

He saw her fingers tighten on the flower stems. 'Do you have a girlfriend, Joey, at home?'

'I did.'

'Did she stop loving you, or did you stop loving her?'

'I came here. What I did here has hurt her. Because of me she has been through pain. After what I have inflicted on her, I doubt she'll love me again.'

'Don't pity me, Joey, because that would be worse for me than anything you brought to your girlfriend. Would you take me back to my father?'

They were the opposites, Jen and Jasmina. He pushed the chair and contrasted them in his mind with each other. One was fit, healthy, the other was crippled, pale. Whatever the physical comparisons, one had a future, the other had a past. He felt an awful shaming, gnawing, consuming guilt. He had bought a girl flowers, he had killed his time with her, given her the charity of his company. He would climb on his plane. He would go up the steps where a wheelchair could not follow. She would be an ever fainter memory until she was brushed from his mind.

They reached the Ministry of Justice.

Joey said, 'I don't know how far we have gone but without your father's help, and yours, I would not have been able to start on that road.'

At last she smiled. It was a thin, fleeting, wan smile, and he thought it lovely. She wheeled herself away from him and up the ramp into the building. Before the gloom of the Ministry's interior engulfed her, he saw the final brightness of the flowers on her lap.

'Hello, Commander, were you trying to get a moment with me?'

The minister basked in the memory of the applause. He had been the last speaker before the lunch break. The audience had been police, editors, social-services executives and education experts. It had been his drugs speech – a velvet hand of sympathy offered to the abusing victims of the trade, a mailed fist to the architects of the misery. He had told his audience that he spoke for a government committed to helping the exploited and crushing the exploiters . . .

and *they*, he'd said, would face the resources of the law-enforcement agencies, united and dedicated. He had clasped his hands together at that moment of his speech to represent the unity of purpose of the agencies. He had quoted, a favourite line when talking about inter-agency unity, from *Ezekiel* 37: 22, 'I will make them one people', and he'd said that had been his promise to the Prime Minister when he was honoured, privileged, to be given the appointment. Evil men, he had said, would find they could run but not hide when hunted by agencies that were, in purpose and deed, *united*.

He was informed of the search that morning of the apartment belonging to Bruce James, and his temper surged.

'It's because they don't trust us, Minister, that they blunder in without sharing – it's divisive, bloody insulting and, worst of all, it runs in utter contradiction to the theme of your excellent speech, and government policy. If you want results, then they've to be reined in. Can I leave it with you?'

'Damn right you can.'

July 1999

'It was a PMA2. That's the most common mine that was laid. It's anti-personnel and designed to wound, not kill. It has one hundred grams of explosive, detonated by five kilos of pressure.'

'But you miss the point, Herr Barnaby.'

In his Portakabin room, in the mine-action centre, in the Marshal Tito barracks, in Sarajevo, the Englishman thought it was against the German woman's nature to allow him to complete a sentence of explanation. Barnaby – he never made it clear whether that was a given name or a family name – was experienced in deflecting the bullying tactics employed by the executives of international charities. Just as he never hurried when cleaning a minefield, so he never raised his voice or lost his temper. 'What point do I miss, Frau Bierhof?'

'You miss the point that the woman, the Bekir woman, was the last to be hurt – that is thirteen months ago.'

'The point continues to evade me.'

'Nothing has been done in thirteen months.'

'Frau Bierhof, do you have any idea of the scale of the problem?' He asked the question without point-scoring rhetoric. Frau

Anneliese Bierhof, Barnaby thought, was a woman unused to detailed rebuttal. As the director (Field Operations) of World in Crisis, from Hamburg, with millions of DMs to spend, she was a powerful hitter. He imagined her bludgeoning her will through endless committee meetings, dictating policy over the hesitations of those unfortunates who feared the jab of her pen at them or her gimlet glance. She was a large woman with shoulders accentuated by the padding of her jacket. 'Allow me, please, as they appear in this office, to tell you the facts of life that must be taken into consideration.'

'I know the fact of life, Herr Barnaby. You will hear the "fact" that I acknowledge. In Germany today we have twenty-three families from the Muslim village of Vraca, and we have eighteen families from the Serb village of Ljut. The stabilization force of NATO reports to Berlin that the Bunica valley is peaceful and does not suffer inter-ethnic tension. Our government wants these people returned to their domicile. They refuse to return while there are still mines in the locality. The mines must be cleared. A start must be made. It is thirteen months since Frau Bekir was disabled, and that start has not been made. World in Crisis has the money in place, waiting to be spent, for the repair of their homes and the infrastructure of their villages – such as the electricity – but we must know that the mines have been removed. When will it happen? Why has thirteen months been allowed to elapse?'

He said quietly, against the rising cresendo of her voice, 'Because there are other places that have a higher priority.'

'That is not an answer that is satisfactory.' She paused, sipped at the bottled water she had brought with her.

Well, satisfactory or not, it was the answer she would have to accept. From his Portakabin, he co-ordinated the work of fifteen hundred de-miners, but the computer database held the locations of many thousands of minefields . . . Barnaby had worked a lonely life in minefields for most of the last twenty years. The only easy work in those twenty years had been the clear-up in Kuwait a decade before. Nice straight lines of anti-tank mines, TMMs, TMAs and TMRPs, laid with the exactness of potatoes in a flat field; find the end of a line and keep going until dusk. Kuwait was the only place it had been easy, and in Kuwait there had been no shortage of money. If Frau Bierhof had been less confrontational, less antagonistic, he might have sympathized with her predicament. He knew, because the evidence of it littered his desk each day, that the pressure was on to expel the refugees from the European havens and send them whence they came.

It was thirteen months since a mine, what he classified as the 'nuisance' variety, a PMA2, had been detonated under the right foot of Lila Bekir, in her seventy-third year, and it was eleven months since he had been to the valley and seen her. She had been home from hospital a week. And she had been lucky . . . If a woman of that bulk, of that weight, had come from anywhere in Great Britain and had lived the soft life, she would have died. She had hobbled to meet him on her crutch, had insisted on making coffee for him, and had served him a sweet cake filled with grated almond. She had told him, disparaging the men who had been there, that she had shouted at them that they should not come forward to help her, should not put their own lives at risk. After the blast, she had put the child on her back and had crawled to the safety of the fence. She had told him that she had reckoned her body would protect the child if she had detonated a second mine. She was as tough as an old boot. It was a miracle, from his experience, that gas gangrene had not set in. The calcaneus, the heel bone, was destroyed at the talus, where the tibia and fibula meet, and she would never walk unaided on that foot. The doctors treating her had decided against amputation at the mid calf. They had not believed a woman of that age would cope with a prosthetic leg. There had been a wheelchair in the corner of her kitchen, but from the shiny newness of the frame and the clean tyres he had realized it had not been used, and he didn't think it ever would be. There had been no compelling reason for him to go and see the family, but his memory of the beauty of that valley had drawn him back. She was one of a few more than eleven hundred killed or wounded by mines since the guns had gone silent.

'Have you actually been there, Frau Bierhof?'

'I am familiar with the situation there.'

'I'm sorry – have you stood on the safety of the track that links Ljut and Vraca, and viewed the valley?'

'I don't have the time to stand in each ruined village. Every minute of my day is spoken for.'

He did not tell Frau Bierhof that the budget for de-mining, which he co-ordinated for the government of Bosnia-Herzegovina, was above twenty-five million American dollars. Nor did he tell her of the numbers of 'accidents' to the men who worked at his direction, who were careless, who would have no worthwhile pension; nor did he tell her of the men killed or maimed in 'incidents' – the pleasantry used to describe suicidal attempts to end the stress of the work. He went to his filing cabinet and pulled out a sheaf of photographs. Like a card-dealer he flicked them, blown-up and in monochrome or colour, across his desk.

He told her about the Bunica valley.

Each time she interrupted him, he made a little gesture with his finger, tapped his lips, then went on. He talked until she no longer interjected, brought the valley into the steaming heat of the Portakabin, and his voice was quiet against the murmur of the arcing fan on the window shelf beside his desk.

He talked until she reached into the pocket of her shoulder-padded jacket, took out a handkerchief and dabbed her eyes.

He said, 'There are a thousand such valleys. I play God. I preside over committees that decide the order in which they should be cleared. Some are disgustingly ugly and ruined with factory complexes, some are as beautiful as this one. What they have in common is that they are all destroying lives . . . When I can justify it, the valley will be cleared.'

'Testicles were pinched, Mr Gough, and it hurt.'

'I'm sure it did, Mr Cork.'

'One to one with the minister – whatever thoughts we have of the relevance of our political masters – is not a happy experience. It was like being in the middle of an incendiary bomb attack. He was powerfully angry. *Unity* is his text for the day.'

'What does the minister want, Mr Cork? Does he want togetherness, or does he want Packer behind bars?'

'He wants a report.'

'We searched the property, of course, and didn't find anything of importance but, then, we didn't expect to . . . Tell him, Mr Cork, in your report that it's about flushing foxes from cover, driving them on to the guns.'

'The only fox he'll ever have seen will have been on Wandsworth Common.'

'What you don't tell him is what I'm asking you to do. I want a total trawl to identify any call on a mobile this morning from the Pimlico district of London to Sarajevo. Shouldn't be that difficult, but I need the help of your old crowd, and GCHQ and the National Security Agency.'

'Are we moving from foxes to rotten apples?'

'Jarring them up, Mr Cork, creating mistakes.'

'I'll do that – and what do I tell, because I don't have time on my side, my esteemed minister?'

'Give him your word that there will be, in the future, total co-operation between the Sierra Quebec Golf team and the National Crime Squad.'

'Starting when? I have to tell him when.'

'Before Christmas.'

'Dammit, today's the nineteenth of March!'

He heard Dougie Gough's fulsome chuckle from the door, and then the chief investigation officer was alone in his room. For a full minute he paced the carpet. Images raced in his mind.

Dennis Cork had never been to the Ardnamurchan peninsula, but he knew Mull, Morvern and Moidart. He saw dark hills set with granite escarpments and rough slopes. The guns waited. Old farmers and postmen, estate labourers, crab fishermen and Dougie Gough, with his pipe lit, made a picket line. They were out on the hillside to kill the vermin that took the lambs. Down the hill came the beaters with their dogs running free. With the beaters was the young man with the heavy-lensed spectacles, struggling to keep up ... Cann. The big dog fox sprang from a peat ditch and tried to double back through the beaters, but the spaniels, Labradors and lurchers turned it. The *mistake* of the dog fox was to run towards the guns. It was a fine animal, strong and healthy, a lamb-taker. Now Cann was first among the beaters chasing it. The dog fox was a bright colour on the dark slope of crushed bracken. Dougie Gough had the shotgun up to his shoulder, aimed, fired, and Packer fell. The beaters and the guns did not bother to retrieve the carcass. They left it as carrion for the crows.

The images were gone.

Dennis Cork dialled the number of room 709 at Vauxhall Bridge Cross. He played the old boys' network and asked for the trawl to be

tasked through GCHQ and on through the Americans' National
Security Agency listening post at Menwith Hill on the Yorkshire
moors, where the great dishes sucked in the pulses of mobile-call
transmissions. He pleaded priority for the precious resources of the
computers. He walked an uncertain line.

He was exposed. He made a second call, to the minister's principal
private secretary. Powerful enemies faced him. He promised that full
co-operation with the National Crime Squad would begin *soon*.

He relied for the survival of his career on the dour Gough and the
young man, Cann, and events in a far-away place over which he had
no control.

'Is it all right?' The Eagle sought reassurance.

'It's fine.'

'Is he all right?'

'He's grand.'

'Did you tell him that, Mister?'

'I told him.'

Not in these days, of course, but a long time ago, when the Eagle
had been at boarding school and showing an interest in law, classics
masters preached the value of the study of Latin and Greek, talked
about 'expansion of the mind' and 'intellectual discipline'. The Eagle,
then sixteen years old, had embarked on a two-year study of which,
now, little was remembered. The fighting had been the most interesting part to a teenager, the description of warfare, and the generals
who directed it. A Greek general and historian, writing four centuries
before the birth of Christ, had identified the surest way to win loyalty. Xenophon had written: 'The sweetest of all sounds is praise.'
The old Greek warlord and writer had been ahead in man management, and Mister had learned the same art.

'. . . I told him he was indispensable. I gave him all the smarm he
needed.'

'You should watch him, Mister.'

'He doesn't fart without me knowing it. Yes, I'm watching him.'

'He's not one of us.'

'Leave it, Eagle. I hear you. You're "one of us", aren't you?'

'You know I am. You . . .'

It was Mister's way, the Eagle recognized it, to win from the disciples, the acolytes, blustered, spluttered declarations of loyalty. It demeaned them, it gave him power over them. He looked into Mister's dull eyes as he made his protestation. His voice died. The Eagle had been left at the street corner above the house while Mister and Atkins had driven on up the hill to the open ground where they'd found the line of sight the day before. Now Mister had walked back, leaving Atkins, the Mitsubishi and the launcher there. The dusk was settling on the city.

Mister said casually, 'His place was turned over this morning – Atkins's place was done by the Church.'

'He told you?'

'He doesn't know.'

'Is he going to know?'

'Not sure . . .'

'Who told you?'

'Crime Squad – there's white heat between Crime Squad and the Church. The Church isn't sharing.'

'I don't want to know about "friends" in Crime Squad, but when did they tell you?'

'A lot of questions, Eagle . . . I heard this morning.'

'Shouldn't you have told me? I am your legal adviser, Mister.'

'What you going to do about it? You're here, they're there. It'll keep.'

'Mister, I am telling you, as your trusted adviser, we have been away too long. Be careful.'

'You worry too much. I pay you to worry, but not to overdose on it.'

The lights sprinkled below them were cut by the dark line of the river, which in its turn was bisected by the shafts of headlights criss-crossing the bridges. With the evening came the cold, but it was not the cold that made the Eagle shiver. The dark line was the abyss into which the Cruncher had fallen. Never could the Eagle have said or thought that he was fond of the Cruncher. Sometimes he'd said, to himself, that the Cruncher was a barrow-boy, sometimes a low-life little shit. The Cruncher had always competed with him, had intervened in matters that were not his. A contract was drawn up, but Cruncher wanted to check out each paragraph and each sub-section. Days of damn work and Mister would tear it up, because of the poison fed into his ear by the Cruncher. The Eagle had never had Mister's ear the way the Cruncher had. But that had not stopped the Cruncher from disappearing into the dark line that was the river cutting through the lights of the city below. He heard a distant squealing of wheels, the scrape of unoiled metal pieces. He shivered hard. He remembered the Cruncher the last time he'd seen him, in the Clerkenwell office over the launderette, and his feet as always on the Eagle's desk, his heels resting carelessly on files, his body tipped back in a chair, the monogrammed cigarette in his hand, and the scent, the conceit as he'd talked about *his* plan for Mister's future in Sarajevo, his vision: *You're a businessman, Mister . . . any businessman who's top of the tree in the UK expands his interests, goes abroad, doesn't sit on his hands, goes looking for wider horizons.* The Cruncher had been in the river for half a night and a day and another whole night, like a drowned mongrel, before he'd been pulled out. It had been a dog's death.

'When are you going to do it, Mister – do something about the Cruncher?'

'You think I'd forgotten about the Cruncher?'

'I didn't say you'd forgot—'

'You think I'm scared to do something about the Cruncher?'

'I didn't say you were scared.'

'You ever known me forget anything about disrespect? You ever seen fear in me?'

'I only asked when.'

'It'll happen, Eagle, when I'm ready. What I said, Eagle, you worry too much. A man with your brain, your brilliance, you don't have a call to worry.'

The wheels' squeal came closer, was beyond the pool of light thrown down by the only high lamp on the street. *The sweetest of all sounds is praise.* He was not a man of violence; his own weapon was in his supreme understanding of the law . . . And yet he had made the devil's bargain. He had never hit a man in his life; he had reduced a grown man, an experienced surveillance executive officer – through the ammunition given to the QC – to a muttering shambling wreck, destroyed him more effectively than if he'd been hit with a pickaxe handle, broken him. With his forensic intellect, it was the Eagle who had sprung Mister from the trial. But . . . but . . . but, for all his *scruples*, the violence inherent in Mister was strangely mesmerizing to the Eagle. He had a place there, beside the bully. He was sheltered by the bully. And it fascinated him. When he thought of the violence, he sweated hot excitement. He wanted to see the launcher fired, because that was Mister's response to a judge who had dared to stand against them . . . and he had the brain, knew it because Mister had told him so, and the brilliance. They came up the hill, into the pool of light, and the city was below them. Mister had seen them.

The squeal of the wheels came with them.

The Eagle doubted it was a labour of love, thought it a labour of duty. He didn't think he, with his weight, his stomach and his heart, could have pushed the wheelchair up the incline. They stopped on the nearer edge of the pool and the man leaned on the handles while the woman hung on to the wheels as if she feared she would slip back down the slope. There was a wheeze in the man's chest. If he didn't have a car it was because he was a fool. The Eagle didn't know a judge at the Bailey, or at Snaresbrook, Belmarsh, or at Uxbridge Crown Court, who treasured principles more than a black car and a driver. He saw the wheels hit a stone and the chair rocked, but it came on, came closer to them. And he didn't know a judge who would have lived in a hovel as the price of guarding his principles – certainly not his own bloody father, for whom the status, the robes, the bloody protocol were all that mattered.

When they were level with their house, what there was of it, and half lit by the one street-lamp, the Eagle felt the punch of a fist in the small of his back, and Mister stepped from the shadows. The Eagle did not have to follow him. He was the voyeur, a mere observer.

'Judge Delic?' Mister asked affably. 'I understand you speak English, that's what my friends say. And you're Miss Jasmina Delic? I'd like a word, please.'

The judge stiffened. His daughter cringed, then straightened herself and her jaw jutted. The Eagle couldn't see Mister's face, but he would have been smiling. He always smiled when he pitchforked his way into people's lives.

'What about? Who are you?' The words were almost obscured by the panting from his exertion. There was pride there, and spirit, but no strength.

'One question at a time, Judge. About the past and the present . . . I am Albert Packer, Mr Packer, Mister. I am the subject, authorized by you, of an intrusive-surveillance order issued to Joey Cann of the Customs and Excise in London, and it has caused me serious inconvenience. That's what it's about and that's who I am.'

Always the voice was quiet, and they would have had to strain to hear him, as the Eagle did, and in spite of the smile they'd have thought themselves locked in a ferret's gaze. There were no cars on the street, no other workers hurrying home, and they'd have known it. Mister walked to them, not hurrying, measured stride.

'What do you want with us?'

The Eagle thought the judge tried to marshal his courage. Mister, in his overcoat, would have seemed huge to them, and they'd have seen the size of his hands, and Cann would have told them the case history. They would know all about this man, the importance of the Church's Target One . . . Mister reached out to them. The Eagle saw his hands drop to the chair's armrest, and grip it. The chair shook, rocked gently by Mister. It would be so easy for him to tip it over, to spreadeagle her on to the street, and he would have been smiling.

'I'd like you, Judge, and Miss Jasmina, to come for a short walk with me – nothing too far, only take a few minutes.'

'Do we have the choice?' she asked.

'I wouldn't want you to feel threatened, that's not my intention, sincerely . . . Come on, Eagle, come and lend a hand.'

With Mister, he pushed the chair on up the hill and into the blanket of darkness. The street went parallel to the side wall of the Jewish cemetery. Above them was a black tree-line topped by clear evening skies and a scattering of stars. There were no lights in the ruined buildings they went past, no ears to hear him if he screamed for help. The judge could not protect his daughter, nor would he leave her. They went meekly together. Mister and the Eagle propelled the chair but the judge walked close behind it, had reached his hand forward and she held it. He wondered at their dignity, that neither shouted or struggled, however hopeless it was to shout, to struggle . . . If Mo knew what he did, she would leave him, be gone in the hour, as would the girls. He smelt the sweat of the long-worn clothes on the judge's body, and the urine in his daughter's bag. They reached the small patch of level ground, where a shed had stood, where the

Mitsubishi was parked. The shed's wooden walls were gone, blown away when the house was holed, but its concrete base remained. The sidelights of the vehicle were switched on and threw enough light for them to see Atkins standing beside the launcher, slung low on the tripod. Mister and the Eagle bumped her on to the concrete, wheeled the chair to the launcher.

'Everything ready?' Mister asked.

'All in place, Mister,' Atkins replied.

Atkins's coat was neatly folded behind the launcher. It was what made Mister special, everything was thought through with care, was planned, down to a kneeling mat. Mister didn't have to say anything more, but tapped the judge's shoulder and pointed to the folded coat. Atkins steadied him as he dropped on to it. The view-finder was infra-red/image intensifier. The judge would be looking at a monochrome image of the roof of his home. The detail of the view-finder would be sufficient for him to see each tile, the bricks of the chimney, the sagging guttering. The judge was whimpering, rattling words in his own tongue to her. It was a snapshot of all they owned: the half-house and each other. She was trying to push herself up from the chair, and couldn't achieve it. Mister caught at the judge's coat, pulled him back, marched him to the chair and turned him so that he faced his house.

'Get on with it, Atkins.'

Atkins crouched behind the launcher. One hand rested on the tripod, the other threw switches. There was a slight but piercing whistle. The Eagle covered his ears.

They were lit in the moment of the firing, then the fire flash was gone. A bright line, with a thunderclap of sound, burst from the fire. The line travelled down the hill, cleared two broken buildings, then impacted.

The roof fragmented below them.

As if he were on duty, showing his paces and playing at a war game, Atkins dismantled the launcher, the spent tube and the tripod, and heaved them into the back of the vehicle.

'You'll be all right from here with Miss Jasmina, won't you, Judge Delic?' Mister asked quietly. 'It's all downhill from here.'

The air around them stank from the cordite firing charge. Atkins drove, Mister beside him, and the Eagle sat in the back clinging to the holding strap. The wheels crackled over the broken tiles that were debris on the street. At the bottom, where it joined the main road, two black Mercedes passed them and sped on up the hill.

'Well done, Atkins,' Mister said. 'Expert and professional.'

She read the message back.

> Dear 'Mister'(!),
> I have to go to Gorazde tomorrow morning. I am driving myself (my driver is sick, the other drivers are already allocated). If your business work allows it, would you consider accompanying me? It would be interesting and perhaps fulfilling. I apologize for the short notice. I will call by the Holiday Inn tomorrow at 8 a.m., and I will look for you in the lobby. If it is 'not possible please do not have concern for me.
> With good wishes, Monika (Holberg).
> PS: I very much enjoyed my day at Visnjica.

She threaded her way from the table in the atrium, through the mass of people, to the overwhelmed clerks on Reception. A woman broke away from attending to the queue waiting to register, took her message, thrust it into the room's pigeon-hole, gave her a harassed smile, and returned to filling in the cards.

Skirting the X-ray machine and the metal detector arch, she walked out through the swing doors. Monika had heard the explosion, but there were often explosions in a Sarajevo night.

It had taken more than forty minutes for the SFOR troops, Italians, to find the source of the explosion. Some of those they asked said it came from inside the Jewish cemetery, some said it was in the tree-line above, some said they had heard nothing and had slammed doors in the troops' faces. The local police knew of no explosion, it had not been reported to the local fire brigade, no local ambulance had been called. Eventually their jeep found a ruined house at the half-way point up a steeply canted street. They saw two Mercedes limousines parked, and found an old man and a young woman, who was in a wheelchair, and a group of men. One of those men – shaven-headed, black-dressed, a gold chain heavy on his throat – explained courteously to the *mareschallo* that the street had been the front line in the war, that munitions were habitually stored in the roofs of such buildings, but were then, sadly, forgotten. It was possible that the roof beams had shifted and in doing so had detonated a mortar bomb. The old man and the young disabled woman had not spoken. The *mareschallo* was thanked for his attention to the matter, but was told with polite firmness that his presence was not required. The jeep drove away.

Joey had heard it. The windows to his room were double-glazed, but the force of the explosion from up the hill across the Miljacka river was insufficient to rattle the glass panes. The sound was muffled, more of a stuttering clap than a crisp detonation. He drifted back to sleep. Maggie had forbidden him to go to the Holiday Inn, sit in the van and watch. It was as if, he thought, for a day he had stepped back over the line, retrieved the die, worn the uniform, forgotten Mister, who was his Target One . . . He thought of Jasmina, she was the dream in his mind as he drifted, and the faint words carved in the *stecak* stone five centuries before: 'I stood, praying to God, meaning no evil, yet I was struck to death by lightning.' His fingers had flickered over the lichened grooves of the writing. The words on the stone were as a talisman to him. Whatever a man or a woman did, however well they lived their lives, the lightning could strike, burn them.

There was a light rap on his door. His name was called.

'Coming, Maggie.' He opened the door.

'You're still a sight, Joey, but it's an improvement.'

'I feel better . . . What sort of day have you had?'

'I've heard the Welsh hero's life story. I think he wants to get his hand up my skirt. He's rather sweet . . . His wife chucked him out. His kids are pining for him. Both sets of parents are on Megan's side of the fence. Yes, sweet and sad, but I think his hands are getting itchy . . . Most of what I'm hearing is that young man talking with the dogs, or down on the floor playing with them and cuddling them. There was some sort of rendezvous tonight that took Ismet Mujic and his gorillas out, but there wasn't an explanation. There's going to be a meeting the day after tomorrow. I don't know where. Sounds like the big meeting where the territory's cut. An Italian's coming. All the talk's in a code.'

'Dirty talk?' She raised her eyebrows – 'talking dirty' in the Church vernacular was conversation with criminal involvement; 'talking social' was about going to the supermarket or the corner shop for fags, or about telling the wife that the new hairpiece suited her. 'Code talk is criminal talk, right?'

'I think so – an Italian's coming, and there are others. I think it's the meeting that matters.'

She'd kept the meat to the last, had teased him. If the meeting was the day after tomorrow, somewhere, then she was inside the time limit set by her own people. She thought that she was out on a parapet, over a precipice, as much as he was; if she fell it would be his, Joey Cann's, bloody fault.

'Thanks.'

'Sleep well, Joey – oh,' she dropped it as if it was an afterthought, 'do you know much about the Italians?'

He grinned ruefully. 'No, not a hell of a lot.'

She thought she was safe, thought it because a belief in her survival made life easier, but it was now two years since she had rejected the *vita blindata* and dismissed her police bodyguards. She had rejected the protective screen and had said to her husband, 'When the Mafia is intent on revenge it will always find a way.' She always made a joke with her husband. Who would want to pay for sex with a woman of forty-nine who was fat, had heavy, dropping breasts, and gross ankles? But last night the word *prostituta* had been daubed in paint on the white exterior wall of their house.

She was Giovanna. She was in her second term as the *sindaca* of the mountain village of San Giuseppe Jato on the western side of the island of Sicily. It was the women's vote that had elected her, again, to the mayor's office. When her deputy, Luciano, had found a bomb lodged under the front wheel hub of his car he had resigned, and she had not been able to find a man to replace him. Her ticket for re-election had been: the Rejection of the Cosa Nostra Path of Violence and Death. She did not give herself sufficient importance, if she were murdered, to be listed as an 'illustrious corpse', but she believed, had to, that she irritated the Family who controlled the village. She irritated them enough for a *pollo squartato* to have been left on her doorstep four months before. She had found the disembowelled chicken, picked it up, and walked with it down the main street. Women had shouted to her from their windows, 'Brava, Giovanna', and she had placed the bleeding bird carefully on the step of the fine house near the church that was the principal residence of the Family. That gesture, more than anything else she might have done, ensured that women came to her, talked to her of the secrets of the Family.

She was told that evening, in a whispered telephone call, that the Family's most trusted nephew, Marco, was entrusted with a mission of importance by his uncle, had gone with a packed case to the airport at Messina, was travelling to a meeting of significance. Giovanna thought Marco a handsome boy and important to the family's future, a boy of intelligence but trapped by the poison in the Family's bloodstream, a boy with a life wasted – a boy who might, one day, kill her.

Mister had gone a dozen paces past the end of the line of black station-wagons, all with smoked-glass windows, past the knot of gossiping drivers, when he jerked to a stop. He was facing the swing doors of the hotel. The noise of a hundred voices, nasal and loud, billowing and American, buffeted him. His eyes narrowed. He peered through the doors. He turned in one swinging movement and faced Atkins. He reached in his belt, took the pistol from it and palmed it to Atkins.

'Leave it in the vehicle,' he said, 'and yours, and get the vehicle down the warehouse – now.'

He waited until Atkins had driven away.

'Right, Eagle, let's see what the party's for.'

They went through the door, shrugged out of their coats and laid them on the conveyor belt feeding the X-ray machine. They went through the metal detector, and were bleeped, because of the coins in Mister's pocket and the metal-lined case for the Eagle's spectacles. By the machine and the arch stood men with cropped haircuts and long, shapeless coats, with flesh-coloured wires coiled between their shirt collars and their ears. They were passed through. Every seat in the atrium bar was taken. Every table was littered with ashtrays, beer glasses, coffee cups and Pepsi cans. At the far end of the bar a woman addressed a little forest of microphones. Cameramen climbed on the soft-cushioned seats to see better. There was bedlam.

At the desk they collected their keys, and Mister was given a note from his pigeon-hole.

Eagle asked the receptionist, 'Who are all these people? What's going on?'

She told the Eagle that the American Secretary of State was due at the hotel in two hours, on a leg from Paris and Vienna, last stop before returning to Washington. This was only the advance party. Mister heard what she said, but hardly listened. He read the note again and felt a small sensation of excitement, better than when the launcher had fired. The Eagle repeated what the receptionist had told him.

'Yes, yes – I heard it the first time . . .' He laughed quietly. 'Would have been choice if I'd gone through without thinking . . .'

'But you always think, Mister, don't you?'

Mister was smiling. 'Tomorrow's not busy, not till the evening, and it's the day after tomorrow that matters. Anyway, I'll be out of town on a little trip. You and Atkins can lose yourselves, can't you, till the evening?'

'Buckets to do here,' the Eagle said. 'Buckets of fun to be had.'

He thought there was a brittle snap in the Eagle's voice. If it hadn't been for the message he might have kicked the Eagle's shin, but he'd read it. They walked to the lift. The Eagle, as always, pushed the outside button for him and stood aside to let him enter first, then pushed the inside button for their floor. Mister was slow to recognize sarcasm: it was too far back in his life for him to remember the last man who had been sarcastic to his face.

Chapter Fifteen

Henry hadn't left a contact address. He'd been vague, infuriatingly obtuse, about where he could be reached when he was abroad. 'May be in and out of several hotels – I'll be on the move. It wouldn't really be a good idea for you to call me or me to call you – it's only for a few days.' It had never been Mo Arbuthnot's habit to quiz her husband on his work, and she'd let it go. He'd kissed her cheek and said he'd ring from Heathrow when he was back in the country.

Three hours before, while she and the girls had slept, the cars had crunched on to the pepper-coloured gravel of the drive. The dogs in the kitchen had woken first, had disturbed Mo, and she'd seen in a half-awake haze the headlights against her bedroom curtains. She'd heard the dogs' barking and the chorus of birdsong in the garden's trees, the slamming of doors, the scrape of feet across the gravel, and the peal of the bell. She'd gone down the stairs, shrugging into her dressing-gown, and peered through the front door's spyhole. They'd activated the security lights. They were well lit: a cluster of men, and one woman, on the step; one face was masked by a plume of pipesmoke. She'd called out that they should identify themselves and small cards were held up to the spyhole. She'd opened the door. Four of the men and the woman had pushed past her, no word said, but the one with the pipe, the eldest, biting on its stem, puffing like a damned chimney, had intoned the text of the authorized warrant to search her home then handed her the sheet of paper as if she might want to check that an error had not been made. She hadn't bothered to read it, but she had claimed, had insisted, that there *had* to be an error. 'I doubt it,' the older man had growled. 'We make very few errors, ma'am.' A police car was parked behind their cars, but the two uniformed men stayed in it, as if this was not their business. She had demanded the names of the intruders, and had been ignored. When the older man had stepped sideways in the hall to go by her she had proclaimed, with all the haughtiness she could muster, that she did not permit smoking in her home. He'd smiled, a chilling crack at the side of his mouth, then strolled back on to the outer doorstep where he had whacked his pipe against the raised heel of his polished shoe and the embers had fallen on to the grouted bricks. He'd left them glowing there and gone by her ... Without proper points of contact, Mo Arbuthnot had no one to call, no one to cry to for help ... She thought her home was violated. Two of them were in her husband's study, his inner sanctum off the far end of the lounge. One was in the dining room and had the drawers and books out of the antique rosewood desk where she recorded the household accounts. Another had chosen the oak chest, Jacobean, in the sitting room. It had been like a wound to her. But the worst of the wounds had not been the rape of her privacy, or the silent shock on the faces of her daughters who clung to each other at the top of the stairs, it was the woman and the family dogs. The woman had gone into the kitchen and left the door open. The dogs should have been leaping at her, or getting behind her legs and snarling at her ankles. She was down on the kitchen's heavy-weave carpet, scratching bellies, crooning to them: she had bought their affection. Then she had started to search every cupboard, every shelf, to open every cookery book kept on top of the dresser.

The older man, his warm pipe pocketed, tramped up the stairs. She saw the politeness with which he requested the girls to move aside and make way for him. He went into her bedroom. Out of her sight he would have been sifting in the drawers of her dressing-table, and that hurt too; but nothing hurt as cruelly as the betrayal of her dogs.

Mo Arbuthnot knew little of her husband's work. He was a

criminal lawyer, he worked through the week in London, and brought little of the work home. At weekends, he did not discuss his caseload with her. 'Not what I come down here for,' he'd say. 'Down here is for getting away from it.' Sometimes, on a Sunday evening, he'd shut himself away in his study for an hour, and she and the girls would be in the sitting room with the television, then he'd bring out his briefcase and leave it by the front door for the early Monday-morning departure. It was always locked. At dinner parties or drinks sessions, at home or at their friends', if Henry was asked about work, he would answer in generalities and effortlessly steer away the talk. 'Legal stuff, anything that comes along, enough to make a crust . . . How's the cricket team doing this summer?' The *crust* – she was not stupid, she could do the arithmetic – was in excess of two hundred thousand pounds in income a year, and there was a stocks portfolio and a pension scheme. She was looked after, as were the girls' schools, and the horses. Few of the women she knew in the village, of her status, had a finger on the pulse of their husband's finances . . . She understood so little of his life and never pressed to be told. Not often, occasionally, not more than once a calendar month, the phone would ring, and Henry would be in the garden or at the stables, and she'd answer it, and a very soft-spoken voice would say, 'Mrs Arbuthnot? So sorry to trouble you, hope it's not inconvenient – can I speak to him, please? It's Mister . . .' She'd go to the front door, or the kitchen door, or the french windows off the dining room, and shout that he was wanted and who wanted him, and Henry would always come running. Mister was, Henry said, 'just another client'.

They left. They took nothing with them, went empty-handed to their cars.

She hated them, but most of all their chief. 'You see?' she said, with venom. 'You made a mistake. As a piece of rudeness this is beyond belief. You bullock into my home, you disturb me, you terrify my girls, and at the end of it the exercise was without the slightest justification.'

The older man said, as he lit his pipe, 'What you should remember, ma'am, and tell your husband upon his return is that – as a more unpleasant creature than myself once remarked – "We only have to be lucky once, you have to be lucky every time." Good day, ma'am.'

She went to the phone, rather than to her daughters. It was the sixth time she'd called Henry's office number – she was too stressed to consider, to ponder on it, that the previous five times she'd dialled out none of the men, nor the woman, had objected. They had not tried to prevent her spreading the word of their search – and she was rewarded.

'Josh? Thank God I've got you . . . It's Mo Arbuthnot . . . I am in the middle of a nightmare . . . No, no, I mean it. Our house, home, us, we've been invaded by people from the Customs. They had a warrant. They've been through every nook and cranny . . . Of course, I'm trying to be calm . . . I don't know where Henry is . . . I don't know what it's all about, they never told me. They were here three hours, they've just gone . . . Where is he? I want him found. Find him and tell him that his home and his family have been subjected to a nightmarish intrusion . . . I don't care what he told you. We've been treated like criminals, and I don't know why.'

'Was that all right, Mr Gough?' the woman, SQG8, asked him.

'That was dandy.'

'We didn't find anything.'

They were out of the lanes and had reached the bypass skirting Guildford.

'It was more than satisfactory. Far from home and a panic call down the phone, sobs and screams, that'll make Eagle's day. I thought it went well, and yesterday . . . Do you know, my dear, you or I would have to work for thirty years – without deductions of tax, pension scheme and National Insurance, and not touch our salary, only bank it – to afford that house? Perhaps it'll be on the market soon . . . Do you mind if I take a nap? I doubt there'll be much opportunity for sleep later.'

The note had come by hand delivery. It was dropped through the letter-box and the bell was rung to alert her to its presence on the mat. The Princess, née Primrose Hinds, took the envelope back to her bed. She settled against her feather pillows and slit open the envelope.

My dearest Princess,
I miss you.
It's going well, but slowly. I hope to leave on the 22nd, 23rd at
the latest. Hope all is good with you.
With love, Mister XXXX

A letter from Mister was a rare treasure. She understood why he
never used the telephone and why she must never call him. Even
when he'd been on remand, in Brixton, and she'd been forbidden to
visit him, he had never written. Verbal messages had passed between
them via the Eagle. It would have been five years, or six, since he had
last written, from Amsterdam. She would have been with him in
Amsterdam but for the influenza.

She kissed the letter, then lay back on the bed for a few moments,
held a pillow and thought of him. Then, she went to the *en-suite* bathroom, tore the page into small pieces and flushed them down the
pan, as he would have wanted her to.

Through the hotel's big ground-floor windows, Joey saw the arc-
lights that burned down on the Secretary of State. The wire services
and the satellite news programmes would carry his words: 'Society
here has to rid itself of corrosive corruption. Citizens of Bosnia-
Herzegovina, you must resist the extremists and the criminals, you
have to turn your backs on the past.' An American officer would
interrupt the great man, cut him short in mid-stride, and would say
into the microphone: 'I'm afraid, ladies and gentlemen, we've run
out of time if we're to make our flight window.'

Joey watched the stampede of the circus around the great man as
they went out with him through the swing doors. The Secretary of
State was hemmed in by bodyguards, military liaison officers,
advisers, stenographers and his own travelling media, and all were
hurrying to the long line of station-wagons, governed by their pecking order of importance. They couldn't get shot of the place fast
enough, couldn't race to the airport and climb on to the 747 too soon.

Troops waved them away, sirens escorted them down Zmaja od
Bosne, which had been Snipers' Alley. A stillness seemed to settle on
the yellow and chocolate hotel building, as if all inside it now caught
their breath, sighed, sagged . . . Joey saw the white UNHCR truck

pull up in the space where the station-wagon convoy had been. She slipped out of the vehicle. He recognized her.

She was only half-way to the swing doors when Mister came through them. They were like kids meeting in a park. No kisses, but their handshake was more about touching and holding than formal greeting. He couldn't hear their laughter, but watched the mute pleasure on their faces.

When they drove away, Joey followed in the van.

She had the wheel, Mister was beside her.

They went past the new American headquarters camp on the far side of the airport, and along the road were stretched little wooden shacks, closed and locked.

She said, 'It's a little part of the black market. Later in the day they will be opened. They sell every CD and video you ever heard of, all illegally recorded. They've paid no duty on them, no copyright. Other than the market of servicing foreigners, the only industry is black. It is worse on the Tuzla road. There are not CDs and videos in the huts on the way to Tuzla, it is women, young women, some from Bosnia but most from outside – Romania, Bulgaria, Ukraine. When they have been "trained" here, they are sent on to brothels in western Europe – it is a disgusting, exploitative trade. Always, Mister, it is the criminals who win here . . . I am sorry, it is gloomy – but that is the reality.'

They climbed on hairpin bends and came to the village of Tvorno. There was lustreless snow beside the road, but the ice on it glistened prettily in the early sunshine. Rows of houses on the approach were gutted, roofless and burned, sandwiched between the road and a tumbling river. Beyond the river were rolling forested hills, then mountains that were snow-swept, formidable and magnificent. He was looking at the wreckage.

She said, 'We call them *cabriolet* houses. Do you understand? It is houses without roofs . . . I am sorry, perhaps you do not think that funny. I promise you, Mister, it is sometimes necessary to have a dark humour if you work here. If you are too serious then you would weep. It is very beautiful, yes?'

The road came down from the high ground into a wide agricultural valley, leaving the snow and ice behind them. She pulled off the road, produced a battered, well-used Thermos and poured coffee for them. They stood beside her vehicle and looked down at the valley and the big river running through it, and at a town beyond the river where there were close-set houses and the chimneys of industrial plants. He looked for damage. All he saw was the collapsed bridge that had spanned the river and had linked the town to the main road. The water now flowed over the bridge.

She said, 'It is Foča. I don't go there. It is a place of evil. I should go there. I could go with troops from the SFOR, but I do not wish to. There is suffering there, the same as everywhere, but I am not perfect. Do you think it wrong to care less for the suffering of some than I do for others? I could not argue if you thought that, Mister. Do you see men fishing? They have no work and they fish for food to eat. The factories have stopped, the chemicals leak into the river – it is the Drina river. I would not eat the fish but they are desperate . . . I do not go to Foča because it is a place where war criminals walk. Everyone knows their names, who the beasts are. You could meet them on the street in Foča just as in Sarajevo you could meet Ismet Mujic. In six years only once have the SFOR dared to try to capture one of them – Janko Janjic, the mass rapist and mass cleanser. He had an eagle tattooed on his stomach and the words "Slaughter Me" on his neck. Every minute of every day he had a hand-grenade hanging from his throat, and he pulled the pin when German troops came to take him. The rapist and the murderer, in Foča, was a hero. Many thousands went to his funeral. Myself – and a good man like you, Mister – we do not know how to speak with such creatures.'

He kissed her at that moment, first her cheeks, then her forehead, then her eyes, then her lips.

'How long will you be here?'

'Just a couple more days.'

'But you will come back?'

'I will bring more lorries – but that won't be as important as coming back to see you.' Mister held her close, hugged her. It was not the way he embraced his Princess. He clung to her as if he had been infected by the misery she spoke of. 'I will come back, not send people who could do it instead of me, I'll come back because you're here . . . I don't talk a lot – Monika, you are the best human being I've ever met.' He saw the openness of her face, and the trust. He had thought of her at first as a contact, a tool to be used, an opportunity to be exploited. They were alone beside the road and his arms were tight round her. She was looking down. The way he held her she could see his right hand. She was looking at his hand and the heavy gold ring on his third finger, the ring the Princess had given him.

'Come on, Mister Charity Man, let's hit Gorazde.'

She disentangled herself. Her face was flushed. It was eighteen years since he had married his Princess and in that time he had not touched another woman.

They drove alongside the Drina river, passed the wreckage of the front line, and went on through the flattened emptiness of no man's land.

Gorazde was a finger town pressed down between the hills.

Mister never reached across her and looked into the mirror, never saw that he was tracked. He would sleep with her. After the meeting he would sleep a whole night with her before going to the airport and taking the plane home. Because he would sleep with her, afterwards, he knew, was certain of it, he would be supreme at the meeting.

A methodical man, with a long training of counter-intelligence operations behind him, Sandor Dizo was a survivor. Eighteen years of his professional life had been in the service of the lll/lll State Protection Directorate, but in 1990 he had effortlessly changed allegiance – not desk, chair or working hours – and had become an executive of the Office of National Security. He had the same view of the roofs of Budapest, from the same room, as he'd had before the collapse of socialism. Then he had worked to stifle internal dissent, now he turned the same standards of intellect to combating the rise in newly democratic Hungary of the influence of organized crime. He had unlearned the practices taught him by the KGB instructors, and had learned those of the Drug Enforcement Administration of the United States and the Security Service of the United Kingdom. He was today's man.

The work of that day, and many others past and many to come, was his surveillance of the movements of Russians who were active in the *vory v'zakone* crime group. If Sandor Dizo had had available to him today the powers of coercion he had enjoyed prior to 1990, the

335

opportunities of the old days, there would have been no Russian criminals on Hungarian territory, but those powers had been withdrawn. He was now a creature of government by computer, provided by the Americans, and fieldcraft, taught by the British. Instead of broken noses and broken necks, he followed the new rules and provided the printouts listing the coming and going of the Russians and filled the files with their photographs. It was not a surprise to Sandor Dizo that the Russians now flourished in Budapest. They ran prostitution, controlled the clubs, moved and sold narcotics, laundered money through the recently opened banks, directed the country's oil-distribution Mafia; they were behind every rip-off fraud of public and private enterprises, they trafficked weapons, and they killed. Being an exact man, Sandor Dizo could list each of the one hundred and sixty killings and attempted murders and bomb explosions on his capital city's streets since he had joined the Office of National Security. On the fingers of one of his plump hands he could count the minimal number of arrests and convictions of those responsible. Without interfering with their operations, he had gained a comprehensive knowledge of the Russian groups.

Nikki Gornikov had left Budapest that morning. He had been photographed leaving his apartment on Prater Street, and photographed again on Line 2 of the Metro. He had then been seen to take the classic anti-surveillance procedure of diving for a taxi, had been spotted at the airport and watched on to the Vienna flight. By the time those strands of information had been sifted on Sandor Dizo's desk, Nikki Gornikov could have driven a hundred miles from Vienna, or could have boarded any of a dozen flights. He called him ironically, when he thought of him, Baby Nikki because he was a forty-nine-year-old bear bull of a man with a face made ugly by smallpox and knife fights. On Baby Nikki there was a fifteen-page computer printout and a four-centimetre-thick file. As was laid down by the American and British tutors of a democratic intelligence service, he noted the departure of Baby Nikki Gornikov, of the *vory v'zakone* group, from Budapest, put another page in the file and hoped the man – wherever he had gone – might slip, stumble, fall under a convenient tram or trolleybus. The place for such a man, so sadistic, cruel and vicious a man as Nikki Gornikov, was the prison yard at dawn.

His tasks of the morning done, Sandor Dizo called to his secretary in the outer office for coffee, and some biscuits if there were any.

'It was their graveyard, but when the Muslims were put out of their homes, the Serb boys used it as a football pitch.'

After her death at St Matthew's hospice, after the funeral service in church, his mother's body had been cremated. Her ashes now lay in an oakwood casket in the crematorium's Garden of Remembrance. It was a lovely garden, clean-raked and dignified in winter, bright with flowers in summer. If kids had come into that garden, just across the North Circular from where he lived, to play football over her casket Mister would have taken a shotgun to them, or a pickaxe handle, or an industrial strimmer, or a chainsaw. None of the little tossers would have been in a state to kick a football again – none of the little bastards would have had the knees to walk again, let alone run. But that wasn't Monika's answer.

'I don't blame the Serb children,' she said. 'They know nothing else. They have never been shown another way.'

'Isn't there a proper pitch in the village where all the kids can play?'

'There was, but it was a park for tanks. It was destroyed. There is no pitch.'

He stood beside her and looked across the graveyard that was a soccer field.

She had gone into the UNHCR field office in Gorazde, left him for less than five minutes, which had seemed an age to him. Then they'd driven on through the town and out of it. Beyond the old no man's land they'd reached a village where the majority of the homes were intact, pretty, perched on hillsides, and had fields where cattle browsed on the first of the spring's fresh grass. The village was called Kopaci, she'd said.

He saw the gravestones, low, old and poorly carved, that had been used as goalposts. The other stones, which had been near the penalty spots, at either side of the penalty boxes and across the half-way line, had been uprooted and thrown aside. They marked the sidelines of the pitch. She had changed him, he knew it. A few kids stood with their parents and grandparents by two houses. The families had returned from exile for their former homes, to find their graveyard was a football pitch, well worn and often played on. It had no grass but had been smoothed by boots and trainers into flattened wet mud.

'I'm going to meet them – are you coming with me?'

He shook his head. 'More coffee with a spoonful of grit, more losing at cards? No, thank you.'

'A quarter of an hour – they have to be reassured. If they give up, go back into Gorazde, then five years is wasted. It is important to spend time with them, if only a few minutes . . .'

'I'll be here,' Mister said. 'Won't be going far.'

He started to walk down the hillside track. The warmth was on his face and his back. He was humming his Elvis. He reached the end of the track, where it joined the road. He was strolling and had not a care. He could not remember when he had last walked on a country track, if he ever had . . . Because of the warmth, he slipped out of his coat and carried it on his arm. He was at peace. He looked up the road, wondering how far he should walk and what he might see . . . and he saw the blue van.

It was parked a hundred yards up the road and faced the junction. The sun, reflected off the van's windscreen, dazzled him for a moment, but when he edged forward and twisted his body further, he could see through the windscreen.

He saw the small pale face, the tousled hair and the big spectacle lenses.

Mister thought the head would turn away, duck, try to hide itself, but it did not.

There was the howl of a klaxon horn. The lorry missed him by a foot, could have been less. Mister felt the sweat coming on his body. He saw the finger on the arm jutting from the window and the gesture of contempt from the lorry driver. He shouted back emptily, uselessly, at the lorry's tail. He had seen them leave the hotel – Cann trailing the woman, carrying the bag and the case – seen them going in time to catch the morning flight out. He looked both ways, up the road and down it, and there were no other vehicles parked, only the blue van.

He turned his back on it and walked off down the road.

Was Mister frightened? He was never frightened. Who'd ever seen him frightened? No one had. He went at a good pace. He had no destination. He strode on the road, and knew he was followed.

338

He gained a target, had to have one. He was walking faster. Ahead of him, sheep and goats grazed by the road, watched by a shepherd and children. Above the animals, up the slope, was the graveyard. He stopped near the shepherd, who leaned on a long stick, a scarecrow figure in his loose clothing. The children had ceased their game, stood in a little knot and stared at him. He turned, looked back up the road.

He began to run towards the van, but it reversed. When he ran faster, it backed faster away from him. When he slowed, it slowed. He stopped, the van stopped. The distance was a hundred yards. He knew he showed his anger . . . Christ, and it was beneath his dignity to show his anger. He retraced his steps, over which he'd run and then walked, and the blue van followed him.

He nodded curtly to the shepherd, then tried to smile at the children through his anger. He sat down on the grass. The shepherd and the children watched him, and the animals grazed around him. As long as he could, he tried not to turn, but the compulsion beat him . . . Cann sat on a rock near to the blue van, cross-legged, like a pygmy bloody pixie. If he'd started to run towards him, he wouldn't have covered ten of the paces before Cann was back in the van, not twenty before the van was backing away . . . and he would have lost his self-respect. From what he knew of the Church and the Crime Squad, the greatest crime on surveillance was to show out – but Cann sat where he could be seen. Mister did not understand. Why wasn't the little bastard frightened of him?

She was standing at the top of the slope, at the edge of the grave-yard, and waved to him. Round her were the few kids from the two families.

Cann was on the rock, a statue.

He walked to her, scrambled up the slope. Twice he slipped and mud smeared his trouser legs. She was laughing and said he was crazy. She held his hand. 'We have to leave, Mister,' she said. 'We need to be past Tvorno before night. We should not be on the ice in the darkness.'

'There's nothing to keep us here.'

Mister had his arm round her hip as they walked to her vehicle. She waved to the kids and to the older people at the graveyard, to the shepherd and the children with him. She was behind the wheel. She kissed his cheek. They drove away towards Gorazde.

The light had begun to fail as they cleared the finger town and began to climb, and her hand rested on his except when she changed gears. His face was turned away from her so that she would not see the fury that winnowed through him . . . No man stood against Mister, then walked away.

August 2000
It was their fourth morning, and that morning it rained.

It was incredible to Husein Bekir. He'd had to scratch in his memory to recall when it had last rained in that summer month. The clouds had gathered the previous evening and at dusk the storm had started. The thunder had echoed into the valley from the west, the lightning had lit the valley as if it was the middle of the day, and the wind had gathered. Through all of the night the gales had howled. By the morning, the fourth, the storm had passed and left only a steady drizzle in its wake.

When the mine-clearers had come on the first morning, Husein had immediately left his home, abandoned his breakfast, grunted at his wife as she'd hobbled after him down the track that he would not be long, and gone over the ford. He had bearded them where they had made their day camp, a battered caravan, a stinking portable lavatory and a parking space for their three pick-up trucks and the two ambulances, up the track from Dragan Kovac's house.

He'd asked the same question of the foreman on every morning since.

He asked it again. 'When are you going to start to clear my fields?'

And he had the same answer on the four consecutive mornings: 'First we do the pylons. Your fields come after the pylons and the restoration of the electricity.'

'My fields are more important than electricity.'

'Your fields are next year, if there's the money.'

On the first three mornings, Husein had then shuffled down the track to Dragan Kovac's home, had beaten on the door and demanded fresh coffee and a substitute breakfast. Then he'd launched into a criticism of the foreman, and the six de-miners, and he'd denounced the priority of the electricity pylons, but he had won no sympathy. His friend, the idle fool, Dragan, had as little interest in the fields as they showed.

That fourth morning he was not going to visit Dragan Kovac. The morning before, when he had launched into the complaint that his fields were not given enough priority, his friend – the old fool – had remarked that Husein was now too aged, too feeble, to work the fields; Dragan had said it was a dream, no more than a fantasy, that Husein, with his withered muscles, would ever be able to plant the new apple orchard that would eventually be harvested by his grandson; Dragan had said that the fields were his history, that his present should be a game of chess, a seat in the sunshine and a glass of home-brewed brandy, or two glasses. The morning before, blinking tears and shouting curses, he had left Dragan's house and waded back over the ford.

The foreman stood in the caravan's door. Behind him the men read newspapers, smoked and drank coffee. In the ambulances the medics had their feet up on the dashboards and their radios played loud music. All his life, Husein Bekir had worked his fields in storms, hail showers, and in the heat that blistered his skin. To Husein Bekir, the foreman, his men and the medics seemed lazy and complacent, showed no understanding of his need to go back to his fields.

On the other side of the track from the junction where the caravan and the trucks were parked was the bunker that had protected the right flank of Ljut village. Leaning against its stone wall, beside its cave entrance, was a new sign. On a red-painted background was a white skull with crossed bones behind it, and one word: *Mina*. All the way down the track, on both sides, little posts had been put into the ground and yellow tape slung between them. There was no tape on his fields, only a slim corridor to the nearest of the pylons from which power cables dangled. He would not speak to Dragan Kovac until he had received abject apologies for the insult that he was too old, too feeble – and the frustration fed his anger.

'Do you not work if it rains?'

'It will clear soon. We will work when the rain stops.'

'Do you have no sense of urgency?'

'What I have is five toes on each foot, four fingers and a thumb on each hand, eyes in my head, and two balls. I have them, old man, because I don't hurry.'

'If you used those machines, I have seen them on television, you .could clear my fields. Why don't you bring the machines?'

The foreman said patiently, as if talking to an idiot, 'We have flails, fastened to the front of a vehicle that is reinforced with armour plate. They don't clear ground to the standard necessary for a certificate of clearance. We only use them to cut back scrub.'

'What about those things you carry, the things that find metal? You could go faster if you had them.'

'We have metal detectors but they're about useless in this situation, for two reasons. First, there is minimal metal in the PMA and PROM mines, they are made from plastic. Second, there are minerals in the ground, in the rock strata, which contaminate the signal, also there are the pylon cables, which confuse the machine.'

Husein Bekir snorted. He was being backed, and he knew it, into a cul-de-sac from which there was no retreat. His voice rose in strident attack. 'How, then, will you – one day, when it is convenient to you – clear my fields?'

'Perhaps we will bring dogs, but the greater part of the work will be on hands and knees, manually, with the probe. We can push the probe four inches into the ground. That is how we do it.'

The foreman's quiet rebuttals seemed as insulting as Dragan Kovac's sneer that he was too old and too feeble.

'I don't know how you can clear the land if you cannot even put in posts, stakes, that will survive one night's storm weather,' Husein said.

'What do you mean?'

'Down past Kovac's house, your posts are already blown over by the wind, because you did not sink them deep enough.'

'The ground is very hard.'

'Oh, the ground is *hard*. It is too hard in the summer, too wet in the winter. I am sorry you do not find perfect ground, not hard, not wet. I work in my fields when it is hot, when it is cold . . .'

'I'll look at the posts. Do me a favour, go home.'

'When I have shown you the posts that you cannot put in the ground because it is too hard?'

'I will walk with you.'

To rid himself of Husein Bekir, the foreman, as if making a great sacrifice in the interests of peace, threw away the dregs of his coffee and went to the nearest of the pick-up trucks. When he reappeared he was carrying a small sledge-hammer. They walked in silence down the track. The clouds were breaking over the high ground in the west, and at the limit of Husein's eyesight were small patches of blue sky. He thought that within an hour there would be a rainbow and then the day would clear: they would have no excuse any longer to shelter in their caravan. In spite of the drizzle the birds were calling sharply. A thrush flew with the trophy of a wriggling worm to an elder bush, a sparrow was chased by finches, and there were little showers of redwings wheeling in formation. The storm in the night had greened his fields. If he had had cattle he would have blessed the rain that gave life to the fields that had been burned by the sun, but he did not have cattle – and there was now a yellow tape strip to separate the fields from the track. If he had had crops – maize or wheat or vegetables – the storm rain would have brought them to a peak before the September harvest, but the fields were not ploughed and he had no crops.

With his rolling gait, his hip and knee both aching, Husein hurried towards the ford and the foreman's boots thudded behind him.

There were two posts down, not more than twenty-five centimetres from the chipped stones of the track. The tape lay on the thick grass verge. Of course, Husein Bekir could have taken the one step on to the grass, picked up the two posts, worked them back into their two holes and tautened the yellow tape. He could have done it when he had walked up the track half an hour earlier to beard the men in their caravan. But he had made his point. How could they talk about clearing his land, more than two hundred and fifty thousand square metres of it, if they could not make two posts secure? He stood triumphant.

The foreman barked, 'You brought me down here because of *that*?'
Husein walked on.

He heard the thump of the sledge-hammer behind him. He stopped, looked behind him, and grinned slyly to himself. One post was in. The foreman stepped back on to the track, moved along it half a dozen strides, and paused by the second fallen post.

'I do not like to have my time wasted,' the foreman shouted after him.

Husein was about to turn. From the corner of his field of vision, he saw the foreman's left boot on the track, but as the man leaned forward to retrieve the second post he settled his right boot half a metre beyond the track. As he bent and reached, his weight transferred to his right leg.

The clap of the sound dinned into Husein Bekir's ears, the brightness of the flash seemed to blind him, the wind caught him, and he heard the foreman shriek.

When the Eagle came out of the hotel's lift, Atkins saw his face: it was pale, wiped with a deathly pallor, and shock was written on it. His eyes were dulled and his mouth slack.

They had killed the day on another tourist drive, but the Eagle hadn't been interested. They had driven, again, out towards Pale, and back again after lunch. At Reception there had been six message slips in the Eagle's pigeon-hole, and he'd taken them upstairs.

'What's the problem? Seen a ghost?'

'We're late.'

They were late for the appointment to meet Ismet Mujic. They drove towards the old quarter. The Eagle's head was bowed.

'Do you want to talk about it?' Atkins asked.

'Talk about what?'

'Talk about whatever your problem is.'

'It is a problem,' the Eagle said quietly. 'A unique problem in my experience. My clerk's been on the phone for me. Under pain of death by garrotting, my clerk is not supposed to contact me unless the world's falling in.'

'Has it fallen in?'

'My home was raided at dawn this morning. The Church came mob-handed with a warrant, all legal, and turned it over. Had my wife out of bed, woke the kids, stripped the place . . .'

'What did they find?'

'They found nothing, they took away nothing.'

Atkins tried to smile, to reassure. 'Then there's no problem.'

'You know very little, Atkins. You jump when you should stand still. The Church – God, give them credit for a modicum of intelligence – know there's nothing in my home, and nothing in my grubby little office. I'm not that bloody stupid . . . What matters is in safety deposits, and in my head. They wouldn't have expected to find anything.'

'So, what's the big deal?'

344

'Posting a letter to me. Telling me where I stand. A man said to my wife: "We have to be lucky once, you have to be lucky every time." That was the text of the message, Atkins. Wife traumatized, girls in shock, neighbours wondering what the hell's going on, at dawn, at good old Henry's pad. Turning the bloody screw, squeezing till it hurts. Going for the weak spot, tightening the wire to breaking point ... That's my problem.'

'Can you cope?'

A wintry little grin played at the Eagle's mouth. 'Probably not much better, but better than you.'

'What does that mean?' Atkins turned, confused, gazed at the Eagle. Hadn't seen the pedestrian who screamed, waved a stick angrily at them.

'Please, watch the road – the Church did your address yesterday.'

Atkins hissed, 'Why wasn't I told? Christ! You didn't tell me.'

'Mister's decision, because you're only on probation.'

'That is so bloody insulting.'

The Eagle pointed to a gap in the cars parked in the narrow street, overhung with narrow balconies. 'There's a space there, you can get into it. You were on the treadmill, you could have got off, you didn't, so don't whine. I've been on the treadmill twenty-something years. It goes faster. Get off, and you fall on your bloody face.'

They left the Mitsubishi, both sombre. They rang the bell, were let in and escorted up the stairs. They heard the dogs pawing the inner door. They saw the big teeth and the snarl in the set of the jaws. They were shown into the bedroom. The bed, Atkins thought, was big enough for a family. Enver was on his stomach and the sheet had ridden down to expose his bronzed back and his buttocks. Serif wore a T-shirt, and the sheet covered his groin. Serif said they were late, and they both apologized. He took a sheet of paper, rested it on a magazine, drew a map for them, said where they should be the next day, and at what time, and they both thanked him. Serif's question: where was Mister? The Eagle's answer: engaged in Ugandan practices. What were Ugandan practices? 'Oh, sorry, just slipped out, beg pardon, Ugandan practices are an expression we have in London for pursuing business contacts.' They were dismissed.

On the pavement, Atkins asked, 'If I was to jump off the treadmill, what would I get?'

'Mud on your face. If I were representing you, I'd urge you to plead. Seven years to ten years. But I wouldn't be representing you, I'd be beside you and looking at twelve to fifteen. That's why we don't jump.'

The talk was in the bedroom when the visitors came, not the living room. And after they'd gone, Maggie's frustration grew because the talk stayed in the bedroom. The giggles, gasps, and the whine of the springs were enough to activate the microphone in the living room's telephone, but the talk was too muffled, too dominated by the sounds of the loving and the bed's heaving for her to comprehend what was said. She'd given the earphones to Frank and his expression had screwed into a sneer. He'd passed the earphones to each of the Sreb Four. Frank was closest to her, in the rented room, and sometimes his hand rested on her hip. She knew now the names of each of the survivors of the Srebrenica massacre, Salko and Ante, Muhsin and Fahro. They'd have seen Frank's hand on her hip, but they showed no sign of it. Being with them, feeling the pressure of his hand, softened the frustration . . . Then the telephone bell. Then the padding of bare feet. Her pencil was poised.
She scribbled.

> *Da?*
> Serif?
> *Da.*
> (Russian language) It is Nikki, I come tomorrow, the agreed schedule.
> (Russian language) OK, Nikki, I meet you. I take you.
> (Russian language) It is all OK?
> (Russian language) All OK.

The call was cut. She heard the feet pad away, then the springs sang, and there was distant laughter. Maggie Bolton was fluent in Russian. She had an Italian coming to a meeting, and a Russian, but she did not yet know the location of the meeting. Quite deliberately, she took Frank's hand from her hip and laid it on her thigh.

The lights had been in the mirror through Ustikolina, and when they'd gone by the nowhere turning to the bombed bridge of Foča, on the open roads before and after Milievina, and when they climbed on the ice surface for the gorge that led to Tvorno. Always the lights were with them, holding their intensity because the distance between them did not grow and did not close.

Each time Mister looked in the mirror he saw the lights of the blue van.

She did not speak. The road and its ice held her attention. She did not hold his hand any longer. She had the wheel and the gearstick and she searched ahead for the longer thicker stretches of ice. Water ran down the rock faces beside the road and spilled on to the tarmac.

Always the lights were with him, and with the mirror.

'Would you stop, please?'

'What?'

'Sorry – Monika, could you stop, please?'

'What for?'

'I am just asking you to stop, please.'

'Ah, I understand. You want a pee stop. You can say so.'

'Please stop.'

Very gently, not using the foot brake but going down through her gears, she stopped. He stepped out. His feet slipped and he steadied himself against the vehicle.

The headlights shone hard at him, and Mister walked towards the lights. If the Secretary of State had not been at the hotel, if there had not been a metal detector arch in the hotel lobby, if his pistol had not been left in the Mitsubishi, he would have had the weapon in his hand. The lights had stopped moving, and the interior lit as the door was opened. Cann came forward and stood in black silhouette in front of the lights. The little bastard faced him. Mister blinked as he came closer to the lights. If he had had the weapon in his hand he would have used it. There was hate in his heart. Men he had not hated were entombed in concrete foundations, were buried in Epping, were weighted on the sea bed, or walked on sticks. Cann stood ahead of the lights, his body diminished by their size.

'Got a problem, Mister?'

He couldn't see the mouth, but light caught the rims of the big spectacles.

'What's a nice girl like that doing with a piece of shit like you?'

He walked through the question. Mister faced his persecutor. He towered over the shadowy shape in front of him. The lights blazed in his face, made tears in his eyes.

'Not going to have a weep on me, are you, Mister?'

Mister lashed out. Right fist, low, short arm punch. The fist buried itself in the slight stomach. The body jack-knifed, would have fallen if the fist hadn't caught the coat collar. He dragged Cann round the side of the blue van, to the back of it. He threw Cann against the doors, then punched him again, first the solar plexus, and as the head dropped, the upper-cut to the jaw. Cann went down. Mister kicked him. Kept kicking him. Nearly fell on the ice. Should have had heavier shoes, should have had the boots the Cards wore when they went out for a kicking, with lead or iron caps. He reached down, found the coat, pulled the body up. No resistance. Arms trying to protect the upper body, hands over the face. He punched until his hands hurt, put Cann down, then kicked until his toes hurt in his handmade shoes. It was hard for Mister to see the small figure on the road behind the van.

He walked away.

The voice was small behind him. 'That was a mistake, Mister, a *mistake.*'

Mister went back to the van. She said, laughing, that it was a long pee stop. His knuckles bled and he hid them from her.

Joey reached his room. He knew she was back. Ante was in the lobby and Muhsin lounged on the landing near her door. He'd been off the road twice, but he'd been lucky: a tractor had pushed him back from the drift once and a pick-up had towed him clear the second time. He'd gone twice into the snow because his spectacles' arms were broken and when the frame had fallen from his nose he'd swerved. There wasn't a part of his body that wasn't in pain.

He went into the bathroom. He held the spectacles, and his hand shook. The mirror showed him his face – blood, scratches, rising welts. He managed his coat, shirt and vest, but the pain in his stomach wouldn't allow him to bend and unfasten the laces of his trainers. He pushed his trousers down, and his underpants, to his ankles. He stood in the shower, clinging to the chrome support. Without it he would have collapsed. The water ran over him and drenched his trousers, pants, socks and puddled in his trainers.

He heard the room door open.

'You're back?'

'Yes.'

'A good day?'

'A useful day,' Joey croaked.

'I needed a new pair of knickers and clean tights.'

'Good.'

There must have been a sob in his voice. He held tight to the support. She was in the bathroom doorway. The curtain wasn't drawn. She was looking at him. The water ran in rivers across his spectacles.

'What happened to you?'

Through the lenses her face was blurred. He didn't know whether she cared, or not. He grimaced, but that hurt his mouth, his jawbone, his cheeks and his brain.

'I walked into a door.'

'Did the door have boots and fists, or just boots?'

'If the door had had a gun I think it might have been rather more serious.'

She came into the bathroom and knelt beside the shower. The water splashed from his body on to her.

'Packer?'

He nodded.

She untied his trainer laces and pulled them off his feet, then the sodden socks, then his underpants and his trousers, and threw each of them into the bath. The water had plastered her careful hair and had made streams of her more careful makeup. She sat on the bath edge, pulled a towel off the rack and rubbed her hair and face.

'You're not the world's most beautiful sight – is there blood in your urine?'

'Don't know.'

'Are you going to live?'

'I hope so.'

'There's a Russian coming.'

'Coming where?'

'Coming for a meeting, for tomorrow's meeting.'

'Where's it to be?'

'I don't have the location ... Clean tights don't matter, not like knickers. I've got to get back. Do you want a doctor?'

'Tomorrow, then, I follow where he leads. My bloody bumper against his exhaust – no, no doctor.'

'We go mob-handed, Joey. I'll not take argument on it.' She said it as if she were his mother, his aunt, or his teacher.

'It's my show.'

'We go in numbers – it's not about whose show it is.'

'Yes, *ma'am*, three bags bloody full, ma'am.'

'Mob-handed, hardware, protection – safe. I wouldn't want to look like you look ... Just so you know – the woman, she's Monika Holberg. She's a Norwegian tree-hugger. She does good deeds for unfortunates, out of UNHCR. You'll find her in Novo Sarajevo, third floor, apartment H, Fojnicka 27. Be a shame, wouldn't it, Joey, if she didn't know what Mister was, what he did? Wouldn't be a shame if, when she's learned it, she kept her legs together and Mister didn't get his over. You up for that?'

'Could be.'

'You want me to dry you?'

'I'll manage.'

She closed the door after her.

Joey staggered to the bed. He was dripping wet. He collapsed on to it. He might have passed out but for the pain and the memory. He was back on the ground, squirming on the ice and the Tarmac to make himself smaller, as the fists and boots rained in on him. *That was a mistake, Mister, a mistake.* The hammering, in his body and his head, was on the door.

He shouted, 'Yes?'

'Are you Cann, Customs and Excise?'

He crawled off the bed, leaned on the wall and then the wardrobe to steady himself, held the towel across his privates, and opened the door. The man wore a grey suit, was five or so years older than Cann, had a good shirt and a nice tie. He looked at Cann with contempt, a replica of the sons of the landowner his father managed for, superiority buried under a caked veneer of politeness.

'Sorry to disturb you, Mr Cann – by God, you've been in the wars. Don't tell me, let me guess, tripped down some steps, did you? I'm Hearn, from the embassy. I've been asked to pass to you a message that came to us via the Ministry of Justice. I do apologize for the inconvenience of calling on you so late, but we thought it the sort of matter that should not have been passed, for fear of misunderstandings, by telephone. You had written authorization from Judge Zenjil Delic for "intrusive surveillance" of the UK national Albert William Packer during that gentleman's visit to Sarajevo. You can go home now, Mr Cann, which might save you another accident. Judge Delic informs us, through the Ministry of Justice, that he has withdrawn such authorization. He's cancelled it. There's no mistake. I have it in writing, couriered to the embassy, over his signature.'

Joey gagged.'But that's impossible.'

''Fraid not . . .' He paused. 'We do have a list of doctors, should you wish for medical attention. If you'd gone through us in the first place then things might have been different, but you chose not to . . . The authorization for you to operate here is withdrawn. Good night.'

The X-ray machine had gone, and the metal detector arch. They walked, flanking Mister, across the empty atrium bar.

Mister said, again, 'I don't want to talk about it.'

Atkins persisted, 'His place has been turned over, searched, so's mine.'

'I'm not talking about it. Don't you listen?'

He gestured with his hand, into Atkins's face, made a cutting motion across Atkins's throat.

They went out through the doors, and the night frost's blast, carried in the wind, caught them. They went along the side of the hotel heading for the city and the old quarter.

'He was my friend,' Mister said. 'We don't ever forget that he was my friend.'

The Cruncher hadn't been the Eagle's friend, and Atkins hadn't known him. Small matter, the Eagle thought. It was enough that the Cruncher had been the friend of Mister. Atkins wouldn't have understood, was frightened, wouldn't have known when to close his mouth and keep it tight shut. They were walking briskly, filling the pavement of an empty street. Atkins would have seen the cuts on the knuckles when Mister had his fist near to his throat.

'What have you done to your hand, Mister?'

'I've done nothing to my hand.'

'The skin's all broken, it's—'

Mister stopped. He turned to the Eagle. He held his hands under the Eagle's nose. The scars were angry, weeping, where the skin was split. 'Do you see anything wrong with my hands, Eagle?'

The Eagle said quietly, 'I don't see anything wrong with your hands, Mister.'

He was Mister's man. He did not then and had not ever dared to be anything else. They walked past the shops with the steel shutters down, and the benches where couples cuddled hopelessly in the cold, past the cafés where the waiters sluiced the floors and lifted the chairs on to the tables. They came to the small park. Round the grass were thick bushes, bare of leaves but heavy enough to toss shadows on to the grass. They saw the boy. He had the earphones on his pretty head, and was gyrating with the music he listened to. The dogs sniffed the grass, meandered between the shadows. Their leashes were hooked to their collars and trailed on the ground after them. He was watched and he did not know it.

Atkins veered away to the right. The Eagle followed Mister to the left, to be behind the boy, as he had been told. He always did what Mister told him. It was about the Cruncher, whom the Eagle had detested, and about the Cruncher's honour, where there had never been any.

They closed on the boy, Enver, who was lost in his music.

Chapter Sixteen

He walked, each step laboured, in agony. He could have taken the blue van.

The excuse Joey gave himself for walking was that exercise would loosen the joints at his hips, knees, ankles, would dull the bruising on his ribcage, the wheeze in his lungs, and soften the ache behind his eyes. The excuse was merely a delaying tactic. He walked because he was in no hurry to reach his destination. He had gone first to the third floor, apartment H, of Fojnicka 37. A young woman had answered, draped in a long-tailed man's shirt, and he'd asked for Miss Holberg. She'd come to the door, wrapped in a heavy dressing-gown, and she'd used her fingers to squeeze the sleep from her eyes. Joey had betrayed her dreams, had told his story. When he'd finished, had demolished her, she'd stuttered questions at him: 'Who are you? How do you know this? Why do you come to tell me it?' Without answering, he'd slipped away down the stairs, and back to the night.

The darkness and the chill of it were close to him.

From Novo Sarajevo, he had tracked alongside the Miljacka river going past the black towers of apartments, the snipers' homes, then had crossed the river at the Vrbanja bridge. It was where she had been shot, where Jasmina and her boy had been, in their turn, betrayed. Cars crossed where she had lain. Oil grease was smeared where she had bled. He was drawn towards the hill, the steep climb, a place he had no wish to be.

He had said: *But that's impossible.* He knew their stories, what they had suffered, and their strength . . . It was not possible.

There were no more cars now, no people scurrying for home up the unlit road. The faster he went up the hill, the sooner he would know the truth of it. Without the moon, full and bright, he would have seen nothing after the last lit pool from the street-lamp. An owl shrieked from the cemetery. He went on. On his watch the hands were past midnight. It was already the day of the meeting. Without authorization for intrusive surveillance, signed by a recognized judge, any evidence accrued from the telephoto camera lens or the directional microphone carried in Maggie Bolton's steel-sided box was inadmissible in court. He could see the old, worn, condescending faces of the new men and the new woman who made the Sierra Quebec Golf team, and he could hear the criticizing merciless rasp of Gough's voice . . . He did not think it could be true, it was not possible.

Joey realized what was different.

Light spewed out at the end of the rutted, holed road from the windows of a house around which was set a skeleton of scaffolding poles. The light reflected on the sleek paintwork of a black Mercedes saloon, and danced back from the radiator screen. At the side of what had been only half a house, captured by the light, were stacked piles of concrete building blocks, and there were two cement mixers. The light, splaying from the window, fell on the slabs of a newly laid patio space between the scaffolding and the parked car, and was reflected up to show Joey the clean new roof timbers that peeped from under a spread tarpaulin.

Joey walked towards the light. He saw through the window the naked bulb hanging from new flex. Before, there had been a grimy, unpolished, inadequate, smelly oil-lamp in the room, humble but it had given out a glow of pride. He went past the Mercedes and banged on the door with his clenched fist, hit it until the pain ran in rivers through his body.

*

The Eagle hung back. He was, of course, too experienced in the matters of criminal law to believe that staying back, not *actually* taking part, would in any way mitigate his guilt. The books to prove the guilt lined the shelves of the office over the launderette; principal among them was Archbold, three inches thick of thin india paper and close print, with a leather cover, setting him back each January three hundred and twenty-five pounds. He would be accused, even if he pleaded he'd stayed back, of 'acting in common' with Mister and Atkins. If he snivelled that he had not known what was to happen, he would still be guilty as an 'accessory to murder'. For 'acting in common' or for being an 'accessory to murder' the sentence was the same – life imprisonment. But that was semantics . . . God alone knew the penalty in Sarajevo, most likely bollocks defenestration then filleting . . . It was his squeamishness, which Mister despised, that caused him to stay deep in the shadows. They didn't need him. God's truth, they hadn't needed him at all . . .

Atkins had done the dogs. All show, all piss and wind, the dogs had been. His dogs, at home with Mo, could make a pretence of ferocity but embarrassed themselves with it. Atkins had slipped into the bushes by the grass, had sat down, had cooed at them, and the brutes had shown that their teeth and menace were a sham. Atkins had held the dogs, and Mister had chopped the back of his hand on to the pretty boy's neck, felled him, stuffed the gagging handkerchief into his mouth and wrenched his arms behind his back. Atkins had hooked the dog's leashes to a park-bench stanchion – which would hold them for a few minutes before they broke free – then had run after them, past the trailing Eagle, to help Mister drag Enver down the side alley that led to the river from the park. There was a dribble of moisture on the pavement, and the smell. The bladder had gone first, then the sphincter. The last few paces, from the alleyway to the bridge, the boy had known what was coming to him and had struggled for his life. Atkins, in that final stampede, had hissed, 'Don't you bloody bite me, you bastard.' The struggling and the way his arms were held up behind his back would have meant they were half dislocated out of the shoulder joints. The Eagle winced. At the end, he couldn't help himself but watch. Mister raised his arm and chopped again, full force, on the back of the boy's neck. They were in the middle of the bridge. A car was turning on to it, but the lights hadn't yet come far enough round to light the rail. The boy slumped under the force of the blow. Maybe he was unconscious, maybe just dazed. It was all one movement. Mister and Atkins had him up, like he was dead weight, and over, like he was dumped trash. There was the splash. The car's lights illuminated the two of them as they walked back to where the Eagle waited. The boy would have been incapable of survival when he went into the water that flowed fast, dark, deep, under the bridge's rail. They came towards him. The boy would drown. The drowning wouldn't help the Cruncher, nor the Cruncher's rent-boys, nor the Cruncher's parents in their Torbay bungalow. It was about Mister's self-respect and Mister's dignity. As they reached him, Atkins was pulling off his glove and looking at his hand. The Eagle heard Mister say, 'You're all right, didn't break the skin – nothing like a good pair of gloves. You did well, Atkins, brilliant.' At worst it was 'acting in common', at best it was 'accessory to murder'. They didn't wait for him.

The Eagle bent over until his head was down at his knees, and vomited up his hotel dinner.

'I am not Falcone.'

Joey shook his head, 'I don't know who is . . .'

'Nor am I Borsellino,' the judge said softly.

'I don't know who you're talking about.'

She interrupted, spoke sharply, 'Giovanni Falcone was a magistrate in Sicily. He arrested many of the Mafia and prosecuted them, imprisoned them. He was killed by a culvert bomb, with his wife and his bodyguards. He was followed by Paulo Borsellino who pursued the Mafia with the same dedication. Borsellino was killed by a car bomb, with his bodyguards. They stood against the tide.'

The room was a building site. They were itinerants, travellers, squatting in their own home. Across the table were layered sheets of newspaper: across the newspaper was a sandy shore of dust. Two of the four walls had been stripped of the plaster rendering to expose old stone. It had been a room, as he remembered it, of dirty, uncomfortable peace when it had been lit by the oil-lamps, but the new electricity threw down a glaring brightness. There were shining new plastic window-frames in place of the rotten splintered wood that was now propped against the wall. Joey was perched on the end of the table and faced her father, who sat on the bed in his shirtsleeves, close to a three-bar electric fire. She rounded on them, with the restlessness of a zoo-caged animal, circled them in her chair.

'I am not a hero. They were martyrs to the reputation of jurisprudence. I am not them. They looked into the abyss, as I have done. They jumped, I stepped back.'

She said with scorn, as if to support her father, 'There were great demonstrations in Palermo after the killings, many thousands were on the streets to denounce the Mafia. The Mafia is still alive, but Falcone and Borsellino are dead.'

'You said you helped me so that you might regain your self respect.'

When the oil-lamps lit the room, the judge had had a face of old dignity. Under the new glare, the face was haunted by defeat. Joey had no business to be there, he was a criticism of them.

The judge said wearily, 'It was a dream . . . Do you know who has had the biggest funeral in Sarajevo, during the war and since? Musan Topalovic. To the people on the streets of Sarajevo he was a hero and a martyr. He called himself Caco. Who killed the hero? He was shot by Muslim government troops during a few days of crackdown on criminality in the last year of the war, to show a skim of respectability to the foreign powers. In the first days of the siege he held a line with what he named the Tenth Mountain Brigade, a formation of rats from the sewers. He was a butcher before he was a hero and a martyr, he slit the throats of Serbs who had stayed in the city, after he had robbed them, and he burned their bodies. He was a man of evil . . . Four years ago his body was dug up and carried shoulder high through the streets, to a new and more respectable grave. Shops emptied, and the cafés, and the bars. I see it in my mind, the worship of those who watched. I awoke, Joey, from the dream. The people of Sarajevo did not want me – they wanted as their hero and their martyr the man who was a butcher, Caco. They would not want me who was an insignificant imitation of Falcone and Borsellino . . . Everything I said to you, it was only a dream.'

The judge's words faded. A week before, Joey Cann would have nodded sympathetically and would have understood. But a long week had gone by.

'So, what happened?' Joey persisted. 'What turned you?'

The judge looked up at him, and his dulled eyes blinked under the force of the ceiling light. 'There were two offers put on the table. The offer to be killed, or . . . Eighteen men came to the house this morning, at first light, with lorries, cement mixers, blocks, timber. They worked all day, until it was dark, and they will be here again in a few hours. At lunchtime the Mercedes came. In the afternoon the catalogues were delivered to us. We will have the bathroom of our choice with a special shower for Jasmina, the kitchen that will suit her and a refrigerator-freezer, and the decoration for the rooms. What do you say?'

Joey, the week-old veteran of Sarajevo, said with spite, 'I say that the whole city will know you had a price.'

'It is Sarajevo, Joey, the city will applaud me, a fool has become sensible . . . In the evening a functionary came from the pensions department of the Ministry of Finance. He gave me back the document I had given nine years before to Ismet Mujic as part payment for Jasmina going to the Vrbanja bridge. With the document was an account statement, the scheme was paid up. They own me, they have bought me, and the world can know it. Don't you have a price, Joey?'

The question hurt, cut deep, and he hesitated. She was behind him, circling them. The wheels crunched on the fallen plaster and squealed. He could not see her face. He had bought her flowers. Anyone who'd cared to look from the pavements, or from their cars on the streets of this shit city, would have seen that a girl in a wheelchair carried his flowers. The question was under his guard.

'I don't know – if it was about someone I loved . . .'

'I did not think I had a price. I urge you, pray to your God that you never have to drink from the devil's cup.' The judge looked into Joey's eyes and asked simply,' Who would have looked after her?'

'Papa, enough of talking,' she snapped. 'He has no sympathy for what you say – look at him. He involved us, Papa. You should not justify yourself.' She came round the table, braked the chair between her father and Joey.

'If it had been about someone I loved I might have had a price. I don't stand in judgement. I hope I don't have that conceit.'

'Will you leave? You upset my father.' He saw the anger blaze in her eyes, and the colour flush her cheeks.

'The withdrawal of the authorization for intrusive surveillance, Joey, does that make it hard for you?' The judge's thin voice seeped from behind her back.

'If I wore the uniform, had the mentality of the uniform, it would be impossible for me to continue.'

'Without the uniform, what is the action of a driven man? What do you do, Joey?'

Because he had come into their lives, the dignity was gone from them. He wondered if, when he was gone, they would curse him. The love that gave flowers was finished. He stood tall over them, and they waited on his answer. He did not know himself, and nobody who knew him would have recognized Joey Cann.

He said, with savagery, 'I go to the end of the road, follow where I am led ... I think it finishes tomorrow. Tomorrow you will know whether you were bought too cheaply, whether you surrendered your pride too quickly ... Look and listen.'

He went out of the room and into the night. They might curse him, they might weep in each other's arms – or forget he had ever come into their lives. In a few hours it would be finished. He walked down the hill, left the building site and the Mercedes behind him, with his decency.

She passed the earphones to Salko, who began to scribble on a sheet of paper. When the call was finished, he gave the sheet to Frank. Frank wrote the translation, and palmed it to Maggie.

'Sorry about that, boys, a little bit of panic there for a moment,' she chimed. 'Turkish isn't one of my talents ... If I was clever, which I'm certainly not at this time of a God-forsaken night, I'd rather fancy a limerick coming on. It's getting quite multinational, don't you think? Line one: "There once was a Russkie, an Eyetie, and a Turk." Then we've "perk", "kirk", "dirk" and "lurk". . . . I'm too bloody tired. You know anything about Turks, Frank?' She eased back in her chair against him, liked the touch of him.

'Mainstream heroin trafficking.'

She grinned. 'You know what I think?'

'Unveil yourself to me, Miss Bolton.' Frank smirked at her.

She pushed him away, but she liked his sauce. It was cold as death in the room. There was a single small light, the bulb heavily shaded, in the room, on the floor. She clamped the earphones back on her head.

'Mister thinks this is going to be *his* meeting – I think he's in serious danger of diving into the pond and finding he's out of his depth.'

'Why would he do that?' Ivor Jowett asked into the phone. His wife, her face frozen in fury, tossed beside him. He listened, thanked the caller, and rang off. He switched off the bedside light, and lay on his back in the darkness.

Ivor Jowett was the drugs liaison officer on a posting from the Custom House to the British embassy in Ankara. The Turkey secondment was a good one. At the embassy, Sehit Ersan Cad. 46/A Cankaya, he was the early-warning siren for the premier cases of heroin importation into the United Kingdom. As an ambitious investigation beaver, with the information fed him by the *polisi* in the cities and the *jandarmas* in the countryside, he would be noticed and fast-tracked to promotion. The stuff poured through the refineries and flowed out over the Bosphorus and across Europe to the British Channel and North Sea ports. Without the contacts, the phone calls at dead of night, Ivor Jowett would have wallowed uselessly. The pity of it was that the calls came, a good half of them, into his apartment in the night hours, not to his office in the working day. Newspaper clippings were sent him each week by the public affairs section of the Custom House; most times the credit for a seizure at Harwich docks, or Felixstowe or Dover, or at the port of Southampton was given to the 'dedication and persistence and thoroughness' of the uniformed staff; the figures soared – a million pounds' worth, street value, of intercepted heroin was commonplace, ten million pounds was not rare. Ivor Jowett, late of the Sierra Quebec Juliet team, was a star ... His wife rolled over and cradled herself in his arm. She was Gloria, formerly of Sierra Quebec Roger. It was said at the Custom House that internal marriages were the only ones that had a chance.

'Do you want a coffee?'

'Wouldn't mind.'

The principal strain on the marriages was the refusal of officers to confide in wives who were not in the family. He could tell Gloria. She did the secretarial in the embassy office, but still grumbled and complained of under-employment. What would he tell her, when she brought back the mugs of coffee?

He was Fuat Selcuk, believed to be forty-eight years old. He was from a village on the Aras river near to Erzurum. His territory stretched along the old Soviet border, now Georgia and Armenia, from Artvin and Kars in the north to Mount Ararat and Mount Tendurek in the south. It was where he had his refineries, where he employed the best young chemists from the universities. The product in which he dealt, raw opium, originated in the poppyfields of Afghanistan. In sacks, lashed to the backs of mules, the cargo was brought north from the collection point at Tāloqān then was ferried across the Pjandz river, where the escort of machine-guns was changed, then taken overland across Tajikistan, and shipped over the width of the Caspian Sea, unloaded at the Azerbaijani harbour of Sumqayit, then moved on to the border posts close to Iğdir and Ardahan. There Fuat Selcuk waited for the cargo's arrival and paid for it with cash, dollars. The money, cut and cut and cut – as the cargo would be – returned on the trail and paid off the lorry drivers, the middlemen, the ferry crews, the border guards, the machine-gunners, the Taliban leaders in Afghanistan, and the farmers who grew the crops of poppies in their fields. He was never cheated. The cargo was never stolen *en route*, sacks never fell from the backs of the lorries or the mules. His arm reached from western Turkey all the way back to the hill fields of Afghanistan. To cheat him would have been the same as tying a heavy stone around the neck and wading out into the Pjandz river. Neither was he cheated in the refineries by his chemists, nor as the lorries rolled off the Bosphorus ferries for the long drive north across Europe and the ultimate destinations in Holland, Germany, France, or Green Lanes in north London. In his younger days, when his reputation as a businessman of honour was not yet confirmed, Fuat Selcuk's speciality was to slice off a man's testicles and stifle the screaming by placing them in the victim's mouth, then stapling his lips together so that they could not be spat out. He was also a man of charity: he had built hospitals and schools, and he paid for the repair of mosques.

The call in the night that had woken Ivor Jowett had been a whispered communication. The men he dealt with always dropped their voices when they spoke of Fuat Selcuk, because they knew the reach of his arm. That morning, Fuat Selcuk had left Erzurum by light aircraft and had flown to Ankara. At the airport, a bright, brave young spark on surveillance duty had chanced his luck and moved close enough for an 'overheard'. The spark's target had met an Ankara-based associate and had said: 'It'll be a dog fuck of a day. All the way there to meet a bastard from England, who thinks he is the top fuck. I'll eat him . . .' and the associate had said, 'Or he'll eat his fucking balls . . .' and they'd gone beyond the hearing of the listener. Fuat Selcuk had caught an afternoon flight to Damascus, then an evening connection to Zurich – his caller had told him.

Why would he do that?

She brought the tea, and Ivor Jowett told his wife about the call.

Her eyebrows arched. 'Taking a hell of a risk, isn't he, the Brit, dealing with a man like that?'

Maggie was hunched over the recorder, listening hard, pressing the phones against her ears. A tight little frown dented her forehead. Frank watched her. Salko and Ante pushed themselves up from the far wall and sauntered towards her table. Her eyes were screwed tight, she concentrated, then she shrugged. 'I can't make it out.'

She passed the earphones to Frank. He listened, scratched under his chin. 'There's a problem . . . something about the peach-bottom boy.'

Frank gave the earphones to the men; they were slipped to each in turn.

Salko said, 'Serif has lost the boy, Enver. He took the dogs out. They have come back, but not the boy.'

Ante said, 'He's talking about an accident. They are going to telephone the Kosevo Hospital. Such a thing has not happened before.'

Fahro said, 'You can hear the worry of him.'

Frank translated and Maggie scribbled down what they'd said. Moments like these always brought a slight joy to her. She pried into her targets' lives. She heard their happiness and she was with them in crisis. At the other end of the tap, she sensed the panic. The first search party had gone out. She imagined them, in their black jeans, black T-shirts and black jackets, the gold chains garlanding their necks, coming back and reporting failure – they were sent out again. She was the witness to the growing chaos. All the days in the basement workshop at Ceauşescu Towers, and the evenings whiled away with the foremen technicians at Imperial College, the nights curled in her chair with her dog and the electronics magazines, had a value when she played the voyeur. She had no interest in the whereabouts of the boy, it did not matter to her if he was prone on a hospital bed, or had gone walkabout, or was drinking himself stupid in a bar, or was in a morgue on a slab. It was her position as an intruder that thrilled her, did now and had in the past. It was her power to insert herself under her target's skin. Those who controlled her walked blind without her skills.

She had neat copperplate handwriting.

My dear Mister,

Tonight a man came to see me. He told me who you were. He described your career as a criminal of importance. I asked his name and how did he know such things and why he told me them, but he did not give me answers.

I hate criminality and its exploitation of the weak, and its very selfishness. Therefore, Mister, I should hate you (I see no reason why the man who visited me should have lied), but . . .

But I think it is impossible for me to hate you. The man said that you had sought me out as a recipient of charitable goods in order to create an authentic alibi of good works; you used me; you wished to create respectability for your Bosnia with Love lorries which would return to the UK loaded with the class A narcotic – heroin. That is cause for me to hate you, but . . .

But I am a good judge (I hope) of a genuine man. I see many who come here with insincerity. Whatever were your first motives for bringing the lorry to the UNIS Building, Tower A, I wish to believe they were replaced by a spirit of true friendship and true affection.

I was not with a criminal in the village of Visnjica. A criminal would not have played cards in the village with the old men, and given them dignity, and would not have held the hand of a child without a father, and given him kindness. A criminal would not have come with me to Gorazde and shown such sympathy for the plight of unfortunates. I was with a man who cared, who had a love for fellow human beings – that is my judgement and it is precious to me.

Perhaps, Mister, when you came here you did not bring sympathy and love. Perhaps you learned them here, in my company (if I am wrong then I am a simple and stupid woman but I think you gained a softness here that you did not travel with) . . . I think you are a good man. Wherever I go, whatever is my future, I will remember you and your kindness. I had hoped – until this man came and told me of you – to see you each time that you visited Sarajevo, to spend time with you, and to grow close to you. You would have made a light where there is darkness, summer to winter, brought hope where there is despair. You should be proud of what you did, with your decency.

We will not meet again,

With love, and may God watch over you,

Monika (Holberg)

She sealed the letter into its envelope.

March 2001

'You'll meet him in a minute, the foreman, Five-D.'

The Englishman, Barnaby, walked down the hill towards the bunker and the junction where the turning led to Ljut village. His guest, an attentive young man, hurried at his side. The lights shone boldly in the repaired houses of the nearer village and were bright pinpricks across the valley, beyond the river, in Vraca. Within a quarter of an hour, the sun's strength would wipe out the electricity's glow from the new windows of the houses of the twin villages. Just before the autumn weather had closed in on the valley, the previous year, five and a half months back, the certificate of clearance had been issued for the corridor of land under the line of power pylons, and the engineering teams had moved on to the site. For a further month, into November, the teams had worked inside the narrow corridor of yellow tape, had lifted the pylons and raised the cables and had restored the power. There had been no further accidents. The power had been switched on. Light had blazed, glowed, shone from each home in the two communities that had been reoccupied. The bulbs were never switched off. The German charity World in Crisis paid the bills.

On the two occasions Barnaby had been to the valley to plan the main clearance operation, he had gained the impression, very distinctly, that the Muslims in Vraca and the Serbs in Ljut kept their lights on through the day whether the sun shone or didn't, and through the night whether they were awake or asleep. It was not for him to tell the villagers that the German aid and generosity were running out. Because all of the donors were now scrambling to turn their backs on the country, and the funding for the de-mining gangs was drying up, Barnaby had brought the journalist to the valley. Fenton, from a London broadsheet with a daily circulation of less than four hundred thousand readers, was the best recipient Barnaby could find. The work had barely begun, the funding for mine clearance was required for another two decades, *minimum*. He needed journalists from mass-circulation newspapers, and he needed politicians to tramp down that lane and a thousand others, but they were beyond reach. Instead, he had Wilf Fenton. He always tried to be cheerful when he brought a guest to a minefield.

'Why do you call him Five-D?'

The way Barnaby told it, there were Five-Ds on a hundred sites. It was a regular part of his introductory patter. He knew, from his dogged persistence in seeking out funding, that anecdotes played better in journalists' copy than statistics.

'All the Ds. He was a De-miner, and was blown up, and damn lucky. He became a Driver, ferried others around but didn't go into the field. He was bored, and went back to De-mining. Was blown up again, was even luckier, didn't lose his leg. Started again at being a Driver. Couldn't beat the boredom so he's at it again, De-mining. That's the five Ds – got it?'

Fenton shuddered as he walked and was eyeing the yellow tape suspiciously, staying on an imaginary line that ran down the exact centre of the track. 'Once would have been enough for me.'

'There's so much shrapnel in him . . .' It was another line from Barnaby's regular patter. All the foremen supported his story '. . . that we always test a new metal detector by holding it up against his backside. The lights flash and the buzzer goes full blast.'

'God – and that's the extent of what you've got to cover, is it?'

'Yes, that's the valley. That's the Bunica river valley.'

It was laid out in front of them. A hawk hovered over the flattened dead weeds of the old arable fields, fluttered on to hunt across the dull weather-stamped grass of the old grazing fields, then soared in the light wind and flew towards the fallen posts and dropped wires of the old vineyard. There was no beauty to it. The green growth of new grass shoots would come in the next month and the flowers would make their carpet in the month after. It was as though the place had lost its soul, Barnaby thought. There was a long, seemingly endless line of yellow tape that marked the extent of the fields, running along the edge of the wooded slopes.

'How long will it take you to clear it?'

'Seven months, eight. That's twenty men working five days a week.'

'How many mines are there?'

'We don't know, the records don't exist.'

'Would you walk there?'

Barnaby shook his head resolutely, 'I wouldn't step an inch over the tape. I am fifty-six years old and I have been working with mines for twenty-four of them. I've learned to *respect* them.'

He told the stories of the foreman, the grandmother and the son-in-law, and Fenton scribbled busily.

They had reached the bunker. The yellow tape was all round the squat construction of stone and damp tree trunks. The paint was cracked on the red surround and had peeled from the skull shape and the crossed bones. Barnaby took Fenton inside and the journalist flashed his Marlboro lighter, turned it up to full. There were scribbled numbers chalked on the walls, the remnants of an old occupation. Did Barnaby know what they signified? He didn't. Fenton said they looked like the bookies' lists you'd find pinned up on a wall of a betting shop. The last date, where the chalk line erased the list of odds, was for a summer day seven years earlier and above the date was the word: Rado.

'I can't help you,' Barnaby said. 'I don't know what it means.'

'A pity, sort of interesting, isn't it? About ghosts.'

They went out into the sunlight, and blinked. The lights in the Ljut windows and the pinpricks across the river were now burned out. A column of de-miners tramped down the track in front of them, the weight of their boots thudding on the stones.

'What are the boots? They look pretty solid.'

'They're supposed to be proof against an anti-personnel mine, or what we call a nuisance mine.'

'That's comforting.'

'Not really – they have rigid soles. They're all right on the flat but they're a liability on a stone slope. You fall over in them, reach out to break your fall, then your whole pressure is on your hand, and your weight. It takes five kilos of pressure to detonate a PMA2. If they're working on a gradient, like the vineyard, they'll kick the over-boots off.'

'Christ . . . why do they do it?'

'For money, so that they eat and their families eat.'

'How do you hold up morale, after an accident?'

'Hunger does the job. Usually, when a de-miner's been hurt, or killed, at least two of them jack it in – they don't eat, and their families don't.'

'You're showing me a bloody – excuse me – brutal world.'

'Feel free to quote me.'

They followed the de-miners down to the ford. The water was in spate across it. Barnaby pointed to a distant farmhouse and spoke of some recent family history: an old woman who moved on crutches and a young man whose skeleton body would not be recovered until the end of the summer because of where it lay, and of an old farmer who survived senility in the belief that he would reclaim and work his fields. He was not yet out of his bed – and that was a greater mercy.

They stood at the side of the track, close to the river. Parallel lines of yellow tape strips ran from the track out into the fields, each wide enough for two men to walk alongside each other. Between these stunted corridors were wide expanses of grass and weed, but the two men in each corridor did not walk, they knelt, their visors down. They probed with thin sharpened steel prods. Fenton said that it was like watching paint dry. Barnaby said, drily, that the chance of losing a leg when home decorating was slight. Fenton saw the dog, and his face lit. A heavy German shepherd, shaggy-coated, was in the longest grass in a corridor between the yellow tape and twenty-five yards from the track. A long thin cord linked the dog to the handler.

'That's what I need.' Fenton raised his pocket camera, aimed at the dog. 'Tell me about him.'

'He's Boy. Nine years old. He's the best, a prime asset. He was trained first by an American de-mining company. They worked him in Angola, then Rwanda and Croatia. They sold him to us. He's going to work out his time here. He scents the explosive ... Not everybody trusts a dog. If he misses a mine he won't detonate it, but the handler following him will. Many prefer to put their trust in the prodder. We argue about it. But Boy is special. When a dog's done its useful work, it's shot. Boy won't be, his handler'll take him home.'

'That's wonderful. Can I go closer?'

'Sorry, no. Mr Fenton, you have to understand that we're in the first week of the season. The men are rusty. They haven't been in the field for four or five months. It's a time of maximum danger for them.'

'I've an angle now, I'm going to write something positive,' Fenton said enthusiastically. 'Something about brave men, and Boy, working to bring a proper life back to two communities in the valley. I like it, I've got the buzz – the valley where the peace will never again be broken.'

'Would you all like a cup of tea?'

It was what the Princess's mother had always done each time the old Bill had come visiting at dawn in their Ilford house, when she'd been a child.

'It's no trouble to me, easy enough to put the kettle on.'

Except when her father was locked up, the old Bill had been regular early-morning visitors. Her mother, Clarrie Hinds, always brewed up a big pot, and cleared the cupboard of mugs for the tray; if there was a senior man among them she'd usually have sliced up a lemon, just in case. She'd always put a plate of biscuits on the tray, opened a fresh packet for them. Like mother, like daughter. Her mother said it helped to make a bad experience more pleasant, and also said that tea and biscuits and talk about the weather – would it rain or wouldn't it? – was distracting for the searchers.

This was a sour lot. Tea declined, biscuits refused, small-talk ignored.

It was now nine months since the last time the Princess's home had been 'visited'. They'd been polite enough then. No sledge-hammers, no shouting, no blue lights flashing, and no sirens when they'd driven Mister away. He'd been given at least ten minutes to get himself dressed, and they'd been discreet when they'd taken him out through the front door. It had only been afterwards that she'd heard from Rosie Carthew, Carol Penberthy and Leonora Govan that the house had been surrounded by armed police crouching in their gardens; the Princess hadn't even seen them. The last time, Mister had gone off as if a few golf friends were shipping him to a far-away course – but Mister didn't play golf. This lot were cold, correct, silent.

They knew the house. They'd have been working from the pictures taken when the house was 'burgled' a year back. They'd each been assigned a room. The oldest man among them had an unlit pipe stapled in his mouth. She'd seen him look around from the moment he'd come in through the front door. There were no ashtrays in the Princess's home. She thought he yearned to produce his matches and scratch a flame, but he didn't ask her. The old Bill always asked if they could smoke, and her mother had always produced an ashtray for them. This man wandered between the rooms, took on the role of a supervisor, and the Princess followed him. They went into the kitchen, the sitting room, the living room, her snug where she did her post, the dining room that was never used, and up the stairs to the bedrooms and the bathrooms. She tracked him like a suspicious dog. When the woman who had searched the dining room, taking everything from the sideboard then replacing each plate and each glass just where they'd been, had met the heavy-bearded man, who'd gone through the sitting room with fine-tooth comb care, the Princess had been at the top of the stairs. The woman and the bearded man were in the hall below.

'You know what's funny about this place, sort of creepy, it's not lived-in. It's like a show house at the Ideal Home. There's nothing out of place – and there's not a book. Did you find one book here? I didn't. It gives you the shivers. Or it's like a hotel room, cleaned for the next guest.'

Then they'd seen her at the top of the stairs, and the Princess hadn't heard another word spoken among them, until they left.

They filed out. Years ago, Clarrie Hinds had said that you never showed anger to them, never flipped, never screamed, because they'd talk about that in the canteen at their late breakfast, and the word would have been passed to the scum, the informers, they paid.

To have shouted at them, to have wept in a corner, would have demeaned her dignity, would have diminished Mister's self-respect. They took nothing with them.

'Thank you for your co-operation, Mrs Packer.'

The older man's match flashed in the dull light.

She didn't answer. The cars were starting up in the road. Usually, at her mother's home or at her own since she'd married Mister, when the police or the Church came with a warrant, searched and left empty-handed without evidence in a bag, there would be tight-lipped annoyance at the senior man's mouth. She didn't see anger, but there was a slow smile, which might have been contempt, or satisfaction. It was no big deal. She'd tell Mister about it when he was back, tomorrow or the day after. Their house rule, which she'd never broken, was that she did not call him when he was away. It would keep until his return. They were a partnership. In his strange, unshown way, her Mister loved his Princess. He didn't crawl all over her, didn't touch her when they were out, didn't smarm her with compliments in front of strangers, but he loved her. It was returned. The trust was between them. When he came back, she would tell Mister where they'd been, how they'd searched, what they'd looked like. He'd listen to her, never interrupting, and every detail of it would be stored away in his mind, his memory. When she'd finished, he'd say, 'Well done,' or 'That's good,' or, if he was expansive, 'You'd have thought they'd have better things to do . . .' and life would go on. She never looked to the future, didn't think about it. A long time ago, when they were first married and Mister was on the up, she'd feared he'd be found in a gutter, or in a fire-destroyed car, and that the uniformed Bill would come to escort her to a mortuary to look at his body. She no longer harboured such a fear. He was untouchable now; as she joked with him, 'God wouldn't dare.' She didn't ask him what the future was, and didn't care.

As the cars drove off, she saw across the road that Leonora was by her gate, in her bathrobe, and miming at her a charade game of filling a kettle and drinking a cup, but she shook her head, smiled – because it was no big deal – and closed her door behind her.

One point confused her. There had been no warning. The night before his arrest, Mister had known they coming for him in the morning. She'd tell Mister that his network hadn't warned her . . .

She went into the kitchen. She made herself a coffee and put bread in the toaster. She took the toast and the mug into the sitting room and switched on the television.

Her eyes roved from the set, from the mug and the plate, over the room. There was no sign that the Church had come mob-handed into the house, it was all strangely tidy and undisturbed. She was almost at the end of the traverse of her gaze over the watercolour paintings, the ornaments, the decanter and the glasses, the fireplace, when she saw the envelope.

It was propped up on a low table beside the chest where she kept her tapestry. She had not put a brown, large-size envelope on that table.

She wondered what they'd left behind.

She laid her cup and the plate on the footstool beside her chair, went to the table and picked up the envelope.

The flap was not sealed, was folded inside. There was no logo on it, nor any handwriting. She opened it and took out a wad of plate-size photographs. Attached to the back of the top photograph was a stick-on message note. 'Room 329, Holiday Inn, Sarajevo. Phone: (00 387 32) 664 273.' She turned the photographs over. She looked.

Her eyes closed, she lashed out with her foot. The fluffy pink slipper kicked against the stool beside her chair. The toast went, margarine-and-marmalade side down on to the carpet, and the cup of coffee flew. The Princess ripped off the stick-on message note, marched into the kitchen and snatched up the telephone.

He had been dressing, his best suit, best shirt and best shoes, and the phone had pealed beside the bed. Mister held it away from his ear, and heard the rant.

'They're not my problem, they can come any time they want, once a week if they want, by appointment or without – you're my problem, Mister. Who is *she*? You are my problem. Who *is* she? Don't play dumb with me, Mister, and don't bloody tell me, "Oh, she's just nobody . . . Oh, she's just a friend, someone I met . . . Oh, she's just a quick shag." Out in the bloody open, like you're some sort of kid out in the park. *Who* is she? Lost your bloody voice, Mister? Did you lose your trousers, Mister? Have to be called "Mister", don't you? because that's about your bloody self-respect. What sort of self-respect is it to be out in the middle of the bloody day, cuddling and cow eyes, in front of the Church's camera? And, don't tell me, "I didn't see the camera, I didn't know they were there", you wouldn't have seen fuck-all except for her tits, you wouldn't have seen a camera if they'd poked you with it. Bloody good laugh for the Church. I have sweated for you, Mister, I've been here when you've wanted me, I've covered your back, I've lived a bloody half-life – and what do I get out of it? It's a bloody Crown copyright surveillance picture of you with a horn on hanging on to a bit of stuff young enough to be your bloody daughter – if you were capable of making a daughter. I've trusted you, Mister, and now you've—'

He put the phone down on the cradle.

He finished dressing, chose a good tie, and checked himself in the mirror.

They were waiting for him in the lobby. How was he? He was fine, he was looking forward to a good day, he was top of the game.

Chapter Seventeen

W as it falling apart? He sat beside Atkins, who drove, with the Eagle behind him. They thought it was cracking, splintering, and were both silent, had been all the way from the city to Jablanica and the start of the gorge that held in the Neretva river. Nothing in Mister's life had ever fallen apart.

He was tired. He said wearily, softly, 'All right, Eagle, all right, Atkins, let me tell you how I see it, because you're asking, and you've the right to, "Is it falling apart?" Fair question. Deserves a fair answer. We've positive and negative, asset and debit. I'll go first on the negative, the debit ... We are going to meet Marco Tardi of the Brusca family, and Nikki Gornikov from the *vory v'zakone* group, and Fuat Selcuk, who owns half of the west of Turkey. They are top-of-the-league people, they're travellers, they reach across Europe and the Near East into Asia and as far as the States. I haven't met people like that before. I meet guys in London, and if the sun's shining and it's a good day I get as far as Manchester, Birmingham or Newcastle, and if it's special I get as far as Glasgow. I deal with Yardies and Chinese and guys who call me Mister because they're scared shitless of me. I'm the biggest fish in a small puddle. I don't know how I'm going to be when I meet these people today. I don't know whether

I'm going to fall on my face, if they're going to think I'm not worth bothering with. It's new ground for me – am I up to it? That's a negative.'

They had left the Jablanicko Jezero lake behind them, where there were wooden restaurants, and fishermen as still as hermits who held their rods and stared at the blue-green depth of the water. Now they were in the gorge. The sun speared down into it. The road was fast and dry, the snow-capped hills were left far back. They went past fields where tractors ploughed. They were three smartly dressed men on their way to a business meeting. His voice was gentle, without passion.

'Since we've been here we have been under continuing surveillance by the Church. It's not a big team, it may just be a one-man token show. I've done what I'd normally do. I've done the warning and the frighteners, and now I've beaten the crap out of him. I don't know whether he's still there, or isn't there . . . They'll have learned about the warehouse we chose, and about the charity lorry. Truth be told, every piece of detail we have put in place this week has been time wasted. That's debit.'

They all wore their best. Mister's suit was light grey. The Eagle wore formal charcoal, what he'd have taken from the wardrobe for a Law Society dinner in Guildford when he sought to impress, his tie discreet, foreign and silk, and he'd have spent time in his room cleaning his shoes before they'd left. Atkins had chosen tan slacks, a sports jacket and the regiment's tie. Mister talked, mused, as if the important audience was himself.

'And it's not just at this end that the Church is working the pressure. Atkins's address is done over, the Eagle's home is trashed – and mine. I'm searched. The Princess called me this morning. She knows better than that, and she unstitched the most basic rule we've got. I didn't have word of it before they came in, and I didn't have word they were doing yours, Atkins, and yours, Eagle. It's like they're stepping over a trip-wire because they know it's there. And it can get worse. There was a picture taken of me when I went to a crappy little village where the Bosnia with Love stuff had been dumped. It's left with the Princess by the Church. It's that sort of moment, a pretty girl and me, and we're close. Christ, I don't get to meet girls like that. Nothing's bloody happened, not yet, but the picture makes it look like I'm kissing her. I've had my ears thrashed by the Princess. She can't handle it, she's bawling, and their recorders are turning on it. That's the negatives. That's why the question's fair – is it falling apart?'

He couldn't see the Eagle, but heard him squirm in the seat behind. Atkins's eyes never left the road.

'Do I turn, cut my losses, and run?'

They were both silent. Neither had spoken since the journey had started. He thought they were both pathetic, but didn't show what he thought.

'It's a fair question, you're entitled to ask it.'

His voice held its quiet.

'I've never run, haven't ever . . . When I was a kid at school, I didn't run. I used to get hell kicked out of me when I was making my patch. Bigger kids, stronger, older, kicked and punched me and I went home with blood on my face and teeth loose, and I went back each next morning, until the day when I could hand back the kicks and the fists. I ruled in that school. I ruled, had control. I would have been nothing if I had shown fear, just another tearaway, and been smacked down . . . When they put me out of school, when I was starting up my own patch – shopkeepers, businesses, fourteen years old and protecting them – people wanted me to cut my losses and run. There was fist fights and knife fights, there was a petrol bomb thrown at me. I went after them. I was a kid, but I went after them in their pubs and in their pads, went after them until they backed off. I had to clear the competition out from Stoke Newington first, then from Islington and Holloway, then from Dalston and Hackney. There was good pickings and the competition didn't want me – it was shotguns and shooters . . . I went inside. I got two things out of Pentonville. I got respect but I had to fight for it, and with the respect came the contacts. The Mixer came from Pentonville, and the Cards, and the Cruncher, and the link to you, Eagle. If I hadn't stood the ground, hadn't fought, at the age I was, I'd just have ended up as another kid who was playtime for the old perverts . . . I came out. I went up to Green Lanes and I started buying, started dealing, started selling on. More territory to move into, and bigger fights. I could have turned then. It was about *will*, about determination, about belief. If I hadn't had the will, if the determination had been short, then I'd have gone under. There was heavy money to be made and too many snouts in the trough, and only room in the trough for one, mine. I put men in hospital, but they didn't talk to the CID because they hadn't the guts to, and none of them came back for more. What I'm saying is that respect doesn't come easy, it's earned. I earned it. I sat in the top of the tree, because I didn't turn or run or quit . . . and the years go by. I am sitting in the top of that tree, and I am thinking. Where do I go, if I don't turn and run and quit? Only one place to go – find a bigger tree, climb it and get higher. Did anyone say it was easy? It wasn't *easy* in the school, not easy getting the shopkeepers to shell out in Stoke Newington, or to clear the territory in north London, wasn't easy in Pentonville, wasn't easy going up to Green Lanes. But I had the will . . . So, now I have problems.'

He eased back against the comfort of the seat. He despised them.

'What's a problem for? It's for solving. Problems are for low-life, they're not for Mister. I go on, I never backed from anything I wanted. I want this . . . Either of you, do you want to get out? Do you want to walk? You going to stand at the side of the road and wait for a bus? Going to the airport? I don't hear you, Eagle. You're not speaking, Atkins.'

He heard the shuffle of papers behind him, and thought the Eagle hid in them, and Atkins's eyes only left the road when he checked the mirror. They came out of the Neretva gorge.

'Well, that's that, then – maybe, because I think we're ahead of schedule, we can stop and get something to eat. Might be a long day.'

Mister closed his eyes and felt the sun beat on his face. He thought only of the meeting. Monika and the Princess were forgotten, and the Eagle and Atkins who were rubbish, and Cann who was a flea's bite. He was untouchable, and supreme, and the meeting would prove it.

They came on to the flat plain, and the signs pointed for Mostar. Joey drove the blue van. He had failed. He had washed up, like driftwood on a beach.

Maggie was beside him, her legs straddling the gearstick, her skirt riding up, and beyond her on the front bench seat was Frank Williams. His arm was behind her neck, her hair against his cheek. They both slept, had the right to. They had been up all through the night to monitor the increasing panic, shouting and belted orders relayed to them by the infinity transmitter. The boy, Enver, had not been found. The Sarajevo police were out searching for him, the hospitals had not admitted him. Only when Ismet Mujic had abandoned his watch for the boy, and had left the apartment to go to the airport to meet the first flight of the morning in from Zagreb, had they come back to the hotel, with time to shower and change, and head off for the Holiday Inn with the van. Joey was the one who had slept, who would drive. He had watched the Mitsubishi pull out from the hotel, and once it was on the open road he had dropped back and allowed visual contact to be lost. He was guided by the small blinking light of the beacon, sometimes intense and sometimes faint, on the screen in front of her splayed-out knees.

He had failed because he had no authorization for intrusive surveillance. He could gather no evidence because the authorization had been withdrawn. He could place the moment when the professionalism he prided had drifted to obsession and the Church culture had been shed. It was when Mister had walked to the cemetery, when he had seen his rolling, confident gait, and he had been outwitted, out-thought; it was *failure*. Everything since had been the feeble, second-rate attempt to claw back from the failure. Joey Cann, and it battered in his mind, was the loser – always.

The beacon guided him and he let her sleep, and Frank.

Two pick-ups followed him. The Sreb Four had split into pairs. On the back of the second pick-up was a wire cage. In the cage was Nasir. Not that Joey gave a damn for the life history of the brute, but it was called Nasir – Muhsin had told him the name and the history as if it were information of importance before they left Sarajevo, information to be nurtured. Nasir Oric had been the commander holding the perimeter line at Srebrenica – who had been withdrawn on government orders, who was not there when the enclave fell, when the throats had been slit. When the beacon light dulled he stamped down on the accelerator pedal to coax the maximum speed from the van.

Joey felt deserted, alone – with only the obsession for company.

The beacon led him to swing right at the main junction, towards Mostar – ahead of him, before he turned, a low line of hills shimmered in the haze. He did not know their name, or that of the valley they hid, and he lost sight of the ground that rose to meet an unforgiving, sun-drenched sky.

Husein Bekir had come down to the ford, but the water was too deep for him to cross. He wore the same protection from the sun as he did against the winter cold. His coat, which reached to his knees, was tightly fastened with twine over his stomach and he had on his heavy rubber boots. His beret cap shielded his scalp from the sun.

The de-miners sat on the track where an ash tree threw shade and their dog was stretched out against its trunk. They ate bread and drank from Coke tins. Husein had come down to the ford to see how far their yellow tape corridors had progressed in that morning's work – one, he estimated, was five metres further forward, one was seven metres, not one of them was more than ten. His fields were more than a thousand metres in length, and a few paces more than two hundred and fifty metres wide. He shouted across at them. Why did they need to stop to eat and to drink? Should they not work faster? How much were they paid to sit in the shade and not work? They ignored him, not a head turned towards him.

He turned. The quiet settled again on the valley. It had been God's place, and it was poisoned. In the heat's haze the fields drifted away from him, were cloaked in silence.

The location chosen by Ismet Mujic was in deference to the Italian. Marco Tardi had flown from Messina to Bari on the Italian mainland, then by light aircraft to Split on Croatian territory. On collection, he had been driven to Mostar.

It was all complications. It was in deference to the Italian because he was the biggest player in Ismet Mujic's business life. The Russian had said they should meet at Brčko, near to the Arizona market, where he had associates. The Turk had wanted Sarajevo, the base of his allies. Fuat Selcuk had reached Sarajevo's airport first and had complained for the entire thirty-five minutes he had waited for Nikki Gornikov's plane to arrive. The Turk and the Russian would not travel in the same car, each insisted that their bodyguards must be with them at all times. The convoy from the airport to Mostar was three cars, and a fourth joined there. It was all shit . . . He had been on his mobile eleven times and the boy, Enver, had not been found.

He made the rendezvous. He watched the Russian and the Turk, not leaving their cars, peer with distaste at the Italian in his car. Small scorpions could be found in the dry hills in summer between Mostar and the coast, and it was the habit of local men to catch them, not wearing gloves for fear of damaging them, then to build a little prison for them of concrete blocks, let them fight, and wager big money on the outcome . . . Ismet Mujic would not have bet on the Englishman.

His car led and, enveloped in the dust trail, their cars followed.

Mister walked, and Atkins stayed at a distance behind him.

Back at the Mitsubishi was the Eagle, who had said his feet hurt in his shoes. They'd left him, with his shoes off, massaging his feet. Atkins, seeing the Eagle's spindly white ankles, had wondered how the man managed at rough shooting over the fields, which he claimed he did. The vehicle was parked outside a big modern hotel, spotlessly clean, money lavished, about the only building Atkins had seen in Mostar that wasn't war-damaged. He'd never reached Mostar when he'd served his twin UN tours.

Mister had led and Atkins had gone after him. Mister had gone off into the Muslim quarter on the east side of the city, down cobbled, shaded streets beneath overhanging balconies, and he'd paused for a long time at the great gap where the Stari Most bridge had been. Atkins could remember when it had been brought down by explosives – on his second tour. The Croats had blamed the Muslims for an act of international vandalism; the Muslims had blamed the Croats for a war crime on a world heritage site. There were two workmen there, and a sign said the bridge was being rebuilt with Italian craftsmen and UNESCO funding. Mister gazed down into the tumbling water below the gap the old bridge had spanned. Atkins thought his face was serene, calm. Had been ever since they'd arrived in the city.

Mister's eyes never left the water of the Neretva.

Atkins said, 'You know, Mister, kids used to jump off here for the tourists, dive off the old bridge, then crawl back up and get paid for it.'

Mister interrupted, his voice still and quiet, 'Can I tell you what's valuable, Atkins? It's time . . . time to focus, concentrate and think . . . Understand me, Atkins, I don't give a shit about whether kids jumped off here. I don't give a shit about this place, anything of it, anything of their war. You ever interrupt me again and it'll be the last time, because I'll have sliced your yapping tongue out of your mouth. You with me, Atkins?'

Atkins reeled. Mister's face never changed. The serenity stayed.

Mister leaned on the rail and stared another minute at the water. He turned, the affable smile on his face. 'Right, Atkins, I reckon we'll be late there, and that's just right. Let the bastards wait, I always say. Let them sweat . . . You all right, Atkins?'

'Of course, Mister.'

The beacon led them from Mostar. They had been through a village marked on the map as Hodbina, a place of scattered homes, small tended fields and grazing livestock, and women worked with hoes and spades on vegetable patches. It was off the main road south to the coast. Smoke came from the chimneys, but diffused into the clean skies. A road, part tarmacadam and part steamrollered stones, took them on, until the beacon's pulse led them to a track veering right off the road, and they saw the fresh tyremarks. It was wild country; the cultivated fields were behind them. Old rock was scattered over the ground and clumps of thorny scrub had found shallow rooting. The sun beat down on it. Joey had slowed. The two pick-ups went by him. They stopped ahead then turned, and reversed into a small wood of dense birch, using a rutted path. He followed and parked beside them. Maggie Bolton went to the back of the van, opened its door, winked at Frank, then dropped her skirt to her ankles. She reached inside and rummaged, lifted out her pair of old jeans and slipped them on. The dog, Nasir, was freed from his cage and allowed to wander in the trees, lift his leg, then was leashed. They went into the depths of the trees.

The guns were cocked. Salko, Ante and Fahro carried Kalashnikovs, and Ante's had a night sight screwed on to the top of the barrel. Muhsin had a pistol at his belt alongside a big water bottle and the leash in his hand. The dog had a dried, weather-desiccated bone in its mouth. They were in front. Frank lugged Maggie's box of magic tricks. She walked with Joey. They went towards the brightness where the sun hit against the last line of the trees. At the edge of the wood they looked down and saw the house.

The track with the tyremarks ran down the hill in front of them

380

and reached an oasis of green. There was a rich garden around the house, clawed back from the stone and the scrub. Sprinklers played over it and made small rainbows. Four Mercedes cars were parked on swept gravel in front of the building, along with the white Mitsubishi. It was Spanish *hacienda* style, with walls of white stucco and closed shutters covering the windows. A carrion crow soared above it and cried gratingly. Two men, dressed in black, worked on the cars – but not the Mitsubishi – polishing away the roads' dust.

Frank was beside him, and murmured, 'Now we're here, can I ask something?'

'Ask away.'

'What are we here for?'

Joey thought before he spoke, as if an immediate answer eluded him. Then said, 'To force mistakes.'

'Yes, yes – OK, very funny man. I'll say it slowly – what do we hope to achieve by being here?'

Joey shook his head slowly. 'I don't know.'

'Wait a minute, steady down,' Frank said evenly. 'If you want to play this out, don't mind me – there are six of us here, and you. You must have an idea where this is going?'

'Regardless of whether you'd come, any of you, I'd have been here.'

Frank stared at him, brow furrowed, and the scratch was in his voice. 'Tell me, if you'd be so kind, what is there that I should know?'

'All you need to know right now is that Judge Delic has withdrawn the authorization for intrusive surveillance on Target One.'

The hiss. 'So, it's not legal, any of it? Jesus – you picked a fine time . . .'

Joey looked away, back to the house and the men cleaning the vehicles.

'Are you stupid, an idiot? What are you? No legality, can't gather evidence, can't put anything before a court, no time for handcuffs. Why are we here?'

'Because I gave my promise to follow this man wherever he led,' Joey said, as if that answer was adequate.

They scrambled down the slope towards the fence that hugged the green of the oasis. Joey saw that the dog never lost hold of the bone. The sun was at its zenith and threw their shadows down under their bodies. They closed on the fence. When one of their bodies, or the dog's paws, caused small stones to cascade down, they all froze, then went on when they saw that the two men had not broken from the work of cleaning the cars. A dozen paces from the fence there was a gully and they sagged into it. Muhsin poured water sparingly into the dog's throat. Masking them from the house was a flat stone, storm-smoothed.

Down on the earth, pressed close to him, Frank murmured, 'You know what? Obsession is dangerous for health – yours and ours.'

'I gave my promise,' Joey said, open-faced.

It was, the Eagle recognized it, Mister's finest hour.

He did not apologize for his lateness. That they had waited for him was obvious from the used plates and dirty knives and forks on the table, the coffee cups and glasses beside the empty water bottles. There had been no hint of apology. Effortlessly, he had created an atmosphere of an equal among partners. They would have fidgeted, cursed, they would have queried the arrangements of Ismet Mujic, they would have listened for the crunch on gravel of the late arrivals' vehicle. 'Don't bend the knee to them,' Mister had said, as the front door was opened for them. 'Let them know it's their privilege to be meeting us.' It was high risk, the Eagle had thought, but Mister always won because he always risked. They'd gone inside, into the dim cool of a wide living room, and Mister had, perfunctorily but with charm, shaken their hands. 'I'm Mister, and this is my legal adviser, Eagle, and I have also brought with me my associate, Atkins. They're fine men, both of them, and as committed as I am to the principles of honest business dealing.' He had been asked by Ismet Mujic if he wished to eat, and had brusquely declined. He had then belittled Ismet Mujic. 'Now, Serif, has this room been scanned?' It hadn't . . . Mister's eyebrows had been raised fractionally in surprise, and the others had gazed at him in a marginal moment of suspicion. Mister had nodded to Atkins. Atkins had left the room. Radios had started to blare through the ground floor of the building, and upstairs. Mister had said nothing until Atkins had returned, then Mister had pointed to the stereo system in the room; that had been turned on, volume up. 'Now can we get to work.' Then he had snapped his fingers at the Eagle and Atkins and had pointed to the table. They'd started to clear it, the Italian began to help, then the Russian and last the Turk, and Ismet Mujic was shouting towards the kitchen for his people, but by the time they came the plates were stacked and the cutlery gathered together, and Ismet Mujic was further belittled.

'We need, my friend, a cloth to clean the table.'

When the table was cleared and wiped, Mister sat down. With the Eagle and Atkins, he took one side of the table, made the living room into a board room with him playing the part of chief executive officer. Mister had said, the last thing before they'd hit the gravel in front of the house, 'We find a room with a table, we sit down one side of it. We do not take off our jackets or loosen our ties. We are not slumped in easy chairs. We are in control – they are bloody lucky to have us.' They sat opposite. They were casual in dress and posture, and their jewellery dripped from them. The contrast was powerful, as Mister had wanted.

It was the nearest he would come to an apology in that finest hour. 'I regret that I do not speak Italian, Russian or Turkish. Neither do my colleagues. I hope we can manage in the English language.'

They gazed at him impassively.

'That's taken, then. Two things I want to say first. I am grateful to you, Serif, for making this meeting possible. I appreciate that it has not been easy for you to bring together three gentlemen with differing schedules, all important. You have, Serif, my sincere thanks.' The Eagle wondered whether they had carried guns into the house. Atkins had left their own weapons in the Mitsubishi, as Mister had instructed, and each of them during the introductions had, off-hand, flapped back their jackets to show they were not armed, as Mister had ordered. 'I work on one strong principle that is not negotiable. My word is my bond. I make a deal and I guarantee that, to the best of my ability, the deal is carried through, and the "best of my ability" is good. Serif will tell you that I have done a deal with him and that the promised monies are now lodged in his account in Nicosia, as I said they would be. You will all have associates in London. You will have checked with them. You will have asked about me. You will have been told that I am a serious player. So, gentlemen, do I have your attention for my proposals?'

The Eagle could not decide which of them had the cruellest eyes.

'You will allow me to give you my evaluation of the common

factor affecting all three of you. In London you do not fulfil your business potential – you fall far short of what could be achieved. That's where I can help, where I can make a difference in your profitability.'

The Italian had the youngest eyes, but there was no sparkle in them to match his smile.

'You bring in, Marco, product from Venezuela and Colombia, but your difficulty is getting it into the European marketplace. I suggest you ship direct to the ports of Montenegro, then take a series of options. You can handle the product yourself and use the Adriatic bridge to Italy, or you can avail yourself of the lorry network I will be setting up in Bosnia. It can be used to move your product either east or north. If you wish it, and your product goes to the UK, I will make available to you the dealer and distributor infrastructure that I already have in place. You will meet with no competition, you will not have to fight a turf war because I will be your ally and no man in London will fight against me. The market will be cleared for your use. That's what I'm offering you, Marco, and I would like you to consider it carefully.'

The Russian had narrow, slitted eyes, and the bags under them were puffed.

'As I understand it, Nikki, you and your colleagues make a great deal of money, but that's where your difficulty starts. What to do with the money? I anticipate that you will find it increasingly hard to use the facilities of Russian banks in New York, Cyprus or Hungary. Those banks are going to come under intensive law-enforcement scrutiny. To maximize the return on your hard-earned profits, you need access to legitimate banking. That's the City of London. I can provide you, for a most reasonable fee, the opportunities to rinse through the City, through introductions. No more grey hairs, stress-free banking . . . In addition, you are engaged in people-trafficking, but it's chaotic and amateurish, and too many of your people consignments go down because you do not have the expertise of a British partner. I can be of help – and I can help with your automobile trade, and your weapons trade. London is not merely a major street-market, it is also a name. London is respectability. The name of London opens doors, as you will find if you take up my offer, worldwide.'

The Turk had small eyes, set close together, and they squinted.

'Thank you for your patience, Fuat. You're a big man. Where you operate you are king, except in one area. I handle your product. I'm at the end of the line, but in Green Lanes I am buying the product you have purchased, refined, then shipped on for importation into the UK. The importation is where you are not king, far from it. I read my newspapers, just as I am sure you read yours. Not a month goes by without the interception of a consignment of product at the British ports. Naturally, you rely on Turkish transportation – Turkish lorries and Turkish shipping. The cargo on such lorries and ship containers attracts the greatest attention. Payment is on delivery, so if the importation is busted you don't get the money. I am suggesting that you deliver into Sarajevo, that Sarajevo is the transit point for both of us. A blind donkey can bring the product into Sarajevo, any lorry with any plates can get through, and that's where you'd be paid. It's less for you, of course, than for importation direct to the UK, but it's less risk. I can use British-registered lorries with British passport-holders driving them, and they're waved through when your transport is stopped, searched. With due respect to you, nothing gets a Customs man's nose sniffing faster than a Product of Turkey stamp on a cargo consignment of ceramic tiles or oranges or whatever you want. What you gain is money, what you lose is the headache and the hassle. That's my proposal to you.'

The smoke of their cigarettes made a wall along the middle length of the table and watered their eyes, but they stared at Mister unblinking.

'I've done my deal with Serif, and I'm very happy with the terms agreed. I can predict with confidence that he is going to be a good friend to me, like a brother . . . Each of you three gentlemen had influence in the running of this country, and I believe that influence will grow as the foreign powers withdraw. I intend to operate here, and I am asking for your co-operation, your partnership, in our mutual self-interest . . . I'd like to take a break now. In the break you, Marco, Nikki and Fuat, have a chance to think over what I've said and to decide whether to take it further. If any of you decide not to, then, please, feel free to back off, and leave. If you feel you wish to move ahead, into those new areas of product profitability that I have outlined, then I will talk detail and percentages. Would a fifteen-minute break be satisfactory? I want to settle it at this session, I want to wrap it up.'

He stood, smiled briefly, then went to the door, Atkins and the Eagle in his wake.

It had been Mister's finest hour, a masterclass. He'd heard it all before, of course, but there had been no mere parrot's recitation of the Cruncher's vision. It had been softly spoken persuasion, and never an interruption, never a yawn. They were the Cruncher's words, but only Mister could have spoken them into the cruelty of those eyes.

'How did I do?'

They were the courtiers. Atkins told him he'd done well. They knew their lines and meant them. The Eagle said he had been magnificent.

'Christ, I fancy some fresh air, away from that bloody cigarette smoke.'

The dog, Nasir, played up, was whining, and Muhsin tried to soothe it. Joey didn't know why they'd brought it. He sat cross-legged on the flat stone in front of the gully. He had the camera slung round his neck, with the big lens attached, and beside him was the dish with the antenna probe, but Maggie had said all she could hear was music, at least four sound sources, and the radios cluttered up any chance of voices. She'd said that if she'd been in her workshop she might have been able to clear the music off the track and get to hear the voices, and he'd said that she wasn't in her bloody workshop but on a bloody hill in Bosnia, and she'd chucked the earphones off her head. The sun was down over the hills in the west. When the darkness had come, Joey had gone on to the flat stone, as if that was escape from them, and from the dog. He didn't know when Frank had told her, hadn't heard him whisper the name of Judge Delic.

The dog wriggled on its back behind him and Muhsin whispered to it, and Joey heard his fingers scratching at the dog's belly.

Joey knew everything about the dog, and the dog's name. Muhsin had thought he'd be interested, when they were in the gully, to know the history of the animal and its name, and Frank had tediously translated.

'He was the best fighter that came out of Muslim Bosnia, better than any of those who were generals or brigadiers, better than Serif. Nasir Oric held Srebrenica for three years. If he had not been there it would have fallen months before the end, perhaps years before. He was a natural leader, only twenty-six years old when he took command of us. He had been a bodyguard to Milosovic in Belgrade, but he came back to us when war was inevitable. He called his men the "manoeuvre unit" and his own weapon, he carried it himself, was a fifty-calibre machine-gun. The Serbs were terrified of him. He went out from our perimeter lines into their villages . . .'

Maggie had interrupted, 'Fuck the shaggy-dog story. What you did was inexcusable. To carry on, not telling us, like nothing had happened when authorization was withdrawn – to tell Frank now, that is a fucking disgrace. It's betrayal. We are illegal. What is this bullshit about promises?'

He ignored her, didn't rise to her carping, and asked Frank to go on with the story, as told by Muhsin.

'When the word spread in the enclave that Nasir Oric was going out that night at the head of the manoeuvre unit, with the fifty-calibre, the people in that part of the front line where he would go out would leave the aphrodisiac of watered honey mixed with crushed walnuts in jars outside their homes, and he would drink, and then he would go to kill Serbs. It was not so that he could fuck better that they left out the aphrodisiac, but so he could kill better . . . And, I called the dog Nasir . . .'

Maggie had said, 'Shit, my people would scalp me if they knew – after all I've done for you.'

Since the dark had come, and the cool, it had been harder to keep the dog quiet, and the big brute had lost interest in the bone, and . . . Light flooded out of the door ahead of him. Joey, from the rock, waved for quiet down in the gully.

He saw the three of them, Mister, the Eagle and Atkins, standing tall.

They left Dragan Kovac's home. It was becoming a ritual, and welcome.

At the end of the day, when the dusk made it impossible for them to work in their taped corridors, a few of them – and the foreman – came to his home, sat on his porch with him and drank his plum brandy. He thought they needed the alcohol because of the work they did. The sun was long gone over the hill to the west of the valley when they lurched off up the track to the junction where their pick-ups were parked by the caravans.

The foreman shouted back, as he disappeared into the evening darkness, 'Thank you, Dragan, and have a quiet night.'

He laughed loudly. 'I have enough of them to know them too well. They are all quiet nights.'

'They think it's going according to his plan,' Maggie murmured. 'Sounds as if there's been a preamble, and now it's a break. The detail's going to follow if the others decide to come in . . . Eagle says that Mister's done well, but he says the others are hostile, suspicious and wary, but they like the money on offer. The money's good but – this is Eagle – they're still cautious. Mister says it'll depend on the percentages . . . God, can't one of you throttle that damn animal?'

She was on the flat stone beside Joey, the earphones on her head, and she tilted the dish with the antenna spike so that it was aimed at the three men who stood on the gravel between the house door and the parked vehicles. Frank was with her, and Ante and Fahro. Behind the stone, in the gully, Muhsin and Salko lay on the squirming dog, scratched its stomach and tousled its neck.

'The Italian, that's Marco, is going to be asked to pay fifteen per cent of the value of cocaine handled by Mister's network in the UK – no, that's the negotiating point. They'll come down to twelve and a half per cent, it's Eagle, he says that's the bottom line . . . Nikki, the Russian – City banking, City of London, laundering. Ten per cent is the minimum, but starting at eleven and a half per cent of all monies washed through Mister's placemen. They've gone on to more per-centages – still with Nikki, but it's people-trafficking . . . God, they are talking big money. Corporation stuff . . . Jesus, throttle it or gag it, but shut it up.'

'The weapons trade, Mister – I suggest not too hard to start with,' the Eagle said, in deference.

'London's the conduit for the trade, Mister. Best place he could work out of – access into Africa and the Middle East.' It was Atkins's first contribution: he felt shut out, sidelined. He was ignored.

'Start at six and three-eighths, on the first million, and go down to five and seven-eighths,' Mister said, with confidence. 'Nine per cent on the second million, ten on what's on top of that, if he goes through our contacts.'

'Sounds about right,' the Eagle muttered. 'Now the Turk, that is some evil bastard.'

Mister grinned balefully. 'I expect his mother loves him.'

'The Turk – we pay thirty-five thousand pounds sterling, delivery in Sarajevo, for refined product, per kilo, as against the forty-five you're paying now.'

'So, I'd be getting, maximum, thirty-six per kilo?'

Somewhere in the darkness above them, a dog barked. It was a sharp, baying, deep-throated bark.

'Three point six million for one hundred kilos. I think I can live with that. If it's not lorries, I was starting to think of all those regattas over the North Sea . . .'

There was a second bark, but it was stifled abruptly, then a low whine, then nothing.

'Regattas in Norway, Sweden, Holland, Belgium, France, all those clubs going over to compete. Can you sail, Atkins? Can't? Try learning. I'm going to have a pee. Fifteen minutes must be nearly up. You want a pee, Eagle? I'll call you when I need you, Atkins.'

It was masterful of Mister. Atkins had heard the bark and knew it was that of a guard or attack dog. It was the bark of the sort of dog used by the Royal Military Police for perimeter protection or for hunting a man down. He heard the door close behind them. Alongside that sort of dog would be a handler and guns and – his mind raced – a listening probe. The dog had barked beyond the fall of the lights around the door. Mister's mastery had been in finishing his sentence, about a regatta route, then suggesting a pee, like he was too dumb to have been alerted, if they were listened to. He shivered. He heard the door behind him open again.

A light was switched on behind him, from the hall. Its beam, maybe two hundred times candlepower, was thrown past him, over the green, well-cut and watered lawns, over the shrub bushes, and the man-height fence that was topped with a barbed-wire strand, into the scrub, on to a grey-white flat stone fifty yards from him. Atkins saw the man he had tried to kill, to run down. The light caught the big spectacles, too large for the face, and the thin shoulders, and the jutting knees as he sat cross-legged, unmoving. A woman with a dish was beside him, and an older man in uniform. Then the flashlight caught two men in dark overalls and their rifle barrels blinked back at the beam. Another man with another rifle, an image-intensifier sight on it, scrambled to join them. He couldn't see the dog but the barking was frantic and the noise billowed over him.

The light went out. There was pandemonium in the doorway of the house . . . He thought that all the bloody security had been in the house, complacent and sitting in the bloody kitchen – none of the idle bastards had been out on the property's fence.

Atkins started to walk. He had come to the end.

There was a shake in his stride, his knees were weak and he wanted to piss, but he went briskly on to the lawns and through the shrubs. He heard his name called, but he didn't turn. The engines were starting behind him, and there was the flash of headlights, the slamming of doors, and tyres grinding the gravel. The cry of his name felt like a knife into his back, then, 'Leave the bastard, fucking yellow bastard!' He heard the bark of the dog and the engines' scream.

He raised the flag – white flag, abject, surrender. Atkins shouted, 'I'm coming over. Please, don't shoot. Please, don't.'

He jumped at the high fence. It bucked, rocked, held under his weight. He did not feel the pain as the wire slashed his hands. He rolled over it, as he had been trained to do. He blundered through the thorn bushes towards the dog. He was thrown down. Hands forced their way over his body, prised between his legs and into his armpits. He was rolled over and his arms were forced into his back, and the handcuffs clicked, tight, on his wrists. He was dragged. Rocks caught his shins. He thought of the steely loyalty of his mother if she came to visit him, and the way the boy had struggled as he'd been lifted on to the bridge rail, and the contempt that would be on the face of his father. They were into a wood of thick-growing trees. Twice he hit the tree trunks and he felt the blood dribble from his nose. They didn't allow him to slow them. He was thrown on to the back of a pick-up. A cage door grated shut. The vehicle jerked forward. Beside him, kept from him by the cage mesh, was the hot breath of the snarling dog.

He thought he was free. He was no longer Atkins.

'Which one are we following?' Frank asked.
   'Mister, Target One.'
   'What about the others?'
   'Irrelevant to me,' Joey said.
   'And the guy in the back?'
   'He's yours, not mine.'
   'I can call up help, cavalry.'
   'I don't want help, not from anyone.'
   'Where do you think, Joey Cann, we are going?'
   'Wherever he leads us to.'

'He'll turn Queen's, won't he? He'll sing, testify.'
   'I'll fix him. Eagle, you worry too much.'
   'Right now, I'm worrying overtime.'
   'Just drive.'
   'You're the better driver, Mister.'
   'If I'm driving I can't shoot. Think, Eagle, switch on.'
   The Eagle knew Mister when in structured situations. He knew him in conference and in meetings, and when there was an agenda on the table in front of him in the office over the launderette. This, though, was new. He did not know Mister in crisis. He was not a part of the other meetings where the maps were studied and the guns loaded; he had been safe from them. The two guns were now out of the glove box. One rested between Mister's thighs, the other was in his right hand, both were cocked. From what he could see of Mister's face, and from his voice, there was no panic. It was as if he had found a welcome fulfilment. The window was down, the cold air of the evening whipping their faces. Mister checked often in the mirror, but the lights stayed behind them. In the chaos of the departure they had, both of them, tried to get into the Russian's car, and been bounced out. A pistol had pointed at their stomachs. The Turk's car had already pulled away. The Eagle had never driven a getaway vehicle. The lights behind were constant, but the lights he followed diminished.

   The Eagle followed the tail-lights as best he could, but the Mitsubishi did not have the acceleration power of the Mercedes fleet ahead. Always the lights were strong behind him. He wanted to piss, and wouldn't have cared if he had messed his trousers. It was all right for Mister, he'd find another bloody lawyer. Suddenly, the lights ahead disappeared.

'They're trying to lose us, bastards.'

'Keep looking.'

'You reckon, Mister, there are road-blocks up front?'

'I don't know – just look for their lights.'

'They'll know the way out, Serif'll know the bloody way – what's that?'

The Eagle would have sworn, far up the road, just past the first sign into Godbina village, there was a flash of a brakelight, and no headlights in front of it. He thought the Mercedes column had killed their lights so that the Mitsubishi would not be able to follow. Of course there would be road-blocks, and bloody machine-guns. His skill was in the reading of the pages of Archbold, not in evading road-blocks and bloody machine-guns. And if they evaded the road-blocks, what then? Where to then? He was slowing. He'd have sworn – on his Bible, on Archbold, put his hand on the smooth leather of the volume and given his oath – that the brakelights had flashed again off the road to Mostar, climbing and going right. He took the decision. He saw the turn-off. There was a high moon rising. He swung the wheel and snapped off the headlights.

'What are you doing?'

'You said to follow them.'

'You sure it was them?'

'Sure, Mister.'

'Positive sure?'

'They turned off because there'll be road-blocks. They know the form.'

The track they were on was good for the first half-mile. The Eagle started to relax. He had made the decision, and stood his corner, and his decision was accepted ... His decision, not Mister's. He was starting to lose the sweat in the pit of his back. He had to go slower, change down through the gears, as the track surface deteriorated. Every minute or so he saw the wink of the brakelights in front of him, higher and climbing. His eyes were now accustomed to driving by moonlight. He leaned forward over the wheel, and by concentrating to his limits he could see most of the ruts, enough to avoid most of them . . . Then came the sinking despair. It came in his gut, his heart and in his mind. At first he did not dare to look up to the mirror. It had been his decision. Mister was quiet beside him, as if he'd parcelled off responsibility.

The low chassis of the Mercedes saloons would have snagged on the rutted track.

He looked up into the mirror and the twin headlights, merging there, dazzled him. The brakelights shone brightly, then were extinguished. As they drew level, the Eagle saw a tractor and two men unloading bales.

As they lurched on the rutted track past the tractor, in the moon's grey glow, the Eagle saw that its front lights were smashed. He had made a decision and it had been wrong. The humiliation and the fear settled on him. He turned to Mister. 'What are we going to do?'

An icy calm in the reply. 'Go overland, walk out of here . . . What are you, Eagle? What the fuck are you?'

'Not very clever, Mister.'

'I'll get you out – what'll you be then?'

'Grateful, Mister.'

The lights behind, in the mirror, glowed more fiercely, and the distance narrowed as they came ever closer. There was, the Eagle thought, an inevitability to this conflict. He'd known it since he'd seen the guns and heard the dog, and when the flashlight had found the young man sitting cross-legged on the flat stone peering at them through heavy spectacles. Mister had said the young man had been 'dealt with'. He recalled what he had said, in the road outside Mister's home, a month before, a bleat in his voice: *You know what I worry about? I mean it, lose sleep about? One day you overreach – know what I mean – take a step too far. I worry . . .* And he could remember Mister's punch just below his heart, and the pain. He pulled over and the Mitsubishi lurched into a shallow ditch.

'You won't leave me, Mister?'

'Did I ever?'

They were at the crest of a hill. The track, ever rougher, fell away from them. Down to the left were lights and the outlines of close-set buildings. There were more lights in the far distance, and a murmur of water. Between the two groupings of lights was a black hole into which the Eagle gazed and saw nothing. He scrambled out. He subsided into the ditch, water covered his shoes and the cold gripped his feet. He came round the front of the Mitsubishi. Mister was silhouetted against the moon. He heard the drone of the vehicles down the track behind them, and in moments their lights would trap him.

'Are you coming or not?'

'Coming, Mister.'

Ante had the rifle to his shoulder. His body-weight was against the bonnet of the blue van. He aimed. He had the whole of the upper chest of Target One in his 'scope. He dragged back the cocking lever, scraped it till it locked home. He settled. Frank swung his arm up. His wrist would have hit the underside of the barrel immediately below the end of the sight's lens, and the aim darted towards the moon. Frank lectured Ante. Joey realized the anger of Salko and Fahro. Muhsin had the dog down from the cage and it peed against the wheel of the van.

'You did right,' Joey said.

'Thank you – but it's not for you. He was going to blow him away. I am an authorized firearms officer, sometimes I'm a team leader. That man is under my control. I am responsible for his actions, and his target is a British citizen. I'd have been before Disciplinary, a full inquiry. I know the regulations – no one's life was in danger. It would have been murder, and if I hadn't intervened I would have been an accessory.'

'I support what you did.'

'I'm grateful for that, Joey.'

'I support what you did because Mister is mine.'

Joey marshalled them. Muhsin would lead with the dog, and Ante would be alongside them. Joey would be a dozen paces behind, with Salko and Fahro.

Joey said to Frank, 'You should watch the prisoner. Please feel free to read him his rights, and you can offer him a solicitor. You can assure him he'll have legal-aid funding for an appeal to the European court should that be necessary, and make sure he's warm, fed and comfortable and—'

But Joey didn't finish. He hurried away into the dark, and there was the thud of the boots around him, and the baying of the dog.

Mister ran.

The Eagle shambled after him.

Every thorn bush seemed to catch at the Eagle's suit jacket and trousers, and he seemed to stumble on every stone. Sometimes they would blunder on to a path and then they could go faster, but each path petered away into denser thorn thickets. On a drop, deeper than half the height of his body, he was thrown forward, winded, and he cried out for Mister's help, but help didn't come and he pushed himself up and followed the crashing, ripping sounds of Mister's flight. Driving him on was the noise of the dog's pursuit. He didn't know how they would lose the dog. There were people in the village, his friends and Mo's friends, who paid seven hundred and fifty pounds for a dog that was little more than a pup, and they talked about their dogs – talked about damn all else but their dogs – spoke about ground scent and air scent. The ground scent was from his shoes, and the air scent was from the sweat as he panted to follow Mister. They said, his friends and Mo's, that 'The hardest thing in this good life is to evade a well-trained dog.' The heel of his right shoe had come off.

'Are you there, Mister?'

'You're doing well, Eagle, keep at it.'

He saw the shadow of Mister and then it was gone. There were thicker trees. Mister had gone into them. Then a path. He was on the path and off it when he heard Mister's feet break dry wood. Mister hadn't told him of the path, hadn't warned him of it, hadn't guided him down it. He tried to run but was capable only of a slow, waddling trot. His breath came in great heaves and his stomach bulk bounced on his belt. He tripped. Moonlight didn't penetrate the canopy of the trees above him. He fell flat. The fall burst the air from his lungs. His fingers scrabbled for a grip, to push himself up. The dog was closer, and the staccato voices urging it on. His fingers found the smooth shapes. Long thin shapes, then wider but still smooth, then the shapes of locking joints, then narrower cross-shapes, then the teeth, and his fingers slipped into the eye sockets and on to the rounded plate of the skull. The Eagle whimpered. The skeleton was across the track. He could not see it, but could feel it and touch it and understand it as clearly as a Braille reader would have. He pushed himself up. The dog's barking drove him on. He had gone twenty more short strides when he realized that his left shoe was off. Thorns, small stones, bramble stems, broken branch wood slashed his foot. He hobbled after Mister and sobbed from the pain. Mister was at the edge of the wood. There was thin grey-white light from the moon and an emptiness in front of them that was cut by a dark line where water ran loud, then more emptiness, then the lights. The lights were a grail. Mister had his foot down on a tape of dull yellow.

'I lost my shoe and the other's broken.'

'Christ, you're my burden.'

The Eagle stepped over the tape. Mister passed him. The Eagle's feet sank into thick grass.

Maggie had her torch on the map.

'I think I've found where we are. The village, the near one, that's Ljut – and over there, the far one, that's Vraca . . . If you look in my bag, Frank, in the back, there's a flask. Won't be hot but better than nothing.'

She switched on her mobile and banged out the numbers.

Muhsin and the dog, and Ante had stopped at the tree-line. Joey reached them, with Fahro and Salko. The dog strained at the leash, but Muhsin held it.

Joey could see the shadowy shapes, separated, slipping away towards the dark cut. He stepped forward: he would follow where he was led. Arms caught him, hands gripped his coat. He struggled to free himself. Wherever the road led, he would follow. Ante lifted the tape and Salko pressed Joey's head down till his eyes were inches from it.

Fahro said the word, and Muhsin echoed it.

'*Mina . . . mina.*'

Chapter Eighteen

The watch on the Eagle's left wrist stopped at one minute past ten o'clock.

At ten o'clock, Mister glanced down, saw the hands of his own watch shine luminously at him, sucked in breath, and looked back. He reckoned he had reached a half-way point in the open ground between the tree-line that he had come through and the black strip that was his target, where there was the rumble of fast-flowing water. He turned his back on the distant lights. He had the PPK Walther in the belt at his waist and the Luger was hanging in his suit-jacket pocket. There would be wheels in the village, where the lights were and, with the PPK and the Luger to persuade, he would take a car. If the dog came close, he would shoot it with the PPK or the Luger.

He didn't know why the dog, the following men and Cann had not broken clear of the tree-line ... Then he remembered the rifles. He realized the target he made and crouched down, the dew on the grass soaking into the lower legs of his trousers. Mister saw the blundering, gasping approach of the Eagle, maybe forty yards away. The Eagle meandered towards him, like a drunk's walk. How long would he wait for him? Half a minute? The Eagle had stopped. He teetered on one leg. In the light from the moon, Mister could see that the Eagle had his arms out wide, like he was a trapeze man walking the wire. He seemed not to dare to put down the other foot, from which the shoe was lost, and swayed. He would not go back for him. But Mister thought himself a good, kind man, a loyal man, and he made a little pledge to himself: when they reached the river – and from the sound of it there would be a wicked current to fight against – he would carry the Eagle over it. He would have the Eagle clinging on his back, or under his arm, and he would take him over the river. He could walk the rest, to the lights, where there would be a car – of course there would be a car.

He thought he'd waited the half-minute.

'Come on, Eagle, shift it.'

He felt no fear. The river did not frighten him, or the thought of the rifles that might be aimed at him. Neither did he feel fear of the young man with the big spectacles who had dogged and followed him. The sensation was pure excitement. He was challenged, tested. The excitement ran in him as a strain that was – not that Mister knew the word – *virulent*. From any challenge thrown at him, any test put to him, he was – always had been – the winner. And when they were over the river, had reached the lights and taken a car, the Eagle would be the witness.

'Come on – or do you want the dog to have you?'

One minute past ten o'clock.

'Coming, Mister – and thanks for waiting.'

Mister was about to turn, to hurry on towards the dark strip and the river, but he watched. The Eagle hopped on his shoe, danced like he was a circus clown, rocked, then reached out the foot that had no shoe, sank on it. The flash was golden in its intensity. The Eagle was caught in the flame, then lifted up as if a fine wire jerked him. After the flame was billowing smoke and the thunder caught in Mister's ears. He felt the wind's rush against him and for a moment he thought he would be driven over but he rocked at his knees and the wind passed him. The flash had wiped his vision. There was only black darkness around him. A silence came.

Mister stood statue still. He had no eyes, and his ears rang tinny from the blast. It was like nothing he had ever seen or ever heard. Then the voice came.

'You are in a minefield, Mister.'

The voice boomed into his consciousness.

'You have walked into a minefield, Mister.'

The voice was nasal, like it was synthetic, and amplified.

'There will be mines in front of you, beside you, and behind you – all around you in fact, Mister.'

The voice came from the tree-line and he thought it was shouted through cupped hands.

'You went into the minefield when you stepped over the yellow tape, Mister.'

The voice was flat-toned and without pleasure or triumph and it cleared the ringing from Mister's ears.

He sank down. He put his buttocks' weight on to the wet grass where his shoes had been, and then he tucked his feet as close to his buttocks as he was able . . . It started as a whimper . . . He had only once before heard the voice, but he recognized it. There had been seven words spoken by the voice, then small, not nasal and amplified. The words dinned at him: *That was a mistake, Mister, a mistake* . . . From the whimper came a low sob . . . He had his arms tight around his body. A light breeze rustled in the grass close to him, waved it. Because he was low down on the ground the lights seemed further distant than before, where a car would have been, beyond the river he would have swum . . . Where he thought the Eagle lay, the sobbing turned to a high-pitched scream that pierced Mister's skull . . . Cann hadn't screamed when Mister had beaten him. He sat hunched in the grass and he could not escape the Eagle's scream. The scream was a knife that sliced into him, the sound of a dying animal. He took his hands from his chest and slapped them over his ears and pressed the palms against his skull, but he could not lose the sound of it. The scream eddied in the grass around him, burrowed in the ground under him, it was around him – as the mines were. Mister did not know what a mine looked like. He must have seen them on television but if he had he did not remember it. There had been no mines at the fair he had gone to with Atkins. He did not know whether they were square or round, black, green or white . . . God, would the screaming not stop? Finally, it did.

It died to a sob and then to a whimper. He eased his hands from his ears.

'Mister, are you there? Tell me you're there.'

'I'm here, Eagle.'

'Can you come near?'

'We're in a minefield, Eagle.'

The voice choked: 'I can't feel my leg, Mister.'

'There's nothing I can do.'

'I want you close to me, Mister. There's the pain everywhere, except in my foot – Christ . . .'

'I can't move. I can't come.'

'Close, so's you hold me – I'm so fucking scared, Mister, and the pain . . .'

'Don't you listen, Eagle? It's a *minefield* . . .' He said it like he was speaking to an idiot. His voice was quiet. It was always quiet when the anger surged in him. When he was angry, men had to lean forward to hear him. 'If I come to you I could be blown up myself.'

'Yes, Mister . . . bloody hell . . . of course, Mister. I'm your burden – isn't that right, Mister?'

Mister knew what was said of him at the Church and the Crime Squad and at the Criminal Intelligence Service: they said that he was careful. It was grudging but it was said of him, 'careful', with sour praise. He did not gamble. Everything was planned before he moved. Only fools gambled. He owned clubs that had rich takings from roulette wheels, but he never played. He never backed horses or dogs unless the names of the winners were guaranteed to him . . . The last time he had not been careful, had taken an action that had not been weighed, he had walked from Monika Holberg's vehicle to the blue van and had taken Cann to its rear doors and had kicked, punched the little weakling creature until his feet had hurt and his hands had bled, and the small voice down on the ground had called it his *mistake*. To move on the field in the darkness would be to gamble.

'What are you going to do, Mister?'

'I don't know.'

'Mister, I need you . . . please.'

'I can't help you.'

'No, Mister, you mustn't risk yourself . . .'

In the moonlight, above the waving grass, he could see, just, the shape of the Eagle's hip and his shoulder, twenty yards away or maybe thirty. The Eagle was on his side, had his back to Mister. The pain must have come as a spasm. There was a low moan and the upper arm thrashed. The Eagle's leg, in the pain spasm, was lifted at the hip. There was no foot. Mister blinked. The raised leg's trouser was shredded to nothing at the knee. Mister did not know what a mine looked like, but he knew what it did. He needed to think. He was beyond anything of his experience, and he had no instinct to guide him. He checked his watch. The time was fifteen minutes past ten o'clock. There was at least eight hours of darkness to cover him. By midnight he hoped that he would know what he should do, and how far he should gamble.

Frank had come through the trees. They'd heard his approach and Salko had flashed the torch to guide him, and the dog had growled. He'd found them.

'What happened?'

Joey pointed down in front of him. At the level of his knees was the yellow tape. Frank whistled, sucked in his breath. 'We heard the explosion – which one is it? Then the screaming . . . God.'

Joey reached across and tapped Ante's arm. He gestured for the rifle to be given him. He let the butt rest against his shoulder, levelled the aim and had his eye to the moulded endpiece of the night sight. He had never been a marksman. The gamekeepers on the estate were expert, but Joey hadn't been. It was a dozen years, when he was a teenager, since Joey had last had a firearm against his shoulder. There was a clinical weight to the Kalashnikov, and it was made heavier by the sight. The cross-hairs wavered. If he'd fired he would have missed because he could not hold the aim steady, but he could see. The image was a grey-white wash, and he tried to hold the cross-hairs on the nearer spreadeagled shape. Target Two was total white – face, body, clothes, and was prone. He shifted the aim and the image in the sight blurred. It went over the trees at the bank of the river, jerked up, caught the lights of the far village, and it burned out. He moved the aim down, raked across the ground, and then saw his Target One. Mister sat, and his arms were around his knees, his head was down and rested on them, but Joey couldn't hold the aim. He passed the weapon to Frank.

He saw Frank's hands move expertly over it, in the near darkness, to check it, then it was at his shoulder, locked there, as if it were a part of him.

'Don't bother to ask,' Frank said, and there was a grimness about him that Joey hadn't heard before. 'Yes, I've handled one, and I've fired one. Have you seen your Target Two? He's short of a leg.'

'I couldn't hold it that well. I didn't know he hadn't a leg.'

'It's off just below the knee. Full weight must have gone on it.'

Frank stared into the rifle sight, and Joey thought him mesmerized by what he saw.

'What happens?'

Frank said, 'Nothing happens, nothing can happen. It's dark, if you hadn't noticed. Any man who goes walkabout in a marked minefield in darkness is certifiable. We could call the people out but they'd only be losing their beauty sleep – if they deigned to come. They won't move before daylight. Looks like he's fainted or something, best thing for him. The solicitor, right?'

Joey took the rifle. He peered into it a last time, then handed it back to Ante. The moon was at its highest point, and its brightest, but it was difficult for him to see either of the men in the field in front of him. 'Will he survive?'

'What do you want, the best bedside manner or the truth?'

'I don't give a damn whether he survives.'

'You have, Joey, a bucketful of humanity . . . I've been with de-miners, some of the foreign ones. They go to the Irish bar up by the Kosevo Hospital at weekends, they get pissed up, and they talk. Try stopping them. You have to move a casualty fast. Right now, in the wound, are the chemicals from the explosion, half a tonne of earth and the shrapnel that's been in the ground for five, seven years – and old cow shit, sheep shit, fox shit, rabbit shit. That's all in the wound. He should be in hospital in two hours, but he won't be. It's not light for eight hours. When it's light they've got to make a path to him – what is it, eighty metres, could be a hundred? They've got to go on hands and knees with probes. That'll take the whole of tomorrow . . . May I tell you a story? It's not first hand but I was told it by the guys at the station when I arrived, they'd been there. Eleven months ago there was a minefield on the edge of Sarajevo – that's not in the back-woods, that's the capital city of this God-forsaken country – and it was marked with signs but not fenced. Ema Alic – I was told the name and haven't forgotten it, won't ever – was a little girl, aged eleven. She was with two boys, both twelve years, and they'd gone out to play. One of them detonated a mine. The boys were killed straight out. She lived. She lived for two hours. She was waving for help and screaming for help. A crowd watched her and listened to her, but they were too frightened to take the risk of going where the kids had. Sarajevo, right, and it's the middle of the day. They can get de-miners there double fast. By the time they reached her, had made the corridor, she had stopped waving and had stopped screaming ... Not even for a child do they hurry. You asked if he would survive.'

Flat-voiced, Joey asked, 'What does Mister do?'

'My question, what is his spirit?'

'At home, Frank, he has support.'

'Now he is alone.'

Joey thought of the hours, weeks, months, years of living with Mister's life. Never close, never able to touch – until now. There was no one in his life to whom he could have described his feeling of driven elation – not to Jen, not to his mother or his father, not to Dougie Gough. The elation was his own, and he guarded it.

Joey said dully, 'At home he has the Cardmen to enforce, he has an accountant and a solicitor, he has the Mixer as his chief of staff, he has the Eels for his transport, he has the Princess – he has a legal system that he holds in contempt because of its corruption and incompetence. He sits on the throne of an empire.'

'Alone, Joey. That's why it's different.'

'Will he break and run?'

In the darkness, Joey thought that Frank Williams, armed policeman, squirmed, seemed to shiver. 'Would you? Would I? I would not. If he stood up and walked away – I don't know the ground, and I can at best guess – he would have a nine out of ten chance of getting to the river, perhaps it is a ninety-nine out of a hundred chance. But that leaves one in ten or one in a hundred. Does he run or walk, or crawl? Does he close his eyes and just go, or does he test each step? He will have been deafened by the explosion, he has no experience of this situation, he is traumatized because he knows that his companion has lost a leg, he is trying now to think clearly but that is very difficult for him. He has not gone to the help of his companion, and that is a good decision because an amateur who tries to rescue is almost always the second casualty.'

The wind was in the trees above them, zephyrs moving the bared branches, the same wind that tugged at Mister, who was alone.

'I like what you say,' Joey said.

'What do you want from him?'

'I want him broken.'

'It's the worst place a man can be.' A quaver stammered in Frank's voice. 'He is trapped in a minefield.'

'I want to hear him scream, in fear.'

'There is a legal process.'

He said, 'I want him destroyed.'

'Are you sick? I think you're sick.'

Frank Williams blundered away. Joey sat with the dog. He leaned against a tree, and his feet were under the yellow tape. He scratched the dog's stomach, and his face was licked, and he laughed. He shouted into the night for all of the valley to hear. 'Heh, Mister, look over your shoulder, and I'm there.'

And Joey Cann laughed louder.

Midnight . . .

. . . as he helped her to undress and prepared her for bed in the shambles that was their home, Judge Delic asked his daughter, 'Do you think of him? Is he ever out of your mind?' Jasmina Delic said, 'I try not to, I try to think of the car and the new kitchen we will have, and our new life.' He thought she lied, but he had not the heart to tell her that he recognized the lie.

. . . Ismet Mujic reached his apartment in the city's old quarter. He had left the Turk, the Russian and the Italian at the airport with a private pilot who would fly them out. He was disgraced, humiliated, and he shouted in fury up the stairs, 'Have you found him?' He was told by a craven man that his friend had not been found, and his world fell further into ruin.

. . . a body that had been snagged among sunken tree branches in the Miljacka river broke free and came to the surface, was carried on by the current past Hrasno and the apartment blocks of Cengic Vila, under bridges, and tumbled over the weirs.

. . . her day and evening in the Unis Building, Tower A, finished, on her way home to Novo Sarajevo, Monika Holberg pushed open the glass swing doors of the Holiday Inn. She went to the reception desk. She saw her letter in the pigeon-hole, untouched, unread, tightened her lips and went back out into the city's quiet.

. . . in the room occupied by the Sierra Quebec Golf team in the Custom House, a secure facsimile message was received from Endicott, room 709, Vauxhall Bridge Cross. It was given to Gough. They were all there and they watched him. Gough said, 'Packer was at his big meeting – it aborted when Cann showed out – there was no electronic evidence – Target Three, Bruce James, is in IPTF custody – Packer and Arbuthnot have gone across country, and Cann is in pursuit. It doesn't matter, though, local authorization for intrusive surveillance has been withdrawn. I think he's beaten us, Packer has. I asked too much of Cann. I thought, and I took a chance with him, that Cann would bring him down. It was too much to ask.' They began to clear their desks and unhook their coats.

. . . Endicott, in his room at VBX, rang the home of a commander from the National Crime Squad. 'Don't interrupt me, please, and don't ask who tasked me. You have an information leak from your building to Albert Packer. A call to Sarajevo was made the day before yesterday, in the morning, from the pavement outside your Pimlico office. We can be that specific. The call was made at ten nineteen and was terminated at ten twenty-one. If you were to check your exterior video cameras you will see who made the call, who went out of the building either side of that window. Act on it, please.' Endicott rang off. Traitors, turncoats, betrayers were a part of the history of his organization; he understood the cancerous contamination of their presence.

. . . the minister came into his wife's bedroom at their grace-and-favour home to switch off her light and kiss her cheek. He sat beside her. 'You remember, when we were in opposition, what you used to do, your good works. You tramped east Yorkshire to raise money for refugee relief in Bosnia. You were fearsome to the stitch-pockets, you bullied till you had your cheques. I'm late because I've been reading about the place. You needn't have bothered. The dream's gone. It's a corrupt haven for criminality, and sinking, and it'll be worse. The end of a dream is always sad, the light going out and leaving a dark, grubby corner.' He held her hand and hoped she slept and had not heard him.

'Are you there, Mister?'

'I'm here, Eagle.'

'What time is it?'

'If it matters, it's a minute past midnight.'

'I know where I am.'

'Good on you, Eagle.'

Yes, he knew where he was and he knew what had happened. There had been a moment, bliss, a happy moment, when he hadn't known where he was or what had happened to him. It couldn't have been sleep, but he might have fainted. There hadn't been delirium, or anything that was a dream, only blank insensible darkness in his mind. He had come through that darkness and he remembered opening his eyes, and he'd tried to swing his body but the pain had stopped him. He felt weak and wanted to vomit. He hadn't the strength. His hands groped over his body, as best he could lying on his side. Each place he touched made the pain hurt worse, and there was sticky warmth on his fingers. The liquid smeared them when he touched his stomach and his thighs. Only when he lay quite still was the pain numbed. He had his back to Mister, couldn't see him and wouldn't risk the pain of trying to twist and look at him. Where his head lay, on his lower arm, there were no lights for him to look at, but the moon's glow showed the stretch of the field and then the black line of the trees.

'Does anyone know we're here?'

'Cann knows. He's in the trees. He's close. He knows.'

'Has he sent for help?'

'It's dark, Eagle, and we're in a minefield. No one's going to come and help.'

'I don't have much time, Mister, if I'm not helped . . . Can't you come close to me, Mister?'

'Don't you listen, what I told you? It's a minefield.'

'Won't you come nearer to me, Mister?'

'There are mines – it's what Cann said – all around me. I can't move. I'm thinking . . .'

The Eagle thought he was free. It was as if a chain had snapped. He could not see Mister's eyes, which cut into men and made them shiver. His back was to Mister. He had no fear, now, of Mister, and he had no need any more of the rewards with which Mister bought him. The freedom was the cool breeze that played across his face, that stilled the pain. He was safe from the fear.

'Mister? Are you listening to me, Mister? I've been with you more than twenty-five years. I know you, Mister, like I know my hand. I want to tell you what I have learned about you.'

It was a struggle to raise his voice. Spit bubbled in his throat. The pain was worse when he tried to speak. The Eagle did not have the strength to shout, and he did not think he had much time. He wished he could have turned so that he could see into Mister's eyes. He gloried in his freedom, and knew it could not be taken from him. He hoped that Mister heard him.

'You are evil, Albert William Packer. You are the most evil man I have met. As God's my witness I am ashamed to have been a part of you. I hope, as those I love say prayers over my body, that I am purged of the sins of my association with you.'

He could not lift his head, which lay on his fallen arm. He spoke into a wall of grass stems and he smelt the fresh-turned earth and the tang, acrid, of the chemicals.

'You are the bully. You inflict pain, misery. After you are dead – whenever, wherever – you will be hated, despised. Don't think a great column of people will follow your coffin, they won't. The coffin will go by and people will slam shut their doors and draw their curtains, because you are vile, a mutation of a human being. But I thank you, I thank you from the bottom of my heart for bringing me to this place. Here, I've learned freedom from you. Thank you, Mister.'

He wished that Mister could have seen his face and seen the truth, the honesty, he felt. His voice fell and he didn't know whether he was heard. He cared no longer about the pain, but tried to throw his voice.

'And thank you for giving me a last sight of you. You're scared, aren't you, Mister? I don't have any fear, not any longer. You're scared, I smell it. How do I know you are scared? Because you haven't run. You can't buy a mine, Mister, can you? Can't corrupt it. A mine doesn't get defused because a bent bastard like me preaches on your behalf in some bloody Crown Court. It's not a jury, you can't intimidate it – it's a mine.'

He heard behind him a slight, very small shifting movement.

'Can you see my leg, is that why you're scared to run?'

The movement was a metal scrape, an oiled lever under a thumb's pressure.

'Show me you're not scared. Run. Run twenty yards, or fifty, then tell me you're not scared.'

For a last time he hurled his voice high.

'Did Cann bring you down?'

The first three shots missed him. They were a thunder around the Eagle and the ground spat over him. The fourth shot hit his raised shoulder and flattened him, pinned him down to the grass, as if a hammer drove a nail into him. He gulped.

'Did Cann—?'

He pulled the trigger again and again and again . . . pulled it until the clicking replaced the blast, and the magazine was emptied.

The voice was away across the fields, from the tree-line.

'The Eagle was your last best man. That was another mistake. Who's going to protect you now, Mister? Are you going to run?'

He let the Luger slip from his fingers and tightened his arms closer around him to make smaller the space of wet grass on which his weight was set. There were six more hours of darkness. He had six more hours in which to make his decision. *Are you going to run, Mister?* If he turned his body, he could see the dark line of the river a hundred yards away, could hear it. Beyond the river were the village lights, and there would be a car. It would take a hundred running strides to get to the river, a hundred times his feet would stamp down on the grass and the earth, one hundred chances of risk . . . He closed his eyes against the night.

The explosion had roused him, but it was the screaming that had pulled Husein Bekir from his bed. He sat on the big ash log outside his home. He was wrapped in his overcoat but that was little proof against the frost chill. The explosion had woken him and then he had nearly slipped back to sleep against his wife's warm back. Then, the screaming had started. Even with his damaged hearing, the sound of it had gouged into him. He could not ignore it: it had dragged him up, tugged him out through the door. He knew the sounds that animals made when in great pain. The screaming was not an animal's. It was a noise that went to his heart – and then it had died, had faded. A long time after the screaming had finished and the quiet had returned to the valley, there had been gunfire. The shots had been faint to his ears, but he had heard them.

Others came. They came in coats such as his, or with wool blankets over their shoulders, and they stood beside him and behind him. Because of his position as patriarch of Vraca none stood in front of him. His view of the black emptiness of the fields over the river was not obstructed, but he could not make out any movement and though he strained his ears he picked up nothing. Some of the men who gathered around him carried double-barrelled hunting guns, but if he had brought his own it would not have protected him against the screaming. It was past three in the morning when Lila brought coffee. He cradled the cup in his hands and felt its heat on his skin.

He held a vigil and waited for the dawn.

When the screaming had started, Dragan Kovac had tossed himself out of his bed, had taken down from the hook the greatcoat from his days as a police sergeant, and his cap. He had gone outside to the shed at the side of the house where wood for the stove was stored, and had groped until he found his axe.

He had leaned against the doorpost, listened to the screams and held tight to the axe handle. They were the most fearsome screams he had ever heard. He thought he was a hard man, conditioned to the suffering of pain. Long after silence had replaced the screams he had stayed on his porch with the axe readied in his hands. There were the lights across the valley, and the lights of his own village behind him, and vehicle lights were at the top of the hill where the track crested the brow before falling down to Ljut, but he had not been able to see into the darkness. Then Dragan Kovac had heard the shots. He had counted the number of discharges and had known that the full magazine was used. The shots had driven him back inside his home.

He bolted the door then turned the heavy key in the lock and wedged a chair of stout wood under the handle. He sat on the bed, did not take off his boots, and his greatcoat and his cap, could not shake from his mind the sounds of the screaming. He held the axe, and waited for first light.

They offered him the flask but he refused it. He could not speak to them, nor they to him, but when Ante held the flask in front of him, he shook his head.

He could smell the brandy. He wondered if brandy had kept them on their feet and fighting when they had come out of Srebrenica, or faith, or desperation . . . and he wondered how it went with Mister and if he had faith to fall back on, or if the desperation grew. He did not know how it would finish, but he thought he had come near to the end of the road, as he'd pledged. When they had finished with the flask, he reached back, tapped on Ante's arm, pointed to the rifle, and it was given him. He looked through the 'scope sight.

He saw Mister, hunched, still, and then at the extreme edge of the tunnelled vision was a gliding movement that came closer to Mister.

It was a grey-dark shadow on the grey-white field.

The shadow flitted in the moonlight.

It came from behind Mister and skirted him warily. Not for two years, perhaps more, had there been a fox scavenging in the garden of his home near the North Circular Road. By tripping the beams, the fox set off the security lights and bleeped the consoles in the hall and in the bedroom. Several times Mister and the Princess had been alerted by the bleeps and had stood at the window to watch the mature vixen. A cautious creature, which Mister liked – and without fear, which Mister liked more. Alec Penberthy had said she had a breeding den just inside the fence of the school's playing-fields. At night in the garden she had looked magnificent. He recognized the shadow.

It came by him in a wide half-circle.

It gave him space but did not seem intimidated.

Past three o'clock . . . The fox was an escape for him. He had told himself that at three o'clock, when his wristwatch gave him that time, he would make the decision, commit himself, move. Of course, he would move. He was Mister. He did not know fear. He would splay out his hands, sink them down into the grass, use them to push himself up, and then he would walk, with firm strides, towards the river. He had set himself the deadline – three o'clock – and now the minutes ticked past and the watch hands sidled further from the hour. He watched the fox and that was his excuse not to move. It watched him.

Having come past him, so light-footed and so safe against the danger, it settled in front of him, sat. He could see the silhouette of its shadow. When it moved on he would push himself up. That was Mister's promise to himself. When he made a promise it was always kept; his word was his bond. When the fox shifted, he would go. He told himself, repeated it in his mind, that a few minutes did not matter. The fox seemed to study him, as if he intruded into its space. Then it ignored him and scratched. It lashed, with the claws of its back foot, against its neck then under its front leg. Abruptly, it shook itself, then its neck rose and its nostrils pointed up. It sniffed. To have reached where the fox sat on its haunches, he would have had to push himself up, offer his weight to the ground, then take ten strides. He heard its coarse snorting, then it was up. It trotted away. He thought the ground and the grass under its feet would barely have been pressured. It stopped, sniffed again, and then its back sank low, and it went forward.

The fox had located the Eagle, carrion.

It started to circle him. The shadow glided over the grass, and each circle was smaller. He had shot the Eagle, silenced him. And the voice had boomed at him in the night from the tree-line, and he had squirmed. If it had not been for the voice, taunting him – *Are you going to run, Mister?* – he would already have gone, started out on the hundred stride paces to the river. It was what Cann wanted, that he should run. Cann wanted his feet, shoes, his weight, pounding down on the earth and grass of the field. Cann wanted the flash and the thunderclap, wanted to hear the scream. Cann was in the trees, waiting on him, a reminder of the consequences of moving: a footfall landing on the antenna of a mine. The fox was close to the Eagle's body.

He could not drag away his eyes.

The Eagle's body was barely visible to Mister. The fox, he thought, investigated the body. He heard the rending of fabric. The fox had found the wound. It pulled on the torn trouser, then began to worry at the leg. He had no more use for the Luger pistol, no further magazine to fill it. He had the PPK Walther pistol in his belt. He saw the shadow of the fox tug at the Eagle's leg. Mister hurled the Luger at the fox. It might have caught the fox's back leg, or its lower stomach, and it yelped shrilly but did not back off. It gazed at Mister. They stared at each other. If the fox had moved away then, Mister would have planted his hands down in the grass, pushed himself up, and started to run or walk towards the river. It did not back off: instead the shadow darted forward. It was a blur against the grass. Mister saw something thrown up into the night air. The fox caught what it had thrown up, then went skittish and ran in tight squares with something in its mouth.

The fox played with the lower length of the Eagle's leg.

It bounced towards the leg and barked over it, tossed it and jumped back from it. Then it settled.

Mister heard the gnawing and the splintering of the bone. He could not fire the PPK Walther at the fox. He would need all the rounds in the pistol when he ran, when he went to the village where the lights burned to look for a car to take him out, away. A stone . . . he looked for a stone. He heard every sound from the fox's jaws. He dropped his hand to the grass beside his buttocks. He tore up the grass and scattered it in front of him. He cleared the grass from a patch the size of the handkerchief in his pocket, scratching into the earth with his fingers. He broke his nails and scrabbled deeper. It was soft earth, finely ground. He did not know that soft earth, milled and worked, had been carried by rain streams from the edge of the field. He burrowed with his hand, moled his way into the earth to find a stone. He was ever more frantic. He would run when the fox had gone, when he had found a stone and driven the fox off the Eagle's leg. He felt the hard smoothness. The little hole he had excavated was dark, too deep for the moon's light to reach into. He started to scrape at the side of what he'd uncovered, and he felt the symmetry of the shape. He thought that what he touched was the same size as the Bakelite top of the two-hundred-gram jars of coffee powder that the Princess bought. His fingers eased from the side of the shape to its top and he cleared away more of the cloying earth until he felt the first of the six points that made the little star. The mine was nine inches from his buttock, buried under six inches of soil and root. It was where his hand would have gone, where the pressure would have been concentrated as he pushed himself up and readied himself to run.

The voice, cold and without expression, carried to him from the tree-line. 'Time is moving on, Mister. I'd have thought, by now, you'd have run.'

When the voice had dissipated in the darkness, Mister was left with the sound of the fox's teeth on the Eagle's leg, and the frost was crisp in his hair.

The first light of dawn came in a soft smear on the hills behind Ljut village.

Chapter Nineteen

The low sun gilded the valley. Gold was painted on the hills, and on the bare trees. The lustre fell on the fields and was trapped in the grass and in the dead stems of the thistle and ragwort; it nestled on the vineyard posts and glistened off the wires between them. Brilliant little shimmers of light ruddied the bristly back of a pig that had come out of the trees' cover to snout for food. The softness of the gold was daubed on the fields and the woodlands, and played patterns on the smoke rising from the twin villages. The smoke turned ochre in the early light as it peeped up from the chimneys and was dispersed. The sun made dazzling reflections in the river where the water ran over shallow stones between the deeper pools.

Joey Cann had watched the dawn come. The valley was laid out in front of him. He rocked with tiredness, and blinked, tried to scrape the confusion from his mind.

If he looked for Mister, he looked into the sun that burned off the frost. He could be patient. The sun would creep higher into the sky and then he would see Mister, would know how the night had gone for him. He sat on the ground with his legs outstretched and reaching to the yellow tape and he propped himself upright on an elbow. The men around him snored quietly and the dog lay close to them.

He had thought Mister would have run in the darkness, would have gathered the courage and gone to the river, would have cheated him. Away to his left, he saw a column of pick-ups and ambulances come slowly down the winding track and they stopped near to the village. He saw an old man come out of the front door of an isolated house further down the track, wearing a uniform greatcoat and a cap of authority and carrying an axe. Across the river, at another house that was separated from its village, children burst through the door and a woman hobbled after them on a crutch. They went to a man who sat bowed on an old tree log.

The sun rose.

Joey saw Mister and he knew that he was not cheated. Above the field grass, he saw Mister's bent knees, his torn suit jacket, his tie that was askew at his throat, and the hands that held his face, and the hair on his scalp. The smile was at Joey's mouth. He cupped his hands together and his shout broke the peace, seemed to scatter the gold dust that had fallen on the valley.

'You should have run, Mister, while you had the dark. Were you too frightened to run?'

He jerked awake. He did not know how long he had slept, or where.

'What stopped you?'

He shook. A shiver rattled him. He was sitting and he thought he was falling. He felt his weight slide, and reached out to steady himself. His hand found the wet grass and the muddied earth, and slipped into the hole. For a moment he could not control its slide. He looked down. He scrabbled for earth, for a grip. His hand was half an inch above the six points of the antenna that would detonate the mine. His muscles were rigid . . . He knew where he was. He recognized the voice, but could not see Cann. His stomach growled in hunger and his throat was parched. Near to him, teeth scraped on a bone. He stared down at the mine in the little excavated pit and saw the mud smears on the green paint. He put the hand under his armpit, locked it there. In the night the trees around the river's roar had made a dark line. Now, the sun shone through them. He could see each branch and each sprig growing from the trees' trunks. The river was safety, a hundred strides away. Mister had never known fear. He took his hand from his armpit, brushed it against his stomach and felt the pistol in his belt. Then he worked the hand under the seat of his trousers, and pushed himself up. He nearly fell because of the stiffness in his knees. He stood, and started to massage his hips, his knees and his ankles. When he had worked over the flesh, kneaded the joints and ligaments under the skin, he stood to his full height, made a bow arc of his back and stretched his arms. He would run – maybe he would close his eyes – towards the trees by the river. In his mind he put the boxes in their place. He would run for the river. A track of grey stone led from the river to the village, where he would find a car; he had the PPK Walther pistol. He readied himself. He thought he would count to ten, and then he would run. He should not have, but he looked at the ground between himself and the river. The carcass of bones was bleached white, was cleaned in the sun, as if fresh paint was on it. Grass grew through the ribcage . . . And the voice intruded once more.

'What you have to think of, Mister, is when it's going to happen: your first step or your last step, or one of the middle steps. At the start, at the end, or in between – you don't know, do you? And you don't know whether you'll scream, like the Eagle screamed.'

After he had seen the first skeleton, Mister counted six more. Some were on their backs, some on their sides, and others had just crumpled down as if their knees had given way beneath them and their heads had fallen forward. Two of the white bone hulks were directly between himself and the river. Three more were to the right, and two were to the left. There was no pattern to them. Should he run the shortest way, loop to the left or right, or zigzag? He gazed out at the bones.

'Go on, Mister, run. Run so I can hear you scream.'

His legs were stiff, dead. He could not take the step. Mister stopped the count. He was short of the last number. The wind played on the grass that covered the earth, and moved the dead dark weed stems. He heard the cry of crows above him, and the gnawing of the fox's jaws on the leg bone. He was leaden. The light and the warmth were on his face. He stood alone in the field.

'God, you're a disappointment to me, Mister. Is the fear that bad?'

They woke, they separated. The ground hadn't moved for Maggie

Bolton, but the chassis of the blue van had. Three times they'd done it. She'd let Frank do what neither the Polish boy nor the young Arab had been allowed to. She couldn't have said which of the three times was the best, but she'd have been able to hazard which was the worst. She was in her forty-eighth year. It had been, for her, the first, second and third time – and there would not be another. She doubted that even a kid of fifteen, on heat, would have chosen to lose their virginity in the back of the blue van, on a bed of coats and rugs, beside the new bucket. If it had been with any of the men in Vauxhall Bridge Cross – they'd tried hard enough – the bed would at least have cost them two hundred and fifty pounds in a West End hotel. Frank Williams lay against her and his cheek's stubble prickled her breast.

'So, is that what all the fuss is about?'

'You, Maggie, are an amazing screw.'

'I don't think so – you are certainly not.'

He turned away from her. Her back to him, she dressed ... It would have been better with Joey. He had smooth hands, and long fingers, but he hadn't offered. She hooked on her bra. The light trickled opaquely through the back windows of the van and she found her knickers on the van's ribbed floor. They were torn – when he'd ripped them off. She wriggled into them, and her tights, and dragged on her jeans. She wanted to be alone in her bed. She wondered if he'd talk about her to people in whatever bar he drank at, if her name would go on a list.

'Well, go on, get on with it.'

'Get on with what?'

'Look after your prisoner – find out what's going on.'

'You're great, Maggie – don't hurt yourself.'

'I am a middle-aged woman and so desperate for it that I'm the original easy lay. Don't worry, I'm grateful – you've cured my curiosity.'

'I thought there might be a future for us.'

'Nothing good comes out of Bosnia – never has, never will. Get rid of them.'

She gestured behind her. Laid on the wheel arch, carefully balanced, were three knotted condoms. She pulled on her blouse and her sweater, then tugged her anorak out from under him. She clicked open the metal-sided box and lifted out the video camera and the collapsed tripod. He was putting on his vest, often washed and a fading dragon rampant on it. She took the mobile phone from the integral battery-charger in the case. His socks, sliding on to his feet, were threadbare at the heels. She hooked the phone's cables to the video. When he had his shoes on he snatched up the condoms, and leaned across to kiss her. Then he went to see to his prisoner, and Maggie took the video camera, the tripod and the mobile telephone out of the van.

She walked a few strides down the track that was hemmed in by yellow tape. She found a vantage-point. She wondered if she would be different when she returned to Ceauşescu Towers, whether the people she worked with would recognize it. 'You know what, I think that tease bitch finally opened her legs . . . I reckon she had it, at last.' She set up the tripod then searched for stones inside the tape cordon and wedged them against the tripod's feet. It would have been better, on all three times, if she'd thought of Joey Cann. She screwed the video camera on to the tripod's head. She had never reached Joey Cann. She held the mobile in her hand, stood back to let the wind snag the tripod and the camera, and she was satisfied that the picture would be steady. He wore no uniform, but she could not have discarded hers . . . She would never reach him. On the track, Frank was in animated conversation with the de-mining team, men made grotesque by their plated waistcoats and visored helmets.

The wind brought her the flat tone of the shouted voice.

'I'm thinking the fear's worse, Mister. Each minute that you put it off, the running, will make it harder, Mister. I want to see you run, Mister, and I want to hear you scream.'

She looked over the sunlit valley . . . Beyond an abandoned vineyard, half-way between the tree-line and the river and far from the yellow tape, in the middle of an expanse of field, Target One stood. The crows circled above him. Near to him was the body of Target Two, and close to it was a blob of colour she could not identify. It was all, to her eyes, so pretty . . . Joey had brought her there . . . so pretty and so cruel. She would never reach him.

She aimed the camera and dialled the number.

Five men lumbered along the slight gap between the tree-line and the yellow tape. Frank was ahead of them, unencumbered. At the back of the line was a German shepherd dog on a rope leash, bigger than Nasir and older.

When they came close, Joey looked into their eyes. There was a weariness, a dullness, that matched the slow speed of their approach. They wore overalls of dreary grey and heavy boots, thick shapeless waistcoats with a flap that hung down over their privates, and bulbous helmets with raised visors of unwashed Perspex. They carried thin metal probes and garden shears, and one had a small handsaw. Another had a metal-detector hoisted on his shoulder, and the one who held the dog's rope had a roll of yellow tape under his arm.

Nasir, growling, was taken by Muhsin back into the trees.

Frank made the introductions.

Joey was asked by the foreman – good English – for his assessment.

Joey scowled. 'Two men, both British citizens, went into the field just before ten o'clock last night. At one minute past ten, a mine was detonated by the fugitive nearest to us – Target Two, we call him. He bawled a bit, then he went quiet. After midnight Target Two started to talk, but Target One shot him. Target One is alone. He nearly moved at dawn. He stood and readied himself to move, but then changed his mind. He's not moved since he stood.'

He hated saying each word to the foreman. The man came into his space, the others with him, and their dog.

'So,' the foreman said, without enthusiasm, 'we have one cadaver and one uninjured person – that is correct?'

'Correct. What is the density of the mines?'

'We do not know. Mines were laid in the valley over a period of nearly four years, but it was not a disputed front line. There is not a barrier minefield. Once there would have been a purpose to where they were buried but time – and principally rain – will have changed that. They can be anywhere. There may be ten, a hundred, or five hundred. We have to assume, always, that we must work through a concentration of mines.'

'Do you use the dog?'

'I think not. The dog is too valuable. If the casualty were still alive then there is great pressure on us to go faster. I think we do not use the dog.'

'What do you do?'

'We make a corridor, a metre and a half wide,' the foreman said. 'It is very slow. It is, my estimate, a hundred and thirty metres to him, that is the work of a whole day . . . The man is a criminal? He shot the man with him, you said that?'

Frank said softly, 'He carries at least one weapon with a full magazine. We have a prisoner. The prisoner said there were two firearms in their vehicle. I have searched the vehicle and there are no firearms in it. However many shots he used for the killing, he has the second firearm, a PPK Walther, with a fully loaded magazine.'

Joey said, 'The man who is dead is a lawyer, wouldn't touch a weapon. Whatever plan you make you should assume that Target One is armed.'

'Do you know about mine clearance?' the foreman asked.

Joey said that he did not.

'It is necessary to be very careful. We concentrate only on the work. We go on our hands and knees and we probe. All our attention is on the ground a few centimetres in front of our bodies. We wear personal protection equipment, but that is of little use to the man who sets off the mine. The second man, or the third, if he is a few metres away, will take the benefit from the clothing. There is a full bomb suit, from Canada, but it weighs thirty kilos, and you cannot work in it, not on your knees. You have in the field a criminal, an armed fugitive . . . Do you think I should ask my men to crawl towards him – and forget that he is a criminal, armed, a fugitive – and probe for mines and never look at him? I cannot.'

'I'm not criticizing you,' Joey said.

'If he were not armed, if that were proved, if he gave clear signs that he wished to surrender, then I would reconsider.' The foreman shrugged.

'Should he run, what would be his chance of setting off a mine?' Joey asked.

'It would be in God's hands.'

'He's not broken, not yet,' Joey said. 'He will be.'

They walked away, taking with them their shears, their probes, the metal detector, the roll of yellow tape and their dog. The sun was rising and bathed the valley's fields. They trudged off alongside the tree-line, and Frank was close to the foreman. Joey thought it was how he wanted it to be. He smiled at the four men who were left with him but none caught his gaze. He sat down. The dog, Nasir, came to him. It lay against his leg and his raised knee threw some shade for it. The Sreb Four made a little huddle and sat apart from him. In front of him, caught in the sun's strength, Mister stood and Joey did not see a muscle of his body moving. He would weaken, Joey knew it. Exhaustion, hunger, thirst and the creeping fear of the mines around him would sap Mister. And then Mister would run . . . He cupped his hands.

'Men were here, Mister, who had the skill to reach you and bring you out, but I told them you were armed and had killed, and who you are. They've decided you're not worth the risk. All that's left to you, Mister, is to run and to hope.'

Midday . . .

. . . Judge Delic, having recessed his court till the late afternoon, wheeled Jasmina from the Mercedes to the doorway of a boutique on Ferhadija, tilted the chair over the street step and pushed her inside. They were no longer window-shoppers. She knew the trouser-suit she wanted, black, professional and styled from Milan. The car was left on the kerb, a no-parking zone, but a black Mercedes would not be interfered with by the police. And up on the hill, over the river, workmen scrambled over and through their home.

. . . the firemen took the strain on their rope, relied on the grappling hook to hold, and pulled the body on to the steep stone-clad bank of the Miljacka. The water dripped from it as it was beached. Around the ice-white throat of the body was a gold chain. A fireman fingered it and read the inscription on the bar: 'To dearest Enver, with love, Serif'. He wiped his hands on his overalls, and activated his radio.

. . . Ismet Mujic sat in his apartment, the curtains drawn, the gloom on his face, his world collapsed, and waited for the telephone to ring. And as he waited, he cursed the day that a man from Green Lanes in London had telephoned to urge him to receive strangers anxious to put to him a business proposition.

. . . Nikki Gornikov slept off his overnight travel in his own Budapest bed, and Marco Tardi dozed in the Rome transit lounge before the Palermo feeder flight was called, and Fuat Selcuk snored in the first-class cabin of the Austrian Airlines flight to Damascus. Going their different ways, returning to their base camps, they had each pledged that they would – singly or collectively – never deal again with Albert William Packer. He was dead meat, might as well have hung from a butcher's hook.

. . . Monika Holberg, her desk and computer screen in the Unis building abandoned, walked into the Holiday Inn's atrium, crossed to the reception desk and saw her letter in the pigeon-hole beside the key. She asked for it to be returned to her. She tore it into small pieces and gave the scraps back to the clerk to be dropped in the rubbish bin behind the desk. As she pushed open the hotel's doors she felt a sense of disaster falling on her. It was the same sense she had known when coming back to her home at Njusford, on the island of Flakstodoya, to be told that her brother had hanged himself in the cattle byre.

. . . the men and the woman of Sierra Quebec Golf stood around Dougie Gough's computer screen on the central desk and stared in tongue-tied astonishment at the image presented to them.

. . . a detective chief inspector reached for his telephone to make a routine call, and found that his line was dead. He looked up and saw that the immediate open-plan area where he worked on the upper floor of the National Crime Squad's Pimlico offices was deserted. In the moment that the first bead of sweat broke on his neck, he heard the door behind him snap open and there were hands on his shoulder and his collar, and he was lifted from his chair.

. . . checking his watch to be certain that his call was in tandem with events two floors below, the commander from the National Crime Squad rang the private secretary to the minister. 'I think we are now in a position to share. The rotten apple is out of the bucket.' Then he spoke to the car pool and told his driver at what time they would leave for the Custom House.

. . . Clarrie Hinds told her daughter to get home and stop moaning, and young Sol closed down the screen on the last computer disk and marvelled at his luck in being chosen, and the Mixer waited for a call to alert him to the return flight so that he could send an Eel to meet it, and around the capital city men who dealt in business and pushed business grumbled at the inconvenience caused by Mister's absence.

. . . the sun blazed down on the Bunica valley.

It burned his face and his hands. It seared into his eyes as it reflected back from the grass carpet.

Mister knew that he had to stay standing. If he slipped down on to the flattened ground under his shoes, then he would never rise again, would never run. The sweat ran in his hair, over his forehead, into his eyes and made them smart. With the sweat in his eyes, the trees at the riverbanks danced and misted. If he turned, he would see Cann, and the shouts would cut deeper. He tried to keep his gaze ahead of him, on the dark pools of the river and the silver spates separating them. If he looked down, he would see the pit he had excavated, and the mine. Each time the voice taunted him, coldly teasing, tormenting and torturing, the fear was stronger. Mister did not know if he could destroy the fear. Behind him was the fox. There was no meat left on the Eagle's ankle and shin; its teeth were scraping bare bone. He started to count, but he knew that when he reached ten he would change the target to a hundred, and then to a thousand. He could not kick his feet in front of him and start to run.

The high sun beat on him, and the sweat streamed down him, and the strength dribbled from him.

'It is a duel.'

They had met at the ford. The water over the stones was too high, too fast-flowing for an old man to cross.

'That is stupid talk,' Husein Bekir called back.

'You say it is stupid because you have not read books. Is that because, like an old fool, you cannot read books?'

'I can read.'

Dragan Kovac grimaced smugly. 'Then, perhaps, like an old fool, you have forgotten what you have read, or forgotten what your teacher told you at school. It is in history – listen, old fool – there are stories in history about duels. Champions fought in single combat, man against man, to the death or until one submits.'

'It's idiot talk.'

'You never listen. I have talked to the foreman of the de-miners. They speak with me because I am a man of experience and importance. Do they talk to you? It is what he tells me, the foreman. It is like the time of Ban Kulin, or when the Great Khan came from the east, or the time of King Stephen Tvrtko, or when Mehmet arrived from the south and the tyranny of the Muslims began. Disputes were settled in single combat, to the death or to surrender.'

Husein spat on to the ground.

Dragan persisted, 'That is why the foreman has come back here to clear your fields – not that you, an old fool, will ever work them.'

'This spring I will plant my new apple orchard, fifty trees, and I will be here to harvest the first crop . . . Do you mean it, this shit about single combat?'

'It is what the foreman said.'

'I don't understand that.' Husein shook his head wearily.

'Because you are an old fool and you do not listen. The foreman is an intelligent man, so he confides in me. A criminal from Britain, Mr Barnaby's country, came to our country, for whatever corrupt reason. He is followed by the British Customs, by our men and the international police. He is in flight from them, and with him is his lawyer. They leave the road and come down the hill . . .'

'Where my son-in-law is dead,' Husein said grimly.

'And go into the field. The lawyer detonates the mine . . .'

'I heard his screaming – like children in hell.'

'. . . detonates the mine. The criminal shoots him. Because the criminal has a gun, and has killed, the de-miners will not move to reach him. That pleases the Customs man. He is called Joey . . .'

'That is a stupid name,' Husein sneered. 'Like a girl's name.'

'Don't, old fool, interrupt. He is young, is junior, he is nothing. The criminal is a big man. It would not be a contest, single-handed combat, if they were in London. But they are not, they are here – and the criminal is in a minefield and—'

Husein was triumphant. 'Which your people laid, which pollutes my fields.'

'And the minefield makes them equal. Joey taunts him that he is afraid to run across the field, to risk going through the mines. If the criminal does not dare to run, his spirit fails him, then he loses dignity . . .'

While they bickered, the long-standing friends – Husein Bekir and Dragan Kovac – gazed out over the fields. Close to them the de-miners worked in their taped corridors, crouched over their probes. Away in the distance, hard for them to distinguish in the sunlight, the single man stood, and around him was the emptiness.

'Who cares about dignity in a minefield? Did Lila? Did my son-in-law?'

'Did the first foreman? You told him about the fallen post, you sent him to repair it, and he will never walk again . . . Dignity to a criminal is everything. Go into Mostar, find Tuta and Stela, dignity is the only thing they have. If they are humiliated, show fear, plead for mercy, then they have nothing. This man, there . . . He tries to hold his dignity, and the young man tries to take it from him. The police could shoot him but then he dies with dignity, and happy, and he becomes the *legenda*. Does he want to be remembered for his dignity, or for his fear that made him surrender? It is subtle, but you would not understand that. At the moment he does not know what to do . . . I believe he suffers.'

'I think it is stupid talk.' Again Husein Bekir spat. 'When a man is in a minefield what value is *dignity* to him?'

The picture on the screen was pastel, rinsed-out colour. Mister, in his suit, stood in a field. In the Custom House room of Sierra Quebec Golf, the team, short of only SQG12, stood behind Gough. Their workplaces were abandoned, the desks littered with file papers and photographs. Above the only tidied place, where the computer was switched off, was the sign: 'CANN do – WILL do'. The picture in front of Gough enmeshed them, and none had the will to break free from it.

The image was of their Target One.

They all had paper mountains to scale but the work had been pushed aside once the call had come through from Vauxhall Bridge Cross, and SQG8 had been summoned to Gough's computer, had rustled the keys, found the network and had downloaded the picture. Gough wouldn't have been able to because he was weak on the new science, but SQG8 was the wizard. Their work that morning and afternoon should have taken them into the final planning stages of the raids that would sweep into the homes of the Mixer, two of the Cards, the Eel who had driven the lorry, and the warehouse where the truck – Bosnia with Love – was garaged. It was Gough's intention that, when Mister returned, he would find his organization disrupted, under microscopic investigation, and doubt permeating his lieutenants . . . but the planning work was discarded. The image fascinated them. The camera angle never changed, and the lens never zoomed. It would have been a still frame but for the occasional wheeling swoops of the crows and the bluster of the puff clouds in the wind. Mister did not move. He did not seem to change his weight from a right-foot bias to a left foot, he did not reach out with his arms to stretch or flex, his hand did not go to his forehead to mop it. The rain pattered on the windows facing into Lower Thames Street, but the shower had no reality for them. The heat of the sun on Mister's head and shoulders were real; they could sense it. Because Gough had lit his pipe, in blatant contravention of the in-house edict, cigarettes were on and SQG4 billowed smoke from a small cigar. The room was fugged. They watched Mister, and each in their minds played with his dilemma and wondered what they would have done, faced with his situation. The shouts, thin and metallic, played over the loudspeakers beside Gough's computer, made them squirm, but they were all addicts.

The door opened. Heads turned briefly. The glances to the intruders betrayed their feelings. The chief investigation officer introduced the commander from the National Crime Squad. There were some among them, and Gough might have led, who would have gone to the walls and abruptly pulled down the sheets on which the cartwheel was chinagraphed, and the plans for the next programme of raids, but the screen held them.

Cork intoned, 'I thought you should know that this afternoon officers of CIB3 entered National Crime Squad offices and arrested a detective chief inspector who was a primary leak source on investigations into the affairs of Albert William Packer. The leak is plugged. I am instructed – yes, *instructed* – by the appropriate minister of the Crown that we co-operate, share, with the commander and his people, the fruits of our investigation. I am told that, united, we will improve immeasurably on the chance of a successful prosecution of Packer and the dismantling of his empire.'

If he was heard it was not shown; the eyes of the team stayed on the screen.

'I intend initially to second one of SQG to the Crime Squad, and for you to have one of their experienced officers in here, and welcomed. When Packer returns, the full resources of both organizations will be turned on him. Packer, is he on his way back? Do we have a flight?'

Gough pointed to the screen. Reluctantly, SQG3 and SQG9 edged aside and allowed the intruders a small space behind Gough's chair. The CIO and the commander craned forward.

'Good God, isn't that Packer? Where is he?'

'He's in a field, Commander, he's standing in a field,' Gough said, with dry civility. 'He is standing in a field and right now his thoughts are far from buying an airline ticket. The field is in a valley that is about ten miles south-south-east of Mostar.'

'Why? Why is he standing in a field?'

'It's not an ordinary field. It's not sown with parsnips or potatoes. Its crop is mines. He is in a minefield. How does he know he is in the middle of a minefield? He knows because Arbuthnot – the Eagle, our Target Two – stepped on one, and is now deceased. He is caught, trapped, in a minefield, and his little mind is working overtime.'

'What about rescue?' The commander's voice was hoarse. 'Aren't there trained people who can bring him out?'

'It's a long story,' Gough evaded. 'Too long for now ... That's Arbuthnot.'

The commander's chin and the chief investigation officer's jaw were over Gough's shoulders as he showed them the corpse, and they peered at the dark shape in the grass that was slight, insignificant, and diminished by the scale of the fields.

'What's that?' The commander's fingernail replaced Gough's. The point he took was beyond the standing figure and near to the prone shape. Against his nail was a russet blob, unclear.

'Don't know,' Gough said.

'Well, go in on it.'

Gough hesitated, and flushed. 'That's a bit beyond me.'

'Should I ring my granddaughter and have her ferried over?'

SQG8 inserted herself, knelt beside Gough's leg and worked the mouse. She highlighted the russet blob, clicked and zoomed, dragged it closer and clearer.

It was not necessary for Cork to speak. They could all see what he saw. Cork blurted, 'Christ, it's a bloody fox ... What's it got? It's got a bone. It's cleaning its bloody teeth on a bone ... What's that on the end of the bone? I don't want to believe what I am seeing. It's a shoe.

It's Arbuthnot's shoe. The fox has eaten his bloody leg, all except for what's in the shoe . . . Christ almighty.'

The smoke of the cigarettes and the small cigar, and from Gough's pipe, floated over the screen. The zoom pulled out, then SQG8 took the centre point of Mister's back, and he was pulled, jerked, closer to the watchers. They could see the silver streaks of perspiration at his temples.

The voice came over the speakers. They were pin-drop quiet as they listened.

'Are you going to run, Mister, or are you going to beg for help to come and get you? Let me talk you through the begging. Throw the gun away first, then strip, get off every last stitch, then beg. You're naked and you're begging, and all the world knows you're finished, and a loser . . . or you run. Those are your options, Mister . . . Come on. Come on.'

The voice was gone. Light wind bruised the camera's microphone.

'Who is that?' the commander barked.

'His name is Cann, he's SQG12,' Gough said flatly. 'He is our most junior executive officer.'

'It's torture, psychological torture,' Cork snapped. 'What's his problem? He is challenging him to risk his life in a minefield. Packer – as damn near as makes no difference – is in custody, if you've anything to charge him with. What you're doing is obscene. Even Packer has rights. I never sanctioned such behaviour. All I sanctioned was surveillance.'

'Then you didn't know your man,' Gough said. 'What did you want, Mr Cork? Did you want a packaged legal process, or the elimination of our Target One? I thought I knew what you wanted.'

'Get him out. That is an order, Mr Gough. Remove Cann.'

'Easier said . . . If you hadn't noticed, Mr Cork, that field and that valley and Packer and Cann are a long way from me. But I'll do what I am able.'

'An order, Mr Gough.'

'How many mines do you reckon are there, Mister?'

Frank listened to the pitiless ring of Joey's voice. He thought Mister's shoulders, out in the field, were lower and he wondered whether Mister's knees were near to buckling. Frank had driven into

Mostar and dumped his prisoner in a police cell, under IPTF supervision, and then had bought supermarket cold food and water.
He had come back to the crest of the hill, then the call on Maggie's
phone had driven him down the slope path, with the food and water,
past the skeleton of a wretch who had tripped the wire of a PMR2A
mine, with the instruction from London. The men had their backs to
Joey Cann. He crouched beside them and listened to what he was
told as they ate and drank. Frank Williams was a career policeman
and he believed in the rigour of law enforcement and in the processes
of the criminal code. He listened to Ante, their spokesman, and then
to the chipped remarks of Salko, Fahro and Muhsin, who had the
dog's leash coiled in his hand. He had seen the monitor picture from
the video camera and had heard the mocking shout across the valley.
What he had seen and heard made a travesty of justice as he knew it.
When they had finished, said what they wanted to, he went and
stood behind Joey Cann, brought bread and cheese and an apple
and what was left in the water bottle. The head wasn't turned, the
eyes were locked on the back in the dark suit jacket that rose above
the hazed heat of the fields.

'Are you listening to me?'

'I'm hearing you.'

'London want you out.'

'Do they?'

'The instruction to be passed to you was made, personally, to me
by Douglas Gough acting on behalf of Dennis Cork, chief investigation officer. Not tomorrow or the day after, but *now*. Out, and quit.'

'Is that what he said?'

'What you're doing is barbaric. Maggie rigged up the video and
it's playing over the mobile. They are watching it in London. They
know what you're doing and, like me, they are disgusted at your
self-serving arrogance. You're going down to his level, Mister's,
maybe going lower than him. If you don't believe what I'm telling
you, out and quit, then use your mobile and call your Gough.
Go on.'

Joey shifted his weight and took the mobile off his belt. He peeled
it out of the ragged leather case, flipped off the back flap and took out
the battery. The battery went into his breast pocket and the mobile
was hooked back on his belt.

Frank spoke, steely quiet: 'Those men behind you, they call you Nasir. They've given you the dog's name ... Muhsin told you that Nasir Oric, defender of Srebrenica, their military leader, was a hero. Salko's just told me that when the town fell the people rampaged and looted in the last hours before the Serbs came in, and they found warehouses stacked to the roof with UN-donated food, but it wasn't for free handouts. It was for black-market sale, and that was criminal ... Ante tells me that Nasir, who had been pulled out by the government to Tuzla before Srebrenica went under, led a column of a hundred and seventy men who fought through the Serb lines to link with the fighters breaking out, hand-to-hand combat, against the odds, and that was heroic ... Fahro tells me that today Nasir Oric is a rich man, not bad for an ex-police bodyguard, with a money-spinning restaurant on the lake at Tuzla and won't talk about the source of the start-up cash.'

'Why do they call me Nasir?'

'Only one side of him was a hero. The other side of him was ... a good man and a bad killer. It's the sort of confusion this place breeds, and you've got it bad. So, I'm telling you now, I want no part of it, nor Maggie, nor them ... Do I leave you food? We want no part of what you're doing.'

'He's not eating, so I'm not eating.' Now he turned. Frank saw the boyish sincerity wreath his face, and the smile. 'I'm going to win, you know. He's the loser, I'm the winner.'

'At what cost?' Frank asked sourly. 'At what bloody cost?'

The smile slipped, the frown was above the big spectacles. 'I've only one favour I need from you. Please, request of them that the dog stays with me. I'll bring him back to Sarajevo, safe and sound, a promise, but I'd appreciate it if I could keep him. The food and the water'll do for the dog, if there's nothing better.'

It was only a dog. Frank put the request. Only another dog. Frank left with the Sreb Four. Before he went into the depth of the trees, he stopped and looked. Joey fed bread to the dog, then poured water into its mouth. He started to walk, hurrying to catch the men ahead of him, and the sun fell in shards between the trees.

It was a soft call. 'Thank Maggie for what she's done for me – give her my love.'

*

He was weaker.

The sun was on Mister's back. It was off his face and that brought slight relief. He stood and did not move. He gabbled numbers but they had no sequence, no rhythm, and he had no target number. The numbers were random, the decision was put off. He did not know the time, but the sun's force had come off his face and away from the top of his head and was now on his back.

He was sinking.

The numbers, in hundreds, tens and thousands, cluttered his mind. When he lost them, they slipped away from him. Then he thought of Cann. Between the scrabble of numbers was the sight of Cann's face. Big spectacles, a wide forehead, curly hair without a comb, a small mouth – the clerk, the paper-pusher of Sierra Quebec Golf. At that age he would be little more than a probationer. The kid stuck leech-like to him. Why? Mister could buy policemen and juries and bankers and the civil service and ... What was Cann's price? Small change, ten thousand, pocket money, fifteen thousand, enough for a down-payment on a flat. The Eagle had said: *You know what I worry about? I mean it, lose sleep about? One day you overreach – know what I mean – take a step too far. I worry* ... Poor old Eagle, good old boy, and right again, always. He could no longer see the trees at the river because the sun bounced on them and his eyes were too tired to focus on them. There was no respect in Cann's voice when he shouted ... He did not know how much longer he could stand and not move. If he were to be beaten, and to beg, it would be soon.

He was slipping.

He played a game with a man's mind, and with a man's life.

Joey was alone with the dog. He had fed it the bread and cheese, and the apple for pulp crunching, and all of the water that they'd left. He'd heard the murmur of the van's engine as it had driven away from the track, and the pick-ups. Sometimes there were the voices, carried on the wind, of the de-miners working from the track by the river but they were little more than whispers and he could not see them.

He said to the dog, who was named after a hero and a killer, 'Doesn't worry me, Nasir, if I'm going down in the filth with him, and get to fight dirtier than he knows how. He loses, I win. What I want is to have him in my hand and to crush him. He's always won, I've always lost, but not here. You can understand that, Nasir?'

His head shook, the hunger and thirst were worse, and he could not cough up saliva to run over his tongue.

In front of him, out in the sunlight, Mister fell.

Joey croaked his shout, 'Don't cheat me, you bastard. Don't beg, don't cry. Stand up . . .'

'Stand up, you cheating bastard. I want you running, running among the mines, and I want you screaming. Get up.'

The sound on the speakers faded and was lost against the traffic on Lower Thames Street; the picture was dying. SQG8 said it was the battery going down on the mobile, or the power pack on the camera was exhausted. She remarked that she was surprised the camera and the mobile, abandoned on the vantage-point by Miss Bolton when she had pulled out, as ordered, had lasted so long. All of them in the room stared, without forgiveness, at Dougie Gough.

'Don't say it, you don't have to tell me. I take responsibility. I think they are about to go into what is euphemistically called close-quarters combat. It'll be in the gutter, Gorbals street-fighting. I ask myself, down there, can Cann win – and then, does it matter, other than to Cann, who wins and who loses? God watch for him.'

The last image on the screen, before the snowstorm, was of the fox careering away with the bone, and of the fallen man trying to push himself up.

Chapter Twenty

The skies were clear and the wind had whisked away the few clouds over the hills in the east. There would be another frost over the valley that night, the same light hoar frost.

But in the last hour of the day, as the sun balanced on the crest of the hill, it still carried strength and threw down a final limited warmth. It hit the back of a young man who sat with the clay mud on his trainer shoes, the dirt on his jeans and the filth stains on his anorak, and it bounced from the inside of his spectacles' lenses on to his grimy, unshaven face. It made fierce colours on the coat of a dog who played at gnawing his fist. It danced on the shoulders of an older man in the field, who tried to push himself up, and failed, and tried again, and made shadows from his crippled efforts. It simpered over a fallen body but still had the power to cook its flesh and to make the stench rise from it.

The sun was on the weed-strewn fields that had once been ploughed, and tickled the weeds' dried-out seed sacs and nurtured the flower-pods not yet ready to bloom, and it rested in the day's death on the grazing fields and on the carcass bones of the heifers and the bullock who had browsed there, and it filtered on to the posts and wires, and the rotted roots of a vineyard, and it splayed out over a patch of ground that might, one day, be an orchard of apple trees. The sun sank, the red replacing the gold, the shadows lengthening, and caressed the rusted frame of an abandoned tractor. It sparkled on a swollen river and caught each wave over the hidden stones of a ford, and it laid down the trellised reflections of bared tree branches on to the dark deep pools where the trout and the pike hunted. It dazzled the eyes of a retired police sergeant and a tired, life-wearied farmer, the one on a chair in his porch with his bottle in front of him and the other on the log in front of his house with the crude rolled cigarette hanging from his upper lip. It flashed on the windscreens of the pick-ups that carried men up the hill with their armoured waistcoats, helmets with visors, their overboots and their sharp steel prods. As the sun dropped, so the valley quietened, and the men who used hammers and power drills to repair their homes came down off their ladders, and the women who had gossiped and laughed and yelled abuse at their kids while the heat bronzed their arms to walnut now scurried to drag their washing from the lines, make a last broom sweep on their doorsteps, close their doors and stoke their fires.

It would be a cold night, because the skies were clear over the valley, the sun had lost its gold and was an angry red.

The crest of the hill to the west cut the first small bite from the sun.

The ghosts came, spectral groups at first, little shadows. The axle pins of their wheelbarrows squealed for lack of oil and they cursed at the weight of the hessian sacks they carried, with the spades and pickaxes on their shoulders. The faces of the ghosts were young and they wore field fatigues of green-blue or of combat camouflage. They went to their appointed places. The quiet around them was broken by the ring of the spades striking buried stones and the thud of earth clods thrown aside. The ghosts were the poisoners. On their hands and knees they put the plastic, the chemicals and the metal working parts into the holes they had dug and loosened the screws that made the poison live, and laid earth and small stones around the poison and filled the holes, smoothed the earth. And the ghosts measured out lengths of wire and used the flat shapes of their spades to knock in peg posts to which the wire would be tautened and tied. Later, the rain would come and drench the ghosts, and silt streams would carry the poison from the wood paths and from in front of the bunkers, from gateways and tracks, and the streams would take the poison and scatter it at random, without shape, in the fields – and the ghosts would be gone.

The drop of the sun, chewed at by the crest of the hill, made the valley tranquil. It was too low, now, to find a strand of wire over which the grass grew protectively.

The gold had gone.

He knew it would be the last time that he would try. Mister put his weight on his hands. They crushed the grass. He pushed himself over on to his knees and then he gasped a big breath, pushed again, his knees creaked in protest, and he stood. In getting himself up, on to his feet, he had swivelled his body. He swayed. He had weakened and had told himself it was the final effort. He stood and rocked, and his feet were numb. More than half of the sun had disappeared beneath the horizon; what was left was low in his eyes and it was hard for him to see into the trees, but he thought he saw the wide spectacles and the pallor of Cann's forehead. It was his last try: he had rallied what strength was left to him. Five times he had tried to push himself up and five times he had subsided on to his haunches. He flexed his toe muscles. The circulation had staunched and the muscles were locked tight, but his balance held and confidence trickled back.

'Well done, Mister, a good effort . . . Now, make my Christmas and run. Don't quit on me now, Mister.'

It was an hour since the voice had last shouted at him, a whole hour since it had goaded him. For an hour he had sat, between his attempts to push himself up, and the valley had gone quiet around him. He had thought of the past and the present, of the Eagle, and the mines, of the Cruncher, and the mines, of the Princess, and the mines, of the Mixer, the Cards, the Eels and the mines, of the *spieler* cafés on Green Lanes, the lorries coming through Felixstowe docks and Dover harbour, and of the power, and the mines . . . It was the pungent smell of the Eagle, like he was rotting already, that kept the mines in his mind.

But he was standing . . . fuck the past and the present. He would not run, he would walk towards the future. His mind was a shambling mess: that was the sun and the hunger. Mister craved the future . . . Lie low, go quiet. Young Sol in the place of the Cruncher, maybe Davey Henderson's boy in the place of the Eagle. The Princess back with him – of course she would be. A new Cruncher, a new Eagle, and the same Princess – and the word would go round the pubs, bars, clubs that Mister had walked out through a minefield, had had the balls to put his feet down, stamp them on ground that was stacked full of landmines. No fear. No bloody fear . . . He was Mister, no bastard took liberties with him.

The shadows of the trees on the hill groped towards him.

He turned his body but kept his feet on the crushed grass. The wind came in a little surge, riffled the grass and brought him the smell of the Eagle. It seemed to cling to him. He could beat the mines, he was the Untouchable. There was a sliver of movement ahead of him. The head of his shadow wavered, far in front of him on a patch of ground that was bare or sparsely grassed. Mister saw the snake slide away from his head's shadow. Its skin was rich brown cocoa in colour, but spread on it were paler blotches, like water pools on an oil sea. It must have been sleeping on the sun-warmed earth in the last of the day's heat, but then he had stood, finally, and the shadow had cooled the place where it rested. The snake's place was on the direct line he would have taken, the shortest route he would have walked, to the riverbank. He had no fear of snakes, insects, spiders. He watched the snake meander across the patch. He saw its head, its needle eye and its jabbing tongue. He was about to take the first step, not running and not blind with closed eyes, walking, so that he held his self-respect. The snake went into the thicker grass that ringed the patch of crusted earth. He looked a last time for it. He readied his leg for the first stride. He breathed hard, sucked the air into his throat, his lungs. He had no fear. It was as if a crisis had gone. His shadow was further on than where the snake had slept. He would follow his shadow to the river – and leave the kid, Cann, bawling and yelling behind him. He touched the pistol butt above his belt. As he tried to follow the last wriggle of the snake's tail, Mister saw the wire.

If it had not been for the snake he would not have seen the wire.

The wire did not have the lustred sheen of the snake's skin. It was coated in dirt. He followed the line it took. In places grass sprouted over it, and then it would reappear, then it was hidden again. He should not have looked for the end of the wire that ran at a height just above a man's shoelace knot. He knew he should have squinted his eyes shut, denied himself the sight of it, and stepped forward. The wire's line took him away to the left, past an old tree branch in which it was snagged, and then it was angled higher. He could see the stake that held it up and its green painted body with the faded stencil markings that had a squat cluster of antennae points just below the height of a man's knee, with a ring above them to which the wire was fastened. The breath wheezed from his body . . . his knees went, and with them his bladder.

The urine steamed on Mister's leg as he went down. When he was on his hands and knees in the grass, he could not see it.

The last of the sun was above the hill's crest and the higher trees were webbed with it. The sky spread blood-reddened light on the valley, washed off it the brightness of the day.

He was broken. His head was on his knees and his fingers were over his eyes, but the tears came, and the urine flowed on his leg. Joey's voice sang out.

'God, Mister, you are a disappointment to me . . . Not going to run? Is Christmas cancelled? What you going to do, sit there all night? There's going to be a lot of laughs round Stoke Newington and Dalston, Hackney, Hoxton, Harringay. You won't be able to hear yourself think up Green Lanes, with all the laughter . . . What's the next big plan?'

He sobbed, and the light failed around him. And the smell of the Eagle and the urine would be worse in the night and the wires would come closer to him, edge tighter around him.

'You know what I was going to do, Mister, if you'd run? I've a big dog here, an Alsatian. I was going to let you get close to the river – if you hadn't stepped on a mine – and I was going to send him after you. You might lose a leg with a mine but this brute's bad, you'd have lost your throat with him. What's to be done, Mister?'

He was mesmerized by the voice and the tears ran on his sun-blistered cheeks and the wind seemed colder on his back. He knew the fear.

'Come and get me.'

'Is that a joke, Mister, is that funny talk?'

'Come and get me out.'

'What? Walk in there?'

'Get me . . . I can't do another night, not here . . . Get me out.'

'Didn't your mummy ever teach you what to say?'

'Please . . . fucking get me out . . . *Please* . . .'

'Got to do better than that, Mister, a lot better.'

He cried into the growing darkness that hemmed in the sun's final light, 'I'm begging you – for charity's sake, for mercy's sake – help me. Please help me.'

'Is it over, Mister? Did I win and did you lose?'

'I lost, you won . . . It's over.'

The voice changed. The mocking sneer was replaced by a brusque rattle of instructions. 'You will sign a statement listing, in your own handwriting, every criminal offence you have committed since your release from HMP Pentonville . . . You will plead guilty at every subsequent trial you face . . . You will name every criminal associate . . .'

'Any fucking thing – but not another night out here.'

'Your word is your bond?'

'Trust me – and help me.'

'You are armed, Mister. Throw any firearm away from you.'

He took the PPK Walther from his belt. He swung his arm and hurled it high. He saw it against the ruddied glow before it fell against the darkness of the hill's slope.

'I did it.'

'I saw you do it, Mister. Strip off. I want all your clothes off you, and your socks and your shoes. Everything. Then stand. Then I'll come and get you.'

'Thank you. Thank you, Cann.'

He tore off his jacket and his fingers fumbled with his tie. He ripped his shirt open and threw it at the grass, then the belt.

In the dropping light, Joey watched as Mister, out in the field, stood and kicked off his trousers.

He took the mobile phone from his belt and the battery from his pocket, married them, and punched the numbers.

He was tinny and distant in her ear. 'It's as if I've killed him, I have destroyed him. I know what I have done. To get there, Jen, I went down lower than him. I was more cruel, more brutal, more vicious. I sucked the strength out of him. He was untouchable, he did not know fear, he is now standing in a field and bending to take off his shoes and socks and then he will be quite naked – I told him to strip. He said, Jen, to me: "Please." For what I've done, you wouldn't want to know me. Two days ago, he thrashed me, and I didn't cry out. He had a big meeting, I wrecked it. I brought him down, I peeled his men away from him. He went into a field. I am at the edge of the field. I have taunted him, laughed at him, I've brought the fear into him which he never had – a good person like you should have no time for me. You asked me, Jen, "How is it that people like that can have such power?" I've taken the power from him, I've exchanged it for fear. He's naked, he's in the palm of my hand . . . I don't have ideology, Jen, I am not serving a cause here, I'm not a crusader – it was about who was left standing, him or me, nothing more, nothing less. It's not because I'm good and he's evil. I am worse than him, have gone lower. It's like I'm contaminated, by him and what's around me . . . I have to go and get him, Jen, and I can't show fear, I have to bring him out. Where he is, Jen, it's a minefield . . .'

The rambling voice went, and she was left with only the tone's purr in her ear.

He was stripped, was bare. The wind was on his skin and it seemed to Mister to heal him, to soothe the burns and sponge off the sweat. He held out his hands at his sides and made a cross of himself.

The sun had gone, but left its fainter glow on the hill's crest, and the lights of the two villages shone distant and bright.

He saw the movement at the tree-line. Cann came for him, with the dog at his knee, to bring him out.

Dragan Kovac watched from his porch, and Husein Bekir from the log in front of his home. It was their valley, and was invaded by strangers. They had the right to watch.

He stepped over the yellow tape.

Joey started to walk towards Mister. He felt a bond with the dog. The dog had no fear and the weight of its body rippled against Joey's leg, and that was comfort. The dog gave him courage. He had asked: *What would be his chance of setting off a mine?* He had been told: *It would be in God's hands.* The dog's paws glided on the grass, but Joey stamped it down with each stride.

He knew everything of the man who stood ahead of him with the arms out: when he ate, when he showered, when he had sex, when he cleaned his shoes. He knew the cartwheel of his organization, the pitch of his voice, the gait of his walk, and the assets secreted away that made Mister first among equals. Only Joey knew what had brought the fear to Mister's mind and had crushed him. At the Custom House, if they had seen Mister naked and holding out his arms in surrender, they would be launching the piss-up to end all binges. Joey alone owned the moment. He felt no elation, but a simple flat lack of satisfaction. No thrill, no triumph. He had gone to the end of the road, followed where it had led him, and the vista was empty.

He did not look down.

Joey reached the Eagle's body. He smelt it, and the dog sniffed at it. He swung to his left and started out on a wide half-circle that would bring him face to face with Mister. The dusk gathered around him. The dog, close to Joey, growled softly and bared its teeth as they skirted Mister's buttocks, then his hip, then his groin. In the half-light gloom, Mister cut a pathetic and pitiful figure, but compassion had long ago been sluiced from Joey. He saw the pleading in Mister's eyes and knew that he had won. He faced Mister.

He could not reach into the future.

He would lead his prisoner to the trees, take him up the path and past the skeleton, up to the crest of the hill, and he would permit him to dress except for his shoes and his socks, and would sit the dog down near to his prisoner. In the morning, when the vehicles came, he would commandeer – beg or borrow – a ride to Sarajevo's airport, and he would fly back to Heathrow. There he would hand his prisoner into the custody of the SQG team, and he would go back to the bed-sit on the top floor of the house in Tooting Bec, and he would sleep. He did not think he would ever again return to the Custom House. He had left the uniform behind, he was not a part of the culture. It was the price he paid – the taking of Mister did not come cheap – he would be shut out. He looked over Mister's body. There was no power, no threat. He had no sight of the future.

Joey went forward to take Mister's arm and to bring him out.

His first step was on to matted grass, and a thistle stem that broke under his trainer shoe. His second was on to a patch of ground that was bare. He was looking into Mister's face. His third step was snagged. Joey felt the restraint, and kicked his foot forward to break the snag.

Barnaby kept the mines on a shelf in his prefabricated office in the Marshal Tito barracks – and when he had visitors, potential donors to the mine clearance programme, he always lifted them down and explained, without emotion, their mechanisms.

'This is the anti-personnel bounding fragmentation mine, which is proven as the most deadly of all those used in the Bosnian war. It has either a trip-wire or a pressure-activated role, but it is more usual in the trip-wire mode. We call it PROM. As you see, ladies and gentlemen, it has a bottle-shaped body, steel, and the fuse is in the bottle's neck. The inside of the bottle has internal grooving, which better aids the shrapnel spread, fragmentation. But this is a clever mine. On a trip, or pressure, its first reaction is to fire a small black powder charge that throws upwards the main charge, held by a tether, a further twenty-five centimetres. That's the "bounding" factor. It carries nine hundred grams of explosive and the main charge detonates – not at ankle level – to cause maximum damage to upper thighs, genitalia, and the vital organs of the lower stomach. The lethal radius is twenty-five metres; the PROM has caused more casualties to our personnel than any other mine. This evening, in your hotel, when you order a good little Slovenian red, look at the bottle the waiter brings, and remember the other bottle I've shown you, the PROM, exactly the same size, but a killer.'

Barnaby put the deactivated mine back on the shelf. The faces of his audience, as he would have predicted, were limp. He doubted many would order wine that evening with their dinner.

A woman visitor paused at the door and looked back at the shelf. He asked her if she would like to handle the PROM. A little shudder crossed her face, but she nodded. He took it down and passed it to her. She held it as though unconvinced that it had been made safe.

He said quietly, because dispassionate factual description worked better with potential donors than melodrama, 'The tether mechanism, the jump before scattering the shrapnel, is what makes it particularly effective. When it's on a trip-wire it only takes a three-kilo pull to fire it. If your foot snags the wire, you'd hardly feel it.'

Her fingers trembled as she gave it back to him.

October 2001

Dougie Gough wrote the name in his notepad: Dragan Kovac. He poised his pen and waited for the translation.

'I am a retired sergeant of police and so I am familiar with the style of statement that an esteemed gentleman such as yourself would expect . . . The memory of that day is very clear to me . . . I now know that the older man was called Packer, and the younger man was Cann. The man, Packer, had stripped off his clothes, he had surrendered. The combat between the two was over. Packer had sub-mitted. It was last light. Cann came with a dog to bring him out of the minefield – that he came into the field was the final marker of his victory. Packer was naked and the dog was near him, guarding him, and Cann set off the mine. It was a PROM, with a trip-wire. Cann went down. I had a fine view of it from the porch of my house. Packer snatched up some of his clothes and ran, as if he had a sense of liberty. He ran for the river. When Packer was nearly at the river, the dog caught him. I went from my house, down the track to the riverbank and called the dog – I am familiar with police dogs. I had with me my long-handled axe. It was becoming dark but there was light enough for me to see that the dog was injured by some of the shrapnel the mine had thrown, and that the dog had bitten Packer's arm. I took them, Packer and the dog, back to my house. The dog guarded him, and I had my axe and I waited for help to come. Then he cried out, Cann did, in the field. The dog heard it. It limped away, went back into the field. I was left with the prisoner. I had the axe but I am an old man, I have been retired many years. I could not keep the prisoner – I was not to blame for his escape. The dog went back into the field and from the time it reached Cann he did not cry out again. You should believe me, I could not have kept the prisoner.'

He was retired now, had 'gone early'. But a telephone call had come to the bungalow on the outskirts of Kilchoan, the chief in-vestigation officer himself, and the request had been made that he should attend the small ceremony as the Custom House represent-ative. A young diplomat, Hearn, had met him at the airport and had

442

driven him to the valley. He had not been able to understand the speeches and he had wandered off. It had been his wife who had suggested he should take his walking-boots. He had sat on the river-bank and changed from his brogues to his boots then used the highest stones to cross the river. He had walked across a ploughed field, newly turned but not yet sown, and across a grazing field where his advance had scattered goats, sheep and two dry cows. He had passed the skeletons. He did not have to be told where to go. The target that drew him forward was a waist-high cairn of stones. It was similar country and he felt comfortable, small fields, wooded slopes and distant mountains, to that which bounded the road approaching his home on the Ardnamurchan peninsula. He stood quietly by the stones and soaked the place of its images, and he'd said the same quiet prayer that he spoke in his mind each Sunday in the quiet of the chapel at Kilchoan. When the ceremony was over, a drifting pro-cession had followed him to the cairn. The diplomat translated the words of the rugged, bluff, self-serving man who wore an old uniform greatcoat and a policeman's cap. He knew he must play the part of a sponge to their stories. There was an official report, which had been drawn up by the embassy half a year earlier, but it had carried no sense of soul in its typed pages. The retired policeman saluted him and stepped back. An old man, his cheeks nicked from the shave to mark the importance of the ceremony in the village, came forward to take Kovac's place, and beside him, hobbling with him, was a German shepherd dog with its left front leg off at the knee.

He wrote the next name: Husein Bekir (farmer).

'I came from my home and I waded over the ford, and I thought I would be swept away, and then I went up the track past Kovac's house – the old fool was whining that it was not his fault that the prisoner had escaped from him – and I followed the de-miners who had been called out. We went on a path they had made between their tape and the trees at the far side of my fields. They had big lamps with them. They worked as fast as they dared to make a corridor across the field. When they had gone half-way, the light from the lamps showed him. I had been told he was called Joey, a silly name. He was on the ground, on his side. He was alive then. They went faster, I think they took great risks. They found one mine, a small one like the mine that has crippled my wife, and a trip-wire but it had become disconnected from the PROM or the PMR2, and then they stopped. Why? Because of the dog. The dog was beside Joey. It guarded him. Even where I stood in the trees behind the tape I could hear – and I have bad hearing – the growling of the dog. The men were more frightened of the dog than of the mines. Each metre they advanced in their corridor, before they stopped, the growl of the dog was more threatening. They said they would go no further unless the dog was shot, and one of them was sent to the village of Ljut to find a gun to kill the dog – the Serbs have many guns, they have not changed. I have worked with dogs all my life, a good dog is as important in my life as my children or my wife. I went down the corridor to where the men were with the lamps and their iron sticks. I talked to the dog. A rifle was brought from Ljut, but I gave my word that the dog would not hurt the de-miners. I saved the dog. We reached him. The dog was beside him and Joey had his arm over it, he held the coat of the dog. It is a good dog. It is of little use for work, but it is a friend . . . There should be a celebration tonight, because of the certificate, we should drink brandy until we can no longer stand – there will be no celebration. We are all honoured, sir, that you came.'

The farmer shook his hand, walked away with the dog, and was replaced at the queue's front.

He could not catch the name, so he wrote: Foreman (de-miner).

'He had lost most of his stomach and one of his arms and his right leg was very seriously injured. There had been trauma and a great loss of blood. If we had been able to retrieve him quickly, within thirty minutes, then we might have saved his life, but he would still have required the amputation of his leg. I think, also, he may have been blinded but I have not seen any autopsy report . . . He confused me. Earlier that day I had met him and I had refused to move towards the man who was trapped in the field and had explained all of the dangers, and he had listened to everything I had said. Why did he then go into the field? Why did he wait until we had all gone, and it was dark, before he went into the field? I cannot say what drove him into the field . . . His life had gone when we reached him. We made this pile of stones where he was.'

At the ceremony, before he had abandoned it and had headed for the field and the cairn of stones, a certification of area cleared had been handed by the de-miner foreman to Kovac and Bekir, and the diplomat had murmured in his ear that the certification was good for ten centimetres in depth – enough for now. The couple presented themselves to him. He remembered her from the airport: 'With the kindergarten, am I?' she'd asked. Either she had aged or she did not wear the cosmetic blanket he had last seen employed, and four local policemen stood sombrely behind them.

He jotted the two names: PC Frank Williams (South Wales Constabulary), Margaret Bolton (surveillance consultant, SWC).

'We felt we had to come. We were a part of it, you see, a part of what he did here. And we found each other here, Maggie and me. We walked out on him, and we'll carry that to our graves. I said to him, at the end, that we were disgusted at what he was doing. I called him arrogant. I'm with the armed-response vehicles now. I do my shift, I check my weapons back into the armoury at the end of my duty, and I go home, but I don't take my work with me. I don't talk about winning and losing, as he did. Did he achieve anything, did he win?'

'Do you know, Mr Gough, what were his last words to Frank, when Frank ditched him? They were "Give Maggie my love" . . . If I'd been here, if I'd stayed, if I'd had to bloody well sit on him, I'd have stopped him walking into the field, but I didn't stay. I'm a consultant now. I lecture on surveillance practices and develop equipment, then I go home to Frank and we have a little meal and we don't talk about what happened here. But he's with us. I see those damn great stupid spectacles, and his kid's grin . . . What's the worst, he didn't want us to stay with him . . . We were just in the way. It was personal, it was between the two of them. I'm glad it was here, in a rather lovely place.'

The man who marched forward had irritation on his face as if not used to standing patiently in a queue . . . He felt he was the bereaved relative at the chapel gate. He sensed that this was a mourner who had travelled from Sarajevo more because of a slack day's diary than a degree of loss. The name was rapped at him. Was he supposed to know it? He did not. He wrote: Benjamin Curwin (SIS, attached to United Nations Mission to Bosnia-Herzegovina).

'I hear they booted you out after the fiasco. Well, it was all rather

445

childish, wasn't it? I'd have thought an organization like yours would have known how to keep its people on a tighter rein . . . I told him he was, quote, "a fucking nuisance here", unquote, and interfering – I told him to do his investigation someplace else because he was upsetting the cart . . . Serif's empire still stands and his reputation is augmented by the rumours that he possesses NATO anti-tank weapons, and a communications system we can't decrypt. His tentacles still reach into the body politic, he still owns the government, but it's harder for us to track his dealings . . . Not all gloom. I was in London last week and heard the latest on your old target. Very far from gloom. You're out of the loop now, so you won't be up to speed. Packer reached Sarajevo, hijacking vehicles *en route* at gunpoint, then holed up there for a couple of days with some UN woman, before moving on – she treated some nasty dog bites on his arm. Now, he's living like a Trappist in northern Cyprus. I would have thought the Scrubs or Wandsworth would be preferable. We monitor him there. He's in a villa up a hill between Kyrenia and Ayios Amrovisios, courtesy of the Turkish Cypriots – the word is it's cost him five million to square them and that awful hood from the mainland, Fuat Selcuk. He's a busted flush. His wife came out to join him, stayed a month, then went home – she's now with her mother. They say his major subjects of conversation, when he can find anyone to talk to, are the price of tomatoes, the quality of the water supply and the frequency of the power-cuts. I heard he'd been ripped off rottenly by his new number cruncher . . . not all gloom. He's behind a big fence, sirens and electronics and lights – must feel quite like gaol. Don't get me wrong, I rather liked your man – a prig, but he had guts.'

A hand was offered, for shaking, but he continued writing his notes, and didn't take it. He had feigned indifference when told of Albert Packer's situation. What he had learned since he had left the Church was that the highest and thickest wall imaginable separated serving officers from former officers. His status had gone with his identity card. He had received, in exchange for current reports and assessments, a carriage clock, a decanter set, and enough whip-round cash to purchase a ride-on mower. On his last day at the Custom House, before sherry with the CIO and the pub session with Sierra Quebec Golf, he had headed the meeting where the Crown Prosecution Service solicitor had pitched cold water on the prospect

446

of a successful prosecution of 'Atkins' without the evidence of Joey Cann (deceased). The little queue had gone, and he put away his pad and capped his pen. He turned and laid his hand on the heap of stones. The diplomat had stepped back, as if understanding his mood. The funeral, down in the West Country, had been private; the family had requested that the Church did not attend, and it had not been disputed. There would be no plaque carrying SQG12's name and his dates in the lobby of the Custom House: 'Clear defiance of instructions, can't have that . . . Broke all the rules in the book, made a mockery of the manual . . . Brought it, let's not muck about, down on his own head . . . Put up a memorial and we send a message to future generations that we sanction personnel operating outside legality . . . It was a vendetta, unacceptable behaviour.' There would only be the stones in the valley. He heard the approach of the car, and the diplomat touched his arm. A Mercedes limousine approached, hugging the hammered-down ruts dug by tractor wheels. The doors opened. A sleek elderly man helped a young woman into a wheelchair, and bumped the chair towards the cairn. He had not seen them at the village ceremony. She held a small posy of flowers. He felt a wearying sadness. A spit of rain was falling.

He took out his notepad again, and wrote down their names: Judge Zenjil Delic, Jasmina Delic.

'We had a choice to make, the present or the future. We chose to safeguard the future.'

'He bought me flowers . . . Before we rejected him I showed him the old burial stones in Sarajevo. On one was written, "I stood, praying to God, meaning no evil, yet I was struck to death by lightning." It is good that they have put stones here, where the lightning struck . . . I return his flowers.'

She gave him the posy of alive strident colours. He leaned forward, and down, kissed her cheek, then laid the flowers at the foot of the cairn. He stared at the heaped stones. Some had dried earth on them and some were covered with lichen. He heard the car drive away over the field. He felt a crushing weight of responsibility. They had all told him he was not responsible – the CIO had said it, and the team had clamoured it, and his wife had sought to persuade him of it – but he knew what he had done . . . Or had there been, in that valley, a young man's fulfilment?

The diplomat coughed, then said quietly, 'If you're to catch that flight, Mr Gough . . .'

He looked around him. He saw the fields, ploughed and grazed by livestock, and a vineyard of new posts and new bright wire, and the wooded slopes, and the gold of the leaves on a big mulberry tree, and the smoke from the villages' chimneys, and the river, and he thought it a perfect place, a place of peace. He took from his pocket the little knife with which he cleaned the inside of his pipe bowl, and opened it, and knelt beside the cairn. He chose a large stone, scratched the words on it, and wondered how long they would last against the weather.

CANN do – WILL do.

The words, above the flowers, glimmered back at him. He turned on his heel.